THE JOURNAL EFFECT

KELLY SIMMERMAN

THE JOURNAL EFFECT
Kelly Simmerman

HTTPS://TUMBLEWEEDBOOKS.CA
A division of DAOwen Publications
Copyright © 2024 by Kelly Zimmerman
All rights reserved

DAOwen Publications supports copyright. Copyright fuels creativity, encourages diverse voices, promotes free speech, and creates a vibrant culture. Thank you for buying an authorized edition of this book and for complying with copyright laws by not reproducing, scanning, or distributing any part of it in any form without permission. You are supporting writers and allowing DAOwen Publications to continue to publish books for every reader.

The Journal Effect / Kelly Simmerman

ISBN - 978-1-998029-11-2
EISBN - 978-1-998029-12-9

This is a work of fiction. Names, characters, places, and incidents either are the product of the author's imagination or are used fictitiously, and any resemblance to actual persons, living or dead, businesses, companies, events, or locales is entirely coincidental.

Jacket Art commissioned by MMT Productions

10 9 8 7 6 5 4 3 2 1

*This book is dedicated to the resilient souls who have survived the shadows of childhood abuse, illuminating a path of strength, healing, and courage.
To Garret and McGregor, may you always know your true selves yet dance gracefully with the winds of change that sculpt your remarkable lives.
To Elle, for your love, support, and endless encouragement. Thank you.*

CHAPTER 1

A gust of wind hits my face from the kitchen window, and it smells like the promise of another late-night Portland drencher. The yellow paper with the attorney's name and phone number takes flight. It flies on invisible strings, soaring and diving through the barely used, foodless space.

I could race around my kitchen chasing the page like a puppy lunging at a chew toy, but I'm more of a logical, wait-and-see kind of woman. With my hands outstretched, it descends, brushing my fingers like the ghost of Grandma Eve has placed the paper directly into my grip. Mom's handwriting is barely legible as she wrote the attorney's information in such anger. All the blood rushes out of my face and body, leaving me as steel gray as the sky. Crushing the paper, I look up at my low apartment ceiling and yell, "Alright, alright, Grandma. What the hell do you want me to do?"

Earlier That Day

It's best to sneak past Mom's bedroom door like I had many times as a teenager. At twenty-eight, returning to my childhood home is both weird and comforting, but as they say, time marches on.

Time doesn't march on.

For me, time folds in, smothering year after year, never stopping.

It holds me in its hazy memory, like those damn school photos Mom has hanging in the hall – one awkward year after another. Knowing it's easier to leave a note saying goodbye, I don't knock on Mom's door. She's sleeping off a wicked hangover and would scream at me for waking her. My ears can't bear any more of her horrible recounts of Grandma Eve. Last night, Mom's shrill, red wine-amplified voice drove me crazy – one story after another about arguments between Mom and Grandma Eve. Good God, the lady just died. Have some respect.

"She always stuck her nose into where it didn't belong, like that time Eve got a housecleaner for me," Mom screeched, disgust staining her face. "Like I couldn't keep up with my own house? Oh, and then she told me I was feeding you too much or the wrong kinds of food. She was all high and mighty with her nursing degree. It was intolerable. That's why we moved to Seattle."

I lug my suitcase down the wooden stairs, avoiding the step that has always had an ear-ringing creak. At the bottom of the stairs, I yank up the back of my sliding jeans. Who thought skinny jeans were a good idea? For curvy girls like me, we're constantly fighting plumber's crack.

The coffee pot gurgles in the kitchen. "Two days is too much with her." My whisper voice cracks under the pressure. Mom's sprained ankle is improving, and work is calling me back to Portland. The small yellow tablet on the stained granite kitchen counter beckons me. Grandma Eve's attorney called last night and left details about how we should take care of her belongings. Staring at Mom's scribbled notes, I tear the page off, fold it up, and jam it into my tight front pocket. Then on the same tablet, I write a goodbye note.

Steam rises from my coffee cup, and my mind searches for memories of Grandma Eve, but nothing comes. What Grandma Eve's attorney told Mom hits me in the gut, and I lose all the air in my lungs. He had said a family member needed to go clean out her house in San Diego. Mom can't go with her twisted ankle. I bite hard on the hangnail on my thumb, ripping at it until it bleeds.

Dogs barked at the front door. I race toward them, tripping over my suitcase. "Stevie, Lindsey, be quiet!" I whisper-yell and point my finger at them. Reaching for the handle, it's obvious how time has performed irreversible deeds on the house. The scratched wood floors, the bronze front door handle peeling from overuse, and the dirty blinds on the front window sagging at the top, kowtowing to sun, time, and neglect. I fling the door open, expecting someone to be there, and the labs thought so, too, with their inquiring greenish-yellow eyes. But there was no one.

A chill rattles me.

I stand there for a moment, shivering. The wet Seattle winter could be to blame, mild though it was, I swear, it felt like someone was at the door. The phone call from the attorney last night ran through my head. "Grandma Eve?" The words burst out of my mouth. Of course, there isn't an answer, and I feel foolish. On the side of the front steps is a feather on the ground. Gratitude moves me to pick up the sleek cinnamon-red quill. I haven't found a feather in a long time. Not since the last time, which was at Mom's house.

Holding the downy feather, a memory of Grandma Eve fills me. It was back when we lived in San Diego years ago. We were in her garden, and the burning sun blazed through the clear blue air. My six-year-old-self slurped on a juicy slice of watermelon while the birds darted in and out of the trees. Is Grandma Eve flying now? Slamming my eyes shut, I shake my head. Stupid thought.

I hate San Diego and everything it means.

The dogs whine and growl as they sniff the front step. "You two be quiet!" My voice sounds like a hiss, shooing them back inside the house. "We don't want to wake the grump." The old door, expanded with dampness, moans as I push it closed. On the bench by the front door, right where I'd left it for Mom, sits the unopened Chausse sneaker box.

These sneakers are special, just for her. They're my recent project at work, hot off the demo line. Showing her the box filled me with pride, but she didn't try them on – not even on her good foot.

"You're wasting that expensive engineering degree designing sneakers," Mom said with her sour lemon mouth. The very next thing she said was, "And if you'd just lose a little weight, you could attract a man." The words shot off her forked tongue like venom as she arranged her red blouse.

She doesn't know about Drew and me. Nobody does, especially not Mom. She'd laugh and tell me I was confused and a fool. She's probably right. But that's how we roll, navigating the untruths and half-truths we tell each other. We both come from a long lineage of secret keepers.

My gaze shifts from the sneaker box back to the red feather, my feather blessing, and I carefully place the plume in my briefcase, smoothing it between a half-finished sci-fi novel and an article about European sneaker designs. My ride to the airport shows up. I snatch my suitcase, pat the dogs' heads, gulp down the last of my coffee, and make my escape.

The SeaTac airport escalator creeps up to the fast-food level. The alluring cinnamon spice smell could mean just one thing. Cinnabon. It makes me powerless. I must devour the three-pound cinnamon roll with the plastic cup of warm frosting. Besides, the extreme pleasure and full tummy will help with my fear of flying. Well, that and the Xanax. The moment I sit down with the roll, all sounds disappear. No luggage wheels rolling across the floor, no passenger names called over the intercom, no beeping cart drivers, no parents snapping at their kids to keep up. It's just me and my sweet, precious Cinnabon floating in ambrosial space.

It's like a ceremony. First, pull a plump strand off the cinnamon roll, dip it into the frosting, and chomp off a big bite. I chew and realize it's all dried out like someone made it last Tuesday. Squinting my eyes and swallowing hard, the nearly impassable bite goes down with a necessary help of coffee. The sugar is both a nemesis and an elixir. I demolish the rest of the dry roll, wiping out every last bit of the sticky sweet, milky frosting deliciousness, and suck it off my finger. My brain captures the sugar, and I know what it must feel like when an addict shoots up – bliss and alarming regret.

I've had a love-hate relationship with food since the ragged cliff of puberty. At fifteen years old, I started making myself throw up, and it worked. Mom laid off me and didn't accuse me of being a blimp. Then one day, she caught me in the bathroom and confronted me. That's when she called Doctor Allen.

Now, I avoid mirrors.

After the flight to Portland, the desire to go home and shower arises, but the necessity of going to work grabs ahold of me. I head to Jake's, the deli I lunch at nearly every day, and order my favorite, a turkey toasty with French fries. Even though I feel disgusted with myself after eating that bone-dry cinnamon roll, I'm craving a quick sandwich before heading to work. Substantial food is necessary, as I'll be working late into the night.

Five people are in front of me in the bright yellow and red oblongish eatery. There shouldn't be customers here at 3 o'clock in the afternoon. I was sadly mistaken. My phone buzzes several times. It's Megan, my assistant. A weighty pressure pushes on my chest as I read the text.

> Where are you? Drew is shitting her pants about the new sneaker line!

This is the third message from Megan, and they are getting progressively more frantic.

> Be there in a few! At Jake's

Jake's is around the corner from Chausse headquarters, where countless devotees wolf down his mannish sustenance.

> Want anything?

> No thanks. Just get over here, pronto!

Opening the heavy glass door to the Chausse building was nothing new for me. However, this time, it felt different. This building is where middle management and engineers work on new fitness products, primarily sneakers.

The elevator delivers me to the fourth floor. My mind ping-pongs between staying at work and going to Grandma Eve's house in California. Thoughts about Eve haven't entered my mind in years, and I avoid San Diego like the plague. Since Mom decided to move us to Seattle, I never looked back. Too many shitty things in San Diego. Doctor Allen recommends compartmentalizing the few scattered memories from that time, especially those of my father and Uncle Jim. Just thinking about San Diego feels like a thousand tiny spiders crawling my body.

A bevy of small red cubicles bedecked with the Chausse logo stretches out in a long scream. I run my finger along the fabric covering the stalls and peer out the window, revealing the shamrock-green turf field below. Once approved, that's where we will test my new sneaker line. Drew mentioned getting the goalie from the US Women's National Soccer Team for the photoshoot. Allowing a slight smile, I imagine myself on the turf field with everyone in my sneakers.

As company regulations dictate, the glass door to my office stands open, and Megan is at her desk. Our two desks share a modest office space. "What the heck! We needed you like yesterday." She springs up off her ball chair and hugs me.

She opens her arms to hug me. I've never been able to do the full both-arms-hug. Sometimes when I'm careless, I think it might be possible, even easy, and then my body stiffens and says, nope! One-armed half-hugs are safer.

"Nice to see you, too, Meg. My trip was terrible. I hate my mom. My grandma died. All of this happened on a short weekend trip to help my mom." I set the greasy to-go bag on my desk.

"Oh honey, I'm so sorry to hear." She takes both of my hands and looks at me with her brown eyes and perfect make-up. Mom would love her. She's all perfect and skinny. "You've never talked about your grandma. What happened?"

"We don't know. Cancer or something." The office looks normal. The stack of file folders on my desk quadrupled during my absence. A fresh pile of 2-D and 3-D CAD product drawings teeter next to my computer. To the right of the piles sits the mug Mom gave me last year. It's a grass-green monster of a thing with the Pebble Beach logo on the side. I don't play golf. All the jocks who come into my office ask what my handicap is as they look at the mug. I've learned to say twenty-six, which usually shuts them up, and they abruptly change the subject.

Megan shrugs. "Well, just be ready. Drew is on a rant. She's been rambling nonsense about this new line and something like..." Megan lowers her voice to sound like Drew. "Headquarters will never run with the existing color palette." She shakes her head, takes a sip of her herbal tea, straightens her pencil skirt, and sits at her desk.

Megan, my exuberant and bloodshot-eyed assistant, gets things done in half the time it takes others. Management should promote her to engineer as she does what I do, but doesn't get paid as well. We're the same age and have the same amount of education and skill. The only difference is that she got pregnant at the end of her last year at UC Davis and took a year off to raise her son, Matt.

There's a stream flowing inside Megan like a dream or a wish. It's visible on her face, somewhere behind the perfection. The story of her blunders keeps her a step behind, like she's lugging around a gigantic sack of guilt. I imagine pressing my ear to her heart to listen to the current of her cravings. Of course, I don't. That would be weird. Besides, that's her business. We are all wrapped in mystery – every one of us – including me.

"A problem with the color palette?" I say over my shoulder.

"Yeah, she's about to blow a kidney over it." Megan angrily flicks a stack of papers across her desk. "Damn, and we worked so hard on those colors."

My most nonchalant tone emerges out of me. "Is she in her office? Maybe I should go talk to her."

"Yes! Oh my God, maybe that'll keep her from coming in here and totally messing with my shit! Besides, she likes you better." Megan winks with a teasing restraint. "I'll look at those fabrics and textiles on your desk." She glances up with wide eyes and a toothy, cheesy smile. "Welcome Ba-aack." Glancing at my blue and silver R2D2 watch, I push away from my desk. "Okay, I'll do my best to soothe the savage beast. Wish me luck."

"*Luck! Missed you!*" Megan shrieks.

My cheeks heat up. Why does Megan think Drew likes me best? Has Megan noticed my eyes glisten at the mention of Drew? I've never told Megan about Drew and me.

My pace quickens, along with confused thoughts. What's wrong with the sneaker colors? My team chose those colors, and it was a long and tedious search.

Before entering her office, I survey myself for the inevitable sloppiness that comes with being me. On my blouse, there is dried frosting that's easy to flick off, and my cinnamon belly is protruding. No amount of sucking it in will help.

"Hi, Drew."

"Hey, Chelsea. How was your trip?" Drew removes her reading glasses and spins around in her leather executive chair.

I step into the lavish, stately office. Signed photos of NBA players looking like they are having a jump shot contest are adorning the walls. My favorite is from Rick Johansson, number 44, flying through the air. Scribbled on the poster with a black Sharpie is a message. "Dear Drew, YOU are the real champ!" It was Drew's idea to develop Chausse Jump Johansson's. An enormous success that landed her here in this position. If my sneaker line is that winning, I will also get one of these big offices.

"My trip? Well, not so good. While at Mom's place, we got word that my grandma had died." It's best to start with the grave news; maybe Drew would soften her stance regarding the sneaker palette.

"Oh, sorry to hear. My condolences." Drew stands up, not making eye contact with me. Unbuttoning her cuffs, she yanks on her blue blouse sleeves and rolls them up, exposing her toned and tan forearms. She knows this turns me on.

Her musky perfume fills my nostrils as she strolls past me and closes the heavy, dark-wood office door. She turns and finally looks at me squarely. "I missed you." She smirks.

Oh, she's giving me that look. I smile, feeling shy. "Oh, yeah?"

It's stupid having an affair with my boss, but Drew is, well, Drew. And having an affair is trite and asinine, but she gives me attention, and that doesn't happen often. Why does she have to be so damn cute with her dark curly hair, high cheekbones, and dark brown eyebrows that slope downward in a serious expression? Drew is like molten lava, pliable but deadly.

Drew grabs me by the hips and pushes me up against the closed door. "Come 'ere, you little flirt." Her crotch is hard against mine, and she kisses my neck.

"Easy there, tiger…" I say, looking side to side.

With one hand on the small of my back, the other tugs at my blouse, revealing my dull, unsexy bra – no lace, no frills. Drew likes lace. I didn't think she'd be down there today. Her head sinks lower, and she kisses and sucks at the tops of both of my breasts, and I squeeze my biceps toward my breasts to make them appear bigger and firmer.

Looking up from the back of her head, which was buried in my cleavage, there on the shelf was my prototype sneaker. My thoughts are scattered in many directions – Grandma Eve, Mom, my sneaker line, the glint of arousal, the smell of Drew's hair product, San Diego. Oh God, San Diego.

Drew's attention is much needed after the horrid time at Mom's, but there's no way office sex could happen today. "Hey, Drew. Drew?" Her chin is soft and firm at the same time as she kisses my neck and then finally lifts her head. "Let's have a drink later, huh?" I wriggle out of her clutch and straighten my blouse, fastening the top two buttons. "So, what's up with my sneaker line? Something about the colors?" My voice cracks.

"Awe, let's not talk about that yet, Chels. I wanna have some fun, first. Trust me. We will get to the sneaker line." She smirks again, showing off those pinchable dimples and mischief. Locking her office door, she playfully catches my arm and whirls me around. "Come on. It's been a few weeks. How 'bout a quickie? Come on. You want this." She holds out her arms as if she is undeniable.

"It's been a few weeks for you and me, but I know you have other women stashed here and there," I say.

Ignoring my comment, she pulls me in again.

"Oh, Drew, I just can't. My mind is on so many other things."

Drew drops my arm. "All right, fine." She reaches over, snatches the sneaker prototype, and slams it down on her desk. "Yes, the color palette is all wrong." She adjusts her pants and belt and cracks her knuckles. She always cracks her knuckles when she's angry. The steamy molten lava has cooled, and now she is back to her rigid self. Was this the same woman who was groping my breasts, desiring me, or at least my body? I look down at myself. This body? Why does she bother with me? "What do you mean, the colors are all wrong?"

She frowns, as if she has eaten something foul. "The Cool Gray is fine, Chelsea, but the Eggplant and Pink Flash have to go. You know, they have that augmented reality computer in Milan now, and *noooo-body* has chosen either of those colors. In fact, pink has been going down every year since that whole pink washing scandal thingy." She hands the sneaker to me. And, of course, I take it, looking at the vein bulging on the side of her neck. "All right then. Get back to me with the *winning* colors. Seriously Chelsea, A S A P." For emphasis, she pauses between each letter. "We have a lot riding on this." She storms over to her treadmill, changes out of her heels to sneakers, and flips the on-switch.

"Sorry about your grandma. Obviously, you were not close. You've never mentioned her."

I've never told Drew anything about my life, not really. The less people know about me, the better. She is right about my relationship with Grandma Eve or, more accurately, my non-relationship with her.

"No, we were not close. It's been almost twenty years since my last conversation with my grandma. She and my mom constantly fought, so we moved away after my parents separated. Never saw her again." I gaze down at my nails and pick at my thumbnail with the jagged edge. "That, um, is something else we need to talk about... I've already missed the funeral as we weren't invited, but I need to take care of my Grandma Eve's house and belongings in San Diego." The words flew out before I thought about the details or if San Diego was even bearable.

"Seriously? With this palette shit-show going on?" She leaps onto the treadmill and sets the pace to a fast walk while looking over some paperwork. It seems like it's from the marketing department. "Chelsea, that fucking eggplant color has to go. It looks like my dog barfed up some shitty Kibbles and Bits. Besides, you just got back from vacation! You can't leave now." She turns up the speed, marching faster.

"Drew, you know that wasn't a vacation. My mom needed help. She hurt her ankle, for God's sake. You know how much we fight. So no, there was no pleasure in that trip." I exhale as suppressed red anger overtakes my cheeks. "By the end of this trip, I thought about taking her out. You know, like rat poison in her coffee or something."

She wiggles her eyebrows up and down. "Feisty. Turns me on." She focuses on the paperwork once again.

Drew pounds her feet on the treadmill like she is stomping bugs. I wish she'd take my side with the color palette issue. She's too much of a self-seeker with a Cheshire smile, doing all she can to please upper management. If only there were just a smidge of her confidence in me, then I would feel more empowered and courageous. But when I try to be bold, it sounds more like a bratty little kid. That's what Mom says.

I hold up the sneaker and do my best to advocate for myself and my team. Don't sound like a bratty kid. "Me… and… and my team think these colors are, well, are good. And it will work fine. We tried hard to find just the right palette." A film of high anxiety sweat covers my body. "And… and."

"Oh, Chelsea, don't flatter yourself. You know it takes more than 'good' and 'fine.' You can't be that blind." She shrugs and belches out an evil half-laugh. "Or maybe you are."

I float closer to the treadmill, unaware of my legs and feet moving, and with a nauseated stare, the word spills out of me. "Blind?" She quickly flips the marketing papers over. I tap the sneaker on the side of the treadmill and look away. If I want to keep Drew interested in me, it will take me backing down and agreeing with her asinine opinion.

"Whatever you think, Drew." My hand clinches into a fist so tight that my fingernails dig into my palm.

"Thought so." She grunts. "Okay, well then, um, get this taken care of. Do the right thing and make us both a success. Remember, we are winners." Drew fist pumps the air, and I want to throw up.

"Yep, I'll try," I say with my tail between my legs.

"Chelsea, seriously, make sure this happens and do not screw it up. Don't just try. Get this done. And don't forget about Justin. He's been a real player, and management likes him. You wouldn't want to give up your promotion to him. Right? Sooo, get rid of that pink shit and the fucking eggplant, and we'll be good to go." She looks up at me for a split second. "Drinks tonight?"

Drew desires two things, well, maybe three. She must be the superstar. She craves recognition. And then having sex seems to be her third goal in life. Not much else jiggling around in that wind tunnel, chimpanzee brain – not to put down chimpanzees.

"No time for drinks tonight. What with this palette shit-show going on? I'll text you later."

"Close the door behind you, Chelsea."

I slink out of her office and yank the door closed with a thunk. She was supposed to gallop over, swoop me into her arms, and tell me how much she loved my sneakers, but that didn't happen. Okay, the Pink Flash is probably not the best color choice, but eggplant will be the next big thing. I just know it. Her words make me cringe. 'Kibbles and Bits.' God, I was a wussy, caving to authority.

Outside Drew's office, I put my head in my hands. "This is unbelievable," I mutter. Jessica, who sits outside Drew's office, looks up from her computer. Squinting a big, fake smile at her, I relax my sucked-in belly. She nods once and then taps on her computer keyboard again.

I turn and clomp back to my office. Megan must hear this crap. She will agree that Drew is wrong. She's got my back.

CHAPTER 2

"You will not believe what Drew said!" My words echo back at me. The baseball clock on the wall reads 4:47. Megan always leaves at 4:30 to get Matt from daycare. Slumping down in my standard-issue black desk chair, the pyramidal pile of work files feels like it is taking over my desk. My emails captivate me as my stomach growls in agony. The damp turkey toasty sticks to the side of the paper bag and then finally gives way. "Damn, slow guy," I say, taking a bite. The tepid sandwich is soggy from the mustard and Caesar dressing, and a piece of floppy lettuce flies out of my mouth and lands on the keyboard. I wanted to eat it at the deli, but Megan's texts were so despairing that putting the Drew fire out became the priority. "Welcome ba-aack." Sipping the bitter coffee and reading the sticky notes on the file folders in Megan's handwriting, it feels good knowing she has reviewed these files.

We are good friends, but I can never tell Megan about my affair with Drew. If anyone finds out about us, I'll get fired. Employees can't date, and here I am, dating the boss. Oh God, how cliché. Okay, dating is too strong of a term. We're more like horny offenders of bad grace who bump into each other every so often. Dangerous, but it works. When she's lonely, in between dating real prospects, we get together.

Luckily, none of my deep, dark secrets interest her. Trust me, it's better to be alone than to be betrayed, so having a boss with benefits is just fine. It's safely distant and private.

The muddy coffee stings my tongue as I reach into my briefcase and pull out the feather from Mom's house. The red quill spins back and forth between my thumb and forefinger. Feathers have been in my path for a long time. They'd show up in my backpack after walking to school or on the ground at my feet. "Feather blessings," my cousin Melissa would call them. "Feathers appear when angels are near," she would say.

At around eleven, it came to me that I hadn't found a feather for some time. No feather blessings. Guess it must be a sign from God.

Back then, I believed in God.

CHAPTER 3

A couple of months passed by, and still no feathers. It was crushing, and the heavy guilt grew inside me. That eleven-year-old girl thought she had done something so wrong that God didn't love her anymore. I scavenged the yard daily, looking for feathers, but found nothing. Each day, this little brown bird perched up in the trees. Her feathers were shiny, and the sun transformed the colors of her back from jet black to brown to auburn. I needed one of *her* feathers. Taunting me, she flew around but never gave up a feather.

One morning, while on my feather-finding trek around the yard, the little bird dipped down and landed in front of me on the ground. I stopped dead in my tracks. This little bird won't mind giving up a feather. I lunged for her, leaping to the ground, skinning my knee. She chirped and gracefully flew high into the fig trees.

Baiting her for two weeks, she would eat the little pie crust pieces from the pies Mom brought home from working at the bakery. She got more familiar with me, almost letting me touch her beak as I offered the crumbs. The flutter of her wings has my heart do the same.

After school, as I ate my part of the pie on the damp grass in the yard, she watched me on the lowest branch. "Cooome on," I whispered. On the grass, the first crumb was out away from me, another a tad closer, and then another even closer. She landed on the grass and ate the first two crumbs. She was close enough that I could study her feet. Even her ancient-looking leathery brown skin with three bony toes sticking out was beautiful.

I pounced on her. The little bird squirmed in my clamped hands, desperately trying to wriggle free. I squeezed tighter and tighter, and her head thrashed against my hand. And then, just like that, she went limp. Her eyes were closed, and I felt her satiny motionless feathers. She was soft and silky, otherworldly, like nothing I had ever held.

Oh God, she's dead. I put her down next to the last pie crust morsel. I killed this fantastic little bird and my lifeline to God. "Wake up! Please don't die! You're so beautiful." Her legs flinched, jerky movements from her tiny pterodactyl feet. And then at once, she jumped to her feet, shook her head, and flew up to the lowest branch.

There was no feather, no blessing. God hated me. She chirped and glided out of sight, graceful and perfect. That crucial day marked the demise of my hopes for attaining a divine feather blessing and earning favor from God. Both seemed futile.

CHAPTER 4

*B*ack in my office, the chocolate chip cookie that comes with the sandwich makes the coffee taste better. Putting the feather from Mom's house back in my briefcase, I think about the situation with Grandma Eve and also about Drew needing me to get the sneaker colors right. I need to be secure with my decision about this new sneaker line, ironically called Chausse FOCUS Sneakers.

With the overwhelming number of distractions today, it is difficult to maintain even a shred of focus. As a rule, I'm as prudent as a young mom walking her three young children across 5th Avenue in New York City, but I am skeptical of Drew's motives. It feels like a trap, something she's not telling me. She's never hidden paperwork from me the way she did in her office today.

"Focus. Focus. Focus." I whisper, taking the last bite of the cookie. Trying to read my emails is futile as Grandma Eve continues poking at my mind, and the family commitment hangs around my neck like dense ocean weed.

It's strange having a grandmother, someone who shares your blood, but my grandma shared so little of my life. Similar to God, did she hate me? Why didn't she reach out to me, send a letter, or anything? At around eleven years old, after moving to Seattle with my mom, I would cry, missing Grandma, but Mom would shush me. Maybe Grandma tried, but Mom probably wouldn't take any of her calls.

Grandmothers should teach the younger generation something important, like making an apple pie or chocolate chip cookies. They should be wild with love for their little ones designing perfect moments together. Grandmas should have alphabet letter magnets on the fridge and be the hand that guides you toward profound spiritual concepts.

From my sketchy memories, there was none of that for me.

Still, if I don't take care of Grandma's things, guilt will overtake me like a dark wave, and my wretched self-hatred and shame will grow even more prominent. I reach into my front pocket and retrieve the crinkled yellow piece of paper from Mom's counter. Studying the attorney's name, my hand moves across the computer keyboard, searching for flights from Portland to San Diego.

Grandma's house won't be that tough to clean out in a weekend. Drew won't even notice. It'll be good to go to Grandma Eve's without Mom. She'd criticize me and how I cared for Grandma Eve's belongings. All of her drama and wine won't be helpful. It'll be better this way. I can be in charge, for once.

Then again, what about my sneaker line and that A-hole Justin angling for MY promotion? A precarious, thready breath leaks out of me. If I leave, Drew will hate me. Her reputation is on the line. So is mine.

Shoving three greasy floppy fries into my mouth, I tap my Chewbacca bobblehead. He stands guard on my desk with his Alaskan malamute matted hair and two bandoliers, ready for action. Remember what Dr. Allen says – control what you can. I tap Chewbacca's head. Your focus (tap) determines (tap) your life. Chewbacca's oversized head nods and bobbles the truth. In my best Yoda voice, I say, "Fear leads to anger. Anger leads to hate. Hate leads to suffering."

I should have said all this to Drew, but didn't have the guts to stand up to her. Instead, I flew into the wire cage of my captivity and let her close and lock the scrawny door.

Then it hits me, and what to do becomes crystal clear. I tap Chewbacca's head, load some of the files on my desk into my briefcase, shove the yellow notebook paper back into my pocket, and head home to my apartment.

CHAPTER 5

My cheek pins against the back of the airplane seat as I struggle to get my well-used, faded green briefcase out from under the seat in front of me. Fumbling around, I fish for the shoulder strap. A pull, and then a harder pull, and finally, it gives way, and a seam comes apart, spilling papers onto the stained carpet shiny from years of wear. "Shoot!"

My flight neighbor, who was a 2-hour 21-minute reminder of the work I should have been doing myself, finally looks at me. She raises her eyebrows but says nothing. She was already standing in the aisle, ready to deplane, with her laptop neatly stowed in a slim brown leather, monogrammed briefcase, which looked like hand-tooled leather from Italy.

Jam-packing all my essential paperwork back into the fat, shapeless case, I thought about getting some work done on the flight to San Diego, but my eyes closed, and sleep overtook me right after takeoff. Too much on my mind last night. Working seemed best. The right color for a project can be difficult when there are so many hues to choose from. However, selecting the ideal shade that captures the project's desired effect is vital. In this case, I proposed a teal hue instead of pink flash to better suit Drew's needs while still maintaining the eggplant color as a possibility.

I was prepared to shield my eyes from the brightness of the San Diego sun. However, an overcast and gloomy sky surprise me. Living in Portland for three years prepares one for a sunless sky. A white Chevy something or other is my rental car, and my bags hit the trunk with a thump. An occasional raindrop falls off the trunk lid. "What am I doing here?" I grunt under my breath. "Eve, Eve, Eve…" Hopefully, I'm doing the right thing. Drew is mad at me for leaving, but I have no choice. Grandma Eve's attorney said a family member had to take care of her belongings, and Mom couldn't.

The traffic getting out of San Diego to La Jolla is horrid. Don't any of these people work? It's only 4 o'clock, and the jammed freeway crawls like a sloth. Even with the awful traffic, San Diego keeps its small-town feel. The uber-tall sentinel eucalyptus trees lining the road look deeply connected to this place as their top canopy sways gently in the rain.

The sea of red taillights illuminates the slow succession of raindrops that hit my windshield. Some drips mingle with others, making friends, laughing, and having a party. And some land and roll solo off to the edge. I relate to the land-and-roll-solo-off-the-edge kinds.

Google Maps leads me to a row of houses overlooking the Cove and the Pacific Ocean. The smell of ocean registers in my nostrils, though I can barely see the water through the clouds and rain. They say La Jolla is the jewel of San Diego, with wide sandy beaches, sea cliffs, rocky reefs, and secluded coves with harbor seals and sea lions napping on the beaches. I take a breath and understand why Eve loved it here. I should have visited her. At least once. A part of me wishes a time machine could take me back and change things, but who am I fooling? I hate my family, and they hate me.

Grandma Eve's driveway is narrow but long. The rain shifts from a sprinkle to a torrent, and I realize my umbrella is in my suitcase, which is stored neatly in the trunk. A chill passes through me, and it's the kind of chill that sends that unintentional earthquake throughout your body. Goosebumps on my arms form like tiny little pills under my skin, so I rub my hands on my jeans to warm them.

Eve's beach house is straight out of a dream. It is a pleasing clash of midwestern red brick and stylish modern California, with small palm trees growing in planters next to the garage. The panoramic windows face the vast shore of the Pacific Ocean, and everything looks homey except for a single gloomy round window high above the front door. The house is foreign to me. Eve must have moved into this house after she and Mom quit talking to each other.

It's a stretch to the back seat to get the notepad with the name of the woman who now owns and lives in Eve's house. Josephine Allard – I called her before my flight to introduce myself and let her know I would come and take care of Eve's estate. Josephine was quiet and seemed angry with me on the phone, and she had some accent. French, I think.

I know little about how Eve died, only what the attorney told Mom. Eve was ill with some sort of cancer and died at home with the help of hospice. Josephine was her good friend and roommate and oversaw her funeral. Mom and I did not receive an invitation.

The car idles in the driveway for a few minutes, and then I can't wait out the rain or my raggedy nerves any longer. Opening the car door, I scurry around to the back, pop open the trunk, grab my suitcase, and run toward the house. My bag clunks on each cement step leading to the front door.

Before I can knock, the door flings open. "You are Chelsea, no? Bonjour!" The older woman wipes her hands on a dishtowel. "Get in out of that rain!"

"Whoa!" I shrill. Is this the same woman on the phone? I step inside the house and offer my free hand to shake, but she opens her arms and hugs me, kissing both of my cheeks. "Oh, okay." My body stiffens from the uninvited hug and kisses.

She smells of Chanel Number 5, and there is a faint whiff of something else but can't put my finger on it. My one-armed hug is the best that my body can do. Warm hugs didn't happen in my family. The only time Mom hugged me, which was rare, seemed to be when she wanted to blend in by imitating what others were doing, so as not to appear out of place. She didn't care about my feelings, only what other people thought about her.

"That rain has not stopped all day! Actually, all week!"

I set my suitcase down and place my tattered old briefcase on its side to avoid further spillage. "Sorry I screamed just then. It startled me when you threw open the door. Josephine is your name, right?"

"Yes, yes, I am Josephine. Please call me Josie." She looks away and then back at me with her hand covering her mouth. "Goodness, you look just like your grandmother. No one calls me Josephine except for my Aunt Genevieve, who taught me American English when I was young." She clears her voice and shoves a towel into her apron strings.

"I couldn't help but notice a hint of a French accent when we spoke on the phone."

"Oui! Born and raised in Paris."

Before seeing Jose, I expected her to be a pallid, thin-lipped old crone. But instead, she's stunning. She's an attractive, silver-haired, lively woman, probably in her early seventies. Her skin is dark brown and has hip, spikey hair like a French Lena Horne. Her solid, sinewy arms are a vivid contrast of mine – soft and fleshy, the color of a halved apple and the squishiness of jello.

A little orange and white dog scampers around the corner, barking at me.

"Pasqual, go to bed. Go on. It's okay." The dog wags his tail. "Go on, now." Pasqual turns and plops down on his dog bed. "That was your grandmother's dog. I am now his caretaker."

"Oh my, let me get a dry towel. You are drenched, Chelsea!" She hurries into the kitchen and back. "Please." She offers me a red hand towel. "Would you like something to eat? I've made a simple roasted chicken with lemon and carrots – the recipe of my mom. Though Mom said Julia Child stole it from her," Josie says with her chin held high.

"I'm starving!" I say, putting a hand on my belly and wiping my wet boots on the colorful entry rug.

Jose picks up my small gray carry-on and turns away. "Chelsea, may I show you upstairs? Is it acceptable that you sleep in your grandmother's room?" Her head jerks around to look at me.

"Um, sure." I'm already uneasy being in this house with this stranger. I don't think sleeping in Eve's room will make it any worse.

"Today is the day of inescapable wetness!" Josi belts out, showing me the way toward the staircase. Obediently, I follow. "The meteorologists say this rain will last the rest of the weekend." Josie dabs her forehead with the back of her hand. "They keep showing mudslides on the news in all the places that had wildfires last summer. It frightens me, considering the hill behind us caught fire last fall."

Feeling awkward and now a bit scared by the rain and its consequences, I think about this, but no words come out of me. A learned response from long ago.

Stay quiet and stay safe.

Josie glides up the stairs in cute little flats, explaining how Grandma Eve re-floored the 1940s beach house a few years ago with Colorado beetle-kill pine wood planks. Grandma Eve had gone to Denver and chose all the wood for the floors. "Did you know that those little beetles eat the tree sap and eventually starve the tree to death? And the beetles die when their tree dies! Tragic, really…" Josie remarks, shaking her head.

Looking down, I imagine those little barbaric gluttons burrowing and binging on the tree sap before killing their host and themselves. I stop and look closer. "Can you still see the beetles in the wood?"

Josie chuckles. "No, no. You cannot see them, but they are there." Josie pushes her eyebrows together. "Will you feel a bit odd sleeping in your grandma's bed? Having never been here and well, you didn't know your grandmother, you will most likely by fine. She knew you, though. But. That is another topic. Anyway." She probed again, speaking in jerky, fast spasms. "I just. Well, I hope you sleep soundly with no nightmares."

"Why did Eve die in her bed?" The words burst from me like a house of cards. I feel embarrassed but can't take them back. I turn the corner to Eve's bedroom with the slowness of a person walking into a morgue. If I could've held up my hand in front of my eyes and looked through my fingers, I would have.

"No." Josie touches the sides of both her eyes. "She did not die in her bed. Eve preferred to sleep in the recliner in the living room." Josie's tone takes a sudden downturn. Her face a painful look, and her fast-paced speech turns slower. "The stairs had become difficult for Eve toward the end of life, so she slept down there. But you wouldn't know anything about that."

In the bedroom, there is an immediate change underfoot. A plush, light cream carpet covers the room. Perhaps the sponge layer of pine needles that once filled those Colorado trees with shelter and happiness was underneath our feet, lending an extra cushion. Prominent in the room is Eve's four-poster bed. And yes, thinking about it, I feel a little squeamish, like when you go into an old hotel or bed-and-breakfast, and they tell you it's haunted. The hairs on my arms rise off of my skin.

"It's a pretty room, no? I would have you in the guest bedroom. But it's full with boxes." Jose disappears down the hall and then reappears.

"I'll be fine, Josie." I hope I'll be fine.

"Well, if you would like, please take a moment to freshen up and then come down for dinner." Josie sets my suitcase in the hallway and not in the room. She points toward the bathroom that adjoins the bedroom but doesn't enter the room like there's an invisible barrier. "There should be towels, washcloths, soap, toothpaste, etcetera, in the lavatory." She's back to her quick talk again. "I need to go and see to dinner."

Knowing I have to catch up on the work that wasn't completed on the plane gnaws at me. Drew hasn't responded to my email about the new colors for my sneaker line. The weathered dark wood sides of the upholstered bench at the foot of Eve's bed give it an antique appearance as I ease down onto it. In front of me is a floor-to-ceiling window. Through a small crack in the clouds, I take in the orangey-red light of the setting sun. I move toward the West-facing window to catch the last glimpse of the splendid, silent sun before the black ocean swallows her up. The rain decides not to fall for the moment, and the sky holds its last discharge of light before releasing itself to the night. The streetlights blink on, and the houses on the street glow softly.

There is distant chit-chat from a radio in the kitchen. My stomach growls, smelling the winter savory aromas wafting from the kitchen. Lively and swift music floats up from downstairs. That music! I crane my head and hold my breath to listen to it better. It's catchy and melodic, and it sounds like the soundtrack of an old movie.

I make my way downstairs, stopping at each step, taking in this foreign house. The walls display framed photos of people, none of whom are recognizable. Drifting like a person in a dream, I squint at each image, but they are nameless faces to me. There is a photo of me, Mom, and Robert, my father. It looks like I'm around five. We are all so young, so fresh, and undamaged. I look happy. We all do.

Josie sniffs, and it snaps me out of my trance. "This music is good, Josie. Who is it?"

Josie turns around from the stove, lifts her glasses, and wipes her eyes. "Excusez-moi. I just miss Eve so badly. I'm not myself without her." She sniffs and pulls out a glass dish from the oven. "That beautiful voice belongs to Edith Piaf. She's a French singer from the '40s." She dabs her eyes, careful to get any smudged eye makeup.

Unlike most women, eye makeup, or any makeup for that matter, does not go on this face. It never made sense to me; besides, I look ridiculous in makeup. Lip balm is safe, and Mom hates it. She used to buy mascara, shiny lip gloss, and blushes, but she couldn't convince me to wear them.

Josie ladles two bowls of soup and clears her throat. "Shall we start with a little amuse-bouche to stimulate the appetite?" Josie sets down the small bowls of a creamy-looking soup with what looked like celery leaves floating on the top. "Here is a little roasted garlic soup with lovage to warm us from all that persistent chilly rain."

It's a supernatural miracle that anyone can cook this kind of masterpiece, like the guy who figured out carbon dating or the binary system. I have lived on takeout and restaurant meals all my life. No Epicurious or Food Network for me. Just some serious Grubhub and

UberEATS usage. That's it, that's all I know. I'm not known for adventurous food choices. Mom never cooked, and I certainly don't.

I take a small tentative sip of the soup. A salty combination of heavy cream and earthy celery washes over my taste buds. I blink, expecting it to taste horrible. Food that isn't on my regular Chinese, sushi, or pizza menus rarely appeals to me. I'm probably too hungry, and my tongue isn't being its discerning, savvy self, but after another spoonful, I decide it is indeed delicious.

"Wow, this is fantastic, Josie! Where do you get it?"

"Oh, I make it myself! It's just a soup." She gives a half-shrug. "Quite easy. Premier, you roast the garlic and then chop the lavage into tiny pieces before putting it into the stock…"

The padded high-backed barstool is the perfect viewing station to watch her cook. I can't imagine making soup. Heck, I screw up Kraft macaroni and cheese. My mind drowns out some of her words, only focusing on her face. Josie has a smile that somehow could make sense of the world's chaos. She doesn't wear worry on her face, not like Mom. Josie's way is stylish and sophisticated, but casual at the same time. I feel myself relaxing, feeling more comfortable. My consciousness returns to the kitchen from the sound of Josie stirring the soup.

"…finally, and this is very important, once the soup has finished cooking, you must taste it to see if it requires more seasoning." She takes a pinch of salt and throws it in the soup, stirs it with a wooden spoon, and then taps it against the pot. As she cooks, she opens and closes the white-painted drawers and cabinets. Josie's well-stocked kitchen has lots of blue and red dishes. Her knives must be magnetized as they hang beside her stove, ready for action.

After the tasty soup, Josie sets our plates full of warm, colorful, home cooking down on the formal dining table. "If you please, here is the roasted chicken and vegetables?"

"Thank you, Josie."

She seems to calm down a bit, not so jumpy and fast-talking. The dining table has two placemats, plates, and silverware; she already put wine glasses out. So comfortable in the kitchen and entertaining. I could tell she'd entertained thousands of times, though tonight was different. Two strangers brought together by someone who was both a grandmother and a best friend. The common denominator, Eve, missing from the equation, has gone the way of the Colorado pine.

"Chelsea, if you would, please open that bottle of wine." Josie asks while she leans over to get napkins from the carved wood cabinet behind her.

"Oh, sure!" It's a French Burgundy. "I've not had wine from this winery." Truth be told, I've never had French wine. Well, I had a tiny sip at a party, but I thought it was awful.

"A Chateau, yes." Josie corrects me. "I'm curious, Chelsea. Why did you come here to help and not your mother?"

"She broke her ankle a week ago and can't travel. She's in a big black support boot and must use one of those little scooters. Besides, it's best if I handle Eve's estate. Mom and Eve didn't get along, as you know, and seeing her home and belongings would probably drive my mom crazy. And then she'd drive us crazy. Trust me. It's much better this way."

"Hm," Josie snorts. "That's unfortunate. Her help would be good." She shifts in her seat. "Well, since you barely saw your grandmother alive, would you like me to tell a story about her?"

"Um, ah, well, sure." My voice raises three octaves, squeaking out the last word. Just when I thought things were going well. I knew it couldn't last.

Her eyebrows lift like her thoughts surprise her. "Well, this is about both your grandmother and me, of how we met." Josie picks up her red cloth napkin and snaps it once hard before placing it in her lap.

"It is quite a fierce story," she warns as she eases herself down on the straight-backed upholstered dark yellow and red dining chair. "I met your grandmother under some extreme conditions." Josie closes her eyes and takes another deep breath. "I was hiding in the doorway of a restaurant in an alley in Paris. The restaurant had been closed years ago, so there were no patrons. Your grandmother had taken the alley as a quicker way of getting to her apartment when she found me." Josie sips her wine and looks away as if to restore her memory.

I put a forkful of seasoned chicken in my mouth, which melts under the softest of my chewing, and follow the bite with a sip of wine.

Josie swallows her first bite, nods at me, and continues her story. "The blood. When I think back, what I remember most clearly is my own blood. It had poured into my eyes. It was draining down, and that metallic, distinctive blood taste was in my mouth. My head hurt, and I tried to breathe. Your grandmother was barely visible to me. She asked me if I was okay? No, no, I was not! I'm not certain I managed to say those words. She understood."

"My God. Blood? What happened, Josie?"

"My stint that evening was over at Boutary, an upscale restaurant in Paris. Regular customers would come in for wine and cheese at the night's end, including Esteban. It turns out he was *fou*. You know, crazy!" Josie motions with her index finger circling her ear, signaling crazy.

I nod while shoving a skinny, long-roasted carrot into my mouth. It's too big of a bite, so I bend the carrot once while it is in my mouth and then cram it in.

"Chelsea, do you want me to continue?"

Not chewing the carrot enough creates a logjam in my throat, and I nervously nod my head.

"My duties ended at the bar at 1 am. He had run up from behind and grabbed my arm. It was startling, and I felt uncomfortable and pulled away from Esteban's grip. He did not like that and retook my arm. He was thoroughly scaring me!"

What a horrific story. Why is Jose telling me this? I take another gulp of wine and realize I'm almost out. I grab the bottle and, like mom, over-pour my glass and fill Josie's as well.

"In his madness he dug his fingernails into my back, and then he pushed me backward onto the brick-paved building. He undid his pants and pulled himself out. I thought this was my opportunity, my moment, to break free. I dealt him a blow with my knee between his legs and ran.

At the dining table, Josie stops momentarily to breathe and takes a couple of bites of food.

"Fuck, Josie! Oh my God, pardon my Fren– I mean my language. I'm sorry." I look down, uneasy, and realize I have plowed through my entire plate. Flashes of my childhood flicker in my head like an old movie reel, and I hear my father's boots stomping down our hall toward my bedroom. Shaking my head helps to make it stop.

"It is very difficult, but important." Josie pushes her chair back. She looks like she is going to clear the dishes.

I stop her, touching her arm. For some strange reason, this feels cathartic. For both of us. "What happened next? Is this when Eve found you?"

"No. I had fallen unconscious for some time, lying in the doorway in the dark alley. Oh God, and I woke up with this odd sensation all over me. It was rodents! They were biting and chewing the blood on me. I screamed and sprang to my feet. Not sure how, as I was in so much pain, but I could not let them crawl all over me. No, no. The rats ran off into the dark."

"My God, Josie! That's horrible! Then what did you do?"

"Barely standing in the alley and hoping Estabon was not out there looking for me, I buried myself in yet another dark doorway, but I told myself to stay awake. My chest hurt. My head pounded. I was trembling from both the cold air and the shock."

"Please, Josie, tell me this is when Eve found you?"

"The next morning, Eve had been shopping at the Marché d'Aligre, and she was walking through the alley. I lunged forward, throwing myself at Eve's feet."

"She placed her bags on the ground and looked up and down the alley. I remember telling her about Esteban and then lost consciousness. I did not know anything else until I awakened in hospital two days afterward.

"And there she was, sitting in my room, writing in her journal. All I could think, both back then and at present, was that here I was, a stranger, and Eve cared enough to watch over me in the hospital. For two days! That, my dear, is the kind of person your grandmother was."

Josie holds a long, pained look at me with her coal-black pupils. "The person you never had the time to get to know." Josie exhales loudly. "Sorry. I'm aware your family had difficulties, but Eve was a special person."

My hands are limp in my lap. Life gets away. I should have visited Eve when she was alive, but it never crossed my mind. Too busy with school and then work, Eve was never top of mind. The Chausse job came shortly after I graduated from Seattle University. And then, there was Mom and all her terrible memories of Eve that echoed through my head.

"Josie, I'm so glad you escaped that situation. That must have been horrible." I sit back in my chair, slouching over. "But you don't know my family or me. You don't know the fights my mom used to have with Eve and the problems Eve caused." My eyes started squinting and tightening. I wanted to scream at her, "You know nothing about my screwed-up life." Josie was just another case of someone not getting me, surely relying on assumptions.

"Chelsea, forgive me, as I cry that Eve is no longer with us. I knew your grandmother well. She was my best friend. From the moment she found me, we became close friends. She was a remarkable individual, self-reliant and courageous, warm-hearted and open-handed."

Got it. Eve was a saint, and I'm an ass. Time to change the subject. "So, did you ever see that man again?"

"No. I told the Police Nationale Esteban's features and where he was employed, but it wasn't sufficient to apprehend him."

A stony expression comes over Josie's face. "That man took more from me than just the money it took to pay the hospital bills. He took my assurance, my confidence. He stole my ability to meet strangers and feel safe. I feel vulnerable when walking alone after dark, always looking over my shoulder. Not only did he break two of my ribs and give me a concussion, but he also reached into my soul, searching around with his sweaty, dirty hands, removing my confidence and joy."

"That guy was a psychopath! You didn't deserve that."

Jose pushes her chair back and clears the table once again. This time, I don't stop her.

My body feels like a sack of dirty laundry. The only stories I was told about Eve were from Mom, but they were all foul and atrocious. Meddling old bitty, Mom would say, and then tell me how Eve would show up at our house unannounced and try to take me away for dinner. Mom didn't cook, and Eve accused her of feeding me too much junk food, but I liked burgers and fries – still do. Mom hated Eve so much that we moved away, and I never saw Eve again.

Josie bangs the dishes around in the kitchen. I should get up and help, but I'm so heavy with anxiety and confusion that standing seems impossible. All my life, I was the family emergency medical technician, tending to the bruises. Mom would inevitably fall into something, usually breaking a glass or a dish.

The dreaded footsteps are in my mind again, coming down the hall to my room. I press my hands tight against my ears, squeezing them so hard I hear the underwater roar. Listening to Josie's story has stirred up old memories and nightmares. Those thoughts I've tried to erase from my memory. Dr. Cohen wants me to talk about this, but I refuse.

Getting myself to stand and help with the dishes takes tremendous force. Josie's lingering resentment fills the room as she moves around me and cleans up from dinner. I'm unsure if she's fuming over that guy assaulting her or if she's mad at Mom and me for not having a relationship with Eve. I know it's best to be closed mouth and agreeable in times like these. Stay quiet. When I was younger, and Mom would get mad, I learned to abandon all small talk and get things done. The family EMT inside me had to become surgically precise with responses, usually turning to silence or minimal animation and then making a break for it.

CHAPTER 6

A sound in the house wakes me. My eyes open, but darkness washes over Eve's shadowy bedroom. The only spec of light comes from a salt crystal lamp that sits on the top of the bookshelf. There was another loud clunk and thump. Was Josie up? Did a glass break in the kitchen? Disoriented from last night's wine and agonizing story, I rub my gritty eyes and hold my breath to listen.

Strange sounds in the night have always terrified me. It meant he was coming into my room. Someone would hurt me and make me do things I didn't want to do, making me feel embarrassed and filthy. That was so long ago now, and with all the therapy, I disconnect from it, from me.

The dog barks intensely, so I peel back the covers on Eve's bed and slide on a pair of loose gym shorts. I try to swallow, but my cottony mouth barely lets me. Stopping to listen again, all I hear is Pasqual's sharp and dangerous barking. Moving in hush mode, I sneak down the hall, tiptoeing. No clunking down those stairs this time. Must go stealthy.

I stop before the last stair and chew on my thumb hangnail.

"Shit. Shit. Shit. Oh, hush. Be quiet! Stupid dog."

Wait... I know that voice. No. It can't be. Easing down the last step and around the corner, I peek into the living room. Oh my God. My eyes were seeing something, but my mind couldn't register what was going on.

"Mom?" I turn on a light.

Crouching on the living room end table with her back to the wall, Mom did her best to steady herself. "No! No! Sit!" Mom says to Pasqual.

"What are you doing here?"

"Chel? Chelsea? Wait. What are you doing here? Oh God, never mind! Get this dog off me before I fall off this God damn table!"

"Come 'ere, boy." I kneel, patting my leg, but he doesn't retreat. He dashes back and forth, snarling and snapping at Mom. "Pasqual!" I trumpet. It seemed certain he was going to bite her.

Josie walks in wielding a baseball bat. "What in the world is going on?! Who are you?" she screams and points the bat at Mom.

The dog continues to bark, lunging forward, pinning Liz to the unsteady and narrow end table. Her feet slip forward on the small, shaky perch as she steadies herself with one hand on the wall. "Help! This dog is going to kill me!"

"Pasqual, come!" Josie commands and slaps her leg. Pasqual, the red heeler, hesitantly withdraws and goes over to Josie. The hair on his back and neck stands straight up as he maintains his stare fixed on the intruder. Mom gets off the table while Pasqual growls and lunges with distrust.

"Lemme help." I hold my hand up, and Mom grabs it hard, hoisting herself off the precarious antique. "You okay? What are you doing here, Mom? How's your foot?"

"Oh, my foot is better, but this dreadful boot must stay on, or my foot balloons up, and then walking is impossible." Mom shakes her finger at Pasqual. "Whew, it had me worried for a minute."

"He's not an it. His name is Pasqual, and he doesn't take to people who break into this house in the middle of the night," Josie snaps. "And again, who are you?"

"Mom, how did you get in?"

"Yes, how did you get in? I lock every door and window each night before retiring to bed!" Josie looks around the room, flush with anger. Josie grips the bat, and in the other squeezes the dog's collar. Pasqual continues to growl. "Chelsea, this is your mother, no?"

"Yes Josie, this is my mother."

"I walked around the outside of the house twice and finally found this window unlocked, so I let myself in." Mom points to the window in the Livingroom. "And then this dog wouldn't leave me alone! Not even for a hot pocket."

"Mom." I pick up the cold, pale disk on the floor next to the broken lamp. "It's frozen."

"So? It's a dog. They'll eat anything! It's meatball and mozzarella flavored." Touching her heart. "My personal favorite."

"Hmm, so, this is Liz?" Josie eyeballs Mom.

"Mom, why are you here?" I question, looking at her ridiculous outfit. She's in all black from head to toe, including a black beanie.

"Well, I didn't know you were here." Mom points at me. "You didn't tell me about that little ditty in your lovely note. I thought I'd have to take care of Eve's things myself. And coming in at night, I figured I'd have to break in. I didn't have a key. Besides, I say never give up the opportunity to dress like a cat burglar, you know, like in Ocean's Eleven or Thief." She sways side to side to show off her all-black outfit. Her backpack swings back and forth on her back.

She's been drinking. "Mom, your backpack is dripping."

Mom hoists her backpack around and off her shoulders, putting her off balance. "Oh no! My wine. I was only having a tad bit while the driver brought me here from the airport." She opens her backpack and pulls out a mostly drunk bottle of red wine and the box of frozen Hot Pockets. "I thought I might need provisions." She winks at me. "So, the driver stopped at a grocery store. He was the nicest guy. His name is Alfred. He's single. And I thought he should have your number, Chelsea."

"Mom! Seriously. Are you nuts?" I slump down in the chair behind me and pull my knees to my chest.

"Well, isn't this the most pleasant family," Josie says in a low, monotone, dispassionate voice. Both she and Pasqual smolder with anger. Pasqual, with his hair standing up on his back. Josie stands stiff, chin up. "This most certainly exceeds the limits of sensibility," Josie hisses.

Mom holds out her hand to introduce herself to Josie. "Hello, my name is Liz. I'm Eve's daughter and, well, Chelsea's mom." Josie refuses to shake her hand as Pasqual is still huffy. Pasqual lunges toward Mom's hand. Mom yanks it back and hides her hand behind her back to save it from being bitten off by either Pasqual or Josie.

"Mom, this is Josie. She's lived with Eve for some time now. Remember what the attorney told us? This house belongs to Josie now."

"Oooh. I see. It's you." Mom lifts her eyebrows. "Well, don't worry about me. I'll just sleep on the couch tonight." Mom put her drippy bottle of wine, plus two more bottles, on the coffee table. "Josie, do you have an extra blanket? And maybe a wineglass?"

"Umm, yes, yes, of course. I would put you in the guest room, but it's full of boxes." Josie turns around and whispers, "Unbelievable..." She now uses the bat like a cane, clunking it up on the wood floor every other step. Pasqual walks behind her, still darting evil-eye looks at Mom.

Mom points at Josie walking away. She shrugs her shoulders and pulls down at the corners of her mouth. "She's the one who got the house? God, what a sour puss. And that dog, he's terrible."

Emotionless, I get up to go back to bed.

Mom grabs my hand. "Chelsea, wait. Have a drink with me."

Mom's eyes are glassy and red. "It's the middle of the night. You're drunk. And I'm going to bed." I twist away from her clutch. "Jesus, Mom, your hand is wet with wine!" I wipe my hand on my shorts and turn my back to go to upstairs.

"Chelsea, wait," Mom pleads.

I turn around slowly, with a sharp look in my eyes. "Mom, you shouldn't have come out here. I wanted to – to do this. On my own."

"How was I to know you were here taking care of Eve's things? I'm not psychic, you know. You told me you couldn't take time off work. Besides, there might be something valuable to sell here. Make a little money. You know, since she gave the house away to that horrible woman."

"I'm here because you said you couldn't come out because of your bad foot. It was the right thing to do. And you are right, I just might get fired over this one."

Josie marches in with two blankets and a pillow. "It's late, ladies. We'll talk about all this in the morning. I'll make up the guest room tomorrow. Chelsea, you can help me carry some of those boxes downstairs, yes? They need to go to the Women's Shelter in San Diego." She sets a pillow and the pile of warmth down on the plush, low couch and walks back upstairs. Pasqual tracks right beside her, hair still standing up on his back.

"A wineglass?" Mom demands of Josie.

Josie spins around and beams an intense look out of her deep-set, unblinking black eyes. I thought she would leap down the stairs and yank mom's larynx out. In a stern, parental voice, Josie responds to Mom's foolish order. "I believe you have had enough wine, Liz." She turns and clicks off the bright kitchen light.

Mom struggles to stand. She leans over the blankets and stumbles forward.

"God dammit, Mom! How is it that I can be disgusted with you and, at the same time, hate myself for feeling that way?" I grab the blanket, shake it out, and fling it across the couch. "Why didn't you call me and tell me you were coming here? You couldn't even walk two days ago. I wanted to do this. Just me. Well, me and Josie. Not you."

Mom's expression crunches as she lets out a grunt. She lies down on her side, fluffing the pillow. Her face presses into the pillow. "You never want me around, Chels."

Ignoring her nonsense, I take the velvety blanket and position it over her, covering her shoulder. Mom's breathing deepens like it always does when she passes out. The featureless rumple in the dark that rises and falls with each breath confounds me. Why is she here? The only thing Mom ever cared about with Eve was her money. But, looking around here, it doesn't appear that she had all that much. The house is nice and clean, but it's not over the top. It's a modest home near the beach in California. Besides, she gave the house to Josie. Mom knows that. The attorney told her.

She IS right about one thing – she's not welcome here. I wish I could chase Mom away and clean out Eve's house myself. She treats me like a child with her goading and bullying. I should call that driver and put her on a flight home.

Mom's presence is unwelcome for several reasons. The desire to handle the situation independently drove me. Demonstrating to Mom that I could do something without her. Be successful. Something I've never done. At least not in her eyes.

Standing over her sleeping face, I look at her crushing into the pillow, and in a raging thought, I imagine bearing down, pushing her face even deeper into the fabric and feathers.

I'd have silence at last.

My hand gets close to her hair. Her coarse, red hair prickles my palm, and she snorts, making me jump. I jerk my hand back, turn around, and tiptoe up the stairs to go back to bed.

CHAPTER 7

Upstairs, I lay down but can't fall asleep. The palpable and unstoppable deluge of adrenaline surges through my body like being struck by lightning. How does Mom always find a way to derail me? She's been showing up at the most inappropriate times, half-drunk, stumbling, and talking loudly all my life.

All my essentials, including the package of M&M's from the vending machine at the airport, are packed in my sad, falling apart briefcase. I pop a few candies in my mouth, and the delicious, crunchy outside melts and softens in my mount before swallowing and grabbing more. My body relaxes as the chocolate eases a little of my anxiety.

A memory from sixth grade takes over my mind. God, it was so embarrassing. It's bad enough just being an awkward twelve-year-old girl than being a twelve-year-old girl with her parents going through a divorce and a recent move from San Diego to Seattle. I didn't know anyone at school, and my smaller self was not good at making friends.

One day, Mom showed up at Hawthorne Elementary and had found her way to my classroom. She waved at me and flashed a big ridiculous smile. It took me off guard, completely shocked to see her. I frowned, and my hand spasmed in a freakish, jerky wave. She walked over and talked to my teacher, Ms. Rafferty, and then Ms. Rafferty motioned to a chair in the back of the classroom. Mom bounded toward me through the aisle with desks on both sides. Her bulky rain jacket draped over her arm systematically slapped each child's shoulder. "What are you doing here?" I said in breathy sternness, not wanting the other kids to hear me.

"Oh, stop being such a worrywart. You won't even know I'm here." There was wine on her breath. God, I'll bet Ms. Rafferty could smell it, too.

Christopher, or glue-eater, which is what most of the other kids called him, wouldn't stop open-mouth staring at Mom and me. He sat at the desk in front of me. Half of the time, he smelled of pee. "Turn around, Christopher," I whisper-yelled at him.

In alphabetical order by first name, my classmates went up to the front of the class and gave their reports on countries other than the US. And then, it was my turn to do my oral report on Brazil. I was suicidally embarrassed. No other parent was there, just my mom. She had plopped down in a chair, rifled through her purse, and started whispering to herself. I shot a look of disgust over my shoulder at her, but the contents of her purse consumed her. I got up. My sneaker tangled in my chair, making a shrill noise as the chair fell back. I grabbed it just before it hit the floor, set it back up, and proceeded to the front of the class. Stuttering and bumbling, I couldn't remember the script I had practiced repeatedly.

"Of course you forgot. You're terrible at speaking in front of people." Mom's loudly whispered words to herself pierce the quiet classroom.

The forest fire of shame inflamed my neck and cheeks. I stared down at the floor and ended my report.

* * *

I'M AWAKENED TO AN UP-CLOSE, wet, black dog nose sniffing my face. "Hi, Pasqual! What are you doin?"

The little white and orange cattle dog wags his tail and, with precision and kindness, licks my nose just once. Pasqual's soft ears comforted me as some of my other senses started coming to life – the welcoming smell of coffee and something else, something baked, wafted into the room. After last night's delicious dinner, I couldn't wait to see what else Josie had up her culinary sleeve. I've always dreamed of someone cooking breakfast for me. Mom never did. Oh sure, she'd say there were Pop-Tarts in the cupboard as she left for work. And Drew? God no. She never spends the night, so there are no intimate morning afters or breakfasts together.

I roll over on my side, pull the comforter over my exposed shoulder, and let my eyes drift around Eve's room. Behind a cello and sheet music is a bookshelf in the corner, loaded with books and other trinkets. I caught one of the book titles, *Zen and the Art of Motorcycle Maintenance*. Why in the world would Eve need a book on motorcycles? There were some classics – James Baldwin's *Collected Essays*, *Don Quixote*, and several Steinbeck novels. But mostly, there were self-help titles like, *Are You Ready to Gain Clarity?* Ugh. Clarity... It's a buzzword that lifestyle gurus and success coaches throw out like bait, just waiting to reel you in.

There were quite a few healing books from Deepak Chopra and Louise Hay on the top shelf, and then a few confusing titles– Final Exit, Death with Dignity, and Assisted Dying. I let out a quick exhale through my nose in a snort. Pasqual raises his head and stares at the door.

"Hey, lazy." Mom pokes her head into my room. "Are you awake?"

"Yep, me and Pasqual are just hanging out." Pasqual growls at Mom. "It's okay, buddy." I pat his head. "It's just that crazy night stalker."

"Hilarious... Come down for breakfast. Josie put out some yogurt and a pastry she calls chaussons with cherries. I allowed myself a small bite. All those carbs, but it's to die for! Also, Josie and I have been talking. Well, sort of. She grunts things here and there. It's understandable why she and Eve got along," Mom snarls. "We need you to get going on cleaning out the attic." Mom pinches her lips.

"Oh, and that rude attorney called. The one who is handling Eve's estate, and he told me a few things." Mom explained how Eve had written in her will that if no one came and took care of her estate within seven days of her death, everything was to be donated to the Big Sister League in San Diego. So, Mom decided she would get all of Eve's financials in order so we could benefit financially from them. And then, she instructed me to go through all the boxes in the attic and garage to ensure there wasn't anything of value that we could sell.

Mom should not be here. I wanted to do this without her telling me what to do and how to do it. She shows up, and boom, that's it. Suddenly, she's in charge.

"Sounds like The Big Sister League was more important to Eve than her family. That much is clear." Mom's tone went from tasky and informative to downright bitchy.

"Come on, Mom. She's dead, for God's sake."

"Humph, she'll probably haunt me from the grave as well. Okay, chop-chop, Chels! Even though you're not the best at sorting stuff, we need all hands on deck."

"I'm bad at sorting? And how would you know that?"

Of course, Mom ignores my question.

"I've decided that we only keep the items that have financial value so we can make a couple of bucks. Otherwise, nothing of Eve's will we keep. Nothing to remind me of her dreadful life. You got it, Chelsea?"

The blunt taskmaster ducks back out of the room, leaving the door open. I try to ignore her rude behavior, but it grates on me. My eyes go back to Eve's bookshelf, and a blue-colored book intrigues me. I get up and pull it down off the shelf. *The Body Keeps the Score – Brain, Mind, and Body in the Healing of Trauma.*

"Chelsea, come on. We need to get this work done!" Mom screeches from downstairs.

I throw the book on the bed. "Coming."

After some strong coffee and the fantastic chaussons pastry, Jose shows me the string to pull the stairs down, accessing the attic. Gritty gray dust infiltrates the air, and we knock down a few cobwebs off the stairs.

"Watch out for black widows or those other poisonous spiders, the brown fleecluse." Mom waves her hands to clear the dust. Her voice is especially shrilly and irritating.

"It's re-cluse, Mom, brown recluse," I say, climbing the rickety wooden staircase and poking my head into the dusty, low-ceilinged space. I know precisely the description of a brown recluse spider. It's those damn little black jumping spiders that give me the creeps. Leery of what might lurk, what dormant creatures might awaken, I creep up the stairs.

"God, Chelsea, I don't care what they're called. Just let me know if you find anything of worth up there."

Luckily, some natural light comes from a small, dirty window at the far end of the narrow space. The beams are dark, not from stain or paint, but from moisture. It smells musty and reeks of mold. Letting my eyes adjust, I see about 20 boxes and some sizeable green garbage bags filled to the top and tied off. Most of them sealed and marked – Eve's keepsakes, Kid's school papers, X-mas décor. And some not marked, or the markings faded beyond recognition. Out of sight, out of mind. A stack of old family pictures leans against the wall. I'm intrigued.

Ever since Mom and I moved to Seattle when I was eleven, I haven't seen or spoken with any of my family. Mom forbids it.

The dust and the age-old stale air give me a sneezing fit. Up here, there is no tissue, so I use the inside of my sleeve to wipe my nose and teary eyes.

I heave several boxes and bags down the unsteady and creaky stairs for Mom and Josie to assess and go through, deciding what to sell and what to donate. While moving the boxes, my back pops. Instinctively, I swing my hand around to my lower back, where the hot knife of pain jabs me. I rub out the pain and plop down on a box. In my hoodie pocket is the fun-sized snicker bar from the airport. The sweetness pacifies the fierce pain, but the candy bar disappears in two bites. Whoever decided on the name fun-sized? I shove the wrapper deep in my pocket so Mom doesn't see it and freak out.

There were eight mystery boxes left. Instead of hauling them down the stairs, I sit in the dank, dusty space to investigate. The first box looks full of keepsakes. I pull out what must be Eve's yearbook from 1948, blow off the dust, and open it up.

"Evelyn Petersson... Where are you?" I whisper, opening the frail red book with a buffalo carved into the cover. "There you are." There is a small photo of her with softly curled hair parted on the left. All the girls wore similar outfits – a dark-looking dress with a white scalloped collar worn on the outside. She looked much more beautiful and put together than I did in my senior photos.

Oh, the travesty when you turn seventeen and beg your mom to get a makeover for your senior portrait at Glamor Shots in the mall, and she says yes. Why they styled me as a 40-year-old streetwalker is beyond me. After the yearbook came out, all my normal-looking classmates were eager to pass their yearbooks around for signatures and gestures. There I was on display for all to see in all my inappropriate burlesque-ness. One girl in my class said, "You don't look that bad. You kinda look like my mom's friend, who is a realtor." With my yearbook concealed in my backpack, I vowed never to look at it again.

Eve's yearbook had something that was not in mine. All the kids had nicknames. There was Lefty, Bluebird, and Eager Beaver. Eve was Pickles. Hmm, why Pickles? Did she look like a pickle, or maybe she loved them so much that she ate them daily? Brought it in her sack lunch? Thoughtful of the fragile pages, I turn them with tenderness. She was in the Commercial Club and the Social Service Club. I've never heard of those clubs. "Huh, she played basketball," I murmur, studying her basketball shoes. They were thin white canvas lace-up deck shoes. We've come a long way with sneakers. Noticing the basketball shoes made me think of work and Drew and Megan. My actual work. My sneaker line.

"How are things going up there? You've gotten quiet. You weren't eaten by a spider, were you?" Mom yells from the kitchen.

"I'm finding some interesting stuff." I shuffle halfway down the steps. "Check this out – Eve's 1947 and 1948 Bison yearbooks from Clearfield, PA."

Mom takes the brittle books from me as I half-tumble down the narrow stairs. Mom starts flipping through the 1947 yearbook. "I forgot she graduated high school in Pennsylvania…" Her voice drops and then goes quiet.

I walk into the kitchen and get a Perrier out of the fridge. "Dang, my back hurts. Do you have any aspirin?" Mom doesn't respond. "Hello."

"Huh? What?" She raises her head from the yearbooks. "Chelsea, I told you. No memorabilia. Just start a trash bag for this junk." She chucks the yearbooks into the kitchen trash can.

"Wait a moment." Josie races into the kitchen and retrieves the yearbooks from the trash. "What are you doing? Throwing away something so precious." Josie wipes off the books with a hand towel. "You don't think her grandkids or great-grandkids might want to see this?"

"No. But, whatever. You think those ridiculous books are so precious? You keep 'em." Mom turns and stomps out of the kitchen. "I do not need that crap."

Josie cleans the books like they are priceless jewels. "Chelsea, do you want these?"

My shoulders drop. "I guess not."

After being on this planet for twenty-eight years, I have developed a few rules. Stay quiet. Stay under the radar. Be plain and even.

Things are better this way, cleaner. I don't get involved with others' affairs, and they don't meddle in mine. Not even Mom, especially her. Too risky.

This rule also means I don't have many friends, or actually, any friends. I don't gush and cackle the way other women do, like in the movies or at work. That's okay. No one wants a friend like me, anyhow.

Back upstairs, the rest of the cardboard box contains a stack of tattered cookbooks and a shoebox. A stunning pair of red leather pumps with an ankle strap and probably a 4-inch heel peek out. The inside stamp reads Christian Dior, and then beside that was Roger Vivier. I'm not much into high heels, as I know more about sneakers, but I know these were expensive – a real splurge. They still look new, maybe worn once or twice. They are European size 41, size 8. I kick off my sneakers and socks and slip on the heels. They fit perfectly! Grandma and I have the same size feet.

I look back down and spot something at the bottom of the shoebox. I pick up and unfold the yellowed paper written with an old-fashioned typewriter.

For you, My Darling~ 4 December 1949
　　With Love, Douglas

Tomorrow Morning
　　Oh, that sun. That busy, demanding master
　　storming through the cracks,
　　expected, but unannounced.
　　I turn my head toward her,|
　　knowing the facts.
　　I wonder once she knows how she will react.
　　Eyes open again instinctively to meet her alacritous smile.
　　Her warm toes on mine, sensual caress.
　　Love tactile.
　　Must deny my quandary.
　　Keep mouth closed.
　　Be present at this very moment.
　　She looks at me.
　　My lips curl.
　　Our hearts swirl,
　　and I melt insuperably.

Oh my God! I wonder if he, this Douglas, gave Eve these sexy ruby pumps? The pointy, shiny heels encircle my feet. I've always had a brilliant, even lucid, imagination, so I close my eyes and try to imagine Eve in the late 1950s. Before my daydream starts, I'm interrupted. Pasqual barks from downstairs, and reality slaps me in the face.

"Don't worry. He always barks at the mailman," Josie yells through the house. "How are you doing, Chelsea?" she calls up the opening of the attic.

"Um, okay. Just a bunch of junk up here." I kick off the stilettos and look at the poem again. Douglas. The name is familiar. Douglas! Could it be Grandpa Doug?

"Junk?" Mom screeches from the bottom of the attic stairs. "Chelsea, what are you finding?"

"Um, nothing all that interesting. Just a bunch of old stuff." I press my palms down on the box, and my shoulders nearly reach my ears. Maybe Mom would let me have these shoes. Who am I kidding? She'll want to sell them. I'm pretty sure these stilettos are worth quite a bit.

The hangnail on my thumb bugs me. It starts as just a minor snag of skin, and then I pick and pick at it with my index finger. The dead skin pulls down, exposing the pinkness of something new. I only claw at it when I'm talking to Mom or trying to stand up for myself, like with Drew or any other boss. But instead of words coming out of me, blood does.

"Oh, no!" Mom shrieks from somewhere in the house. "Josie! Chelsea, come here!"

Without thinking and in haste, I stand straight up and smack my head on the rafter. "Oowww!" I rub the top of my head, turn from the small window, and rush down the stairs, trying not to hurt myself further.

"Help!" Mom's voice comes from Eve's bedroom. "The roof is leaking!"

Josie runs into the room with a trash can to get the drips that come down in succession like water torture. Drip, Drip, Drip. The drops hit the plastic vessel and splash up the sides.

The bathroom towels soak up some rainwater as Josie and I dab the carpet on our hands and knees. Mom watches, but does nothing.

Disaster follows Mom like a new boyfriend or bad karma. She has a knack. Whenever Mom walks into a room, it's guaranteed that something awful will eventually happen. A painting falls off the wall, mysterious fires in the kitchen, broken coffee cups, computer crashes, or gigantic hornet nests appear.

In no time, the trash can was filling with rainwater. "We're gonna need a bigger one," Josie confirms as she hurries out of the bedroom, pushing Mom to the side as she rushes out. "If you're not going to help, then step aside."

Josie calls a roofer as she sprints back in with a larger can to hold the deluge of water. It was now gushing from the ceiling. I pull out the full can, and she replaces it with a bigger silver metal can from the garage.

"With all this bloody rain, nobody can come out for at least three days." Josie jams her phone into her back pocket. "So, we'll just have to keep capturing the water 'til it stops." Josie flops down on the edge of Eve's bed and puts her head in her hands.

The carpet is starting to dry, and the towels are soaking wet. "Josie? Are you okay? It's just a little water. We'll get it cleaned up."

"Well, the leak IS horrible, and I wish someone could come out here to fix the roof. It's just…" She lifts her head and gazes around Eve's room. "I haven't been able to come in here since she passed." Josie sniffs. "I miss her so."

Still on the floor, I knee-walk over to the box of tissues on the nightstand and offer a tissue to her.

"She was my best friend in this crazy world." Josie dabs her eyes. "Life is going to be so hard without her. It's hard to imagine going on without her. It's like this leak is Eve's tears coming from heaven. She would have loved to have the two of you here in her house when she was alive."

I look at the filling trash cans and then over at Mom. Her eyes are flat and cold, like two pieces of stone.

"Well, yes. Okay. Back to work." In a jerky movement, Mom turns on her heels and leaves the bedroom.

"I'm sorry, Josie. My mom has zero tolerance for emotions. She thinks everyone should just be happy, or at least look happy. Anything else, forget it. She's never known what to do with me all my life, with my anxiety and whatnot."

I get up, hang the heavily soaked towels over the tub in the bathroom, and step back out. Josie was not sitting on the bed anymore. I inspect the room. "Josie?"

CHAPTER 8

The unstoppable rain batters the roof. It floods down, sending a steady river into the trash cans in Eve's room. My phone alarm goes off every thirty minutes to remind me to empty the heavy cans of water into the tub. My back strains each time I move these slippery, shifting whales. According to Josie, the rain is Eve's ethereal tears flooding her room, but I hope she stops crying soon. Otherwise, I'll need a chiropractor.

The next box in the attic is full of sweaters and winter clothes. I stuff all the clothes into a large garbage bag. I'll make sure Mom sees this bag. It will deter her attention from the other keepsakes I want to save. Mom pops her head into the attic, making me jump.

"Chelsea, it's so boring in Eve's office. I'm going to go through these boxes up here now. The garage needs some work, so you have to work down there. Did you find any of the old bitty's journals or diaries?" Mom climbs up the stairs, her gaze darting from box to box.

"Mom, we decided it was best for me up here," I state, struggling to sound firm. "And no, there have been no journals. Besides, we plan to donate everything that we can't sell." I feel blindsided by the sudden change of plans. Spiders. Scare her with the spiders. "Mom, there are a ton of spiders up here." I open my eyes wide for effect. "I've killed a few biggies!" That'll do the trick.

It's good up here. It's quiet, and my mind can conjure up ideas about Grandma Eve. At least I can be the boss of the attic domain. "Lots of spiders up here, Mom."

"Yes, spiders. That is what this is for." She holds up a bright orange fly swatter. "Found it in the garage."

"Mom, I wanna stay up here." At my feet is the shoebox with the stilettos and love poem, and I step between the box and Mom, shoving them back.

"Enough, Chelsea! I need to go through these boxes. Now go downstairs. It's bad enough we're here. I don't need your back talk as well. Now go." She waves her hand toward the opening of the stairs and turns around to assess the attic.

Mom puts her hands on her hips. "What the hell have you been doing up here, Chelsea? More of your foolish daydreaming? All these hours, and it looks like you have done nothing."

"Mom, all these boxes are sorted as we planned." Throwing another sweater into the donation bag, I lean down, retrieve another trash bag, and toss it on top of the shoebox with the red stilettos.

Mom scowls at me. In this lousy light, her blue eyes look deep set and black. "Never mind, just leave. I knew you were no good at this." She spins around and pulls clothes out of the open box, throwing them on the floor one at a time. "We need to get this job done. Go, Chelsea, now!"

Picking up the trash bag, I attempt to conceal the slightly squashed shoebox.

"What is that?" she barks.

"Oh, just trash. I'll take it down with me and dump it." Before slinking down the stairs, I see Mom's hands shaking like she had too much coffee. Mom is acting weird, even for her. What is she up to? I know, Mom. She's usually not interested in someone or something except as a vehicle to allow her to gain control. And then, suddenly, she has you under her spell, and you become a participant in her plans. She takes what you say and do and twists it all around, detouring the truth and muddying the situation. The master of confusion, she makes you feel as if you're the one who's insane. Trust me. Living with that woman for eighteen years teaches you a thing or two. I've seen her bag of tricks. Every time she's around, it makes me feel like I'm going crazy.

Instead of the garage, I go into Eve's office and sit at her desk, imagining what it was like to be her. From Eve's window, the view of the beach looming above the other houses seems constant and steady – the earthen and muted sand against the expansive but snaking line of blue. Spinning the desk chair toward her desk, I spot it. It was a brand-new spiral notebook with EVE written on the cover.

I open it and see the unfamiliar handwriting of my grandmother.

November 11, 2019 – Well hello, diary. It's been a while since we last chatted. I was on a roll writing journals years ago, telling my family's story, travels, recipes, and life lessons. This may be my last journal, though, as I have refused to do any more radiation and chemo.

Spoke to Epinimon, our shaman and dear friend, and he told me that cancer represents deep hurt and pain that I've been carrying around for a long time. He's correct. I have longstanding, still, unresolved suffering, and a deep secret and grief are eating away at me. Epinimon is very smart and tuned in. Holding this secret all these years has damaged me.

But what should I do? How is one to communicate with people who want nothing to do with you? Maybe I didn't try hard enough, didn't do enough. I sent letters, birthday cards, and presents to Liz and Chelsea after they moved away, but never heard back from either of them.

There is sadness and profound pain that fills me. It feels like I'm pressing my heart into a sharp sword. My love is deep for Chelsea, sweet little Chelsea. I should have tried harder. I told Liz what I saw. The way he touched her. Liz was so mad at me, defending her husband and his creepy twin brother, Jim. Damn you, Jim.

I HAD to stand up for Chelsea. Keeping my mouth shut was not an option, and it cost me. Boy, did it cost me. But love lives on, and I never stopped loving Liz or Chelsea. My spirit will always love them because my soul knows no loss. And I know the truth, the factual truth of what happened with Chelsea, Robert, and Jim – that Goddamn lie. Someday it will come out and be exposed to the light of day.

I flip through the notebook. Eve only wrote a few pages. There's another brief entry in a different colored pen.

November 12, 2019 – Josie has been such a big help. She brings me tea and puts a cover on me when I fall asleep on the recliner. I love that lady. I'm so weak, barely making it up and down the stairs – this body. You're not supposed to break down on me, but I guess it must.

And then, on the next page, she wrote another passage. This entry is not dated.

In America, we let our families die in hospitals and rehab centers, cold and sterile, hooked up to monitors and needles coming out of hands or arms, or both. People in lab coats, force-feeding pills, and Jell-O. Not for me.

Rather than allowing this stupid dis-ease to get the better of me, we've decided to throw one last party. If we cry, we cry. If we laugh, we laugh. No rules. Just good people gathering for love. Many will be traveling both a physical and an emotional distance for me. My heart overflows. I want friends to stay with us if they can. Josie will help me put sticky notes on my possessions to claim and take with them if they want. If they don't, that's okay, too.

We will be kind to ourselves and know that endings are also beginnings.

Let's turn death into a reason to celebrate, a chance to lift out of the fear of the unknown. I want to do this while I can still enjoy the love of my dear friends.

Should I call and invite Liz and Chelsea to the parting party? It scares me. Liz still hates me. They should know that I'm, well, not long for this planet. I will call Liz in the morning.

I frantically flip through the rest of the journal for more, but that's it. I want more. No, I need more. The journal rests on my chest. It should have been a priority to get to know Eve better. God, I'm a fool. My stupid life consumed me such that Grandma Eve never crossed my mind. Mom was so believable, saying Eve was horrible, but what did other people see in Grandma Eve? Josie loved her. It sounds like she had many other friends who loved her as well – all those people framed on her walls. I feel my heart tearing. I've lost a person I didn't know I had. Even worse, I didn't care.

The journal stuffs into the back of my pants, under my long-sleeved plaid shirt. This journal needs to be kept safe and out of Mom's hands. I grab the veiled shoebox and walk out of the small, first-floor office. Be cool. Look nonchalant. Peeking up and down the hall for Josie, she's nowhere to be seen. Mom is still up in the attic, so I duck into my, err, Grandma Eve's room and jam the journal and shoebox under a pair of jeans in my suitcase.

Sitting on my knees in front of the suitcase, I try my hardest to remember. What was Eve referring to in her journal entry? "The way he touched her." My eyes squint, but only fuzzy, flickery memories come back. Blurred flashbacks of me sitting on the floor coloring, walking home from school, and seeing my father with a beer. Then another memory of Uncle Jim taking me fishing. Ashen and dull, the memories in black and white creep in and through me. I hold my breath. Can people forget and then remember memories? Can someone suggest a false memory, and then over years, it seems like the truth and feels natural and identifiable? Did Grandma falsely implant a memory in me? Or the other is true. And why did Mom systematically block my memories with her distinctive, hostile rhetoric about Grandma Eve?

Grandma Eve said she wrote other journals. If Mom finds them, she'll throw them away. That cannot happen. I need to read them – to know my past. I slam my suitcase closed. My heart speeds as my palms get sweaty. I grab at my shirt and push my fist into my chest. No, No. I can't lose control. Not now! I squeeze my eyes closed and curl up in a fetal position on the floor. With no sense of control, my primordial, subconscious beast takes over my body. As I writhe, curling my knees to my chest, the realization dawns on me that Grandma Eve's journals hold the key to all my most private questions. The truth is right here, under this roof.

That sound! It penetrates my mind, so piercing, the pitch and squeal of wood scraping on wood. My ears are hot as I clamp my hands against my head, but it doesn't help. It's not coming from outside of me. The horrible sound comes from inside me. "No!" I plead with my mind. It doesn't listen. It does what it will, sending me into a full-blown unstoppable anxiety attack.

The anxiety attack lasts a few minutes, though the extreme pressure behind my eyes feels like it lasts for hours. My head is entirely drenched in sweat, and I push my wet hair away from my face with numb hands. Familiar nausea and stomach cramps grab as my trembling body shuts down. The lights are bright, so I shield them like a prisoner coming into the light after being in a dungeon. I need my Xanax, but moving is impossible. I surrender to the abysmal fatigue and eventually collapse over my suitcase.

CHAPTER 9

My phone alarm sounds its raucous and bloody tone – time to empty the water buckets. On the floor, with my head crushed into my suitcase, I feel for my phone in my back pocket and shut off the cruel alarm. The blurry room upsets my stomach, and I wipe the drool from my cheek and check the time. Twenty minutes. Usually, it takes an hour to shake off a panic attack, but that'll have to do.

Breathe in through your nose and out your mouth, like Doctor Allen says to do when a panic attack occurs. My breath-in chokes from the wet carpet smell from the leaky roof. It's sour-milky and stale like a giant, shaggy, wet dog. Fixing my gaze on the filling cans of water, I remember being in Grandma Eve's room. I push myself up to sit, then onto my knees, and attempt to stand, but the room spins around me in whirls and beats. I stop and rest my hands on the floor. With all four on the floor, I stabilize myself in a tabletop position. Count to ten. Remember the technique Doctor Allen recommended. Count to ten! I close my eyes. One, two, three, four–

There hasn't been that terrifying wood-scraping sound in my head in years, not since I was a teenager. I had woken up screaming every night from the terrible grinding squeal. And then it stopped, just like that. And now, it's back. I'm going to take an extra Xanax.

"Chelsea, do you need help with the water?" Josie yells from downstairs.

Struggling to stand again, I lurch forward and then back as if I had been on a three-day drunk. "Ah, no. It's okay. I... I got it." Pull yourself together. Count to ten. Okay, okay. Five, six. No one should see me in this dreadful state. Seven – there's no time for this counting crap. Ten! I wipe my damp face and crooked stand like Lucy, the half ape-half human.

If Mom gets to those journals first, it'll be impossible to read them. I need a plan. "Grandma Eve, help me," I whisper, looking up. Good God, Chelsea, you are a scientist. She's not up there. Sitting on the bench at the end of her bed, the dragging, weary aftershocks of the panic attack plague me. My back relaxes, and my heavy hands flop next to my legs. My fingertips sweep over the coarse and thin textured fabric covering the bench. The room spins again. I grab the edge of the seat to steady myself. It will take an hour to recover. I know that from experience. Breathe in. Breathe out. Count to fucking ten. I'm squeezing the bench so hard my knuckles turn white.

Easy. You don't want to break the thing. Loosening my death grip on the bench, I feel a gap between the seat top and the sides of the legs. The antique Spanish-looking bench has metal hinges. I shift my weight to the left, lift on the other side of the bench top, and it gives. I'm sure they're not in here. Why would someone put precious journals in the bench at the foot of your bed?

After slothing off the bench and opening the lid, I pluck out mundane paperwork and receipts from Home Depot and Ralph's grocery store. Moving aside some loose notebook paper, I rifle through the small, rectangular opening but only find a bunch of nonsense paperwork. I pull a piece out and study it closer. It says New Year's Eve Party and then has a list of names of people I don't know – Gary, Ellen, Tom Wellington – with doodles around the edges.

Digging deeper through the papers, I feel something more substantial. It's two small, pale yellow floppy notebooks out of the bench cubby. They have nothing written on the outside. Some loose newspaper clippings and photos fall out of one. I fumble to catch the clippings and flip it open, and read.

At some point, you must let go of what you thought should happen and live with what IS happening.

Yes, Eve's handwriting! I recognize it from the last journal that was in her office. My heart rate quickens, but not from panic. There are loose photos tucked into the journal. One image is of me coming out of school. I remember that blue and white sweater from eighth grade. It was my favorite. Another photo is of me walking with Mom, pushing a grocery cart to our car. Total zit-face looks like my Freshman year. I've never seen these photos. Who took them?

Losing no time, I flip to the first page of Eve's journal.

January 15, 1987, Well, here we go again. Dear Diary: This is my second journal. The first one filled up with little effort. I shouldn't say that, exactly. What I mean is that I had quite a bit to say, and it just poured out of me, unlike fine champagne. No, it splattered out of me more like shaking out hot sauce from a bottle, random and messy. And spicy.

Punching the air in a one-two, I squeal. "Yes!" I nod triumphantly and turn to the first pages of the other journal. Holding the journals out in front of me, I see numbering on the inside jackets. They say One of Three and Two of Three. I sit on the floor, cross my legs, set Journal Number One on my lap, and open to the first page. Grandma's handwriting is careful and round with that same unique older person quality of cursive writing. I read the first entry.

Dear Diary: I am Evelyn Petersson, and today is March 1, 1983. My friends call me Eve. I am on a search. At 57 years old, I need to understand the meaning of my life. Not too much to ask, right?

Two years ago, Sally gifted this journal to me. I didn't start writing in it until now. Now, when desperation hits me, I write to get my feelings and thoughts down. Now that my life is a mess and Doug is gone.

My heart and soul are clenched and closed. All I crave is sleep. Can't eat. But my dear friends won't leave me alone. Thank God. JoAnn comes over every day and makes a pot of tea. She endures my psychotic Jekyll and Hyde antics. At times, I cry hysterically; other times, I punch a pillow and scream his name.

Pat brings lunch, alternating salad, and homemade soup. I do my best to eat but pick at it. "Just eat a few bites." She says, patting my hand.

Damn you, Doug! I loved you. It was a deep, stunning, spacious love. And now you're gone.

What was real? Were you angry and didn't say anything? Did you know how important you were to me? Did you love me? Or? Were you just a stupid, selfish jerk? Why didn't you tell me about her?

And now, it's too late. I suppose I could scream at your grave.

She's talking about Grandpa Doug. He died before I was born. Mom loved Doug, always singing his praises, but she thought there was foul play surrounding his death. There's more to read in this journal, but I'm worried Mom may barge in and take these journals from me.

With everything out of the bench and thrown on the floor behind me, I scan the room. The third journal must be here, somewhere. It's probably in another in-plain-sight hiding place, but upon further investigation, there's nothing under Grandma's bed or on the bookshelf.

I look down at my raggedy hangnail and think, for once, I don't want to rip at it. There were still a bunch of boxes in the attic. Mom cannot get her hands on any of them. I know if she does, she'll want them demolished. I'm sure Mom is planning a bonfire of the bones of Grandma Eve's existence, a big Celtic celebration to ward off Eve's evil spirit. She wants it all up in smoke.

My phone alarm sounds again, pulling me out of my journal search. Outside, the fitful, violent rain is now slowing. Thank goodness. The relentless pelting has turned to fine, misty tears whispering down Eve's window, and the water cans fill up slower than before.

Josie walks past my room and then back again. "Oh, there you are. I've been looking for you all over the house. I thought you were up in the attic, but when I popped my head up there, your mom was throwing clothes around and talking to herself. She seemed distressed." Josie raises her eyebrows. "So, I didn't disturb her."

"Yeah, she shooed me out of the attic a while ago. Dealing with Grandma Eve's stuff seems to stress her out." I stash the journals under some receipts and random papers.

Josie walks into the room and inspects the cans. "How's the tsunami watch going?"

"Seems the sudden, tempestuous flood has slowed down a bit."

"What're all these papers?" Josie questions, putting her hands on her hips.

"Oh, just junk. I pulled it all out of the storage area in the bench. Looks like receipts and notes, bits and pieces of things." The mess covered the floor around the bench. "Should I keep this kind of stuff or toss it?"

Josie comes closer to the jumble of papers. If she notices the journals, she'll want them or give them to Mom. This cannot happen. I need to read those journals. I'm intrigued by Grandma Eve's life. All the parts I've missed and to learn more about this deep, dark secret she kept.

My body jerks, and I step out in front of Jose, tripping and bumping her arm.

Josie lurches forward and then catches herself on the windowsill. "Oh, my!"

"Oops, my feet don't seem to work today. So sorry, Josie." Helping Josie by lifting her arm feels good to me. She's one of my lifelines to Grandma Eve. "I'm a total klutz. Just ask Mom. That's what she calls me all the time."

Josie turns, rubbing her forehead. "If I live through this, it will be a wonder," she says in a whisper voice.

"Yeah, I'm sorry."

"Well." Josie clears her throat. "I guess I'll need receipts from this year. Otherwise, throw out the rest with the rubbish." She lifts a couple of pieces of paper from the floor, studies them, and sets them on the bed in a pile. "I didn't know you would be sorting out Eve's room?" She squints at me and walks toward Grandma Eve's bathroom.

Her keen black eyes probably see right through my enigmatic, suspicious behavior. I look down and away. My ears are hot, and I'm sure they are turning red. "You saw Mom. She's acting like a crazy woman. She kicked me out of the attic, so I thought it best to stay in here and monitor the leas." My voice cracks. "The leaks."

"Well, if you ask me, I think you both are questionable. I'm doing my best to stay in the present and find just a smidge of joy in this process, but you and your mother are making it rather impossible."

Okay, I deserved that. "Josie, why were you looking for me in the first place?"

"Oh, never mind." Her voice drifts off as she walks out of the bedroom.

I hate being strange and misleading. It makes me cringe to think so, but I'm acting like Mom. These journals need a safe place. Nobody can know about them until I have time to read every page. The journals hide in my suitcase under some clothes with the top closed. The rainwater cans are slightly lighter with less rain in them, and all the receipts and papers stuff easily into a trash bag. I'll make sure Mom sees the garbage bag. She'll think I'm productive.

The journals call to me from my suitcase. I close the door and find the first journal. Reading them in succession, as she wrote them, is essential. The stories will unfold, and there will be a better understanding of Grandma Eve and my childhood. While rummaging around in my suitcase, I find the large bag of Skittles I packed. Provisions, yes. Mom has her wine, and I have my sweets. As a Skittles lover, the orange and yellow flavors are the best. The brand continuously makes new flavors, but nothing beats the originals. And what is up with the purple ones? What the heck is that? Poop flavored? I push those aside and put them back in the bag. Sometimes, I get desperate once all the good ones are gone but the poopy purples. And then, it's hard to admit, but when one needs a sugar high, one will dip down into a dark and poopy place.

Back to Journal One.

March 2, 1983, Betrayal cuts deep. It makes you feel you are the lowest life form on the planet, like the bottom-feeder amoeba that gets scooped up by a scientist to study something obscure, like human liver abnormalities.

Betrayal never comes from your enemies. It comes from someone you love.

What was real? Was he angry and said nothing? Was he dissatisfied? Did he know how important he was to me?

"Chelsea? Where are you?"

I slam the journal closed and shove it in my suitcase. The bedroom door flies open. Mom stomps in, ungracious and rude.

"Sheesh, Mom, you could knock, you know." I tug at my jeans and straighten my shirt.

"Jesus, Chelsea, you look like crap!" Mom reaches out to fix my hair. She pushes a straggler behind my ear. "Seriously, you look bad, even for you. God, it pains me at how plain you are."

"Gee, wow. I can always count on you, Mom, to make me feel like a piece of shit." I scan the room, double-checking for the salvaged keepsakes. "Well, you know, Mom, this house has been a ton of work. Just look at that." The full white trash bag sits on the floor beside the bench. She glances at the bag and then angles her body away from me. "The attic is all yours, Chelsea. I got what I needed. So you can get back up there and finish the job."

She got what she needed? What did she get? "Finish the job? What am I? A hitman?"

"Yep, yep, yep. I mean, no, you're not a hit – Oh Chelsea, get back up there, right now! Get it ready to give to the women's shelter. I sorted it all out, so you don't have to think. Because, well, we both know that when you overthink, you daydream off to Darth Vaderland, and nothing gets done. Just put it all back in those boxes and load them in your rental car." Mom studies the bedroom while fanning herself. "Maybe I'll stay in here for a bit."

"Mom, are you sweating?"

She shoots a fake, forced smile at me, but it hits in my gut. Nausea rises in me again. Something is going on with her. The deception behind her eyes makes me bristle. She blots her upper lip with the back of her hand and then swipes it away with force.

"Look, Chelsea." She walks straight over to me with that look in her eyes. She has that look of uncontrolled anger.

I wince and step back. This is not the first time she's acted like this.

She bursts toward me. "We need to get this house cleaned out," she hisses, pushing her index finger into my chest. "Go back up there and get it done." Liz raises her eyebrows to add emphasis to each word.

"Mom, I'm a grown woman. I'll work wherever I want to in this house. I'm not taking this from you anymore."

As soon as the words emerge from me, I feel the hot sting of her hand as she slaps my cheek. My gaze flings to one side. "Enough! I have had just about enough of you, Chelsea!"

"Jesus, Mom!" My hand covers my mouth. The prick of her violence makes me both angry and empty. Every time she hurts me, I get emptier and emptier, like cold air in my veins.

"Oh, sure. Now you're gonna cry. Poor little Chelsea. You have never failed to disappoint me." Mom paces the room. "All your life… Everyone had to walk on eggshells around you. Don't upset Chelsea. Or else she'll make up some horrible story and go around telling everyone."

I could feel my cheeks flaming. Don't cry. Don't cry. I look down, away from Mom's piercing stare, but turning my back to her is not an option. I know better.

"Go on, go tattle to one of your teachers. Oh, that's right, you don't have any teachers anymore. Do you?" Mom juts out her chin, threatening my space again. "Got anything to say?"

My shoulders tighten, and my back runs into the wall, giving me more space than her arm's length. I shake my head no and look down at her foot with the black support boot. My heart pounds like a trapped mouse battering its cage.

"Thought so." Liz turns and looks out the window. "Go on, you little brat. Get out of my sight. And don't disappoint me. It's making me crazy being in this house."

Her words land hard on me. I'm like a cornered animal wanting to snarl, scratch, and fight, but I can't. She makes me feel like a child again. Helpless and small.

Opening my mouth, but nothing comes out. My jaw clamps closed.

Stay quiet.

It's better this way – no further confrontations. I'm tired and hungry and still recovering from the panic attack. Touching my cheek where she'd slapped me, I want to say something, but the only sensation inside me is the cold rush of air.

Mom marches into Grandma Eve's bathroom. There's no stopping her. She has complete control, and she knows it. "I'll handle the rest of these rooms. Finish the attic, Chelsea," Mom squawks from the bathroom.

CHAPTER 10

Stoic and silent, I walk out of Eve's bedroom, down the stairs, and toward the kitchen. Mom doesn't deserve the satisfaction of seeing me cry.

In the kitchen, Josie chops up onions with a chunk, chunk, chunk. The stinging smell assaults my nose. I stop and gaze at her hands. It's like the knife is an extension of her hand. "Josie, do you have any diet coke?"

Josie spins around. "Heck no! We don't drink that junk. That stuff'll kill you."

"Oh, okay." Looking down, I turn toward the attic.

"Would you like a glass of water or iced tea, Chelsea?"

"No, thanks." I tug on the rope.

"Are you okay?" Josie asks, softening her tone. "Wow, honey. Your eyes are super red. Is the onion the culprit?"

"Must be the onion." The stairs to the attic open with a puff of dust. My red eyes are not from the onion.

Mom made a colossal mess in the attic. Clothes, papers, and trinkets litter the attic floor. There's a pile of books in the corner – more cookbooks and some self-help titles. I stuff a big black garbage bag with all the clothes and most of the books and then take them downstairs and out to the trunk of my rental car.

One box in the attic that Mom tore into like a ravenous bear looks promising. I take one thing out at a time, inspecting each item. The old cardboard box with all four sides crinkled in still had a few potential treasures in its coffer. There's a small book that looks like a journal. I turn it over, but it's another cookbook. Grandma must have loved to cook.

The familiar red and white checkered Better Homes and Gardens Cookbook is in the box. The much-thumbed and dogeared book had other recipes on note cards and loose paper folded inside. I'm learning Grandma Eve's handwriting style. There was a vintage Holiday Cookbook and a Casserole Cookbook, and then I found the best of the bunch, Dishes Men Like – New and Old Favorites, Easy to Prepare, Sure to Please! "Ha! What the heck?" I had to flip through it – macaroni camp-style, pork and beans, Welsh rabbit, and London loaf recipes fill the pages. The only recognizable recipe is pork and beans, and that's about it.

No man or woman would want me to cook for them. I'm terrible in the kitchen. There are few LGBTQAI movies, but in all the regular movies, when the guy stays over, you make him breakfast. One time, I invited Drew over and thought she might actually spend the night. Anticipating this monumental stage of my mostly dry dating life, I had bought a 6-pack of eggs. It was around 6 AM when I had put the eggs in water, secured the lid, turned on the burner, and returned to bed. In about forty minutes, we heard gunshots coming from the kitchen. Bam. Bam. We flew out of bed. *Bam!* Stalking into the kitchen, we saw the war zone. Drew ran in and shut off the stove. Lesson learned. When you boil eggs, and the pan runs dry, they explode like bombs. After that debacle, Drew got dressed and went home hungry, and I spent the rest of the day scraping the machine gun of splattered eggs from the ceiling and stove.

Piled together on the attic floor are the Man Cookbook and the Better Homes cookbook. I'll bring those down and show Josie when

Mom isn't around. Josie will appreciate these. She might even have some stories about Grandma Eve's cooking.

I pick through the box to get all this cleaned up and get on with the search. But the cardboard box offers no journals, so I fill it back up, haul it down the stairs, and out to my car. I had backed the car into the garage to keep everything dry from the steady rain. My car is filling with Eve's life. Once all this goes to the shelter, it will be gone forever. I pick up one of her sweaters on top of an open box and hold it to my face. It smells of perfume, cardboard, and dust. Tucking the sweater under my arm, I step into the house.

With the attic cleared of most of the boxes and bags, I could see more clearly. Heavy, unpainted timber covers the walls and ceiling, and stuffed insulation stands between each timber. It smells of wet wood and moldy bread with a touch of the salty ocean. Silence reigns here. I like that. After moving all the boxes around, the small room seems free of danger – spiders and other little critters who enjoy old cardboard boxes and shadowy spaces. Unable to stand up straight because of the pitched ceiling, I bend over like a geriatric cave dweller.

"Dinner in twenty," Josie yells from the kitchen.

"Okay, thanks," I holler back, waiting to hear if Mom responds, but she doesn't.

There is one last little box in a dark corner under the rafters that Mom must have missed. Keepsakes, it says on both the side and top of the box. This whole attic holds mementos. I open the box, pull out a wad of packing paper with care, and start to tremble. Get a hold of yourself, Chelsea. It's probably more cookbooks.

A framed print of just me and Grandma Eve grabs my attention. I look to be around five years old with long, red, straight hair and bangs. Grandma Eve's eyes are piercing blue. The unfamiliar appetite for sentiment rises through me like chimney smoke. I've never been interested in family. It usually scared me to think about family, but now, being here in Grandma Eve's house, I'm eager for more. I hold up two pictures of Mom and my father at their black and white, uninteresting wedding and toss those aside. A beautiful blue vase and a pale-yellow book are toward the bottom of the box. Excitedly, I open it, but there is no writing. It's just a blank journal that matches the other two. Where could that last journal be?

I jump up and glide down the rickety stairs. Josie faces forward in the kitchen and doesn't turn around as I scurry like a thief through the kitchen and up to Eve's room. My cheek and ego are still sore from the slap. What Mom said echoes through me. 'Making up stories and telling my teachers…' I didn't make up any stories. Those so-called stories were the truth, but Mom has never believed me.

Quick and careful, I peek into Grandma Eve's room. Thank God Mom's not in here. Even though it's coming apart, my briefcase is the perfect hiding place for some of these keepsakes. Under some of my papers, a snicker bar winks at me. Disappointed, I pick up the flat empty wrapper, and like a desperate stray dog, I lick it for the last of the melted chocolate. The empty wrapper hides under a few used tissues in the trash. Mom will really flip out if she sees any candy bars in my possession. Checking the hall for Mom or Josie, I dart out of the bedroom, my broken briefcase in tow.

Mom comes out of Eve's office just as I scurry down the hall. "Chelsea?"

Ignoring her, I slow my gait, attempting to look normal. One thought consumes me. Get up to the attic and put those keepsakes in my briefcase.

"Chelsea!"

"What?" I stop walking but don't turn around.

"Did you do anything with Eve's journal? The one on her desk?"

I turn halfway around but don't make eye contact. "Don't know what you're talking about."

"Eve's last journal. In her office? The one she wrote in during her final days?" Mom steps toward me.

"Never saw it."

"You sure you never saw it? Hmm. I'll ask Josie if she did something with it." Mom lets out a heavy sigh. "Why do you have your briefcase? You better be working on this house and not those stupid sneakers."

I feel a roiling heat in my belly. "Work emails." She chooses the worst times to take notice of me.

"Did you fully clean out the attic?"

"Mostly."

"Okay, Chelsea. Enough with the one and two-word answers." Mom puts her hands on her hips. "You know, I had to slap some sense into you. It's the only way to get through your thick skull." The engorged vein on the side of her neck looks like a taught rope about to snap.

"What's that in your pocket?"

In my back pocket are the photos that fell out of Grandma Eve's journal. I didn't want to share them with Mom. "Oh yeah, I found these. Just some old photos. Nothin' really."

Mom holds her hand out. "Lemme see."

I give her the photos and study her expression. Her eyebrows squish together as she looks from one image to the next.

"Mom, who took those of us?"

"I've never seen." She stops herself and scratches her cheek. "This one was right after we'd moved up to Seattle." Mom holds up the one with me in my favorite R2D2 long-sleeved t-shirt. "How did Eve get these?" Mom stares at the ground with a blank look. "How?"

"How the heck would I know?" I snort, discovering that there is much to discover about this family of mine.

"I'll keep these. You'll lose them. Now, get that attic done before dinner! Or else, I'm gonna lose it. Again." Mom spits her words out through gnashing teeth.

"Mom, can I please have those photos back? They are pictures of me, you know? Besides, you said you wanted nothing of Grandma Eve's that is not of value."

"Well, I'm in these photos as well, Chelsea. We were together when they were taken – whoever took them." Mom turns and walks away with the photos.

In the attic, the blank journal and the other keepsakes safely go into my briefcase. In an attempt to draw a deep breath, my lungs refuse to be replenished with oxygen. Instead, my throat constricts as

I turn around backward, preparing myself for the descent down the attic stairs – one foot, then the other. My clammy hands can barely hold the rails. The briefcase strap gets hung up on the top lip of the staircase. I yank on it, but it doesn't give. Giving it another tug, it slips out of my sweaty hand, tumbling heavily to the wood floor. It lands with a thump lump. The empty journal half-spills out of the case.

My only choice is to let go of the stair rails and freefall the last few steps to recover the ornery briefcase. I land on my feet and then fall toward the briefcase.

"Bordel de merde! Whoa, Chelsea!" Josie drops a serving spoon on the floor, tomato sauce splattering all over. "Are you all right?"

"I'm fine. I'm fine." But I'm not fine. My back hurts from the impact. Looking down, I push the stray journal back inside and stand up. My hand finds my lower back to help support my spine. I pick up the briefcase, treat it like it was explosive, and make my way out of the kitchen.

Josie's voice drifts off as I turn the corner. "I hope your computer wasn't in there..."

The worst challenge is yet to come – Mom. Walk calmly, Chelsea. I think about Drew and how I've watched her confident swagger. However, I'm neither calm nor confident. But I can't allow the exploitive and opportunistic wolf to get her hands on any of Grandma Eve's journals. They're mine, and I'll do anything to protect them.

"Ladies, again, dinner is ready," Josie calls from the kitchen.

With some effort, I stored the briefcase and all its contents under Grandma Eve's bed. With the roof still leaking, I peer into the water cans, haul them to the bathroom, and dump the water in the tub, catching a glimpse of myself in the bathroom mirror. Mirrors are my enemy, but this time, I look at myself with a sheen of sweat covering my cheeks, upper lip, and forehead. I dab my face using a hand towel, probably Grandma Eve's hand towel. Josie thinks I look like Grandma Eve. That thought makes me smile. Closing my eyes, I prepare myself for an hour of sitting across from Mom.

I rush through dinner, shoveling in the goodness. Josie calls it pork chops in sauce tomat. The scrumptious, savory dish makes my mouth water with each bite. I raise my head and look at Josie. "Josie, will you send meals to me in Portland? I've never eaten this well, like ever."

Mom takes a drink of her wine. "You know, when you were younger, Chelsea, I had to work. Always too busy to cook a decent meal."

"It's in my genes to make beautiful and nourishing food." Josie glances at me. "I get a chance to show my love by making a delicious, home-cooked meal. And Chelsea, the more you cook, the easier it gets." Josie sits back in her chair. "Once we became friends, um, your grandma and me. She would try new recipes." Josie smiles at me. "She went to Paris for cooking school, you know. Sometimes the dishes turned out delicious, and sometimes they would go terribly awry. In the end, she developed into quite the excellent cook."

"So, Grandma found you in that alley when she attended cooking school?"

Josie nods. "Yes."

"Wait, what alley?" Mom slurs.

We ignore her question. I visualize Grandma Eve's journals sitting alone in my room. Not even Mom's sour and sharp attitude can bring me down. I stand up from the table and start collecting dirty plates. "Thanks for the amazing meal, Josie. And I'm not kidding about my Portland meal offer."

Josie nods and smiles. "If you want me to show you a thing or two in the kitchen, I'd love to help."

"Thanks, Josie." Embarrassment washes over me that my mom doesn't have this wholesome value around cooking and didn't pass that on to me. Loading the dishes in the dishwasher, I turn to Josie. "I'd need more than a few tips in the kitchen. I'm a terrible cook. Besides, my sneaker line work is calling me this evening. I'm going upstairs in my… err… Grandma's room."

"Chelsea, I've never seen you so driven! Sheesh, usually you procrasssinate on everything," Mom slurs, barely getting the sentence out. Once she drinks wine, she can't stop. It's a nightly occurrence, and I noticed she opened a bottle of wine at around 2 o'clock today.

"Thanks for pointing out that lovely character flaw of mine."

"Well, it's the truth." Mom gulps her wine and looks away. "Oh, lookie there." Mom staggers over to the buffet table, where there is a picture. She picks it up and pokes at it with her finger. "God, Chelsea, you were a scrawny little thing. And then, when you were like eleven or twelve, you just blew up." She sits back down at the table, carrying a framed photo. "You were probably nine or ten. Look how skinny you were."

She's trying, but it's not working. She can't push my buttons. Not tonight. I can't wait to read the journals. Mom will never get her grimy paws on any of them. Through those journals, I'll learn about Grandma, the actual person she was. Not Mom's distorted version of her. I'm intrigued. Those sublime red stilettos. That poem? What was he trying to say to Eve? She kept the poem with the heels, the practically new heels.

Josie gets up by pushing her palms firmly onto the table. She bends over, rubs her thighs, and limps into the kitchen. She comes back holding a teacup. "You sure you wanna get back up there, Chelsea? Would you like some pie and hot tea first?"

"Not right now. Are you limping, Josie?"

"Oh, this limp? It's just Arthur visiting."

"Arthur?" I question.

"Arthur – It is." She smirks at me. "All this moisture from the rain wakes up that old grouch!"

I half-smile at her and look as to say I'm sorry. I'll bet she's told that joke a hundred times. "Pie sounds amazing. Maybe later, Josie? Right now, I'm going upstairs to, um, work."

CHAPTER 11

Up the stairs, I run into Grandma's room and close the door behind me. Fearful Mom will make another unscheduled entrance, so I grab the first journal, dated 1983, and a pillow from the bed. I hurry into the bathroom and close and lock the door. Throwing the pillow on the floor, I settle down, resting my back against the cold wall. Holding it made my heartbeat faster than a greyhound winning a race.

March 6, 1983, It was hard, but I called Liz again. She finally picked up. Hadn't talked to her since I first broke the news about her dad. She barely spoke to me. I cried, but she didn't. And then she hung up on me.

March 8, 1983. Late night tonight. Work was hectic today. So busy that the ER went on to an unscheduled divert. Nothing like getting right back into the harried pace with ER docs and supervisors yelling orders.

All day, there was one surgery after another. No breaks. That's better for me right now. Can't be alone with my thoughts. The uninvited flashbacks. It feels like I am back on that mountain, doing CPR, cutting Doug's chest open, trying to save his life.

Dianne, the only supervisor who kept her cool today, gave me the name and number of her therapist – never been. I'm not crazy. But the memories won't stop. I keep reliving that evening over and over. My heart pounds, and

I break out in a cold sweat. I need help. It's probably best to reach out to the therapist.

Audible noises emanate from the kitchen, followed by the unmistakable sound of footsteps coming up the stairs. "Chelsea! You still awake?" Josie taps on the bedroom door.

I attempt to jump up from the floor, but my foot has fallen asleep and refuses to work. The journal stashes under the pillow on the bathroom floor, and I do my best to stand. Pins and needles jab with each hobbled step. I finally get to the bedroom door and yank it open. "Yes, still awake. Um, working."

Josie sets a piece of pie and a cup of tea on the bedstand. "Lemon meringue. It is delish if I say so myself." Josie clears her voice. "Your mom wouldn't touch it." Josie covers her mouth as she yawns. "Tomorrow, we must endure another rainy day; I'm afraid to report. Are you okay? Getting your work done?"

"Getting some of it done. Thanks for the pie and tea. I never met a pie I didn't like. Did Mom go to bed?" And won't come in here and bother me.

"Yes. Your mother made her way up to the guest bedroom. We cleared out enough boxes to find the bed. That girl can certainly consume wine." Josie shakes her head and peers up at the rain-soaked ceiling. "This rain, this weeping, will end soon. Otherwise, the roof won't hold." Josie inspects the water cans. "Your mom questioned me about Eve's last journal. I left it right there in the office, next to Eve's computer. And now, it is gone. Did you take it?"

"No – never saw it." I turn toward my bed, straighten some papers, and keep my stare down. She can't know that I'm lying. "I'll bet Mom has the journal, and she's trying to throw us off her scent. If I know her, she probably lit it on fire and danced a circle around it."

Jose grimaces in a twisted frown. "Look, your mom didn't get along with Eve, but what you said is not right. Eve was my best friend!" Josie wipes her eyes, turns, and slumps out of the bedroom.

Pushing the door closed, I rest my forehead on the sturdy door. Each tiny grain of the door stares at me. Those grains know the truth. This room knows the truth. My hand lingers, wrapped around the

THE JOURNAL EFFECT

cool silver doorknob. I want to open it and tell Josie that, *yes*, I have that journal and the two others. One journal is still missing – the third one. There are three because of the numbering on the first page of each journal. Without looking, my sweaty palm finds the lock and secures the door. I can't risk Mom or Josie knowing about Grandma's journals. They will go safely back to Portland with me. I will find the truth, the truth of my life. The truth of Grandma.

I sit back down on my pillow on the tiled bathroom floor and take a bite of the pie. It's soft and delicious. The meringue swirls around with light brown peaks. The journal opens perfectly to the following passage.

April 4, 1983. Went to therapy. The therapist had a huge forehead and long skinny eyeglasses, the man behind the big, metal clipboard. I'm sure he means well. I don't think therapy is for me. The icy river between us didn't provide any warmth or trust. No connection. He talked me into one more meeting. I'll go, but I'm not holding my breath.

Called Liz again. She's busy with two jobs. I'm proud of her work ethic, but I wish Robert's work proved more reliable. The construction industry must be slow. She told me they'd like to start a family soon, but she's worried about money. In my opinion, twenty-three is too young to start a family. I want to help them financially, but it's tight without Doug's income. His sudden departure leaves an indelible void in my heart, and the weight of grief presses heavily upon my shoulders.

Asked Liz if I could come over tonight. Not a good time, she said. She's avoiding me. Liz is in pain about Doug's passing, but won't reach out to me. I love my beautiful daughter. I know it's horrible to lose your father at such a young age.

Losing your father at a tender age is a profound and shattering experience that will forever alter the course of her life. Memories of his laughter, comforting presence, and words of wisdom will become treasures to cling to, desperate to preserve the essence of who he was. Liz is grappling with a profound sense of loss and an understanding that life can be heartbreakingly fleeting.

There was a long pause while we were on the phone. Then Liz told me she talked with her doctor, who told her I shouldn't have tried to perform an open-heart stimulation on Doug. What was I supposed to do? CPR wasn't working. He was dying in my arms. I had to try, at least.

Started having nightmares about it.

Attempting to process Grandma's words, I look up from the journal. My half gaze finds a vase of dying flowers on the vanity. The once simple but profoundly beautiful arrangement had decidedly gone past its prime. A few petals gave up the fight and dropped where they died. I get up from the floor, swoosh them into my hand, and pass them by my nose. The soft petals still smelled of perfume and sweetness. I hadn't noticed the gift card until now and pull it out of the floppy, browning flowers. It reads: Our dear Evey, we will miss you. Save some good wine for us in heaven, as we will join you one day. Love, Jody, Elle, and Karen.

Gently pressing the petals and card into the center of the journal, I settle myself once again on the pillow.

August 21, 1983 Coffee is strong this morning as the fog retreats to the sea. I feel my heart cracking open like the emerging sun, the aurora. Almost six months since Doug passed now. I'm becoming myself again. Deep connections. Spirituality. Curiousness. Wildflowers.

Gave up on that expensive Uncle Poker face therapist and joined a support group at the hospital. It's great! We meet every Tuesday evening. Excited to go tonight. I'm growing fond of Peter. Not like that. No. I don't think I'll love a man ever again. Peter's wife died of breast cancer last year, and he seems like he's come to terms with her passing—mostly. He told the group that when he most feels like crying, He puts on a funny movie or listens to Eddie Murphy or Robin Williams. So, I started doing that. While I love Tootsie and the Airplane movies, Monty Python and the Holy Grail take the cake. It helps, especially after I'm jolted awake from that frantic, awful recurrent nightmare about Doug.

It's the same every time. I'm asleep in our bed, Doug beside me. And then weird sounds come from outside. I reach over for Doug, but he's not there. Can't see a thing in the pitch-black room. Somebody knocks on the windows and shakes all the doors downstairs. This manlike creature leaps to our bedroom window from a nearby tree branch and opens it from the outside. It slithers in, and a burst of foul-smelling, moist air enters the room. His face looks like Doug, but his eyes are burned out, leaving dark, horrible indentions. I try to jump out of bed to help him, but I can't move. I open my mouth wide to scream, but only desperate whispers come out. He steps back, and now his entire body is visible. He's in his hiking clothes. The same clothes as the night he died. Ominous burned hands emerge from the wall behind him. Doug can't see the hands as they grab him and pull him back. I wriggle my legs, twisting and turning, but movement is impossible; I'm trapped. My whisper screams don't help. The burned hands fully engulf Doug's body, drag him into the wall, and then he disappears.

I wake up covered in sweat with the soaked sheets tangled around my legs.

I shift my weight and get up off the floor. My back, my feet, my skin, everything screams in pain from all the physical labor of cleaning out Grandma's house. I employ my best-learned skill and muffle the taunting agony. Ignore the pain. It'll go away. More pie would help, but Josie may wake up, or worse, Mom.

Picking up my phone from the nightstand; it reads 1:25 AM. I missed a text from Drew.

> Hey, Chels – I miss you. Yeah, I'm texting pretty late. Booty call time. Lol. What time does your flight land tomo? R U still mad at me?

With frustration consuming me, I forcefully slam my phone onto the nightstand and choose to ignore the incoming text. Instead, I locate the journals in my suitcase and place all three on my bed. Both of the older journals are open to the first pages, where Grandma had numbered them. The numbering in the upper right corner of the first page is clearly written. Journal One of Three, Journal Two of Three. Three of Three is missing. I need to find it! It must be in this house, but where?

Tenderly, my fingers glide across each book, caressing their spines as if tracing the contours of a lover's body. I hop into bed, and the books jump and shudder. Seeing them come to life makes me smile, if only for a moment. All right, Grandma, what more can you tell me? I stick my legs under the covers, lean back under the four-poster bed, and open Journal One again.

September 21, 1983, Sometimes, you find the most beautiful souls in the black sheep, the odd ducks, loners, eccentrics, the lost, and the forgotten.

I had the best conversation with a homeless woman today. The door nearly blew out of my hand while entering El Pescador fish market, and this young woman approached me, asking for spare change. I thought about her request and asked her what she planned to buy with the money. She said she used to be a chef at a high-end restaurant and wanted good-tasting food. Not the crap she's been eating lately. Wondering why she was homeless and asking for money, she said that was a long story that included lots of heroin and cocaine.

I invited her to sit with me and get whatever she wanted. She accepted shyly. She was quiet at first, but once I got her going, Alice was a pleasure. She had interesting stories, but I sensed a cocktail of emotions. Guilt, shame, pain, and sorrow swirled behind her eyes. I didn't ask, and she didn't say. There is a hushed and mute wrenching of her life that must seem incurable. I asked her if I could call her Alice Wonderland. She smiled. Invited her to have lunch again with me next week at El Pescador. We'll see if she shows.

It did my heart good just offering her one meal and an hour of my time. All my friends came to my rescue when Doug died, and now I get the chance to help another person. Seems like perfect karma.

Grandma exudes compassion and generosity, a stark contrast to the person Mom always depicted her to be. Mom called Grandma money-grubbing and stingy. Why would a selfish, miserly person buy an expensive lunch for a homeless person? And then, ask her back the next week?

I reach over and get my phone. It's now 2:40 AM. Drew's text sits there like a stray dog. My heart softens as I text Drew.

> Landing at 10 PM. Home by 11ish. Come over then?

I do my best to keep my droopy eyes open, though each blink lasts longer and longer. One more page. Just one more. I turn the page and raise my eyebrows, hoping to lift my eyes open.

September 25, 1983, When Doug first passed, I clinched closed. My shoulders slumped in, and I craved depressed sleep. No eating, but my dear friends wouldn't leave me alone. JoAnn would make a pot of tea and then sit with me and allow me to cry or punch a pillow– whatever it took. Pat brought lunch over almost every day, alternating between homemade soup, salad, and sometimes chocolate cake. I'd pick at it. "Just a few bites." She'd say, patting my hand.

I've been thinking about Alice Wonderland. She can't be over twenty-seven or twenty-eight, and to feel that her life is somehow over breaks my heart. That because she got hooked on drugs, she is a bad person? No, that is not the truth.

This morning I did something I've never done. I grabbed a pen and paper and wrote a poem for the first time in my life. If I see Alice again, I'd like to give this to her. Don't know if it's good or not. It doesn't rhyme much, but here goes.

Appreciation not Possession (For Alice) September 24, 1983

> My rosiest, pink friends
> picked and finished.
> A regular event, a grave ascent.
>
> I am a bud, a flower
> loved and honored as I tower.
> Tell myself I will not be
> like my friends,
> chosen for my bloom and grace.
>
> I will be wild, fierce, hard to identify.
> Finding space.
> refuse to be civilized,
> planted in a neat row
> with a plastic label.
>
> Then again, others say they swell
> from the sensual, pleasing touch,

    the arousal of being relieved of their towering
        command,
    to be placed in the arms of a beloved.

    It might be nice not bearing the value of savage and
        solitary.
    Perhaps I won't be thorny or invisible.
    And maybe, just maybe
    I'll be impossible to forget.

CHAPTER 12

⌳

*J*osie places a grapefruit, two plates, and a knife in front of me. "You know what to do with that, right?"

"Um, yeah? Sort of." I've never cut up a grapefruit, only ordered one in a restaurant. They are horribly sour, even after drowning them in sugar. I'm tentative with the knife, like a tightrope walker on opening night. I know enough to cut it in two.

"Well? What's your plan now, Chelsea?" Josie says with her hands on her hips. "Just staring at it won't get it cut up."

I look at Josie and scrunch up my face. "Josie, I didn't want to tell you I don't like grapefruit. They are awfully sour."

"When was the last time you had one?"

"Like ten years ago."

"Alright." Josie takes the two halves and places them down on the plates, flesh side up. It smells citrusy, acidic, and pungent. "You know your grandma showed me these nifty cutting tips. She loved grapefruit. If I show you how to cut these up, do you promise you'll give it another try?"

"Can I have it with sugar?" I bargain.

Josie puts the sugar bowl in front of me and then cuts the grapefruit. "See, you go around the outside first. Then take the knife and separate each section. Easy-peasy."

"Cutting grapefruit is *not* easy-peasy." Mom shuffles into the kitchen in her bright green bathrobe and slippers. "I hate cutting grapefruit. Eve made me do it all the time when I was young."

"Well, there you go, Josie. Now there's another reason I don't eat grapefruit. Evidently, my mom thought they were too hard to cut." My comment lands like a pancake flat on the kitchen floor.

"Actually, Chelsea, as I got older and moved out of Eve's house, I never wanted to see another grapefruit. Just smelling it turns my stomach. We had a grapefruit tree in our backyard, and she'd make me cut up that foul fruit every day."

"Well, today's the last day!" Josie abruptly changes the subject. She does this every time she and Mom disagree about Grandma. I'm sure Josie can't wait to slam the door on Mom and me and finally have us out of her house. We haven't exactly been model guests.

"Right, Josie, not much left to do here." Mom helps herself to a cup of coffee. "Josie, do you have any fat-free, sugar-free creamer?"

"You mean, do I have cancer-in-a-can creamer? No."

Mom scoffs at Josie, takes her black coffee, and sits across from me at the table. With bloodshot eyes, she looks at me. "Are we riding to the airport together?"

"Yes. We should leave no later than six tonight."

"Why so early? That's crazy. My flight isn't until 9:30."

"Mom, just for once, please trust me. I've checked traffic and have considered travel time to the airport, drop off the car, and check-in. And we have different flight times."

"Fine. Whatever, Chelsea." Mom sits back and crosses her legs. She looks at me again. "I told you to put that silly t-shirt in the trash. You look like a twelve-year-old nerd, just like in that picture you found."

I look down at my Star Wars long-sleeved tee that Megan gave me for my birthday four years ago. Yea, it's a little faded and stretched out, but still. "It's comfy. Besides, R2D2 is the best. Who gave me that Star Wars t-shirt when I was younger in that photo?"

"Oh, it was your father. He got it for you before we left for Seattle."

A sick feeling takes over my stomach, but I stay quiet.

"He gave it to you against my will, and here is some news for you, Chelsea. Luke Skywalker is never coming for you." Mom chuckles to herself, amused by her own comment.

Tuning out her caddy remark, I need to ask Mom about the details surrounding Grandpa Doug's death. But how? Mom held a deep affection for Grandpa Doug, and I am hesitant to disturb her again by evoking the memory of his passing. I tap my fingers on the small antique kitchen table. Grandma leaps into my mind, and I swallow hard. "Mom? I, um, barely remember how Grandpa died. It happened before I was born, but how did he die?" My words fly out in a nervous burst.

Mom lifts her head from looking down at her coffee. "Why are you talking so loud, Chelsea? Jeez, I'm two feet away. I can hear you."

"Right. Sorry. I'm just curious about Grandpa Doug."

"Well, I haven't thought about that in years." Mom raises her eyebrows. "You know, Eve was a surgical tech nurse, always trying to keep everyone alive. Ironically, both her husbands died before she did. Humph, it turns out she was responsible for my father's untimely death." This time, Mom's voice gets louder.

Josie, who had been gliding around the kitchen preparing and cooking breakfast, came to an abrupt halt. "Wait, what? She was *not* responsible for his death!"

"Oh, no? I spoke to a few doctors who said she should have never opened him up on that mountain."

"He was dead. Zero heartbeats." Josie's voice is flush with anger. "She had no choice." She slaps down a large mixing spoon on the stove and turns around.

"That may be, but she should have never done that up there with no sterilization or replacement blood."

"Wait, wait, wait, you two." I try to stop another smoldering battle between Mom and Josie. "Someone, please tell me what happened while they were hiking?"

Mom squints at me. "How did you know they were hiking?"

"Well, um, you said they were up on a mountain. I just assumed–"

Shit! I need to be more careful. There may as well be a sign around my neck that says I have the journals.

"Whatever." Mom looks away, focusing her gaze out the kitchen window.

Josie walks to the kitchen table with a cup of coffee and sets it down hard. "Chelsea, I'll tell you what happened. Your Grandma told me in great detail. She fell into a profound state of depression for the longest time after Doug died."

"Oh, that'll be golden. Yes, Josie, PLEASE tell the story of how MY father died." Mom pushes her chair away from the table. "You didn't even know Eve at the time."

Josie sits down. "My apologies. Liz, please tell Chelsea what happened to your father."

"No, no, you seem to know everything about Eve. You go right ahead." Mom crosses her arms, sets her jaw, and looks away. The cold battlefield between Mom and Josie clashes on in ear-ringing silence. Modern warfare makes my cheeks burn red.

She stands and recoils into the kitchen. About a minute goes by with no one speaking. I feel like a cancer patient about to get my test results.

Josie clears her voice and starts in a slightly breathy tone. "One afternoon, Eve and Doug took a hike to their favorite spot, Mission Trails-Kwaay Paay Peak – one of the best places to see San Diego at sundown. Eve said they had hiked to the top of the trailhead and looked around at the spectacular views when Doug grabbed his chest. He broke out in a sweat and fell to his knees. Eve jumped right in with her long-known people-saving skills and put him on his back to start CPR. She looked all around, but there were no other hikers. She pinched Doug's nose, gave him three breaths in his mouth, and then screamed three sharp words, 'HELP! HELP! HELP!' You know, the universal signal for distress." Josie places a plate of croissants with butter and two different colors of marmalades and jellies on the table.

Josie turns toward me and continues with the disturbing recount. "Eve started chest compressions. Putting all her weight into her hands, she said she could hear and feel Doug's ribs breaking under her heavy downward compressions."

"Jesus, *really?*" Mom finally breaks her silence. "I guess you *do* know *every* gory God damned detail. Don't you, Josie?"

"Sorry, Liz. But yes, I do. Your mom told me everything about her life. She told the truth, unlike others in her family." Josie's seated posture stiffens. She places a croissant on her plate, takes the butter knife, puts a pat next to the croissant, and returns the butter knife. She spoons some marmalades with a small silver spoon, puts the orange glob on her plate next to the butter, and then returns the spoon. "Liz, would you like to continue?"

Still looking away, Mom waves her hand in the air and shakes her head no.

"Very well," Josie says, flat-faced and emotionless. "Eve continued with the breaths, the compressions, and the screams for help. She felt for a heartbeat, but there was nothing. No beating. No life. She pounded on his chest. Nothing. She looked around the trail for anything sharp. She knew she would lose him if she didn't do something drastic."

"... *and* this was when things went wrong," Mom blurts out.

My head ping-pongs from Josie to Mom and back to Josie again.

Josie's unwavering stare fixates on me, seemingly oblivious to Mom's presence. Her gaze, impenetrable and intense, captivates every fiber of my being. "Eve jumped up and grabbed their backpack. She told me she struggled to unzip the main compartment. Her hands were shaking so badly."

"What was she looking for?" I ask.

"A God damned corkscrew," Mom explodes.

Josie closes her eyes and continues. "She kneeled over Doug and felt for a pulse one more time. She put her head on his chest, hoping to hear the familiar heartbeat. Nothing. She opened the corkscrew and stuck it into Doug's chest. She had to push hard. Harder than she expected to make the first penetrating cut. She ripped off her sweatshirt and dabbed the blood streaming down the side of his chest."

Mom has both her hands covering her face.

"When the cut was deep enough, she reached in, feeling her way to what she thought was his heart. She grabbed it and squeezed. His eyes popped open, and he took one quick breath. Eve continued squeezing his heart, hopeful he would come back to life. His face lost what little color it had. He took a long breath out and died right there."

Josie pauses and exhales a big breath. "There were two bodies on top of that mountain, but only one walked back down in the dark of night."

"See, there you have it." Mom sits forward and grabs a croissant. "She killed him."

Mom assumes a defensive posture, forcefully stabbing and tearing at her croissant with a sense of frustration and probably deep pain. Then I look at Josie with proud posture and proper knife and fork skills. Then back to Mom. "Mom, it sounded like she loved him and was doing her best to save him. Honestly, it sounded like a tough decision. I wouldn't have the guts or the courage."

"Right, Chelsea, it was brave and bold," Josie adds as she stands up. "It took much courage. He was going to die if she didn't take action."

"No, you're wrong. It was her action that killed him."

Josie stands. She places her chair under the table accurately and tidily. She picks up her coffee mug and plate and walks into the kitchen. Josie didn't make any further eye contact with either Mom or me.

I cradle my coffee mug in my hands, and I keep my eyes down and fixed on my plate with only crumbs. In my periphery, Josie spoons something into a bowl. I think it's oatmeal. She sprinkles something on it, but it's not sugar. I have the sugar bowl. And then, without a word, she walks out of the kitchen.

I reach for another croissant. "Sorry about your dad. No matter how it happened or who's responsible, Mom, it's tragic and sad. And it's too bad I never met him."

Mom's demeanor softens now that her opponent has left the ring. "Thanks, Chels. All of this stinks. It feels like I'm in a washing machine permanently set on high-speed spin. I can't wait to get out of this house. Chelsea, I've never told you this, but memories of my dad's presence linger inside me, intertwined with a bittersweet longing to hear his voice and his comforting laugh once more. The void he left behind is huge and it cannot be filled. The world felt different after he died. Even the simplest of joys were sour. It's terrible losing someone you love. What made you think of Doug?"

"Um." Think of something. "There is a picture of Grandma and Grandpa on the top shelf in Grandma's bedroom. It made me curious." I walk into the kitchen, spoon two bowls of oatmeal, and bring them to the table – one for Mom and one for me. "All Josie has is real sugar, not Splenda or anything like that. Sorry, Mom."

"Figures." Mom rolls her eyes. "Can you go get that photo from Eve's room? I'd like to see it."

"Well, it's packed. Yeah, it's in a box that's all taped up." Four helpings of sugar will be good in my oatmeal. "Mom, let's just get this crap done and return to our homes. We both have our lives to get back to." I go back to the kitchen and get the grapefruit Josie cut up.

"You're not going to eat that, are you?"

I shrug my shoulders. "Thought I'd try it." I have to! It's Grandma's favorite.

"Be careful. It's vile. Tastes like bitter vomit."

I spoon a section out and eat it. "I kinda like it."

Mom watches me. "And with that much sugar, anything tastes good. Twenty calories per teaspoon, Chelsea."

"Mom, there's no calorie counting for me. If I did, I'd lose my fucking mind."

"Well, maybe you should start counting calories and carbs. It might help you trim down and find a man. Anyway, which box would that photo be in? I'd like to see it. I have very few photographs of my dad, if any at all. Hopefully, it'll fit in my suitcase. Keep it safe, you know."

"Um, gosh. I do not know which box exactly." Once more, a surge of heat engulfs my neck and cheeks, flushing them with a renewed intensity. I'm not a good liar. There wasn't a photo on top of the bookshelf. That was made up. "I've not been paying attention to any of Eve's stuff and like which box has what."

"Seriously, Chelsea? My fuse is dangerously short right now. Is it in those boxes going to my house?"

"Yeah, I think so." God, she's going to catch me in this lie.

"How old do they look in the photo? How were they dressed?"

"Um, young? Mom, I didn't really–"

"Okay, fine." Mom stirs her oatmeal aggressively. "That photo better be in that box."

My phone buzzes in my back pocket. Thank God I can look away from Mom. There's a text from Drew.

> Hey! How's the old-fart house cleaning going? Ha! JK. Seriously, how are you? Miss you! I've been horny for you.

I respond.

> It's going well enough – I guess. Except my effing Mom showed up out of the blue. She's such a pain, and it's been a bit of a roller coaster over here. I'm finding some interesting stuff that my grandma wrote.

CHAPTER 13

𝓐 plane ride can be the best time to reflect, and my mind drifts to Josie and how reasonable and likable she is. Missing someone you've just met and gotten to know can be a bewildering experience, like a fleeting connection that leaves a mark on your heart. It's as if the universe conspired to intertwine our paths, only to pull them apart abruptly. The memories of Josie's captivating presence and the intriguing conversations echo in my mind, causing an ache that defies reason. It is an unexpected longing, a poignant reminder that some connections defy logic and time. I'm surprised at myself to realize how much her presence impacted me in a short weekend.

An abrupt landing and the hustle to get off the plane shakes me out of my thoughts. Eager travelers surround the baggage carousel, ready to zip off to their next destination, either home or vacation. I'm ready to get home and dig into Grandma Eve's journals. The flashing red light turns on, and the suitcases tumble down the lethargic conveyor belt. One by one, fellow travelers haul them off the belt, some in business clothes, others in sneakers and sweats. I stand there waiting until every suitcase disappears. Even the hippie guy with long dreads and smells of weed, who sat next to me on the plane, picked up his leather duffel. The monotonous drone of the conveyer belt sounds like distant battle drums. I jump when the horn sounds in the baggage area next to me, signaling another flight of suitcases. People swarm around the other carousel. My conveyor slows to a trickle and then stops – no more bags. My stomach sinks as the red light turns off.

This has never happened to me. What if the airline lost my suitcase? It's unthinkable. All of Grandma's things are in my bag, and I feel my heart racing as a bead of sweat forms on my upper lip. That suitcase has all but the first journal in it. It has the second and her final journal, the Stilettos, the love poem, photos, the blue vase, Grandma's sweater, and the Cookbooks. It has all the belongings I worked so hard to squirrel away, successfully hiding them from Mom.

At the baggage office, I look at all the bags lined up along the wall and scan each name tag. "No. No. No." None of them are mine.

A woman from the airline fast-walks over to me. "Miss, you must stay behind the blue line until one of us calls you."

"My suitcase. It didn't come up on the carousel!"

"I understand, but you can't be back here. Please move back behind the blue line on the floor." She motions to the floor at the opening of the doorway to the office. "Okay, please give me a minute, and I'll look at these unclaimed bags."

I take an anxious step forward. "Just did. None of those are mine."

"Miss, stay behind the blue line."

My heart pounds, and the loud swooshing in my ears makes it hard to hear the woman. Confused and angry, while staying behind the blue line, I look at all the suitcases lined up one more time to be sure.

"I'm sure they rerouted your suitcase to another airport, and the staff will send it back soon." The woman turns around to inspect the names of two suitcases behind her on the floor. "What's your name?"

"Chelsea Price." All I can do is stand here watching the woman. Not looking at her face, but at her blue United Airlines sweater and perfectly quaffed ponytail. She turns back to me. My gaze drops to the wings pin on her lapel. She appears official, like she should know where *every* suitcase is in this airport. "Look, that suitcase is essential. We must find it."

"Can you wait for a few more flights? It might show up, or you can give us your phone number. We'll call you when it comes in. Or we can have it delivered to your house." The faceless blue woman takes out a pen and a form for me to fill out. She motions me to come over the beloved blue line on the floor.

I rub the back of my neck and look down at my watch. It's already 11:45 pm. It will probably be too late to meet Drew tonight. A vision pops into my head of strangling this woman with that ridiculous blue and red scarf that's tied around her neck.

"No, do not have it delivered! I'll pick it up." I don't trust anyone with my precious cargo.

I throw my purse, torn briefcase, and jacket down on the blue waiting chair, then turn and grab the pen and paper. "It's imperative you find my suitcase. It's not just about some stupid clothes, you know." Filling out the form, I push so hard on the pen that it squishes out some ink and smudges the page. What if they thought there was a bomb in my suitcase? They'd find it in a heartbeat.

The woman takes the finished baggage claim form and starts pounding on her computer keyboard. Jesus, what is she typing? A fucking novel? My emotions are out of control, like being caught in a turbulent storm, where waves of intense feelings crash against my mind and heart. It's late. I'm tired. I've had to put up with Mom all weekend and my unusual feelings surrounding Grandma and Josie.

"Hm, that's strange... I do not see you or your suitcase in the system." She types again.

"What, like it vanished? How does this happen? In thin air? I paid the $30 bag fee. Do you see that? I *hate* this incompetent airline! Are you that stupid?" I'm astonished at all the words that fly out of my mouth. God, that sounded like something Mom would say. It's like being overwhelmed by a powerful force that is difficult to contain or understand.

"Miss. Please calm down."

"Calm down? That suitcase has everything important in my life!

Calm down?" I want to grab her blonde ponytail and swing her around the room.

"If we can't find your bag, we will pay you one hundred dollars for the contents."

"I don't want your stupid money! I need my luggage! Now!" Stopping myself is beyond my control. I'm screaming at her like a mad, perverse hyena.

I overhear the other blue woman saying on the phone, "Security. Now."

"What if I told you there was a bomb in my suitcase, huh? You'd find it then, wouldn't you? You little peon who is forced to wear a stupid uniform. A uniform! Where's your little beanie cap? Like the ones those Hot Dog on a stick girls wear?"

Something simultaneously snatches both my arms from behind, and I'm lifted a few inches off the floor and spun around. Two humongous men pull me out of the baggage office.

I wriggle, but it's futile. "Don't shoot me!" I howl as the two men put my face down on the tile floor. "My suitcase. I only want my–"

"Do not say another word," one of the security guards grunts. They pull both of my arms behind my back, and I wince as they put the cold metal handcuffs around my wrists. The clicking sound pierces my ears as I realize what is happening. They yank me up to standing.

Lowering my voice, I attempt to sound calm. "Look, this is all a mistake. I'm not a criminal. It's my–" Tears release from my eyes, but I can't wipe them away. They fall down my cheeks, neglected.

"Enough!" the boorish-voiced man on my left says. "You are in a lot of trouble, young lady. You best stay quiet and stand still. Right now."

The security guard on my right lets go of my arm, turns to blue uniformed woman, and talks to her under his breath. The other shorter but freakishly wide man stands at my side, holding my left arm, his fingers digging into my bicep. And then I hear the dreaded word "bomb." Blue woman number two points to my purse, briefcase, and jacket sitting on the chair. And like that, I'm dragged out of baggage claim and into an elevator. They whisk me into a small office where two agents stand, ready to frisk me.

They look through my purse, dumping all its contents on an elementary school-looking table in front of me, and then they make me unlock my phone. The second I do, Drew's text shows on the screen. The agent pulls it back before I can read the message. Another officer pats down my jacket and pulls the empty M&M wrappers from my side pocket. Everything gets placed everything on the table.

Feelings of abandonment dig into my heart. The sting from Mom's slap chills me to the core once again. Almost worse is the fact that Grandma Eve is gone. I will never have a relationship with her. My lonely belongings lie there lifeless and strewn across the sturdy but plain six-foot table.

I can't believe how stupid I was with the baggage claim women. How stupid to mention anything about a bomb. Stupid, stupid, stupid. What is wrong with me? I'm pathetic and incurable.

One of the officers flips through the first journal I had in my briefcase to read on the plane. At least I have that one. That is, if the officer gives it back to me.

"What is this?" He holds the journal in the air.

I sniff my nose. Warm liquid streams down my lip, and it tastes salty.

"Jesus, somebody get a tissue," he barks at the officer standing at the back of the room.

Still handcuffed, the young man wipes my nose. I'm grateful for the tiny bit of kindness. I look at him in the eyes and nod a thank you.

"That's my grandma's journal." Tears want to explode from me. "She just died, and I was at her house this weekend." I sniff again. "We were cleaning out her house. There are two other journals in my suitcase. I haven't had a chance to read all of them. That's why I freaked out with the baggage claim ladies."

The officer put Grandma's journal on the table next to my jacket.

I sit forward. "Officer, I was irresponsible and acted furious and delusional. It's not like me to get so angry. I'm very sorry. There's no bomb. I only mentioned that because I wanted to light a match under that woman. Sorry. You have no idea how important that suitcase is to me." "What's in the journals? Why are they so important?" The officer lifts an eyebrow.

"It's all about her life. We were estranged for many years, and now she's passed on, and all I have are her journals. There are some family secrets that I think she can unlock for me. There are some recipes and rules of life. That kinda stuff."

"Secrets? Recipes? What recipes? Like how to construct a bomb?" He opens Journal One and reads with more scrutiny.

"Oh, God no! Recipes, like bean soup and tacos. You know. How to make great food."

He grunts at me, continues reading the journal, and motions for the other officer to gather my scattered personal contents.

Three hours later, they released me. They put all my stuff, including Grandma's journal, in large see-through plastic bags. Still no suitcase. They inform me that if I set foot on any airport grounds in the US within thirty days, I will be arrested. How am I to pick up my suitcase if they find it? I don't ask.

Just stay quiet and get out of here.

What if they can't find my suitcase? Grandma's journals will be gone forever. The thought scares me. I'll never know the truth. Talking to my father is not an option, and Mom explodes every time I ask about Grandma. How will I ever know what happened to me?

Walking out of the private screening room, I pull my phone out of the zip-lock bag to call Drew, but the screen is black. It's dead. And all the food areas are desolate, with the black prison bars pulled down. My stomach growls. God, something sweet would be perfect right now.

My car clock reads 3 AM, and I plug in my phone. Even though it's late, I call Drew. It goes to voicemail. I call again. Voicemail. "Goddammit!"

Tomorrow at work, I'll explain to Drew what happened. She'll understand. She might even comfort me. Or probably not.

CHAPTER 14

My failed sneaker sits in front of me on my desk, mocking me. It seems surreal that, just yesterday, I was at Grandma's house, smelling her smells, sleeping in her bed, and having meals with her faithful friend, Josie. My frazzled, sleep-deprived mind trails to my missing suitcase and all the stories I'll never get to read. Not caring that I'm at work, I blurt out, "Why me? Why my suitcase?"

"Don't worry, Chels. They'll find your bag. And those beautiful journals will be right where you left 'em," Megan says from behind me. She's always the enthusiast – the polar opposite of me.

"I'm not holding my breath." The words crumble out of me without turning around.

"Chelsea?"

I whip around in my chair and see Drew standing in our office doorway.

"Why aren't you answering your texts? I texted you three times. Need you in my office. Now." Drew turns on her heels and walks away, not revealing her planned ruse. It turns me on when she plays boss and I play subordinate.

Megan's eyes widen. "That does not sound good."

"How did I miss the texts from Drew? My phone is right here." I get up and make my way to Drew's office. The horn dog, I'm sure she needs a little sexy attention. I may go for it today. A brief distraction would do me good.

"Close the door," Drew says as I enter her office.

"Yes, ma'am," I say playfully. After closing the door behind me, I take hesitant steps forward, echoing softly in the room. The air seems charged with anticipation as I make my way toward Drew. She's sitting in her retro swivel chair. I try to sit in Drew's lap.

"No." She recoils and pushes me away. "Sit over there." She motions to the chair on the other side of her desk.

"Oh, okay."

"You couldn't just keep your mouth shut, could you?" Drew whisper-yells.

"What? What are you talking about?" The chair facing her is stiff-backed and uncomfortable. "What's going on?" I whisper back.

"You told Megan."

"I told Megan what? Drew, what's going on? My sneaker line?"

"*No*, you fucking idiot! They found out about us." She jerks up to stand, shoving her rolling chair back so hard it bangs into her credenza. "Goddammit, Chelsea. Do you know what you've done to me?"

"To you?" Air seeps out of my mouth. "Drew, I didn't–"

"Just shut up. Of course, you told Megan about us. You spend all day, every day, together. And then Megan gossiped around the office." Drew circles the desk and walks over to the large office window. "I got a nice little call from Suzanne this morning. That was not fun."

"Suzanne? Oh, tell her it's a lie. We can mitigate this. We deny everything and tell her it's just dumb office gossip."

"Chelsea. Are you deaf? It's all gone! My promotion to Global Sports Marketing and you taking over my position here in this office. Both opportunities have vanished, thanks to you."

"I'm the one to blame?"

Drew turns toward me, red-faced and angry. "Well, I sure as hell didn't tell anyone. Why would I? You're not exactly someone to brag about, you know."

It hurts, but she's right.

"So, what did Suzanne say?"

"She was crystal clear. She said, end it, or I will end you. And we better believe her."

"What should we do?"

Drew looks down and away. "I never want to see you again."

Her face looks weird. So hard. I know she has a rough edge and an enormous ego, but these qualities I can ignore most days. "You don't mean that, Drew. We can work around these allegations."

Drew walks back over to her desk and picks up a stack of papers. She tosses them to me. A few pages float to the floor. "You and Megan are laid off. It's the only way, Chelsea."

"What!" I pick up the pages that fell on the floor and read.

"No. Drew. This is not fair. You can't–"

"Look, I'm being kind by laying you both off."

"Drew, I'll stay away from you. Megan is innocent, I swear. You don't have to go to this extreme."

"Don't fight it, or I'll hit you both with workplace sexual harassment and assault. Unwelcome sexual advances and requests for sexual favors. It's all documented with photos."

My mouth opens, but nothing comes out. My heart pounds, and I can't breathe. I jump up and run out of Drew's office, leaving the door open. She slams it behind me as I half-run down the hall and into the bathroom. Tears fill my eyes. On the toilet, my pale, fish-white, flabby belly hangs over huge thighs. The termination papers are shocking. I'm in disbelief that I've lost both my job and Drew all in one day.

Megan! She's a single mom, barely making it. What the hell have I done? I need to get to her before Drew to soften the bomb. Getting laid off feels like a blow to my self-esteem and identity. The job that once provided purpose, structure, and a sense of belonging is suddenly gone.

I rush into my office.

"Oh my God, Chelsea." Megan stands near her desk with her hands out, palms up. "Are we getting laid off because of the color palette problem? I cannot lose my job! You know the financial bind I'm in."

"Let's go get a coffee. Out of this lousy building. We need to talk."

"No, I'm not going anywhere with you until you tell me what's happening," Megan growls and crosses her arms.

For the first time in three years, I close our office door. Chausse has an open-door glass-everywhere policy, except for upper management like Drew. "Meg. Look. Do you think something is going on between Drew and me?"

"Chelsea, everyone suspects you two are doin' the nasty. Jessica swears she's heard you two having sex in Drew's office. I was going to ask you, but you've had to deal with all this family stuff. Why didn't you tell me? I thought we were friends."

My head rests in my hands. "You have got to be kidding? Everyone thought we were having an affair?" My mouth goes slack. "Jessica heard?"

"Is it true? Are you dating? Is this the explanation for the pink slip?"

"I'm afraid so. And yes. We've been seeing each other for a while. Not really dating, though." I walk toward Megan. "Please don't hate me. We needed to be discrete."

"Don't come any closer to me, Chelsea, or I'll scream. Swear to God." Megan's voice hitches as she grips the pink slip. "Let me get this straight. YOU have the affair, and I get fired! This makes no sense. Do you love her?"

"God, no! Meg, we, you know, had a little fun here and there. I'll talk to Drew. She thinks you gossiped about us. She thinks you told Suzanne. She's mad and probably embarrassed. You know, I'm not much of a catch."

"For the record. I did not participate in any gossip, and talking to Drew's boss, Suzanne, is out of the question! That nasty USC law school bragging, Suzanne. She's nauseating." With a pained expression, Megan throws her phone in her purse and turns toward me. "Chelsea Price, you better make this right. My entire life will fall apart without this job." She opens the glass door and storms out.

What have I done? Drew's right about one thing – I AM an idiot. Why does Drew get to stay and we have to leave? It makes no sense. One of my deepest aversions is having my picture taken, but Drew made me feel sexy that one night, saying she wanted pictures of me naked. I thought it was what people do in relationships and would impress her. So stupid. Stupid. Stupid. What a catastrophe. I pound my palm against my forehead.

My phone buzzes. It's an email from the airline. I grab my purse and jacket and bolt out of the office. Looking up and down the hall, I don't see her. Meg, where did you go? I frantically push the elevator down button. Once downstairs, I jump out of the elevator, running straight into a woman.

"Oh, my!" She jumps back. "Chelsea, what's the hurry?"

There she is in plain clothes and no make-up, so Portland. "Suzanne! Um, something in my car. I need to." Words tangle in my mouth. This is Drew's boss. The last person on Earth I'd want to bump into. Looking ridiculous, I'm sure. I spin around and continue running toward the parking lot. Her eyes burn two black holes into my back.

"Megan!" I yell. She turns around, looks at me, and then gets into her car. "Megan! They have my suitcase!"

The bald tires on her small light blue car screech as she backs up.

I reach her car, just to the driver's side of it. "Meg, wait!" I'm out of breath and desperate for her help.

She puts down her window. "What! Chelsea, I am so mad at you. You're the reason why–"

"The airport. They have my suitcase!" I put my hands on my thighs and try to catch my breath.

"It's always about you, Chelsea. You just got me fired, and now you want me to help you with your stupid suitcase with all your useless memorabilia."

I pop up to stand. "It's not useless, Meg! Please understand. I'm changing. It's Grandma. Just today, I drank water instead of diet coke. And that's not all. I must know what she thought about me and my life. Whether or not my father molested me, I *need* those journals and your help! *Please!*"

"Wait, your father abused you? Who are you, Chelsea?" With her hands glued to the steering wheel, she puts her car into drive.

"No, don't go. Wait!" Desperation fills my lungs and voice. "It's a long story, but I have always suspected my father molested me. But I have no clear memories or evidence. My mom denies it altogether. We have lots of family secrets. Anyway, it makes no sense to go into that right now. My grandma is gone, and all I have are her journals to piece my life together."

"Can't tell me about Drew. You can't tell me about your father. What the…" Megan expels a deep breath, the kind that comes from deep in the soul. "Chelsea, I don't know who you are. And the look in your eyes scares me."

I soften my facial expression, realizing I had been scrunching up my face. "Okay, okay." I lower my voice. "Please understand, Meg. I'm a terrible friend. I hide and hold everything in. Sharing myself has never worked for me. But maybe, just maybe, the answers to all my questions will be in my grandma's journals." With my hands together in a prayer position, I beg. "Please? Please, Meg, take me to the airport."

Megan rubs the back of her neck. "For God's sake, Chelsea." She bangs her head on the steering wheel and then motions to the passenger seat. "Get the fuck in."

CHAPTER 15

Pacing the blacktop of the short-term parking at the airport, I feel like some wicked beast waiting for her next meal to be thrown through the bars. Megan is still in there, attempting to retrieve my suitcase from TSA for twenty minutes now.

The Girl Scout cookies help pass the nerve-racking time. A young girl and her mom were going around the office this morning before my life blew up, and I got four boxes of my favorite, the peanut buttery Dos-si-dos.

I decide to text Drew.

> Drew – stop being ridiculous! Megan had nothing to do with this. Evidently, the whole God damn floor knew we were having an affair. We weren't careful enough. It was Jessica who gossiped, not Megan. She told everyone she heard us in your office. We need to talk.

Drew texts back.

> I never want to talk to you again. Do not text or call me. And don't bother coming back to work. Somebody will clean out your desk, and they will let you know when you can come and get your belongings.

> Ok, fine. But please don't fire Megan. She needs her job, and she's a fantastic employee.

My throat tightens, and my eyes sting from tears again. I'm responsible for getting her fired, and it burns inside me. Feelings of sadness, disappointment, and even anger emerge as I grapple with the sense of rejection and the abrupt disruption of my personal and professional life. The cookies and pacing beside Megan's car are the only things keeping me sane.

Ever since we met three years ago, I have felt responsible for Megan. We are the same age, but it feels like I'm older. It's because I'm her boss. She caught on fast at Chausse. Without realizing it, we became close friends. Well, as close as I can get to anyone. She tells me what I need to hear. If I'd told her about Drew and me, she would have told me to end it immediately. Tears trickle down my face. I'm not ready for all this. I can't give up my relationship with Drew, and it kills me knowing they fired Meg because of me.

Drew is just acting like she's playing hardball, like that other time when she tried to split us up last Spring. She said she needed space. It felt like we were in a rut – no communication, boring sex, no flirting with each other. We were in her office when she told me I was holding her back from having a meaningful relationship.

She was right. We both knew we were not each other's forever person, if that even exists. The attention from Drew felt good. It supplied just enough of the essential human touch and sexual release. After three days, she called me late on a Friday, asking if she could come over. We had the best sex. I'm sure she'll call in about two to three days, just like the last time.

Megan makes it to the car with my suitcase in tow. "Here's your Goddamn suitcase."

"Thank you so much, Meg. And thanks for not hating me for getting you fired." I wipe my eyes, put my hands up in a prayer position, and bow my head in respect. "I'm trying to get your job back."

"Huh, not likely that egomaniac Drew will let either of us back. What did you ever see in her? Never mind, don't answer that." Megan puckers her lips. "Now that you have your suitcase back, will you let me be mad at you again?"

"I'm ignoring that last comment. How'd it go in there? Did they give you a hard time?"

"It was scary. The security people were really fierce and acted like they would need a pint of blood from me in exchange for the suitcase! First, they frisked me, inspected my license, looked me up and down, then compared my signatures against my license. Then once I had your suitcase, they forced me to go through it in front of them."

Listening to Megan, I lay my suitcase down on the parking lot blacktop and, with a mix of trepidation and hope, unzip it. "Good. The Stilettos are still here. I thought one of those TSA chicks might steal 'em."

"God, Chelsea. We have to look for jobs." Megan breathes out her words while staring at her phone.

"I know, Meg. I'm so sorry." I grab sweatshirts and socks from my bag and throw them on the pavement. "And if Drew doesn't come to her senses, we can be the two musketeers looking for jobs together."

Megan frowns. "Don't put your clothes on this gross parking lot." She opens the trunk door of her car. "Now, what are you looking for?"

"There's a journal missing." I frantically pull everything out. "Journal Two. I can't find it!"

"Calm down. I'm sure it's in there." She picks up the clothes from the sour oil-stained pavement and places them in the trunk.

Every last article is out of my suitcase. "How did this happen? They were both in here – Journal Two and her final words. Why would TSA take just one?" I look up and over at the terminal.

"Chelsea! Don't even think about it. YOU cannot go in that airport." Megan unzips an outside compartment on the suitcase. "Nope, nothin' in there. Shoot, Chels. I don't know what to say."

In a fireball of energy, I pick up my suitcase and slam it back on the ground like a frustrated eight-year-old with a broken toy. "Why is everybody out to get me?"

"Everyone is not out to get you. You've just had an awful couple of days. Well, I guess it's going on weeks now." Megan pats my back. "It'll turn up, I'm sure." Folding Chelsea's clothes carefully, she puts it all back into the bag, zips the beat-up suitcase closed, and gets into the driver's seat. "Come on, Chels. We have way more important things to do. We have to find jobs!"

It feels surreal, like this is all a nightmare. I'm stunned. We were supposed to get past this color palette issue, and then we'd be promoted. But now, everything is wrong. My emotions fluctuate rapidly, swinging from one extreme to another, leaving me disoriented and uncertain.

Megan puts on her turning signal. "This morning, I had a good job, and within hours, I'm unemployed. Poof! Like that. Why Chelsea? Why did you have an affair with Drew?"

My body crumples into the car seat. Shame fills me with a heaviness in my stomach. "I'm so sorry, Meg. It's understandable why you feel shaken up. My actions were disgusting and wrong."

"Well, next job, don't sleep with the boss."

"You don't have to remind me. I've learned my lesson." The passing cars are a blur as we get on the freeway heading back to the office. "Where could that journal be? There's nothing in them that TSA would want. It's just life stories and recipes and such."

"Stop fixating on that journal!"

"It's important to me, Meg!"

Megan rubs the back of her neck. "You sure it made it in your suitcase? Could it be in your briefcase?"

"God, my briefcase. It exploded on the plane on the way out to Grandma Eve's and Josie's place, and it needed some tape and lots of begging to stay together. Oh, I hope it didn't fall out." My fingernails grip the edge of the seat. "I'm so mad at myself for losing that journal. Two journals that I won't be able to read. All of Grandma's stories are gone."

Megan looks over at me, squinting her eyes. "You should be madder at yourself for losing our jobs!"

"Well, maybe you shouldn't have gossiped about Drew and me!"

"Jesus, Chelsea, don't look at me like that! You look like you could kill me!" Her breath hitches. "I didn't gossip. You are the reason we are both unemployed!" Megan jerks her car into the office parking lot, sending me off balance, and throws on her brakes. "Get out of my car."

My suitcase is heavy as I lift it out of the trunk, and her tires screech as she speeds away. She turns the corner, and then she's out of sight.

The office building looms in front of me, taunting and mocking me. I feel weak and sit down on the curb. I've lost everything – my job, Drew, Meg, and the second journal. Not knowing what to do, I sit on the unforgiving, cold, gray cement curb. Young professional twenty-something's rush by me on the sidewalk. They look at me in horror. Their gaze slides over my face, reading the wrenching pain in my neck and jaw. I hear faint whispers as they walk past me. They probably know and are whispering to each other that I'm the idiot who slept with her boss and got herself and her assistant fired.

Like the airport, my office is off-limits as well. I'm sure Drew would dial security in a matter of seconds and have my ass drug out of there. Getting cuffed twice in one week is not a good idea.

I will my body over to my car, wipe away my tears of guilt and sadness, and sit in the driver's seat. Pounding on the steering wheel and starting to scream, a desperate guttural sound blows out of me from deep inside. No one outside the car can hear my screams as I have all the windows up, but if you happen to catch a glimpse of me, you'd think I am deranged. You'd be right. My reflection in the rearview mirror shows a dirty strawberry blonde with red eyes and a wet, fat face. Mom is right; I'm not capable of doing anything right.

* * *

At home, I pour myself a whisky on ice. The brown liquid goes down hot. My mind drifts to Josie and how her house must feel palatial without Mom and me. Hell, it is palatial compared to this lifeless coffin that is my home.

Mistybrook Apartments in Portland grew in the early 1980s, and you can tell. The pale white, wood-sided building holds two hundred and twenty units. My third-floor, interior, one-bedroom apartment has never felt like a proper home. To save money, the property manager agreed that I would repaint the dark blue interior walls, but I never did. They grow on you after a while, like the mold on my bathroom windowsill. The gothic walls clash with most of the furniture I moved from my grad school apartment in Seattle. Even so, it's where I've existed for three years.

My suitcase stares at me. I take each piece of clothing out with care, shaking each article. Out of my baggy, tweedy gray sweater, an earring falls out. Picking it up, I examine it. The heavy artisan silver earring with inlaid turquoise had small diamonds encircling the stone. I continue to shake out each piece of clothing and yield nothing more.

Maybe it dropped into my suitcase at Josie's? I hold up the earring again. "Who do you belong to?" It doesn't look like something Mom would wear. Too southwestern. Instead of Journal Two, I get this earring. "Why?" My scream reverberates off the apartment walls.

I look up, both hands in fists. "Grandma, help me." There are so many unanswered questions. I close my eyes, wishing a memory would take form. My childhood is a blur. For me, memories start at about eleven. I know others who can site memories from when they were five and six, sometimes younger. A few months ago, Megan told me a story about when she was in kindergarten. Me? Nothing. Mom reveals nothing. She's always waved me off, saying she was busy working two jobs and couldn't remember anything from my early childhood. Mom is not trustworthy. She's covering something or for someone. Talking to her is like swimming against a riptide – lots of effort, but you get nowhere.

I don't speak to my father, Robert. There's been no communication since Mom moved us to Seattle and he moved to Denver. Uncle Jim is dead. Grandma Eve is gone. No siblings. These journals are all I have to piece together my wretched terrestrial existence.

Another whiskey over ice might help to calm me even though I'm breaking my one-drink rule. Exhausted and strained to my limits, there is a stirring inside me. I need a solid plan right now, though every time I make plans, disaster prevails. Take today, for example, rooting myself into a position with Drew where my options are bad or worse. There is no room for any good outcome.

Getting Megan's job back should be my first goal. If that's at all possible. Then, see what happens with Drew and me. And finally, find all of Grandma's journals, figure out all these family secrets, and solve the jigsaw puzzle of my life. I've created three hurricanes, a triangle of disasters that I need to clean up before more fallout occurs. Regardless of my atrocious track record, I'll follow this plan.

"Okay, Grandma. Talk to me." The Journal opens where I left off on the plane.

Sept 27, 1983, Went back to the fish market today to see if Alice Wonderland would be there to join me. Waited outside for about fifteen minutes. The warm fall breeze was lovely today. Just when I thought she would not show, she rounded the corner and walked straight toward me. She wore a green army jacket and stained baggy jeans, cinched tight with a rope belt. Her dirty blonde hair was tied up in a band. I greeted her, and she nodded in acknowledgment.

Like last week, we had the same wine but ordered different food. This time, we ordered the Kumamoto oysters with extra horseradish. And then we shared the Pacific white sea bass with pan-fried tomato-caper relish, served with roasted vegetables and fishwife rice. De-lish!

Alice was a little more talkative today. She told me about the restaurant business and how it ate her up. The more tips she made, the more cocaine she'd buy. Her life became a blurry mess of food, drugs, and bars.

Alice dreams of living on a vegetable farm, growing organic food for restaurants. Alice said she'd like to raise chickens because they are the perfect animal for a farm. They poke around the garden, eat the bad bugs, fertilize it as they go, give eggs, and eventually give their own life as food.

She told me about how food manufacturer's label unhealthy foods as healthy, and people believe it. This fascinated me. She scoffed at the low-fat trend in our foods. She said that taking the fat out of foods that should have the fat will make us more fat. I challenged her about skim milk. "Yuck!" She made the funniest face. "First," she said. "Milk is disgusting! Am I a baby cow? Are you?"

She said, "Don't even get me started on butter vs. margarine or egg whites vs. the whole egg,"

I explained how my mom and dad came from farms in Pennsylvania, and my parents said that we should leave things the way we find them. That messing with our food will mess with us, and not in a good way.

Alice told me to eat the rainbow, and my body would feel like it was a pot of gold. She laughed and said that she wasn't talking about Lucky Charms.

That was a friendly reminder. I will eat more veggies and fruits – the rainbow of the planet.

Gave Alice the poem I had written for her. She cried when she read it. Then I started crying. Good stuff.

Wait a second, Lucky Charms is fortified with vitamins? Isn't that healthy? I like the idea of my body feeling like a pot of gold. Right now, it feels more like a pot of crap, like some little evil, green-toothed leprechaun shoved rotten potatoes into my thighs.

My legs drop out from under me as I stand up from the couch. "What the–" My knees crash to the ground, and the room spins. I grab my head, squeeze my eyes closed, and wait out the dizziness. When it feels somewhat safe, I blink my eyes open. My shirt is soaked in sweat. All I've had to eat today is a box of cookies and one and a half whiskey drinks. Breaking my strict one-drink rule did not serve me well. I can't call anyone – not Megan, and certainly not Drew. I'm scared and all alone.

Alone, for me, has been a source of comfort. Silence is free of judgment and pain. I could escape in its pillow of disregard by staying quiet or keeping my head down. I have always been the gliding ghost that nobody saw or acknowledged, leaving no footprint, shadow, or trace. Not being seen was both perfect and shameful, pleasure and sorrow. Today it feels alarming.

The vertigo passes, and I stand unbalanced. In my kitchen is a bag of potato chips. I crunch on a few of the salty disks and decide to make an appointment with my therapist tomorrow, as this is the third time this had happened in the last month – once before I left for Mom's house, one time at Josie's, and then, just now.

I sit back down with the bag of chips, push my drink away, and turn the page.

Oct 4, 1983, This has become a regular thing with Alice. She has been looking better each time. She told me she took a shower this morning at the shelter. With clean clothes and clear eyes, she actually smiled when she saw me.

Even though it has been busy at work, I have eaten a salad every day this week for lunch, and I feel great! Lost two lbs as well. Eating the rainbow is working. I'm also staying away from diet drinks. In the Los Angeles Times, I read that diet drinks make you think you've had something sweet when you haven't, tricking your taste buds but not your cells. Talked to a doc today at work about this theory, and he just glazed over. He said that they don't teach nutrition in med school.

Called Liz, and she was grumpy with me on the phone today. Told her I was lonely, and that I missed her father. She blew up. She thinks it's my fault he died. I'm feeling confused. It seemed like the right thing to do, but I doubted myself. Feel guilty. Feel alone. I should have never let him take that hike with slight heart attack symptoms. Should have heeded the warnings, but he said he felt fine. I believed him. Should not have let him take that hike. Then we would have been closer to a hospital to EMS. How could I let this happen?

I'm so sad. I've hit rock bottom. I'll never see Doug again. Never feel his lips on mine. Never talk to him. Never sit together Sunday mornings and read the paper to each other.

Liz hates me. All I need now is to lose my job, the trifecta of collapse.

I know how you feel, Grandma. Having that destructive, secretive affair with Drew was the worst decision. A wiser person would have run in the opposite direction. Then Megan and I would still have our jobs. Mess avoided.

Rock bottom doesn't come with any grand entry or stampede. It's swift and cutting and vacant. I have no job, no best friend, no girlfriend, no grandma, and no answers about my father and Uncle Jim. And now, I'm digging around to find the explanations I have been avoiding all my adult life. That horrible wood-scratching noise that used to wake me every night haunts me. My distrust of men. My deep fear and hatred for my father. What if I get the answers but can't handle them?

The potato chips are helping. I'm not sweating anymore. Because I'm wet, my body starts shivering, so I pull the dark blue couch throw and put it over my legs. It's the only thing in my apartment that matches the walls. Megan got it for me a couple of years ago.

Turning the page, I realized there was a gap in time between the journal entries – about two years. There's no explanation, just a new entry.

Nov 4, 1985, Had dinner at Liz and Robert's tonight. Robert's brother, Jim, was there. Just don't like that man. Not once did he look me in the eye tonight. He flashes that Cheshire cat smile when he answers my questions. It makes me nervous, like I can't trust what he's saying.

Robert and Jim work in construction and say they might go into business together. Hope not. From what I can sense, that would be a disaster. Robert told me they wanted to partner because they couldn't afford to hire anyone. Red flag. Plus, the two men don't seem compatible. Their personalities are quite different.

Despite this, we had a lovely evening. I picked up Chinese food takeout, and then we played Trivial Pursuit most of the evening.

I am worried that Liz drinks too much. She said this was her first night off in nine days, and she was cutting loose a bit. Still, there were a lot of Long Island iced teas going down.

Not knowing how to fill the spirit, Liz uses alcohol. I use food. I'm seeing this now more and more clearly. We both fill our emptiness with outside distractions that turn into demons. I brought this up. Liz wouldn't discuss it further, but Robert and I had a good discussion. He's a deep thinker and enjoys philosophical conversations.

Mom's still filling her spirit, and her liver, with alcohol. She must have drunk two to three bottles of wine daily at Josie's. I rub my temples. Grandma Eve refers to all those in my family who are not in my life anymore, except Mom. She was just as defensive as she is now.

Dr. Allen says that defensive behavior is usually a deflection of the truth.

There is not much memory of Uncle Jim, my father's twin brother. He died in a hunting accident when I was around ten. Mom said he was with Robert, and they were deer hunting when he died. That there was a small investigation, but nothing came of it. Mom says that no one could tell Uncle Jim and Robert apart, not even her. She says that it used to drive her crazy. They dressed alike, drove the same truck for their construction work, and their voices were identical.

I flick the thoughts of my father away. He's the reason I've been in therapy all these years.

Jan 1, 1986, Was at Mary's annual New Year's Eve party last night. Fun! Looked around, and everyone seemed to have their lives together, way better than me. With envy and astonishment, I stare at their porcelain skin as they chatter about their successful kids, smoothly ticking through life. Have all these people found the magic, or is it all wizardry? Feel the need to look hard, to force my mind to listen to my heart. I'm not the smooth, white vessel holding a perfect bouquet. No, I'm more like the chunk of blue glass that washes up on the beach, eons from home, worn and weary from the powerful tides. It's okay; I have stories; boy, do I have stories.

Everyone kept asking me last night if I had any new year's resolutions. I prefer to write down my top 100 projections for the year. Do this every new year. Write down my desires, wants, and aspirations. Once done, I'll put the Top 100 in my desk drawer and pull it out once per week. Here are my top five:

- *I will challenge my brain more. I'll read at least two books per month – one fiction and one self-help.*
- *Lose forty pounds. I need to eat better, exercise more, and lose weight. I've been carrying around this extra weight for way too long. No more Taco Bell and McDonald's. Yes, they are convenient, but I have to do something different. Pain plagues my body so much of the time, and I know it's because of my weight and unhealthy food. (My daily salad at lunch turned to comfort food. Pizza at the hospital cafeteria won out.)*

- *I will walk three miles each morning before work. Not only for the exercise, but I want to notice my surroundings more – sense into my body. Take in the smells and sights.*
- *Have more below-the-surface conversations. No more talking about the weather kind of stuff. I will ritualize deeper conversations with almost everyone.*
- *Be more grateful. Every morning before getting out of bed, I will close my eyes and think of all the big and small areas of my life and the people who bring me joy and serenity. And then, I will express this gratitude outwardly to my loved ones.*

Jan 20, 1986 While on my way to Liz and Robert's, thought it strange that I saw Jim sitting on a bench in the park adjacent to Liz and Robert's house. Jim has no kids, but he was watching a girls' soccer scrimmage. The girls looked to be middle school-aged. I asked Liz. She just shrugged and said to each their own.

Liz and I constantly fight anymore. She goads me every chance she gets. Been awful. I try to use my new year's affirmations, but unfortunately, it's not working. Sobbed all the way home.

It's common knowledge that Mom and Grandma fought all the time. That's why we were estranged from Grandma, but I did not know Grandma was overweight, like me, and ate fast food like me.

I'm feeling buzzed from the whisky, and my stomach growls. I need food – more than just chips. Like Grandma, good health needs to be a priority for me. If a couple of pounds come off me, Drew might come back. There is nothing in my apartment to eat, so I call Uber.

"Chelsea?"

"Yep, I'm Chelsea." I slur to the driver as I slide into the back seat of his silver SUV.

"So, where can I take you?" he asks in a cheerful tone. "You didn't specify where we were going."

"Um, sir, do you know of a good salad place or something healthy to eat?"

"You don't have to call me sir. I know I'm older than you, but you can call me Roy." He smiles.

"My friends call me Roy-ber. Get it?" He giggles to himself.

"Ha, that's clever! Roy, the Uber driver. Royber."

"Hm, salad place. I stay away from those myself." The trim, silver-haired man says.

"Shoot, I want to eat healthy, like my grandma."

"There's a Popeye's Chicken around the corner. That's pretty much all I eat when I eat out. Well, that's 'cause my wife's home cooking is the best. But she's a vegetarian, and a man needs meat sometimes."

My stomach roars again. "That's fine. I'll take Popeye's." My apartment building looks dismal and gloomy out the rain sprinkled car window. "I'll eat healthy tomorrow."

CHAPTER 16

My sunrise alarm clock starts its ascent from dark to light. I jump to shut it off before it finishes the cycle to complete the bright sunrise. Mom calls me a nerd for having this alarm clock, but it's much better than waking up to an obnoxious, loud beeping sound. It was a splurge, but it's like the sun is in my room and wakes me gently – the alarm clock transitions from dark to light within thirty minutes. With no sun in Portland, this has also helped with my seasonal depression.

But this morning, there was no need to get up early, no work, and nowhere to go. I close my eyes, not only to sleep more, but to shut out what happened yesterday.

The familiar sound of salsa music seeps through the wall from next door. When I first moved in, my neighbor Gabriella brought over a plate of homemade cookies. They were delicious. She'd said there were not enough hours in the day, so she gets up early to make family breakfast and lunches. It's soothing, the music. It sounds like love, caring, safety, warmth, and homemade food.

Though I want to keep my eyes closed and enjoy the comforting tempo of the music, they pop open, taking in the still life of my bedroom. In the corner, the exercise bike mom gave me as a house-warming gift now doubles as my clothes-drying rack. I have a single chair under the window and a stack of engineering books on the floor in the corner. The top of my dresser holds one of my prized possessions – a 1983 steel tech model of the Millennium Falcon. The kit was on eBay. It took all night to put it together, but I couldn't stop. The curtains billow, signaling wind outside. Yes, they move even when the window is closed. The curtains are opaque with dust, casting a murky shadow over the room. Then, I hear it hitting the window, the Portland mist, or, as normal people call it, rain.

I reach over to my nightstand, unplug my phone, and look at the screen. There are no new texts from either Drew or Megan. I dial Mom.

Mom clears her throat. "Well, it's awfully early to be calling."

"Good morning to you, too. Yeah, sorry, I didn't look at the time."

"It's eight o'clock. Shouldn't you be at work?"

"Oh yeah, they gave me the day off."

"What? You said you needed to get back to work. That some other guy was gonna get your promotion."

"Well, he'll probably get it, Mom." My voice drifts off. She's trapping me again. I pick up the stray earring, push the curtains aside, and dangle it in front of the window. The clouded light catches the tiny diamonds, sending sparkle dots across my wall like dancing stars.

"Are you missing an earring from our trip to Grandma's and Josie's?"

"You always change the subject, Chelsea. You never answer me. Why won't you answer my question? Why aren't you at work today? You made such a fuss about it when you were here."

My hand slams down on the bed. "Mom! I don't want to talk about work right now."

"Well, somebody woke up on the wrong side of the bed."

"Yes, actually, that's true. So, tell me one thing, Mom. Did you lose an earring at Josie's?"

"Geez, you don't have to yell. No, Chelsea, I didn't lose an earring."

"There was an earring in my suitcase, and I wondered if it was yours." I bite on my thumb cuticle. "It's turquoise, with little diamonds around the edge."

"Nope. Not mine," she says with sureness in her tone. "I don't have any turquoise earrings."

"Yeah, that's what I thought."

"Could it be Josie's?" Mom inquires.

"Not sure. I'll text Josie when we hang up." I get up, sit on the edge of my bed, and try to soften my tone. "Mom? I want to ask a question, but please don't be mad at me."

"What is it, Chelsea?" Her voice deepens. "And no guarantees about the not getting mad part."

"It's about Uncle Jim. I know he died in a hunting accident. But I'm sure you know more of the details."

"Oh, Chelsea. Going to Eve's really screwed you up."

"It stirred up some questions, yes. I'm just curious, and all my memories are fuzzy. Some memory jogging might help. Tell me something about Uncle Jim. I barely remember anything about that part of my childhood."

"Ha, tell me about it," Mom snorts. "I can't even remember what I had for dinner last night!"

"Sheesh, I know, Mom." It's hard to remember anything consuming two bottles of wine a night. "Anything more you can tell me about Uncle Jim and how he died?"

"God, Chelsea, hold on. I'll need another cup of coffee before I answer that doozy." She rattles around in her kitchen.

I push the grimy curtain open a bit more and look outside – more rain. The healthy, tall trees that line the parking lot sway in the light wind.

For most adults, memories kick in at around four years old. For me, memories start when I'm about twelve. Leading up to that, I have only flashes here and there, no sound bites, only flickers and glints of recollections. It's like watching an old black-and-white talkie movie with no subtitles. The images jump around, not making any sense. All my life, I've avoided remembering or connecting with my childhood. It was just something that happens to each person – you're born, you grow up, and then you're an adult. There is no need to fixate on the details, but being at Grandma's and reading her stories stirred something inside.

"I'm back," Mom mumbled, exhaling a deep sigh. "Chelsea, even for me, the details are sketchy. They always were. Your father never wanted to talk about it. All I know is that Robert and Jim went deer hunting, as they did for years. They'd go out each weekend in September and October, hunting rifles in tow. They'd load up the truck with a cooler of beer and some sandwiches, sleeping bags, and ammo. They'd be gone all weekend. Those two were the best of friends, but they say that about twins." Mom slurped her coffee. "They'd camp at the same desolate spot every year, somewhere on the California-Arizona border. Jim said it was their good luck place."

"Did you like Uncle Jim?"

"I liked Jim well enough, but he was a little jumpy, a little shifty."

"Like you couldn't trust him?" Grandma did not trust him. She said so in her journal.

"I don't know. I could never put my finger on it. Jim went out to the bars most nights but never had a proper date. No girlfriend, ever. I thought that was strange, as he was handsome and charismatic. A real talker and convincing. I told him he could sell ice to an Eskimo."

"How was he shot?"

"Well, according to your father, Jim shot himself with his own gun. Robert didn't see it happen, but the investigation proved it was Jim's gun. Robert called it an accident. And the police believed him." Mom coughed her normal morning cough like she needed to clear years of accumulating goo from dodging the truth. "This wasn't the first time Jim had tried to hurt himself. His senior year in high school, he had cut his wrists, unsuccessfully, of course."

"How did he shoot himself?" My coffee finishes gurgling, and I pour the brain-reviving drink into my yellow and blue Chargers mug.

"The bullet hit his upper thigh from up close. Robert said he had placed the gun there to look at the stock, and then, somehow, it discharged. He bled out before Robert could get him back to the town hospital. That's the story, anyhow."

"Mom? Did you believe Robert's story? You don't sound convinced."

"Well, the police believed him, so I did as well."

"That's not what I asked."

"Good God, Chelsea! All the questions. It's so tiring."

"Please, Mom. I need truth. I'm sick and tired of everyone treating me like a child. I can take it. Tell me if you believed Robert's story."

"He's your father, you know. You could call him Dad."

"It's my choice to call him Robert. He hasn't been much of a father, so he doesn't deserve to be called Dad. Not in my book." My neck blazes with redness just thinking about my father. "Mom, the truth. Please?"

There was a cruel moment of silence, and then she responded. "Oh, God… Well, in the beginning, I believed your father. But then he started acting weird. After a few drinks, he'd talk some gibberish like he had killed his brother, that he was responsible. That he should have driven him to the clinic before he'd died. And then he'd clam up."

"After a few months of this, your father became an aggressive time bomb. Every time I asked him about Jim, he would explode. Now, of course, watching your brother die would really screw with a person, but his erratic behavior was too much. He wouldn't talk. He couldn't work. I loved Robert, but he was making it hard on us, on our marriage. Plus, your grandmother kept accusing him of mistreating you. I think it was more than he could take." Mom takes a deep breath. "It was unforgivable what Eve said about Robert."

"Then Robert flipped out and left us, and after drifting a bit, he moved to Denver. That's when I received the divorce papers."

I rub my thumb across the knobby arched lightning bolt of the Chargers logo on my mug before taking another sip of coffee. "Mom, did Dad mistreat me?"

"Well, he used to take you to McDonald's for dinner almost every night, if you call that abuse. But Chelsea, that's not what we're talking about," Mom says in a sharp tone. "You wanted to know more about how your Uncle Jim died, and I told you. Now, that's enough." Mom's pithy timbre halts the conversation. She exhales a loud breath. "How was your flight home?"

"It was fine." There she goes again, covering herself in a veil of vagueness. She needs to tell me what she knows and what she thinks might have happened to me. Waves of nerves rush over and through me.

"Why, again, are you home from work?" Mom inquires. "Oh, and I went through those boxes you had shipped from Eve's, and the picture you had mentioned was not in any of them. Where did you put it? You told me it was in one of these boxes."

"Oh, hang on, Mom. Someone is calling from work. I'll talk to you later."

"But wait, you remember that photo?"

"Mom, I gotta go." Why did I say there was a photo? I'm such an idiot. There was never a photo. That was to cover one lie with another lie.

The air in the tiny kitchen is thick with the aroma of coffee. I pour another cup of coffee and slink down onto my kitchen chair, putting my feet on the other chair. Two chairs have been enough for me. One for me and one for my feet. No need for an extraneous empty seat. My mind floats to what Mom had just said. Maybe, just maybe, she told some truth about how Uncle Jim died.

I've never shot a real gun, only fake guns on Xbox. But the way Uncle Jim died sounds weird. Why would a seasoned hunter put a loaded gun toward his own body? A meaningless and foul death. Closing my eyes might help conjure a memory of Uncle Jim, but there are no memories, and my mind is gray. Then a few sparks of memory invade the grayness. Robert and Jim were identical twins, and most people could not tell them apart. I remember looking for discriminating marks, scars, or twitches. Anything to tell them apart. How did Mom ever know one from the other? Which guy was she getting into bed with each night?

A bang makes me jump. The sound came from the parking lot. Out the rain-streaked window is an old black beater chugging along. And then it backfires again, sending a billow of smoke into the falling raindrops.

The thought of having your leg shot at close range makes me shudder. If Uncle Jim attempted suicide, he hit the correct place, other than the head. Put one hand over your ear and the other pulls the trigger. Brilliant, really, if you're into that kind of thing. I prefer pills – they are much cleaner. Take a handful, go to sleep, and never wake up.

I redial Mom.

"Did you find that photo?" Mom barks.

"Oh! God dammit, no, it's not in my suitcase, either. Um, there is another question." I swallow a hard knot of anxiety.

"Now what, Chelsea?"

"When Robert left us, was it because Uncle Jim died, or was it because of you and me? Did he hate us?"

Mom moans. "I don't have time for this, Chelsea. Nobody knew what went through his erratic Swiss cheese mind. Why don't you fly to Denver and ask him yourself?" I hear her cackle and then click.

"Mom?" Nothing. I toss my phone on the kitchen table and pick up Grandma's journal.

August 8, 1987, Chelsea was born today! Rushed to the hospital and waited and waited. Twelve and a half hours of labor. Poor Liz. But she did it. We all do – Moms' that is.

I held Chelsea all burrito-wrapped in that white blanket with blue and pink stripes. She's perfect, beautiful in her brand-new body with old wrinkly-looking red skin and blueish-green eyes. I do not know how babies do it. They hook your heart the moment you lay eyes on them. She has my heart. I love that precious little being.

Not wanting to overstay my welcome at the hospital, I left the new family. Got a daily paper from the gift shop at the hospital. It has the date Chelsea was born and all the day's news. I'll wait and give it to her when she's old enough to read and relish it, maybe on her eighteenth birthday.

I'll bet that paper is long gone by now, thrown out. Mom never gave it to me when I turned eighteen. Come to think of it, Mom never gave me anything from Grandma. No pictures, no notes, no trinkets, nothing. Did Grandma forget about me as I forgot about her?

August 9, 1987, The doctor wanted to keep Chelsea at the hospital overnight as she was a bit jaundiced. So excited to see her, I hurried over to the hospital this morning and spotted her among the other sleeping babies in their see-through beds.

Seeing all the newborns made me reflect.

From the moment we first open our eyes, we know we are individual expressions of life extraordinary. We lie in our cribs or parents' arms, playing with the light, experiencing it in this human form, as it's been dark in the womb for almost a year. Smiling and cooing, we move our hands around, swirling the light, watching it dance between our fingers. Everything feels good, different, but good. Peaceful now that the transition period between spirit and incarnate spirit is complete.

Incarnation brings innocence. Each of us is born unaware of the planet's limitations on our bodies and minds. I wonder if there is a force in play like its someone's job to create and show us restrictions and Earth rules. Maybe they're called The Confiners, and it goes something like this.

The Confiners fly over and circle the newborn. "Who are you?"

"I am a person, an expression of life. See? I was just born," the little one says.

"You are on the planet Earth, kid," the Limiters squawk. "You have to contend with limitations, with gravity. You don't eat. You die. You don't breathe. You die. Separate from those big people over there, your mom and dad, you die. Do you hear me, kid? So get your feet on the ground. Forget about the light and the fairies and the angels. Better focus on getting some milk in your little mouth."

"But, but..."

"But nothin', kid. There are billions of people on this finite planet, so keep your mouth shut and do what you are told. And look over there at that wall. Do not walk through it. You are not spirit any longer. You'll wind up with a big, painful knot on your forehead!"

You'll grow older. Wiser, some would say. I think most humans grow dumber. But that's from my viewpoint.

So after we bump our heads and skin our knees, we listen to the Confiners. We become deaf to the truth of our spirits, turn off the stereo, break the knob, and throw it in the trash.

I don't want this to happen to Chelsea. I wish for her to have a whole, satisfying life where she feels safe.

The trick is to remember. Remember who we really are. Remember the light. Remember our spirit friends, flying and talking with our consciousness, not just our mouths. Keep the curtain lifted – the great escape from the straitjacket, the locks, and chains. Find new frequencies, even if you have to dig around in the trash can and find that knob.

Wow, that was very esoteric. I've been attending a meditation class and am having some interesting conversations with some of my fellow meditators. Angie, the woman who leads the group, sparks us to think outside the box.

My voice pierces the brittle silence. "Yeah, kind of out there, Grandma." Not sure when it shut off, but there's no more delicious music coming from Gabriella's wall. Just me and my chilly heartbeat. I pull a sweatshirt over my head and stuff my hands in my pockets. There's something in my pocket, and I pull out the yellow piece of paper with Grandma's attorney's name and number scratched on it. Setting it on the table, I smooth out the crinkles.

There are more questions than answers. I have blips and sparks of memory of my father touching me inappropriately. Or did he? Mom says I'm making that up, but I don't think so. My mind goes back and forth.

I may have pushed those memories so deep inside me, and I can't seem to find them anymore. Reading Grandma's journals makes me want to dig around and find an actual memory.

My attention goes to the yellow paper, and I have neurotically smoothed the yellow paper over and over that the ink smeared to almost illegible and my palm is black with ink. "Jesus, Chelsea, why do you think about this stupid stuff? Think about what you know."

Fact. Mom wanted, no, she needed everything of Grandma's destroyed, given away, or thrown out.

Fact. Grandma is dead. She can't harm Mom, and her belongings surely can't. Fact. I have only a few memories of Grandma, and now her keepsakes keep her alive in me. I should have collected more of Grandma's things, but Mom would've blown up even worse than she did.

Here's another fact. Grandma suspected Robert was abusing me. If Mom thought Robert abused me, why didn't she do something about that? What stopped her? Embarrassment, shame, disbelief?

It must be about shame. Shame that Mom didn't challenge Robert when she suspected he was touching me inappropriately. Shame that she didn't understand or stop the abuse. Shame that Mom didn't side with me or believe my stories. She didn't even pretend to accept them. And then, it became too late. Too late to talk about it. Too late to uncover and confront the issue of abuse. And then Dad left us and moved to Denver.

Problem solved.

A sick combination of embarrassment and paralysis stiffens my body. The limiters sell you on the lies and half-truths that keep your mind from turning inside out. Mom didn't want to believe anything was happening, even though I was being abused right under her nose.

I drag myself into the kitchen and look in the cupboard for something for breakfast. The only food is a box of crackers, macaroni and cheese, and a container of Twinkies and Cup Cakes. Nothing else there. A loaf of white bread and some cheese slices stare back at me in the refrigerator. I pull out the cheese and look at the wrapper. It reads processed cheese-like food. Cheese-like? What the hell is that? Isn't cheese just, well, cheese? Like from a cow? Wow, like what Grandma said to Alice in that restaurant. I fling it back into the fridge. Toast is fine. I grab the bread and margarine. Oh no, margarine. Shit. I've been eating all the worst food.

The crunching sound of my toast is deafening in comparison to my quiet apartment. And yes, I put margarine on my toast. Sorry, Grandma. Gabrielle, my neighbor, and her little chicks must have flown the nest. Silence used to be my restorative warm blanket, my companion, easy. It used to soak into my pores and bring comfort. I could read or play video games by myself – no one to bother me. Today, I'm frightened by this silence. It feels strange to me, foreign, even dangerous, like the seconds before a bomb explodes.

Fragments of yesterday jumble in my head, splinters of words said, words thought. My body recoils. I'm still in shock that Drew fired both of us. I look at my phone again – still nothing from Drew or Megan.

I have to confront this situation and cannot stick my head in the sand anymore. Poor Megan. We will get through this together. I text.

> Hey, Meg. You OK?

I wait for her reply, crunching my toast and sipping my coffee.

Ten minutes go by, enough time for my mind to replay yesterday's horror film. I'm sure Meg is furious at me. She's not to blame. It's all my fault.

> Come on, Meg. Please don't be mad at me. I fucked up, and I'm sorry. What's goin on? Working on your resume?

Still no answer, so I add.

> Come over later for wine and whining. Let's work on our employment game plan together.

Meg takes her time answering my text. I jump when the text finally dings.

> I'm swamped.

> Come over. Misery needs some company. We can work on our resumes together. I'm so sorry for what I've done.

A few minutes go by before she texts.

> I talked to Drew, and she gave me my job back. When I asked her about you, she said you'll never get your job back. I'm sorry, Chels. So now I'm doing the work that both of us would be doing. Yay me.

It feels as though someone has punched me in the gut, an intense, painful mule kick. Just like that? She goes in and gets her job back. I'm glad Megan can keep her job, but we won't ever work together again. Team Chelsea and Megan. The Star Wars Jedis. Now, she has my job. My job. My sneaker line. My Drew.

The thought sinks in. I lie.

> That's great news, Meg.

> Gotta go. I can't let Drew catch me texting. Especially with you. Cya.

I sprint over to the kitchen window and crank it open. Raindrops flick across my face as I take in the moist air through an open-mouthed pant. My entire life is tearing apart. The torture is complete. Every possible bomb has exploded. No more silence as my ears ring and my head pounds from the rush of blood surging. Gripping the counter, I dry-heave into the sink. Nothing comes up as there's no life left inside me.

Wiping my mouth with the back of my hand, I watch the tree in front of my window sway. What kinds of things happen to trees? They either live or die. No job. No commute. No sneaker line. If a limb breaks in the wind, a gardener lops it off, and it grows another. Soil, sunlight, and water – simple needs. For me, there are no reasons to live. It's so quiet. Even the birds refuse to sing, or maybe they have better things to do.

CHAPTER 17

*P*art of me wants to crumple. The other part, the part that's taking me over right now, is aching for answers. While the two emotions duke it out, I dial Josie on my cell, and luckily, she answers.

"Hi Josie, this is Chelsea. I want to come clean about something, and please don't be mad at me."

"What is it, Chelsea?"

Propping my phone on my shoulder, I wipe my sweaty palms on my pants. "When we were at your house, there were some of Grandma's journals in the attic boxes. I didn't tell either you or Mom. I feared Mom would destroy them, so they hid well in my suitcase." My nervous words fly out of me like a jet plane taking off. There I did it – the truth. I immediately want to hang up and blame it on a poor connection. Then later, deny that I said anything. Instead, this other Chelsea has hold of me, and I hesitate and wait for Josie's response.

"I understand," Josie says in a flat tone. She used the exact manner with Mom while we cleaned Grandma's house.

"It seems Grandma wrote a series of journals. I think there were three in this series as she labeled them One through Three."

"Okay." Josie's voice sounds overly calm, repressed even.

This crushed sound reminds me of myself all too well. It comes out of me all the time. My needs, dreams, and desires have gone unmet for so long that repression is my typical language.

"And, well, two of Grandma's journals are missing. I've been reading the first one, and it is intriguing. I always thought my family was so screwed up, but Grandma makes us sound kinda normal, you know, like a real family." My voice shakes, and I swallow hard. "Josie, I'm sorry, but it's hard for me to trust anyone. Are you mad at me?"

"Dear, I do understand. It would have been best to tell me about the journals, but they belong to you just as much as your mother or me. Did you tell your mother?"

"Heck, no! And please don't tell her. She would freak out and demand they be destroyed. These are Grandma's words, the history, my history. It's all I have, and she stays alive through her writing."

"Yes, mon tresor. Well, Chelsea. It seems we both have a secret to tell."

A moment passes before either of us speaks. She has a secret? Josie seemed like an open book, always telling me stories about Grandma, about herself. A secret?

Josie clears her voice. "I was in Eve's room checking the water cans to make sure they weren't overflowing. Your suitcase was slightly open, and that's when I noticed it – one of her journals. Eve was in a dark place when she wrote that one. I didn't think you should read it – not yet. She was blaming herself for the death of Doug up on that mountaintop. She sounded almost suicidal."

"So Josie, you have Journal Two?"

"Well, let me check. I didn't look to see any numbers. Hold on." Josie shuffles through some papers.

"This is number two, Chelsea. After reading a few entries, I did not think you should experience it. That's why I took it out of your suitcase, and I'm not sure about Journal Three. You did such a thorough job of clearing out Eve's belongings. Do you suspect your mother has it?"

I chew on my cuticle. Josie says this so casually, even airily, like she does not know what Mom is capable of. "Oh God, I hope not." Air expires out of me like an old balloon. "If she does? I'm sure she has already used it as a fire starter. Josie, do you think it would be okay if I were the guardian of Grandma's journals? I swear to you I'll protect and save them. Can't guarantee if there will be another generation that comes from me, but they will be safe with me." I sit forward and stop gnawing at my cuticle. "Josie, please understand that these stories are like gold. I'll treasure and watch over them."

"Very well. I will send the journal to you in the mail."

"No! What if the post office loses it?" Remembering the airport debacle. That cannot happen again. "They are not the most efficient, you know." I wouldn't be able to bear that. Losing it twice!

"Okay, should it remain here with me?"

"Yes, that would be great. And Josie? Please, please, please don't tell my mom, or anyone, for that matter." I walk into my bedroom and pick up the foreign earring. "Josie? Did you lose an earring last weekend?"

"Yes, I did. How did you know?"

"Is it turquoise?"

"Yes, with little diamonds around the main stone? It went missing the weekend you and your mother were here."

"For whatever reason, it was in my suitcase. It must have dropped when you picked up Grandma's journal." I hear Josie clanking dishes. "Are you in the kitchen? What's for breakfast, Josie?"

"Oh, just a little porridge, you know, oatmeal. First, you cut up a bit of apple and boil it softly with some cinnamon and maple syrup. Then the oats go into the boiling water. Tastes better than that instant slop. That's for sure."

"I'll be right over!" We both laugh. If only I lived closer, there would be a warm breakfast at Josie's every day. So tasty and comforting. Homemade with love, like my salsa-music-loving neighbor.

Josie chuckles nervously. She's relieved I don't live closer. "Chelsea, you know that once you read all of Eve's journals, you can't walk around in the dark anymore, no more blindness. You will know things. Things you never knew before. Things about yourself, about your grandmother, about your family. Are you sure you are ready for this, dear?"

I'm not sure. I've tried hard to keep childhood thoughts out of my mind and body like a trained assassin, tracking and shooting down all the painful emotions. Occasionally I'd get curious when there was a blip of memory, and I'd ask Mom, only to get her stock answer. Chelsea, don't be ridiculous. You're just daydreaming again.

With all this family dynamic surfacing, I can't escape the thoughts plaguing me. The emotional assassin must be off duty right now, allowing questions to erupt. What happened to me? When did our family turn that corner from somewhat normal to all screwed up?

Oh, it's just your colorful imagination. But who thinks that kind of stuff up? Me pulling my dresser in front of my door when Dad got drunk. Why? Especially at ten years old? I'm sure I was still eating my boogers, not thinking about someone touching me inappropriately.

After college, I wanted it simple – a good job, a nice relationship, save up for a little house. So far, I have none of that like a fool waiting for the wrong train. My cooling coffee is bitter. There's nothing here for me, and quite frankly, there is nothing to lose at this point. No job. No Drew. And Megan, who can't, or won't, talk to me.

Grandma didn't believe in coincidences. That everything happens for a reason, she said. That there is a purpose or underlying meaning behind every experience in life. It implies that there is some divine plan, fate, or greater force orchestrating the events that unfold. I gave up on God a long time ago. All I know is that it feels like I'm possessed with an unbelievable hunger to learn more about Grandma's life, my life.

"Chelsea? Are you okay? Did you hear me?" Josie says gently.

"Thanks, Josie. I think I'll be able to handle the truth of Grandma's life. This first journal is incredible. I'm finally getting to know my grandma – who she was and the life she lived. I'm finding that I love her."

"Awe, Chelsea, I'm so glad to hear. You know, I loved her, as well." Josie sniffs. Neither of us talks, allowing the sublime moment a little breathing room.

Josie clears her throat. "Well, okay dear, I want to be clear. This is important. There will be good times and bad times in all of our lives, even in your grandmother's life. The sun goes down each night only to come up again the next dewy morning. This Journal two reflects a rough time for Eve as she had to deal with death, grief, and guilt. She could not see the rebirth just yet – all dark. No sun. But it sounds like you've made your mind up, Chelsea. I'm proud of you." Josie taps a spoon on a bowl. "Dear, my breakfast is ready. I will keep this journal for you until further notice."

"Thanks, Josie. Do you want me to put your earring in the mail?"

"Well, now I'm worried about the mail service. No, can you hold on to that for me? We will have an exchange in the future, an earring for a journal."

"Deal. Until further notice."

"Bye now, dear."

At that, I hang up the phone and smell the warming cinnamon oatmeal from the thousand miles between us. I close my eyes and pretend to eat a spoonful of the soft, comforting breakfast.

My eyes gently open. Nope, still here in this depression chamber of an apartment. "What the hell am I gonna do?" Opening my bank app, my savings account balance has a nice little pad. "Grandma," I whisper. "Please help me."

Journal One – January 11, 1988, Attended the meditation circle again. I'm doing my best not to feel so much anxiety about Doug dying. I go through times of grief and anger. I'm angry at myself for not saving him, and then I'm mad at him for leaving me.

This insight came to me while in the guided meditation.

What if we have it all wrong? What if we are not on a journey? What if there is no end destination? No heaven or hell. No wrong turns. Only gathering learned lessons, like foraging around a garden for nourishment.

My meditation was highly vivid. I had this thought about the journey of life. But maybe I AM the journey. My journey doesn't lead me. I lead. I'm in control. That's empowering. All is experience. My experience. My journey.

Am I just being an egomaniac? Maybe. But the idea comforts me that if you do your best, there is no right and no wrong, no perfection or imperfec-

tion. There is only learning. When I see, hear, touch, and taste, how can any of that be a mistake?

The arguments with Liz are getting worse and worse. She's furious, and I don't know why. She's always on edge. I want to help Chelsea, as Liz always works, and I don't think Robert and Jim can handle her. But the more I offer to help, the more Liz pushes to get me away. I love Liz, but we can't seem to get along. It's terrible.

I stick my finger into the Journal, holding the page. What's my journey? My experience? No right and no wrong? That's a hard one to bite off. I can't get my head around that one, Grandma.

My journey to this point has been a well-thought-out procurement. Go to college, get an engineering degree, and get a good-paying job. I have never seen myself getting married or having kids. Definitely no children. I don't want to screw anyone up.

March 14, 1988, Chelsea Chelsea Chelsea – what can I say? I love this little one! Super cute stage – seven months. Although, every stage for her has been adorable. Today, she was scooting around on one knee, then switching to the other. Put both her knees under her. She looked right into my eyes with her dreamy blue/green eyes, and then both knees flopped out from under her, and she landed on her belly like Bambi on ice. I laughed. She examined me carefully and then laughed. Then she started pulling herself forward with her arms so strong, going forward. My latest nickname for her is Scooch, as she scooches along!

Watching her, I realized perfect lives in imperfection. Her imperfect scooching will lead to a perfect crawl. The perfect crawl will lead to a wobbly walk, leading to a perfect walk to a perfect run. Babies don't know the concept of perfect. They don't judge themselves. No critic or inspector calls them out with a whistle for a poor attempt at crawling.

Chelsea uncontrollably giggles whenever I blow my nose. So, whenever she cries, all I have to do is pull out a tissue, wave it around, and whammo, she stops crying. It's my grandma superpower!

August 8, 1988, Made sweet potato muffins for Chelsea's first birthday. She loved 'em! Liz got home late from work and seemed distracted tonight. She works so hard. Luckily, Robert has a new building project. Should help with their money situation.

Chelsea is almost walking on her own! She pulls herself up and cruises along the couch around the coffee table, holding on to both. I encouraged her toward me, but she wouldn't let go of the coffee table. Took her arms and walked behind her all around the house. She was so curious.

She has dimples everywhere – her cheeks, her knees, her elbows. So cute!

I'm feeling less and less happy about work. Ever since Doug died, I haven't been able to get back into my groove. I've tried therapy and meditation. I'm walking every day – that feels good. But I'm thinking about doing something else. I've been a nurse my whole life. It's the only trade I know. But Alice suggested I take some cooking classes to work at a restaurant. She chuckled the other day when we were at lunch, saying we should go in on a restaurant together. She'll be the chef, and I'll be the sous-chef. I'll start with cooking classes and see how that goes.

OCTOBER 6, 1988, *Decided to take cooking classes in Santa Fe, NM. I can't wait! It's a new place that teaches people how to cook modern southwestern. The chef opened a new restaurant two years ago in Santa Fe, The Hungry Coyote. Hope I'm not getting in over my head. I can barely cut up an onion, but I've been trying. They told me they take all levels of cooks.*

The only way to make genuine progress in life is to put yourself out there. Sure, it may be less painful just to put up walls and always make safe decisions, but the agony of avoiding life will eventually worsen, and the regret will linger with its stink and oozing bitterness. I have made plenty of mistakes in this life. Do my best to learn and not repeat. I'm listening to my heart more, which feels good – potential failures over regret.

Told Dena I needed some time off from the hospital. She encouraged me to go on a hiatus instead of quitting. She gave me six months. I took it.

I'm a little scared, but I'm going to Santa Fe! And until then, I will cook every night. Practice makes perfect, and mastery is not achieved instantly but rather through gradual progress and continuous refinement. And lots of work.

However, after being on this planet for a long time, I recognize perfection is an ideal that may be unattainable in many cases. Instead of fixating on achieving flawless perfection with my cooking, focusing on progress, growth, and personal development can be more helpful.

I never try new things. It's terrifying. If I fail or screw up, people will not think I'm intelligent anymore. Mom used to tell me if you don't want to look dumb, stick to the things you know how to do.

Grandma is this fantastic combination of vulnerability mixed with the ability to learn and grow. She believes that her learning and intelligence can grow with time and experience. I've always thought that basic abilities, intelligence, and talents are fixed traits, that you are born with a certain amount, and that's all you get.

Grandma is not a failure or unintelligent, and certainly not dumb. She's trying new things, being adventurous, and being spontaneous. Not to the point of hurting anyone. She's living her life. Grandma's preparing to go to a new state and learn a new skill. Just like that. Out of the blue. I'd be scared to death.

The hairs on my arms raise, and goosebumps appear. My thoughts go from Grandma to my life journey. "If you can do it, Grandma, maybe I can too." I stand up and look out at the swaying trees. My brows draw closer as my face tightens in fear. The emotional assassin wants to eliminate my hopeful feelings. I can feel her loading her gun, but this other brave part of me turns the gun on her and dismisses her from service.

* * *

SHOVING my last and final suitcase into my trunk, I struggle to close the hatch. The back seat of my car is jammed with books, a photo album, and a couple of light jackets.

Megan sounds angry with me when I call her and explain my plan. She says the ten-hour days at work are crushing her. She is entirely in charge of the sneaker line. My sneaker line! Drew will not have it any other way, she says. Pangs of jealousy tremble through my belly. That sneaker line was my creation from the bottom up, and now, it is violated and changed from perfection to something else.

Megan reminded me, again, that I can't call her at work. We always used to chat at work. We always got our job done, but then we would talk about which TV shows we were binge-watching, which books we were reading, or about Matt, her son. I ask her if I could call her back tonight after work, and she says she will be busy with Matt. She's still mad at me. I ask her if she is, and she just says she'd better get off the phone. Yep, she's mad at me.

Parts of my job were creative and exciting. I would create something new, work with my team, brainstorm side-by-side with Megan, and flirt with Drew. Now it's all gone. Like Grandma said, 'the trifecta of failure.' Work, best friend, and lover. Over and out. My safe cave is collapsing in on top of my indifference and apathy.

I pull into the grocery store parking lot for road trip food. Walking around the store, I unconsciously place random items in my basket while humming to the song playing in the store. The handbasket handle digs into my hand. In the basket is a 6-pack of Diet Coke, M&Ms, potato chips, and beef jerky. My initial thought is it is a good start for an eighteen-hour drive. Then Grandma's words play across in my mind.

Eat actual food. Eat the rainbow.

The handbasket drops onto the floor with a clunk. "Screw you junk food!" I say in a not-so-quiet tone. All the contents jerk up and down as they hit the floor. The young mom strolling toward me jumps, and with a look of horror, she swings her cart around and scampers away from me, shushing her kids away from the crazy lady.

The handbasket lies on the dirty nondescript tile floor in aisle six, and I stomp to the front of the store, grab a fresh basket, and head straight for the produce section.

"Alright, Grandma. What should we eat?" I get a small bag of apples, a carton of strawberries, and a bottle of water. In the checkout line, I grab a Snickers bar. It has peanuts.

I get in my car, check my route on Maps, and grab an apple. Is this the right thing? Leaving everything? My job. Drew. Megan. Portland. My apartment.

A squirt of apple juice hits my tongue with every crisp bite, and the crunching sound reverberates in my head. I look around the parking lot. It's actually a lovely day in Portland. It's not raining.

When I told Megan about my plan, it sounded wild, even to me. Let's face it. I have time on my hands right now. She didn't laugh like she used to. She said I was escaping my problems and needed to stick it out and be realistic. Drew needs to cool down, and once she and Megan figure out that they need me, she'll call.

For now, I need honest answers. My sketchy memories aren't enough, and I'm skeptical of what Mom tells or doesn't tell me. She always holds back information, protecting herself, some emotional manipulation, and dismissing my feelings. I need to know my story, not just be told my story by others around me. This trip is to discover me. The only way is through Grandma's journals. I'll finally get concrete answers

My image in the rear-view mirror catches me, and doubt creeps into me like black ooze seeking deep crevices. Maybe Megan is right. I want to escape some emancipation or freedom from my emotional cell block. My blanket of doubts has always kept me safe, not warm, but safe. Avoid danger, be watchful, and look around the corner. But I'm fed up. I can't carry on like that anymore. Maybe an escape is the perfect remedy.

In my car, I look over at the passenger seat, and there sits the journal with the seatbelt across it like Grandma is riding next to me. She loved me. I should have seen Grandma through the years, but I believed Mom. If Mom was so off about her, what else could be wrong?

The blue sky is like the color of the turquoise in Josie's earring. Tears fill my eyes. I dab them and wipe the wetness on my khaki pants. There's a desperation inside, like someone has played a horrible joke on me. And now, I might get the chance to discover the punch line. But who was the mastermind behind the prank? As much as I'm irritated by Mom, I don't think she can hold on to secrets for this long. On the other hand, she's one hell of a liar. I've seen that first-hand all my life.

If I discover that my father abused me, and Mom covered for him,

I will confront her and offer a few choice words. "Why? Why didn't you tell me?" I'd slap her across her face, and she'd look at me, stunned. "You chose the wrong person! You are my mom. You're supposed to protect ME above anyone else. My mom."

I lay my arms and head down on the steering wheel and sob. Tears overflow my eyes, and my entire body shakes. Of course, I could never do that. I can't confront her. She won't tell me the truth. She'll tell me I'm a disappointment, that I'm making it up like she always does. What if she covered for him? And then systematically drove out Grandma. Mom protected the wrong people and sent the wrong person away.

After a series of deep breaths in through my nose and out of my mouth, like Doctor Allen taught me, I lift my head and wipe my eyes. The truth is in Grandma's journals. I start my fully loaded car, Grandma riding shotgun, and get on I5 heading South.

CHAPTER 18

It's only been a week since we were at Grandma's, but I'm foggy after driving all night and jittery from the energy drinks and coffee. I find the house in La Jolla and pull into the driveway. The smell of the beach is a delightful combination of salt, fresh, and earthy aromas mixed with wet stones.

Josie doesn't answer her doorbell, even after several attempts. I should have called her, but the anticipation of reading Journal Two got the better of me. That and also, Josie could have said no to me coming back to her house so quickly.

Sitting on the porch chair, I pull out my phone and call her. It goes to voicemail, but I don't leave a message. My eyes sting, but the comfortable chair and the mid-morning sun kisses comfort me. My weary eyes close, finding a bit of relief. The sound of the ocean surf fills me. The rain was so fierce the last time I avoided going outside.

"Chelsea?"

I jump and blink rapidly, trying to get my bearings. The calming effects of the sounds and aromas of the ocean had put me to sleep.

"Chelsea. Are you okay?" Josie says, patting my arm. "Goodness, what are you doing here? You don't look so good, dear."

"Hi, Josie. I wanted to surprise you." My eyes feel gritty.

"Well, I'm surprised! Come in." Josie punches a code into the pad above the doorbell. "What is going on, Chelsea? What are you doing here? Is everything all right?"

Hauling my groggy self out of the porch chair is a chore. "That's a bit of a story. The condensed version? I am unemployed, friendless, have no significant other, and need that journal you kept." I follow Josie inside and look around the house in all its comfy, classy beach style – a stark contrast to my moldy orphanage apartment. Grandma's, now Josie's house, feels warm and inviting. I can breathe here.

"Would you like some iced tea or coffee, dear?" Dolled up in a gray skirt and white silk blouse, Josie's eyes shine bright as the day.

"I've had enough coffee, but iced tea sounds refreshing! Thanks, Josie." I pull out the familiar bar stool and watch her in the kitchen. "Yeah, you probably didn't think you'd see me so soon." A half-laugh tumbles out of me, and my voice has an unpleasing strain, like the vibration of a rope drawn out too fast.

"You are right about that!" Josie raises her eyebrows. "Sugar?"

"No thanks. I'm trying to cut back." The mild and delicate tea goes down easily. Sugar would taste better, but I want to follow Grandma's routine. Like Grandma, my desire to lose weight and feel better outweighs the need for sugar. Though in the past, trying to lose weight was like tinkering with the Titanic. Futile.

"So, why didn't you tell me you were coming back here?"

"Journal two!" The words blast out of me. "Josie, no matter how sad she felt, I have to read it. We don't have Journal Three, so that means we will only get two-thirds of her life. Of my life." My throat hitches as it feels like I've swallowed a lump of clay. "This is important to me!" I push my glasses up on my nose and look her deep in the eyes. The weight of this presses on my chest. Grandma held the only source of truth and authenticity.

I stick my hand in my jeans pocket and fish out Josie's turquoise earring. "We had a deal."

She looks at the earring with a half-smile. "Yes, we did, and keeping my word is important. But why didn't you let me know you were coming here?"

"Oh, Josie, I thought you might turn me down and shelter me from Grandma's pain in the journal you kept. Since we sorted through Grandma's belongings, I haven't felt like myself. There's been a profound shift within me, a noticeable change. My mind has become fixated on Grandma's journals, and an insatiable need has taken hold of me to delve into every word she ever wrote."

Grandma writes about our family systems so clearly. It's as if someone suddenly left ajar a door into some world unseen. I've had a small taste of what our life was like. Now I want a big gulp. "It's been just me and Mom for so long that I had put the rest of my family out of my mind, but Grandma writes about all of us in a way that feels normal."

"Well, there is no such thing as normal when it comes to family." Josie rubs her arms.

For the first time, it feels like Josie has had some regrets about her own family. I've been consumed in my family drama that it never crossed my mind that she might have gone through some hard times, too.

Josie clears her voice. "Chelsea, before I get journal two for you, there is something you must know. I was going to call you this evening because there is more news from Eve's attorney." Josie straightens her blouse. "I was just at his office going over her will, and there were some interesting details that were revealed today."

"What did he say?"

"There are a few references about you and your mother. You're going to like this. She had whole life insurance policies on both of you that are now mature, and you can borrow against them if needed. They are worth $100,000 cash, and death benefits are half a million." Josie smiles at me. "She mentioned you might need to pay off student loans or a down payment on a house. Basically, you can use the money however you see fit."

Josie's words echo inside my head. All these years, Mom had said that Grandma was stingy. "I was happy with just the Stilettos and journals. Wow! A hundred thousand? And it doesn't need to be paid back? You're not kidding?"

"No, I'm not kidding. And… what Stilettos, Chelsea?" Tilting her head to one side, Josie blinks a few times.

Guilt about stealing Grandma's things hangs around my neck like a dead skunk. "Did the attorney say anything else?"

"Chelsea, what Stilettos?" Josie edges closer.

Oh God, I'm going to have to tell her. "Sorry, that's one more thing of Grandma's that found its way into my suitcase. They belonged to Grandma. There were those heels and a love poem from my grandpa Doug to her. Did you know Grandma and I have the same size foot?" A jolt of excitement hits me.

"Well, no Chelsea, that's one detail I did not–"

"Josie, they are the most beautiful I've ever seen. I'm more of a sneaker girl, but these are sublime! Do you want to see them?" I look down in embarrassment, knowing Josie is such an honest, good person. "My car's stuffed to the gills with all my things. I'm not going back home for some time."

"Really? What are your plans, dear?"

"Well, there is no plan. After losing my job, I just up and left Portland and didn't look back. Reading Grandma's journals and tracing her steps is my priority. She talks about me. No one talks about me like that." Josie refills my glass with more iced tea. "Josie, I've never felt this way. I've never felt lovable enough, smart enough, anything enough. And when I read those journals, all these things are possible for me. Reading Grandma's journals makes me feel like a breath of life is moving inside me. I've been half-dead for so long that I need to revive atrophied parts of myself. Do you understand?"

"My, you and Eve are similar in so many ways. One time she told me that her heart was so starved and malnourished that she kept filling herself with food, feeding her mouth, not her soul. That was an important turning point for her weight loss." Josie looks at me with her brilliant dark eyes. "There's another thing… Chelsea, you look exactly like her!"

"My mom used to say that to me, but not in a good way. One time I had been eating ice cream, and it tasted so good that I threw my head back and laughed. Mom said never do that again because it reminded her of Eve."

Josie furrows her brow. It was the same look she gave Mom when she broke into the house.

I never laughed and smiled like that again. Keep it all in and stay quiet. It was safer that way.

"Chelsea, how 'bout you stay for a few days with me while you read the journals? Give yourself space to process. I am sure you have lost your job and boyfriend for this reason. I am glad you came here." She smiles that warm, all things are good kind of smile, and it feels like the planet spins in perfect concert with the stars and the sun. It's like there are no wars, no terminal cancer, no bleeding terror coiled deep down inside, and no men coming into your bedroom uninvited.

"You do not think your mom will show up in the middle of the night again?" Josie chuckles.

"Ha, no! She has no idea I'm here. And let's keep it that way." I feel lighter telling Josie some of these secrets. She's motherly, not mean. "Josie, while I'm baring my soul, it was not a boyfriend. It was my girlfriend who broke up with me."

"I'm sorry to assume you were with a man."

"It's okay, Josie. Mom doesn't know that I have been dating women, either."

Josie takes a stack of photos out of a drawer. "It is uncanny how much you look like Eve." She smiles and hands the images to me. "I kept these from your mother in hopes of giving them to you, dear."

Judging by the hairstyles and clothes, the photos were from the 1970s and capture a unique blend of nostalgia and cultural transformation. The grainy, vibrant images evoke a sense of freedom, expression, and the distinct fashion trends of the era. Josie thought it was safe to give me these photos. If she trusts me, I should trust myself.

Together, we unload my car and drag two overstuffed suitcases upstairs to Grandma's room. This time, there is no fear, apprehension, torrential rain, and no more roof leaks. I can't wait to sleep in Grandma's bed, immerse myself in her life, and learn about my life.

Josie's right. Absorbing this newfound family information will require time for it to sink in truly. I plan to finish both of the journals we have and continue looking for the lost journal. A pit forms in my gut thinking about asking Mom if she saw Grandma's third journal. Not sure how to handle that one. If she has it, I'll need to get it from her. If she doesn't, I'll never know that part of Grandma's life.

The red stilettos still look brand new as I model them for Josie. She giggles and covers her mouth. As she reads the poem from Grandpa Doug to Grandma, her giggles quickly turn to tears. Her eyes overflow like a dam breaking its barriers. Josie came along after Doug had died, but she loved him because Grandma loved him. She's like that.

After a long, luscious afternoon nap, I sit in Grandma's bed, prop up some pillows, and want to read, but my stomach seizes. I'm starving. Josie is nowhere in the house, but there's a note on the kitchen counter.

Chelsea, I'll be back around 10p, out with girlfriends. There are leftover lamb chops and salad in the refrigerator. Help yourself.

I open the fridge, and sure enough, there's dinner on a plate wrapped in plastic. Absolute magic.

At some point, Josie comes in through the garage. Pasqual, Josie's dog, barks a friendly bark. Not like the ferocious way he barked at Mom when she broke into the house. I look up from the journals, eyes blurry.

"You are still awake?" she says, setting her purse on the coffee table. She flops down on the couch next to me. "How are the journals? Can I read the first one? Have you finished it, yet?" "Yes! You'd love it, Josie! I just finished." Making room for Josie, I move my sock feet off the couch. "Ready to start Journal Two."

"Okay, it is in my office upstairs." She pushes herself to stand, taking my empty plate and fork still on the coffee table. "I see you liked the sorbet."

After dinner, I scanned the freezer and found a small carton of raspberry sorbet. "Oh, sorry, it's all gone." I look down. "I'll buy some more tomorrow to replace it."

"That's okay, dear. I am glad you enjoyed it."

I don't even remember eating it. I'm entranced with Grandma's journal. It's been fantastic learning about her. Grandma mentions me during my infancy, portraying me as undeniably adorable. A smile naturally graces my face. It comes from some inner place. That place I have denied for so many years. Pure joy. However, it's mixed with an avalanche of questions. Lots of questions.

After putting my dishes in the sink, Josie saunters back into the living room. "Chelsea, I need to tell you something more that the attorney told me today." Josie sits back against the couch and kicks off her flats. "There's more than that insurance policy."

"What is it, Josie?" My muscles stiffen, forcing me to sit up straight.

"Well, he told me some things that feel like a bomb. I needed to get a better understanding before telling you. That's why I was out with some of my girlfriends, and they said that you were old enough to hear what Eve had told the attorney and that you should know everything." She turns toward me and takes a deep breath.

My mind races. Is it about me? About Grandma? About my family? I stay quiet and study Josie. She looks uncomfortable and seems to search for words.

"Okay, well, here it is... Your grandmother was romantically involved with a man who lives on the Walaletta Pueblo in New Mexico."

"She has another family?"

"Um, no. This was long after Eve had kids when you and your mother didn't talk to Eve. When you lived with your mother in Seattle."

I lean back into the couch cushions, clenching my legs together, waiting for the news.

"This was a long-distance affair. Eve loved him but could not make it work. His life was in New Mexico on a pueblo, and hers, well, was here." Josie gets up off the plush, low couch and walks into the kitchen. "Would you like some hot tea, dear?"

"Sure, thanks. But Josie, what does this guy have to do with me?"

"His name is Tito Romero. Eve would talk about him frequently. He controlled some political position on the Walaletta Pueblo. She exalted him. She said she trusted him. Trust was very important to Eve. Little did I know she had entrusted him with some of her most precious belongings. It seems that Eve had some little secrets up her sleeve, things I didn't even know about." Josie dunks the herbal tea bags in tandem. She looks disappointed. She values knowing everything about Grandma and seems blindsided and disoriented by this information.

"The attorney told me that Tito has one of Eve's journals and a few other things. A few things for you, Chelsea. He did not have a phone number, only an address for Tito, and doesn't know if he still lives there or even if he's alive."

"Oh, my God! Does he have Journal Three? What else does he have?"

"I am unsure, but only you can get these things from Tito. He won't release the journal or the other belongings to anyone but you, Chelsea."

"Me!" Overwhelmed by Josie's intensity and the weight of this news, I avert my gaze, needing a moment to process it all. The intensity and the suddenness of it are too much to handle. "Me? Why just me?"

"I do not know, dear. The attorney didn not know either. I asked him specifically about her journals. Only one journal is mentioned in her will – the mysterious Journal Three. It's crazy, I understand." Josie sips her tea. "Chelsea, based on your reading of her first journal, what causes Journal three to be so special?"

"I don't know. Grandma has yet to mention anything about the third journal. She talks about daily stuff in that journal. You know – it's about work, my first birthday, reading to me, fights with my mom, stuff about my father and uncle. And then, it seems she was a deep thinker. She has these philosophical ideas. Oh, and then there's Alice and a fish restaurant they frequented."

"What? She talks about Alice Wonderland? And the restaurant?"

"Yeah. Do you know Alice?"

"Yes. I met Alice once. Nice woman. You know she and Eve went in on a restaurant together?"

"She did it! Grandma writes about how Alice asked her to be her sous chef, so Grandma went to Santa Fe to learn how to cook." My excitement is reaching such heights that it feels like I could burst out of my skin. All these stories I'm reading are now making sense. "Did they buy a restaurant together?"

"Yes. Eve was the financier, and Alice was the chef. Eve would often work there on busy nights. And then Alice took over the restaurant after a time in rehab."

"What was the name of the restaurant? Is it still around? Is Alice still around?"

"They called it Eve and Alice's Kitchen and Bar, and..." Josie taps her index finger on her chin. "I believe it is still a thriving neighborhood restaurant."

"Josie, we have to go!" I jump up from the couch.

"Now?" Josie looks at her watch. "It's 11:30. I'm sure they're closed."

While searching my phone, we discover the restaurant is still in existence and is closed at this hour. The About Us tab features a picture of Grandma and Alice Wonderland, both in white chefs' coats, outside the restaurant entrance. "Whoa, look at this!" I show Josie my phone. She raises her eyebrows and exhales a deep breath. She's holding back some tears again. "Okay, tomorrow we'll go there for lunch!" I proclaim.

"Yes, Ma'am! Does the website say if Alice still owns the restaurant?"

I read the rest of the About Us page and then scroll around, looking at the Menu, but it doesn't say who owns the establishment. "We'll call them in the morning. Maybe they'll tell us if Alice still cooks at the restaurant."

"Now, Josie, tell me everything the attorney said about this Tito guy. New Mexico? Grandma mentioned taking cooking classes in Santa Fe, New Mexico. Maybe that's where they met?" I'm feeling more and more confident speaking to Josie. So many feelings I'm experiencing in places unknown, foreign, but good. "A pueblo? Do people live in pueblos? Josie! Tell me, what's going on?"

"Oui, oui, I will tell you everything I know. It is important, yes. One subject at a time." Josie raises an eyebrow.

"Oh God, sorry, Josie. I'm acting like Mom. I need to calm down, but it's impossible." What could be in Journal three? Why only me? How did she know I'd read her journals and come back and piece our lives together? My head jumbles up like a ball of string. My nose dips down into my mug. The warm cinnamon apple steams my face, and I take a sip.

"You know, dear. Once you know about your family, about your grandmother, there is no looking back. It's like trying to stick toothpaste back into the tube. Are you sure you can withstand this information?"

"I've been questioning that, too." Consciously collecting my thoughts, I make a deliberate effort to meet Josie's gaze, ensuring a connection between us. "Yes. I'm ready to know the truth."

"At any cost?"

"Yes, Josie. At any cost."

CHAPTER 19

In bed, my mind races, and sleep evades me. Josie understands with confidence that I am ready to gather the facts to learn the truth. Oh God, I'm unsure if I'm prepared. Actively avoiding the truth has been my operating standard, thinking the unpleasant revelations would be too much. This avoidance has also led to a profound sense of loss, as essential milestones, celebrations, and shared experiences have proceeded without me. Feelings of guilt, sadness, and longing bubble up, but self-preservation is still top of mind.

I'm feeling a little stronger as Grandma is on my side. I think I can take the truth. My internal dialogue goes back and forth like a hollow table tennis ball. If my suspicions are correct, my father molested me. If I'm wrong about that, then what the hell are these flashes of memories? I fluff up my pillow, roll over on my side, and close my eyes.

There it is again. I slam my hands against my ears and scrunch my eyes closed, but the sound does not stop. Scratching and edging, the sound of wood scraping against wood. My lips and chin tremble, and beads of sweat form on my forehead. Like never before, the memory jumps me like a mugger in the darkness. And there it is, playing in my mind like an old movie.

"It's all in your mind. It's all in your mind," but the memory won't stop.

Even with my eyes squeezed closed, I see the scene from up above. I'm a hovering spirit over this tiny little strawberry blonde-haired girl in light blue shorts and a grubby, washed-a-million-times, off-white tank top. I remember that tank top. I wore it all the time that summer, as it had the Teenage Mutant Ninja Turtles on the front. My terrified ten-year-old feelings are now in my twenty-eight-year-old body. We are one, this little girl and me. One mind, same body, same feelings.

I shake my head, hoping this memory, this encoded flashback, won't intrude on me. Throwing the covers back, I grab my Xanax. Doc Allen told me to double up on pills occasionally when necessary. It's necessary! The pill goes down with a gulp of water from the glass on the bedside table.

Still, the movie of my ten-year-old self fills my mind. From up above, I watch my ten-year-old self scramble around my bedroom. My scraggly hair sticks to my face from the summer heat and terror. And then my twenty-eight-year-old person sinks down into the bedroom, into my young body, and our thoughts are one. I am her, and she is me. We share this memory and will forever.

Because this had happened occasionally, I asked Mom for a lock on my bedroom door. She scoffed and said no way. So, I'll have to haul my dresser in front of my door. It's the only way. If I don't, he can get in. I've done this every night since that first time last week. If I don't block my door, the potential for disaster is enormous, like an unsuspecting family picnicking on train tracks.

Last week, when he came in, he had said he just wanted to rub my back so that I could go to sleep. It started with that, and then his hands touched me in places that felt weird, wrong. Mom told me many times not to touch myself down there. One time, when I had to go to the bathroom so badly, I held myself so that pee would not leak out of me. Mom swatted my hand and said, do not touch yourself there. It's rude.

The sun sets, and the darker and later it gets, the more potential for more danger, more exposure. My dresser will hold back my door and my forceful intruder, so I pushed it with my hands, body at a diagonal, putting all my little ten-year-old strength into it, turning red and heaving on the white painted wood dresser nudging it and pushing it over inch by inch, wood on wood, screech, and growl.

The process took about twenty minutes, caught my breath, swiped away my sweat, and then pushed again. The dresser finally barricaded my closed door, and I peer down at my skinny, pale legs. My plan is to do this every night of my life, or at least until I'm old enough to run away from home. It's not safe here, and Mom is of no help.

Why do dads want to touch little girls' privates? Those rude places. Do other girls have to do this? Pull their dresser in front of their door so he can't get in. I'm afraid to ask any of the girls at school. I'm sure they would laugh and torment me, as usual.

My miniature body sits in front of my dresser. Even though I'm slight, the more weight against the door, the better. Stay awake, I reminded myself, as this has become a repeated event every night. "Not tonight. Please, not tonight." I whispered to myself. Time goes by, and my room gets murky from nightfall. Turning on my light would bring attention to my room, to me. Shifting my body, I did my best to stay awake. But it's late and dark. I rest my eyes for a bit.

I'm jolted awake by the abrupt scraping of my dresser on the wood floor, making a screeching, penetrating noise. A thin, shrill voice ekes out of me like the cry of an expiring mouse. Thump, thump, thump. He shoved on the door over and over. My skinny body lurches forward on each heave. I gasped. Stay quiet. No sounds. Digging my heels into the floor, I pushed back.

"Come on, Chels. Don't you want a back rub?" he said through the door crack. And then he pushed and shoved again, bumping the dresser against my back. "Chelsea! What the— why do you keep putting your dresser here?" He thumped the door against the dresser, jerking my head forward.

I heard him stomp down the hall in his work boots. "What are you doing here? Dammit, you startled me. No, you can't go in there. She's sound asleep." His voice drifted off.

My chin and lips trembled as my heartbeat drummed in my ears. Stay quiet. I waited. And waited. And listened. Who came into the house? Was it Grandma? Could it have been Mom? I imagined sliding my dresser back, running down the hall, hollering to whomever it was, and telling her about *all the gross touching. But I didn't. I can't. Dad told me not to tell anyone, that this was our little secret time. If it got out, he would not bring me gifts anymore.*

The necklace he gave me last week hung on a nail on the wall next to my bed. I loved it when he gave it to me. He put in the nail and hung it for me. I wore it every day until he came in four nights ago and touched me in that wrong place. I wanted to yank it off the wall and break it up into a million tiny pieces. The girls in my class at school flooded my mind – Jessica, Nicole, Ashley, Amanda. I bet they didn't shove their dresser over to secure their bedroom door.

Some time goes by, and there is silence. No voices. No footsteps. Just the extreme quiet of my room, overcast with heavy shadows. I pulled the comforter off my bed and sat back down at my watch station in front of the dresser to keep my vigil. On the floor, knees pulled up to my chin, pushing my back into the dresser, just in case he tried again. This is my new night watch and sleeping position.

When Dad touched me wrong, I didn't stop him, unlike Mom, who swatted my hand away from its rude placement. When he asked me if I liked what he was doing, I stayed silent, stiff. What's he to think if I don't answer? Was it an assumed yes by not saying no?

He'd be mad at me because I blocked him from getting in. I'm so stupid. He probably wouldn't give me any more unique gifts. No gifts, no love.

I wake up in Grandma's bed, back in my twenty-eight-year-old self. The extra Xanax knocked me out. Though I'm half asleep, my mind races in spinning and questioning loops. Did that happen to me? Or did my imagination get the better of me, like Mom always accuses? No, it felt real. It was real. Imagination, my ass! Damn you, Mom.

The La Jolla morning sun peeks through the blinds, casting sliced shadows across the walls. The fear of darkness and fear of my father slowly melts as my scrawny ten-year-old self integrates back into me. My sticky, cottony mouth suffocates, so I drink the end of the water. The cool wetness washes over my dry, prickly tongue before it sneaks down my throat.

Who came into the house that night? I didn't hear the other voice. He asked, what are you doing here? It doesn't sound like it could have been Mom. Unless she came home early from work that night. Whoever it was, he seemed surprised.

Well, at least I now know what happened during that shrieking, scraping sound. The details of pushing the dresser had never played out. This was the first time there was any cognitive memory of that dreadful sound. During my teenage years, I would wake up in the middle of the night, all sweaty, screaming and crying from nightmares of that sound, but I never could remember what had happened. Then, after a bunch of therapy, the nightmarish screeching sound stopped. I stopped having the nightmares, but sleeping through the night was, and still is, impossible.

On the nightstand, my phone rests on top of Journal One. Lifting my phone, I check my messages, hoping to find a text from one particular person. But Drew didn't email, text, or call. Even though she's wrong for me, I can't help it. There's a part of me that misses her.

I'll send a friendly, quick text about the journals and what I'm discovering about Grandma. Maybe we could be friends. Typing a few sentences, I look up and over at the journal. My thumb pushes the delete button hard, over and over, until there's nothing but an empty message. I set my phone face down on the bed and pick up Journal One.

These journals are like a puzzle with shifting edges. Who is this Tito? Why him? How did the two of them meet? Why New Mexico? Why, Grandma? There better be more about this mystery man in the journals.

It's like Grandma wrote this script years ago, leaving breadcrumbs and clues. Now, she directs the play from another realm. Did Grandma know I would find her journals? How would she know I'd go on a search for the lost journal and my lost truth? I yearn for the climax and cliffhanger, and, at the same time, I'm frightened. Take a deep breath. Don't become anxious – one step at a time.

I throw off the covers, pull on my sweatpants, and head downstairs.

"Mornin, Josie."

"Good morning, dear." Josie pours coffee into a bright red mug. She sniffs and wipes her eyes with the corner of a dishtowel.

Josie wore no makeup, and her eyes were red and puffy. Not that Josie always looked top-notch, but I wanted to know if she had a rough night as well.

"This Journal Two… Whew, it's a difficult one. Really sad. Eve was in a low emotional space." Josie places the coffee and sugar bowl in front of me.

"Thanks, Josie." Carefully, I measure out one teaspoon of sugar, just one, and put it in my coffee. "Did you read it all the way through?"

"Not quite. I still have a little bit to go. It's quite raw and sensitive."

I let that sink in for a second. "Does it say anything about Tito? Did she meet him in Santa Fe when she took the cooking classes?"

"Yes." Josie finally looks at me. She studies my face. "Chelsea, are you alright? You look like you've seen a ghost."

My cheeks puff up, and a deep sigh leaks out. "I think I've seen the ghost of me from years past." I stir my coffee. "Reading about my past has whipped up some terrible memories. Forgive me, Josie, but let's not talk about it right now. Okay?" The warm mug is comforting in my hands. "Back to Grandma and Tito?"

"Yes, Okay. Eve met Tito while she toured the Walaletta Pueblo while taking those cooking classes. He was a part of the Pueblo tribal government. Eve describes New Mexico most wonderfully. She used to love it there. I've never been but would love to one day." Josie pulls out a carton of eggs and some strawberries from the refrigerator and puts them on the kitchen counter. "Falling for a man threw Eve into a tailspin. She thought she'd never fall in love again after Doug died. Eve described her relationship with Tito as confusing, exciting, and painful." Josie frowns. "Then Eve goes on about the way Doug died. She blames herself for his death. Though the details she goes over sounds like she did all she could do."

I push the sugar bowl away, knowing it's dangerous to have it close, and a sense of pride fills me with my shifting consciousness. I feel pleased with myself, like the way skinny women must feel when they put up their hand, saying no to a piece of birthday cake.

"In the journal, Eve talks about arguments with your mother." Josie grimaces. "Liz limits the time Eve can come over and take care of you, Chelsea."

"Goddammit, Liz!" I throw the spoon down next to the sugar bowl. It jumps and then lands on the countertop. "What is wrong with her? Sorry Josie, but I'm furious at my mom right now. The way she kept me away from Grandma. She led me to believe Grandma was an ogre, a monster. It's just not fair. I'll never get those years back! Mom stole Grandma from me." I've seen other grandma's doing grandma things with their grandkids, like taking them to the movies, playing at parks, and going down slides with their fledgling tucked safely inside their grandma's legs. I'll never have that with my grandma.

"Chelsea, life is not about fairness. It's about balance. Imagine a great cosmic balance sheet that we take part in co-creating. Every relationship, every interaction accurately recorded, and then an equal and opposite balancer shows up in our lives." Josie pats my hand. "Karma, my dear. It's quite perfect." Josie motions me into the kitchen. "Cooking always helps with frustrations. That's what my mom used to say." She places a cutting board and a large knife down on the counter. "Okay, prepare to cry."

"Cry? I'm too mad to cry."

Smiling, Josie hands me an onion. "You cut up the onions and peppers, and I'll start on the strawberries."

Josie shows me how to take the papery skin off the onion and chop it so I do not cut my fingers. Then she helps me with the bell pepper and cuts it so the stem and seeds come off easily. She's handy and nimble-fingered, a natural.

We cook the onions and peppers in olive oil, sauté Josie calls it. Then whip up the eggs and add them to the onions and peppers. Josie adds garlic powder, salt, and pepper. She doesn't need to think about what comes next. She flows through the kitchen like she has thousands of times. Watching Josie, my heart swells like a sponge. In no time, we are sitting down to a fabulous omelet on a bed of spinach with strawberries on the side. It's so appealing and colorful that I take a picture of my plate.

Over breakfast, we compare notes to help us better understand what might be in the missing journal. I feel Grandma watching and directing me from beyond, in spirit form. Josie and I muddle through her life, questing for the truth.

My hands clench into fists of rage as anger for Mom builds in me again. "Josie, why do you think my mom had such a horrible image of Grandma? I mean, why do you think Mom hated Grandma? What in the hell happened between them?"

"I'm not sure. I only hope that the missing journal will reveal those details. Maybe you could ask your mom?"

"I'm so mad at Mom. If I try to talk to her, my words will get all jumbled up, and then she'll make fun of me. Besides, she wouldn't answer me. She never did. She's always dodged family questions." I cross my arms and exhale a deep, nasal breath. "I just wanna scream at her." This foreign feeling of standing up for myself is both scary and liberating, like skydiving through an unknown sky. The metallic taste of adrenaline fills my mouth.

"Oui, there, there, I know how you feel." Josie scoots her chair up, sits directly in front of me, and grasps both my arms. "Chelsea, I know one thing about anger. It's like you are looking at a situation from only one angle. Anger blocks the whole view. One must peek around the backside of anger." She shifts forward in her chair. She's so close to me I can see her pores. "It's like you can pick up the situation as if it were a triangle made of, let's say, dried, stiff spaghetti pasta." Josie pretends she's holding the pasta triangle with both hands out in front. "Look at all the sides. You can put your hand through the middle of it. You can throw the pasta triangle on the ground and break it into a million pieces." Josie acts out the gestures. "You could drop it into boiling water and soften the pasta, soften the situation."

"Take your anger and turn it to curiosity," Josie continues. "Look at all the angles, and then you'll see the situation from all its edges and viewpoints." After breakfast, Josie picks up our dirty plates and takes them into the kitchen. The dishes clatter as she places them in the sink. She turns toward me. "Chelsea, you are angry because you care."

Josie sees me. I mean, she really sees me. I've let no one do that before. It's always been too frightening, too exposed. But here, I'm safe. There's no need to pretend, no lies, no manipulation. I can be my flawed self, and Josie is okay with me.

If you had told me just a few months ago that I would be in my estranged Grandmother's house, becoming best friends with a seventy-five-year-old woman I only met a week ago, I'd have laughed right to your face. And then, if you said I would be strengthening my ties to family and untangling our complex bowl of spaghetti life, I would have turned and sprinted in the other direction. Nope, this is quite remarkable and out of character. Unemployed, unencumbered, and ready to pack up my car and head to New Mexico are things the old Chelsea would never do. How did Grandma put it? Confusing, exciting, and painful.

We settle in for a long day of reading and taking notes – me on the couch, Josie in her office, and a fresh pot of coffee in the kitchen. Back to Journal One.

December 11, 1988, Been cooking up a storm in prep for my Santa Fe cooking classes! Here's one of my favorites. Friends love 'em too! Had Mary and Jay over the other night, and they couldn't get enough of these yummy tacos.

Shrimp Tacos
For the Garlic Cilantro Lime Sauce
¼ cup oil
¼ cup water
½ cup chopped green onions
½ cup cilantro leaves
2-3 cloves garlic (less if you're sensitive to garlicky things)
½ teaspoon salt
juice of 2 limes
½ cup sour cream
For the Shrimp Tacos
1 lb. shrimp, peeled and deveined, tails removed
1 teaspoon each chili powder, cumin, and southwestern seasoning (see notes)
¼ teaspoon cayenne pepper (more or less to taste)

2-3 cups shredded green cabbage
8 small corn tortillas
1-2 avocados
Cotija cheese and additional cilantro for topping
lime wedges for serving

Pulse all the sauce ingredients except the sour cream in a food processor. When mostly smooth, add the sour cream and pulse until combined. Taste and adjust seasoning as needed. Set aside.

Heat a drizzle of oil in a large skillet over medium/high heat. Pat the shrimp dry with paper towels and sprinkle with the spices. Add the shrimp to the hot pan and sauté for 5-8 minutes, occasionally flipping, until the shrimp are cooked through.

Toss some of the sauce (not all) with the cabbage until the cabbage is coated to your liking. It should resemble a coleslaw – you want it to be enough sauce so the cabbage weighs down slightly. Use the leftover sauce on top of the tacos or in other recipes. Yummy!

To serve tacos, smash a spoonful of avocado on the tortillas, top with a few pieces of shrimp, top with coleslaw, and finish with Cotija cheese, cilantro, and lime wedges.

Chelsea update – 6 months old now, and she's in a state of constant motion – playing, kicking, walking, climbing. I told Liz and Robert that it was time to triple-check the childproofing throughout the house and to put a rug beneath her crib in case of jailbreaks. Robert agreed, but Liz accused me of being ridiculous, saying that Chelsea could never climb out of her crib. I didn't get into it with her, so made a mental note of what I should bring over to make things safer for Chels.

Brought over a small ball and took Chels to the park next to the house. She had such fun kicking it around. Her little wobbly run is just fantastic. She loved our picnic. Brought mac and cheese with steamed broccoli to eat. We ate the noodles with our fingers between getting up and kicking around the ball. Watching her warms my heart. Brings me absolute enchantment to watch her grow and learn.

I close my eyes to summon any memory, but there's nothing, no recollections, no mental pictures of being with Grandma, no feelings. Nothing. It's like my mind empties when it comes to my childhood, like a black hole inside me has collapsed and sucked in all my memories.

At least, I have that one memory, terrible as it is. The scraping dresser sound is one of the scant memories in my brain. That one is a doozy. At least now, I know it was my father who came into my room without my permission and touched me inappropriately. That is one puzzle solved. My suspicions were correct.

A good or soothing memory of Grandma would help balance that ugly memory. It seems impossible that I cannot remember being with Grandma. I've been reading all these stories of her taking care of me, loving me. But I have no memories of Grandma. Come to think of it, I don't have many early childhood memories at all. But the time me and Grandma spent together sounds so lovely in the journals. It's terrible to suppress those memories. I flip my hair over my shoulder and push my glasses up my nose.

February 11, 1989, It has been a while since I've journaled. Been super busy wrapping up at work (today being my last day at the hospital) and packing for my trip. Tomorrow's the big day! I have everything lined up and ready for my trek to Santa Fe. Car packed, tank filled, and have my maps folded in the glove box.

I'm hesitant, maybe even scared, to leave the hospital and do something that excites me. It feels like jumping from a plane. I can almost feel the sensation as the parachute opens and you glide through the air, and a remarkable feeling of freedom and liberation takes over. The breathtaking views, the sensation of weightlessness, and the realization that you have conquered your fears can be genuinely empowering. I'm in that moment of pushing beyond my comfort zone and embracing the exhilaration of the unknown.

Dropped over to say goodbye and give Chelsea a big hug. I will miss her. Two weeks without my little pumpkin. I told her Grandma's leaving for a bit but don't think she understood. She just kept offering me dry Cheerios from her bowl.

Last week, I grabbed a few cookbooks from my favorite used bookstore – Betty's Book Barn. Got The Silver Palate Cookbook by Sheila Lukins and Julee Rosso. Betty told me I should take this one with me. Lukins and Russo are the co-owners of Silver Palate, a Manhattan gourmet takeout shop.

I tried making miniature Chevre tarts from the Silver Palate book, and they went terribly awry. One must be aware of the dough you're using when baking. Never knew there were different kinds of dough. Just thought dough was dough. I will pay more attention to the details. So next were the miniature quiches. A little less disastrous. They weren't pretty, but they tasted good.

Alice offered to teach me some knife skills, and I took her up on it. She came over last night, and we cut up a bunch of different things and made a nice salad – onions, cucumbers, even tomatoes. I've always been afraid of garlic, but she showed me the best way to chop the garlic first by whacking a clove with the side of a large knife. Those skins came right off the clove. Also, she showed me a fancy way to chop basil. Roll all the leaves into a ball and then chop 'em up. I'm not good with a knife, but I'll get there.

Going to bed. Plan to leave tomorrow morning at 6. Be in Flagstaff by two. Can't wait!

Josie steps into the living room. "How's it going?" I ask.

"Been interesting to read. Some of these stories I've heard, some are new." Josie lets Pasqual out into the backyard. "Makes me sad, though. God. She left too soon."

"If only she was here, and we could talk to Grandma and not just read about her." I place a bookmark in Journal One and point to the cover. "She's just about to leave for Santa Fe. She's been making tricky-sounding recipes and preparing for her cooking classes. What's in Journal Two?"

"Some references of Tito and Santa Fe and Walaletta that might be helpful. I made note of them down for you." Josie puts her hands on her hips. "Speaking of recipes, Chelsea, what shall we make for dinner tonight?"

"Shrimp tacos! Grandma put her recipe in this journal."

"That sounds wonderful. Your Grandmother loved to make those, especially when we had company over."

We decide Josie should do the grocery shopping, and I will continue to read journals. Reading them next to the pool will be nice. The warm sun and light coastal breeze register on my face, so tender and sweet. A dragonfly dips and soars across the pool. So much better than Portland weather.

I pull my hair back and put it in a band. It's getting long enough to donate it again. Every two years, I cut my hair and donate it to make it into a wig for kids or women who have had chemotherapy and have lost their hair. The one condition is that I only have it cut when I'm not home. For about a decade now, I've been donating my hair. I'll ask Josie for her hairdresser's number. I think chopping off this old hair and old memories will be refreshing. It just might help me concentrate going forward and understanding the balance between Grandma and me.

Without Grandma here, all we have is oddly shaped interlocking clues to piece together her life and mine. Each familial puzzle piece has a small incomplete image or picture tessellating with the next, forming a life story. The elements and the story are like an intricate recipe. Two parts Eve, a bit of Josie, a dash of Tito, and… me.

I must get my hands on Journal Three, the lost journal.

My mind wanders to the stories about Alice. Maybe Alice met Tito. Perhaps she knows how to find him and what he meant to Grandma. She's right here in California, right under my nose.

Eve and Alice's Kitchen and Bar appear to be open for lunch, so I call but only reach a full voicemail box. There's no way to leave a message, so I call every five minutes. Finally, someone picks up. "Hello? Eve and Alice's," a young woman answers.

"Yes, hello. I was wondering what time you open today?"

"Oh, we won't be open today. We are closed for renovations."

"Renovations! For how long?"

"Another week. So maybe check back then."

"Um, is Alice there?" Click. "Hello? Hello!" I dial back. It rings and rings. No one answers. "Goddammit!" I yell out and throw my phone down onto the open journal in my lap. It jumps off the journal, hits the ground, and bounces into the pool. I leap at the phone but don't catch it. It sinks fast. Reaching into the water, it's just past my fingertips, and I watch my phone hit the bottom of the deep end, still lit up with the call to Eve and Alice's Kitchen and Bar.

CHAPTER 20

As fast as a superhuman runner, I race over and snatch the pool skimmer from the shed wall, dip it into the water, and fish out my dripping phone. Wiping off the phone with my shirttail, I touch the black screen. Nothing happens. "Please work! Please, please, please!" Poking and jabbing at it like a woodpecker doesn't work.

They say phones can get wet, but they probably won't work after swimming in six feet of water. Drips come out of the charging and speaker holes, and then I blow hard three short times to dry it out like mouth-to-mouth resuscitation.

The phone still doesn't turn on. It probably needs some time to dry out, so I set the phone on the side table next to me in the sun. Discouraged by my phone, I flop down into the poolside chair, pick up the journal, and see there are only a few more pages left.

2/12/1989 Well, one day down, one to go. Made it to Phoenix. Was on I-8 the entire way out from San Diego. Got a flat tire on I-8 just outside of El Centro before making it to the Arizona border. Luckily, a friendly family stopped and helped me change my tire. While the mechanic fixed my flat, I got homemade green chili and cheese tamales from a small stand across the street from the mechanic. The beautiful young woman who served me put a few extras in a bag for the rest of my trip. She told me her aunt and grand-

mother made them, and luck would be on my side for the rest of my journey if I ate them. So, I ate up!

Right time of year to be driving across the desert. Not too hot, and the wildflowers along the side of the highway were a stunning blanket of purple and yellow. It made me miss Doug, as he loved the desert landscape. I kept looking over at my empty passenger seat, wishing, aching for him to be there. Stopped on the roadside, picked a small bouquet of wildflowers, had a good cry, and put them in my spent iced teacup in the drink cup holder.

Their fragrance was not that of perfumy, cut flowers. They had more of a hot, green, earthy aroma, smelling unrestrained like children's laughter. Like Chelsea's giggle.

I love you, my dear Dougy.

Tomorrow, I will trek the final seven and a half hours to Santa Fe. And then my cooking classes start the next day. I'm both excited and scared, like on the first day of kindergarten.

I want to feel that way about a woman or a man someday. After being away from Drew, I know it was not love between us. I was killing time, filling a hollow space inside me. Wanting someone special involves opening yourself up emotionally. It means allowing yourself to be vulnerable, to share your thoughts, feelings, and dreams with another person. This vulnerability can be both intimidating and exhausting. I'm not sure if I'm capable of this type of vulnerability. The more I think about my relationship with Drew, the more our dysfunction becomes apparent. Drew was calling all the shots, and I survived on a few crumbs of her time. She would decide when we could get together, and it always had to be at my apartment. Drew never wanted any of her neighbors to see us and ask questions. She made all the relationship decisions – if you could call it a relationship, sneaking around, hiding from everyone, even Megan.

I can't help but feel sad, though, at the loss of a potential love with Drew. I've never been in love, that deep desire to nest together, to encourage my lover's growth, seeing past her flaws, and she ignores mine. The way Grandma and Grandpa Doug must have felt.

Relationships have always been a challenge. I was an awkward teenager, and in my early twenties, I was stiff and bumbling, and now,

I'm a hermit with two left feet. I've been in lust a few times, but always at a distance. If I saw a guy I liked, it would turn out he either had a girlfriend or the attraction wasn't mutual. Mom's words echo in my mind. "Well, if you would just lose some weight, you'd find a man." There must be men or women out there who don't care about a few extra pounds on their partner. Not every woman possesses a rail-thin body. Some are big, small, heavy, and light. They all find love.

Why not me?

Maybe I'm not the best judge of character. No one ever looked at me in high school. In college, there was Brandon, who had a cute face but the brains of a turnip. I was on a guy-kick back then. Then there was Eric, and we had met at a bar. I should have known that one would not go well. After a few drinks, he searched his pockets and claimed he had misplaced his wallet, so I picked up the tab. On our first date, about one week later, he had said his money was all tied up in some "Kick-ass, lucrative investment that he only needed to hold out a few months 'til the big payout came." Believing him, I paid for the following three dates. Eventually, a mutual friend told me he lived in his mom's house and played video games all day. After confronting him, he said he was only dating me because I was ugly and desperate enough to pay for everything.

After that, I swore off men. They were either as dull as a dishwasher or would rattlesnake around me, flicking their tongue in the air, waiting for the perfect time to strike. After a long, and I mean a super long, dry spell, Drew sauntered into my life. I thought, for sure, my arid girly bits had dehydrated from the scarcity of attention. I tried to stay away from her, but she was very convincing, and I was lonely. And she flirted with me – actually flirted with me. I'm ashamed to admit it now, but it turns out Drew possesses the foul combination of both dishwasher and rattlesnake.

The way Grandma loved Grandpa, deep and trusting, gives me hope. I want to be passionate about someone and for them to treasure me. My experiences with love are not even remotely close, but there have been some changes inside me, a deep stirring. I feel the possibility. A slight shift. A sliver of light is coming through the blinds. The journal feels comforting held to my heart, and silently I thank Grandma and Josie for starting to crack my heart open.

Josie introduces me to things I never thought I'd want to or could do. My heart has been stone cold and lifeless for so long that I thought those feelings were normal. I'm finding it's not. It's not for Grandma and Josie. These women have lived fully with open hearts and open minds. Not without faults, but open to experience life and love. Grandma found love after Grandpa Doug died. It sounds like she found love and trust with Tito.

I want my heart to unfurl, but I'm cautious and afraid of the outcome. That openness will harm me, hurt me as it has in the past, like the difference between being thrown off the fifteenth or sixteenth floor. A broken heart is a consequence of living and loving openly, so I've found it easier to keep people at a distance. My mantra has been to stay back and stay quiet. Stay safe.

Josie comes into the house from the garage. "Chelsea?"

"Yes?" I set the journal down, jump up, and open the screen door to the house.

"The groceries, dear. Can you help?"

"Of course." Josie's heavy grocery totes have carrot tops and lettuce peeking out.

Josie smiles at me. "Tonight, I think we will start with charcuterie… What do you think?"

"Charcuterie?" I try to pronounce the word just the way Josie said it.

"Oh, I'm sure you've had it before. Charcuterie is a board full of cured meats, cheeses, olives, crackers, and marmalades."

"Right, okay, yes, I've had that before. Sounds delish!"

I heave the last bag onto the kitchen counter. "Josie, I did something idiotic, as usual. My phone dropped in the pool, and I'm afraid it won't work. My two left feet are to blame, like Mom always tells me. And I need to call Alice and Eve's Kitchen and Bar. We have to get through to Alice."

"Oh, no!" Josie wrinkles her brow.

"Yeah, I know, really dumb."

"Well, it sounds more like a silly mistake to me. Not dumb or stupid."

"I have it in the sun, hoping it'll dry out." I point toward the back-screen door.

Josie opens her purse and pulls out her cell phone. "Here, use mine."

"Thanks, Josie." I take Josie's phone and look up the number again. Leaning back on the kitchen counter, I tap my fingers to the beat of the rings, counting them. Eight... nine... Making eye contact with Josie, she looks expectant. Eyebrows raised.

"Well?" she asks.

"No one answers. One person answered before my phone took a swim, but now no one answered. They are under construction or something."

"That's quite frustrating," Josie says as she puts carrots and celery into the fridge.

"Yes, frustrating like the rest of my life." My voice drifts off in discouragement. Setting Josie's phone on the counter, I turn and shuffle out of the kitchen.

"Chelsea? Are you all right?"

"I'm just so confused. Do I go to New Mexico on the off chance I'll find Tito and the lost journal? Do I go back to Portland, patch things up with Drew, and attempt to get my job back? Or should I drive my car over a cliff and end my misery?"

"Sweet girl." Josie takes a few steps closer to me. "This is a confusing time right now. You've had so much thrown at you. Your grandmother loved you. You know that much, right?" "Yeah. But, Josie, I'm scared. I've never driven that far away. Walaletta, New Mexico, will take me two days by car! And I'm afraid to meet new people, especially men. How am I going to pull off this Tito thing? Josie, help me."

"Oh, dear. I would go with you, but you should experience this on your own. Facing your fears and overcoming a situation is empowering. You'll feel stronger for pushing myself, no matter how painful."

Josie is in light blue Bermuda shorts and black flip-flops. Her flouncy white blouse says she's a true California transplant. I remain quiet and let her words seep into me like warm water through a tea bag. The force is strong in Josie. Yoda would be proud.

"Chelsea, have you heard the saying, feel the fear and do those things, anyway? Some even say that you should scare yourself every day." She returns to the grocery totes and pulls out two small blocks of cheese. "The sense of possibility can stem from your personal growth and development. As you learn and evolve, you may start seeing new opportunities and potentials previously overlooked. This growth can bring a fresh perspective and a greater belief in your abilities. Believe in yourself, Chelsea. It's okay to trust yourself as well."

Imagining the drive to New Mexico and attempting to find this stranger makes my entire body shiver in fear. "Josie, please, please, please come with me!" I hold up my hands in a prayer position. "Please?"

She looks down at the cheese. I can tell she's considering my proposal. "No, Chelsea. It's your discovery. I can't take away your adventure."

"Please! It's not possible to do this without you." My heart pounds in my chest. "This is not an adventure. Trust me. It's more like a horror movie!" My throat tightens. "Please, Josie! Go with me!"

"Chelsea, dear, I have full confidence you can find Tito and the lost journal." Josie walks over to me and takes me by the shoulders. "You can do this. You don't need me. Believe in yourself. Trust yourself."

That's just it – I've never believed in myself, and neither has anyone else. I stand quietly, looking into Josie's eyes. Not flinching, she looks directly into mine.

I break the stare and look down and then outside. "I'm gonna go check on my phone." Walking out the screen door to the sun-drenched backyard, I lift my phone, close my eyes, and take a deep breath. "Come on, baby. You have to work." I open my eyes and push the on-button. The screen flashes in a kaleidoscope of colors before it goes black again, and then my home screen shines for me. It's a photo of Megan and me in our office. "Yes, it works!"

That day, a coworker took this photo while we celebrated

Megan's second anniversary with Chausse Shoes. We looked happy. Really happy. My shoulders slump, and my body feels limp, like an uprooted weed. I miss Megan and seeing her every day at work, and the lunches we'd eat at our desks. She, with her leftovers from dinner the night before, and me with my Cuppa Noodles. They came in a 24-pack from the discount store. A buck a day, I would tell her. She used to razz me about the noodles, but I thought they were delicious.

Calling or texting Megan on a Thursday is dangerous, especially if Drew is around, but I miss her. Opening my text messages, I read the last message from Drew, saying not to contact her. My head hangs.

Don't do it. Don't text Drew. God, I want to. What would Grandma do? What would Josie do? I know what Josie would do. She'd dropkick Drew, walk away, and never look back. Easy for someone like her. She's a strong woman with smarts, beauty, and wit. But for me? I am – just me. Okay, I'm smart. I've got that going for me. Some things like engineering concepts come easily to me, and I can recite metrics, performance, and data all day long.

I dial the restaurant one last time and hold my breath. It rings and rings. No answer. My whole body clinches.

"Chelsea?" Josie comes outside and sits down in one of the wrought-iron chairs. "I have something for you." She opens her hand. A silver bracelet shimmers in the sunshine. "It was Eve's. She wore it all the time."

It was curiously heavy. The engraving on the face of the bracelet said, ALIVE. Josie has that calm, motherly look on her face. "This was Grandma's?"

"Yes. I had given it to Eve when she was first diagnosed with cancer. It was her mantra. She wanted to be alive in all senses of the word – lively, vital, animated, spirited. Her list of ALIVE words was pages long. She would recite them every day. Awake, alert, dynamic." Josie takes the bracelet from me and opens up the clasp. She lifts my wrist and puts it on me.

Josie clasps the bangle around my wrist. I search my mind for words relating to alive. "You mean, like agile, enthusiastic, or ready?"

"Yes!" Josie's high cheekbones gleam as she radiates with a kind smile. "More, Chelsea! Can you think of more?"

"Ummmm, powerful and strong." Studying the word on the bracelet, I blurt out words as they come. "Bright? Oh, how bout intelligent or game or on the move!"

"Yes, Chelsea!" Josie sits back in her chair, tips her head back, and laughs. "Oui! You got it! ALIVE!"

"Alive." My finger runs back and forth over the engraved word. "God, why is she gone?" I look up and watch the treetops sway gently in the light summer breeze.

"I know, dear. Every day, I miss her beauty, pleasant voice, and laughter."

Josie's caring brown eyes are about to overflow with tears. "If Grandma were here, I wouldn't have to do these scary things like go to New Mexico by myself." Now tears fill my eyes. "The three of us could be here together, and it would be perfect."

Josie sniffs. "Oh, it wouldn't be perfect." She scoffs. "We would eventually get on your nerves. Huh." Josie leans toward me and holds my wrist, touching the bracelet. "It's so hard to see, but everything is unfolding just as it should." With a light squeeze, she continues to hold on to me. "I know. Traveling to New Mexico sounds frightening and hard, and I'm sure it will be at times. And if you get off course, change your direction and accept what is. Allow grace and synchronicity to fuse. Collaborate with the universe and be curious about the outcome."

"But what if I can't find Tito? What if he moved or, even worse, what if he's dead?" I barely get the words out. My throat feels thick.

"Then, I guess you don't find him."

"Then it was all a waste – my time, my money…" My voice cracks. "Josie, I must find him. I must find the lost journal!"

"Yes, yes, you do." She pats my wrist and the bracelet and then sits back in her chair. "So. What are you going to do?"

I slump in my chair and read the bracelet one more time. What is my plan?

Josie pushes herself to stand. She picks up the pool skimmer, places it against the pool house, and walks back over. Standing next to me, and she blocks the sun with her body. All I see is her silhouette with an aura so bright I can barely make out her features. "Well, dear, you have some thinking to do. And I have more groceries to put away." At that, she turns and goes into the house.

Someone needs to take me by the hand and lead me. I want Josie to help. She should tell me how we are going to find Tito. Josie should say pack the car like this. Drive like that. Go there. And then, we can retrieve the lost journal, read it together, and everything works out, just like that. But that's not the way Josie operates.

Unconsciously, I pick up my phone and dial. I'm brought back to reality when someone finally answers. "Alice and Eve's Kitchen and Bar." The first question I blurt out is about Alice and does she still work there? "No." The young woman utters. I can barely hear her for the construction noise at the restaurant. "Alice manages our farm half-hour north in Poway."

"So she's not there? Can you give me her phone number?" My posture perks up as I get all my questions out before she hangs up on me again.

"I can't give out her phone number. She's pretty private." I hear an electric saw as she talks. "She comes in every Thursday in the truck with the veggies for the weekend."

"Can I leave a message for her?"

"What?"

I yell into my phone. "Can you tell Alice that Chelsea called? Eve's granddaughter, Chelsea."

"Chelsea, you say. I'll tell her."

"Okay, thanks very much." At that, I hear a click.

Waiting around here until next Thursday is not an option. Eventually, I'll drive Josie crazy. My mind flits and flashes with ideas. Should we go to Alice's farm? Would she go to New Mexico with me? Doubtful. She's a private recluse. Anyone who can live on the streets of San Diego won't jump in a car with a stranger and drive eight hundred miles only to find yet another stranger.

It sounds like Alice got her dream. Grandma said she always

wanted to work on a sustainable farm, and now she manages the farm for the restaurant. How perfect for her. Grandma helped her get her life back. Now, I need to get my life back. Back? No. I need to get a life. I've been living, but I have no life. My finger traces the word on the bracelet.

ALIVE.

We only have two-thirds of Grandma's journals – Journals One and Two. I need Journal Three. Without that lost journal, I'm never going to know the truth, the parts of my life I can't remember. All I have to do is drive to some teeny town in New Mexico, track down a stranger for whom I have no address, and convince said stranger to trust me enough to give me Eve's sacred journal. The same journal Grandma asked him to watch with his life. Well, I'm guessing she said that. Maybe she didn't actually say, "Watch it with your life." She might have said to keep it for her until further notice. In either case, Journal Three must be chock full of family secrets. Why else did she ask Tito to guard it, and why am I the only one who can retrieve it?

The attorney didn't say Mom. Grandma named me. I'm the one, the only one. Grandma put me in her will. How could she have known I would find the other journals, that I'd be binging on them like a kid with Halloween candy?

Here's another question, why New Mexico? I've never left the West Coast, other than that Chausse training in Rochester, NY. I've gone up and down the West Coast all my life, but it scares me when it comes to traveling away from the Pacific Ocean. New Mexico is a brand-new territory, and I'll be driving to a strange and foreign place. What if my car breaks down or there are no gas stations? What if I get a flat tire like Grandma? What if a wrong turn takes me to the Mexican border, and I can't find my passport? Then, they're holding me at gunpoint, like at the airport.

And then there's meeting this man, a stranger. I'm not good with strangers. I'm not good with anyone – strange or otherwise. Because I'm naturally suspicious, I never feel like I'm on solid ground around people, so I often avoid meeting new people. My thoughts pierce me like thorns. The cruel, creeping tiger of anxiety inches closer. Get a hold of yourself, Chelsea.

Grandma must have trusted that Tito was the right person to hold on to this precious journal. Trust. That's quite the word of the day. It takes much proving for me to trust anyone. I don't even know Grandma, and now I'm entirely trusting her plan. I'm going to pack up my car, risk my life, and drive to New Mexico. What am I thinking? That's not safe. I can't do this.

The journal calls to me, so I read the final entry in Journal One.

Feb 14, 1989 *Santa Fe, NM, Finally made it! It was a long haul, but I feel energized. A great surge of energy surged through me after I gassed up in Albuquerque (I'm sure the fresh air and coffee helped). That hour it took from Albuquerque to Santa Fe woke me up. Driving into Santa Fe, I witnessed how the sun shone through the impossibly blue sky. At first, the low-slung buildings blend into the landscape, but looking closer, I saw the adobe houses that dot the hills and valleys. They blended into the reddish-brown dirt and looked like old, earth-colored California missions. The closer I got to Santa Fe, the mountains surrounded the highway with low pine trees and a type of bush with beautiful yellow flowers (I'll have to ask someone what those are called.) As I exited the highway onto Old Pecos Trail, I decided to roll down my car window, and what greeted me was an extraordinary scent. The air carried a refreshing aroma unlike anything I had ever experienced. It was a delightful blend of crispness, tinged with the gentle essence of wood burning in nearby fireplaces. Following the winding road, it eventually led me to the heart of the town and my hotel, an enchanting journey immersed in captivating fragrances.*

CHAPTER 21

The dirt parking lot behind The Walaletta Hotel is dusty and about half full, mostly with pickup trucks. Their website says, "An Adventure for Visitors. A Tradition for Locals." After Josie's pronouncement that this trek would be an adventure, the slogan seemed like a sign. By the looks of it, The Walaletta Hotel was probably never a four-star hotel, unlike the Four Seasons Drew once took me to. People probably didn't give star ratings when this was built, back when dinosaurs roamed the planet. One review said it was cozy, which is code for old and decrepit. The two-story pinkish adobe stands tall with bright blue windowpanes and doors that lean to the left. Hopefully, staying here isn't a mistake. I get my bag from the trunk and gaze up at the sky. I made it, just like Grandma! The dazzling sunset with animal clouds of orange and pink playing overhead fills me with pride. I made it to New Mexico on my own.

Stumbling up the two uneven and cracked cement stairs, I push open the purple-blue painted hotel door. I'm not one for décor, but I'm dazed by what is before me. A vast ocean of brown leather and heavy wood overtakes my senses. Worn wood floor planks, dense furniture, and floor-to-ceiling beams that resemble shiny old trees support the southwestern adventure. Red, blue, and orange Native American blankets tumble over railings, and faded rugs lay under the couches in the reception area. Inside the hotel, that same intense purple-blue color lives everywhere. It lines the inside of the arched doorways and echoes in the stripes on the throw pillows on the cracked leather couches and oversized leather chairs.

"Hello!" a young woman with long dark hair and a striking red sweater says from behind the reception desk.

I zigzag around the furniture to the large, ornately carved counter. "Hello. I'm Chelsea Price. I'm here for two nights."

After the receptionist checks me in, we take my bags upstairs to my room. I slog up the stairs as my legs feel thick and slow from sitting all day in the car. The young lady opens the door to my room and sets my duffle bag on the end of the bed. "Will this be okay for you?"

"Yes, this will be fine."

She nods a quick yes and walks toward the door. "Oh, do you want firewood?" She points to a rounded built-in firepit that is wide at the base and narrow at the top. It almost blends entirely in with the white mud walls.

"Oh, is that a fireplace?"

"First time to New Mexico. Huh?" She whisks back into the room and over to the fireplace. "It's called a kiva. We only burn local wood, pinon, and juniper. When you make a fire, place the wood pointing up so that each piece rests on the other, kinda like a teepee. I'll get some wood." She spins around and dashes out of the room.

I stroll into the bathroom – the small, ornate mirror with narrow blue tiles framing the glass fits well in the cramped space. My flat hair goes with the circles under my eyes, both tired and road weary. The small bathroom has this bright blue everywhere – on the tile and painted on the front of the vanity.

There's a tap on my doorjamb. "Here's your wood and some newspapers." She sets the firewood down on the ledge next to the kiva and quickly turns toward me. "The ledge that goes around the kiva. Everyone calls it the banco." She pats the small bench that surrounds the fireplace. "It's nice to sit on when there is a fire burning. Breakfast starts at seven." She smiles. "Try the huevos rancheros. Let me know if you need anything else."

"Hey, just quickly. I love all this blue." I swing both of my hands out, palms up. "Is it like your logo color or something?"

"Oh, that's the Walaletta blue. You'll see it everywhere. It represents one of the four sacred directions of Pueblo life. Blue speaks for the direction of the Southwest. So, to honor our heritage, we put blue everywhere." She tips her head to the side as she speaks. "Some of the old guys who hang out at the bar here say the blue also keeps out evil spirits like a talisman or a good-luck charm."

"Old guys at the bar? Say, do you know Tito Lujan?"

The woman considers my question. "Um, no, I don't think so. There are a ton of Lujan's in Walaletta, but I've not met Tito Lujan." She turns and speaks over her shoulder. "I'll be downstairs if you need anything."

As I gently shut the door, the noticeable accumulation of numerous layers of blue paint draws me in. The thick buildup serves as a visual reminder of the passage of time and the various transformations this door has probably undergone. Each coat tells a story, a history of change and renewal, creating a textured canvas.

I flop into the chair next to the kiva fireplace and check my watch. It's getting late for dinner, and I stink from the road, but I'm hungry. A splash of water on my face and a reapplication of deodorant will have to do. A pang of fear hits me when I realize I don't have a book to take to dinner. Reading at dinner keeps my attention off the fact that I'm eating alone. Rifling through my duffle bag, I remember it's still in the car, but hunger overtakes me. Grandma's Journal Two is in my other suitcase, snuggling with my t-shirts. "Yes!" I kiss the cover and then tuck the journal under my arm. On my way to the hotel bar, the information kiosk catches my attention, and I pick up a map of Walaletta and a few other brochures.

Under a blue arch is a sign pointing me toward the aptly named Kiva Bar. The quiet bar smells of delicious food – hints of cooked burgers, fried potatoes, and a slight whiff of old cigarette smoke. Four men sit at the bar, and all four crane around to watch me as I walk in. One of them holds his stare at me for an uncomfortable amount of time, forcing me to look down and then back up. Those penetrating dark brown eyes and strong jaw rivet me in place, and I stand there like a dunce.

The bartender nods at me, breaking the spell, and I can move. "Sit anywhere," she offers, and I sit at a small two-top next to another kiva fireplace. Kivas are all over this hotel. She comes right over with a glass of ice water. "Just you, tonight?"

I'm so tired of that question. The result of eating alone almost all my life, from my elementary school cafeteria to bars and restaurants. When someone asks me, "Is it just you?" I hear, "So you're all alone in a bar, at night, all by yourself. Just you? Looser."

"Yes, just me."

"Can I get you something?"

"Yes, I'm starving and thirsty." Remembering Josie had said to drink as many margaritas as possible, I decided that's a good idea. "I would like a margarita."

"House marg okay? Salt?"

"Yes, sounds great."

The man at the bar again is a cute thirty-something with long dark hair and olive skin. His hair, tamed and tied in a bright multi-colored band, contradicts his masculine clothes. Stop it, Chelsea. Don't be a stalker.

One of the brochures from the lobby was for a B&B. It read, "Perhaps it's the Walaletta mystique that binds us all together despite a history of revolt and rebellion. Or maybe the electromagnetic emanations from the Sangre de Cristo Mountains keep us coming back. In any case, stay and play with us!"

I furrow my brow and glance at the menu, and it feels like all the eyes at the bar are peering over at me once again. As casually as possible, I look up from the menu, and sure enough, everyone at the bar stares in my direction. Again! One of the older guys has a dopey little grin. My eyes dart back and forth from the cute one to my menu. This is a great bar! And, the male attention is fabulous but unusual. I check myself, ensuring there's not a big glob of something spilled on my shirt. All good. Well, as good as it gets after road-tripping for two days. I sit taller and pull my shoulders back, glancing at the men and then back down. My cheeks pinken as I fight back a smile that wants to break out. I touch my hair, making sure it isn't standing on end, and then tuck it behind my ears and lick my lips the way Drew used to like, or I thought she liked.

At that moment, a white-haired older man enters the bar, walking in from behind me. They all get off their barstools, shake hands, pat each other's shoulders, smile, and sit back down. Tall and lithe, the cute one swings around the stool to sit again. Through his jeans, I can tell he's athletic and substantial with thick thighs.

All the men turn back toward the bar, away from me. I thought they were looking at me. All those men, young and old, checking out the new girl in town. It turns out they were all waiting for him – the guy behind me. Embarrassed, my shoulders slump as I sink into the chair, giving me a paunch belly. Of course, they weren't looking at me. Nobody looks at me. Ever. I'm just the lifeless and hungry outsider, no matter where I am or where I go.

The server sets down a bowl of green chile and a house salad to go with my margarita. The chile is spicy and warms my tongue and the back of my throat long after I swallowed. To divert my thoughts from the men at the bar and my feelings of foolishness, I consciously direct my attention toward my dinner and stay present in the moment, focusing on the flavors, textures, and aromas that grace my plate. The fire in the fireplace crackles and jumps as one of the flaming logs falls from the teepee stack.

Why did I let myself get excited about those men? Stupid. That doesn't happen to me. I'm not that girl. Not that big fiery flame that all the men and women gawk at and circle, trying to get close to the sensual fire. I'm more like the regular embers that turn ashen, where sometimes they'll poke at the coals to get a rise out of me. I should have known better with those men at the bar, just like Drew.

When Drew and I went out to eat, which wasn't all that often, she would give the wait staff a hard time. She would order one thing on purpose, and then she'd say there was a mistake when it came. When they offered to take it back and get the order right, she would hold up her hand and say, "No, I'll eat it even though the order is all wrong." The first time she pulled this on a server, it appalled and embarrassed me. After the server left our table, Drew winked at me and said she was trying to lower the bill or get free drinks. I told her never to do that again, but she didn't listen. Knowing it embarrassed me made her pull the stunt even more.

Put Drew out of your mind. You have more important things to think about. I scrape the bottom of the soup bowl, getting the last bite of chile. How to find Tito? It should be easy enough. Being a tiny town, I'm sure everyone knows everyone, like in all the movies set in small towns. I'll bet one of those guys over there knows Tito and would give me his cell phone or address. Maybe I'll ask the cute one. Craning my neck, I scan the bar but don't see him anywhere. Damn! It would have been an excellent excuse to talk to him.

The fire crackles again as the bartender puts another log of wood on the fire. She's a one-woman show as she picks up my empty bowl and plate.

"Would you like another round?"

"Not sure just yet. Do you know those men at the bar?"

"Oh yes. Those guys are regulars here. They call this bar their living room."

"A younger guy was sitting with them. Did he leave?"

The server points to the empty barstool. "The handsome hottie? That's what I call him. Sammy. And then, he calls me foxy lady. Pretty funny, considering we've known each other since we were kids. We fool around like that." A sincere smile from down inside her beams out through her eyes. "He said he was going home."

"Well, in that case, I'll take the check."

She finishes clearing my dirty dishes and wipes the menu with her bar rag. "On second thought, I'll take another marg. Can I bring it to my room?"

"Of course, sweetie. You can take alcohol anywhere as long as you stay on our property." She wrinkles her nose and scrunches both her eyes in a double wink.

"Hey, also, do you know an older man, Tito Lujan, who lives on the Pueblo? Or at least, he used to live on the Pueblo. My grandma knew him before she passed on."

"What in God's—" She swallows the rest of her sentence. The dark-haired bartender quickly scratches her head. "Tito Lujan!" She shrieks and shakes her head back and forth as to say no. Her lips press together in a grimace. "Listen, I need to get these dishes in before the dishwasher goes home for the night." She spins around, and power walks over to the blue swinging door to the kitchen.

My head snatches back from her abruptness. I monitor the door to the kitchen as it moves this way and that, and then she finally emerges.

She makes and delivers my drink, and I jump when she thumps my second margarita on the table.

"Here's your check." She slams it down and spins around before I get the chance to offer my credit card.

I take the check and feel into my back pocket for my credit card. The bartender emerges from the kitchen and sweeps my card off the table.

"So just quickly. Tito Lujan. Is he a regular here, by chance?"

"No! I mean." She taps her index finger against her bottom lip. "I can't. Talk about that asshole." Her smiling eyes turn dark, and her nostrils flare as she turns and walks away.

Oh my God. That asshole? My chest tightens. I want to ask one more time, but I shouldn't. Stay quiet. Stay safe. You don't want her to get even madder at you. My lip stings from the salt on the glass.

I can't stay silent anymore. Grandma's lost journal is at stake.

The server walks quickly back to deliver my card. A jolt runs through my body, and I stand up, body stiff, feet firmly grounded on the wood floor. "I am determined to find Tito Lujan. You know him." My words force past the dry lump in my throat. "You do not know how important this is to me."

"Miss," she sighs. "I cannot help you." Her words and demeanor are cold and resolved. "Don't go digging around Tito Lujan. Go back to wherever you came from." She turns and stomps away.

Paralyzed, I stand there. The bar's animation plays on in front of me, but the only sounds are the whirring in my ears. There are no clanking glasses, no chatter, no swinging kitchen door, no crackling fire, no background music. The bartender pours another round and disperses the drinks to the men at the bar. They raise their glasses in a toast. Not one of them looks over at me. The phrase, "Don't go digging into something you know nothing about," keeps looping in my mind.

My phone buzzes. It's Mom. I can't talk to her right now. She doesn't know what Grandma's attorney reported, so she's unaware that I'm in New Mexico hunting for Tito. Mom doesn't know about Grandma's journals and that I'm searching for the lost one. I never told her that I lost my job or about Drew. Well, she never knew about Drew.

Waiting for Mom's voicemail, I pick up my margarita, lick the salt from the edge, and drink. That bartender knows something about Tito. She thinks he's an asshole. Why would Grandma love an asshole? Why would she entrust one of her journals with him if he's an asshole? I will not leave this bar until she tells me.

Not taking my eyes off the bartender, I listen to the voicemail. "Chelsea, this is your mother." Like, I didn't know it was you. "Carrie, at work, gave me a Starbucks card for my nineteen years here at Robert and Sons Insurance. Wasn't that nice?" What's your point, Mother? "Oh, I got out of that awful boot, though my ankle still swells and hurts. Did you send that photo you mentioned at Eve's? Remember that photo you found of my father? Anyway, call me."

Why did I lie to Mom about a photo of Eve and Doug? I can be such an idiot. Once Mom fixates on something, she never lets it go, like a golden retriever with a bone.

Picking up my drink and tucking Journal Two under my arm, I make my way to the bar and sit at one of the empty bar stools but don't make eye contact with anyone. One by one, the men pay for their drinks.

"Bye, Jen!" One man says, and as a group, they walk out through the side entrance and into the night.

I check my watch, and it is almost midnight. I'm the only one left in the bar. "Jen? I only wanted to–"

"Look, I don't know why you are here asking about that man." Jen cuts me off mid-sentence. "There is nothing to say about him," she whisper-yells while aggressively drying bar glasses.

"Okay, okay." Somehow, I need to get through to Jen and understand why she is so angry at the thought of Tito. "Hey Jen, can I buy you a shot?"

Without saying a word, she reaches up and takes down a tall, thin blue bottle of tequila. She pours the light-brown liquid into two shot glasses and clanks them down in front of me. She slams two cut limes on the counter next to the shot glasses. Then she licks the backside of her hand between her thumb and index finger and shakes salt on the wet spot. She hands the salt to me, but I've never done this before. The bartender, Jen, nods one quick time, signaling that I should do the same. So, I lick, apply the salt, and wait for her next move.

Jen picks up her shot, so I do as well. She taps it on the wood bar and then puts it to her lips, sending the glass back. And then, she licks the salt on her hand and bites into the lime. So I do the same. The tequila is hot in the back of my throat, and swallowing the stinging liquid is almost impossible. I lick my hand and bite into the lime, hoping to disarm the sharp knife attacking my throat.

"I think we got off on the wrong foot. My name is Chelsea Price. I'm staying here at the hotel." She takes the two shot glasses and puts them in the sink behind the bar.

I lower my outstretched hand. My head swirls from the tequila. "Jen, all I need is Tito's address. And then I'll be gone and won't bother you any further."

"Humph! Like you think you can get onto that property? You know you can't. You're not Indian. Forget about it."

"I can't go onto the Pueblo?"

"Nope." She jerks the cork out of the blue bottle again and pours herself another shot. "Nope. I can't even get on that Pueblo, and I'm half Walaletta." She sniffs and sends back the tequila.

"So, Tito still lives on the Pueblo?" I'm starting to slur.

Jen lets out a long deep breath. "Yes. That asshole lives on the Pueblo with no running water and no electricity. A place I am not allowed to live because of HIS laws and HIS rules." She looks down. "Some father," she whispers.

"Wait." I lean forward. "Tito is your father?"

"Yeah, lucky fucking me." Jen walks around the bar and plops down on a stool beside me.

"What laws and rules?" I ask.

"Well," she says in a breathy tone. "One must be eighty-five percent Walaletta to live on the Pueblo." Jen reaches over the bar, grabs a handful of tortilla chips from a large bowl, and sets them on the bar between us. "My father didn't loosen up on that rule when he was tribal Governor. Noooo." She tosses a chip into her mouth and crunches. "Not even for me."

"But you look Native American." The words slip out of me. My mind is fuzzy, like cotton balls shoved in a glass jar.

"What did you say?"

"Oh. Well. Um." Change the subject. Change the subject. "Does your mom still live here?"

"She passed a long time ago of breast cancer. I was only nineteen." She pours herself another shot and offers one to me. "Mom wasn't Walaletta. She was just from Albuquerque."

I put my hand over my shot glass. "I'm done. Thanks."

"So, how does your grandma know?" Jen clears her voice. "Tito. How does she know my father?"

"She used to be friends with Tito. My grandma just passed away. He has one of her journals that I'm supposed to read. That's why I'm here." I point to Journal Two. "It'll probably look like this one. There are three in a series, and my grandma said that Tito has the third one."

"Well, good luck getting that." She snorts. "He gave up almost all of his possessions when he moved into his family's home on the Pueblo.

He refuses to own a cell phone, and now all he speaks is Wala, our native language."

"Do you have his address?"

"Ha! That's a funny one!" Jen gets up and walks around the bar. She puts both of our glasses in the sink. "There are no addresses on the Pueblo. Everybody knows everybody. There's no need for street signs or numbers." Swiping the chip crumbs off of the bar, she looks at me. "Look, Sheri? Is it?"

"No, my name is Chelsea."

"Oh, okay, Chelsea, it's late. I wish you luck in your search. I've told you enough about Tito." She turns and shuts off the lights over the bar.

I ease off the stool, hoping my feet and legs work after the tequila. I'm unstable and stand for a moment, then turn and sway toward the blue arch where I came in.

"Oh, and if you see him? Slap him right across the face for me. Tell him that's from Jen." Jen flicks off the final light switch and lets herself out the side door, locking the door from the outside.

Back in my hotel room, I lie down on the made bed. Kicking off my Chausse sneakers, the white ones my team designed last year, there is a thud as the sneakers hit the carpet. Seeing my sneakers makes me think about Megan. I miss her. Fishing my phone out of my pocket, I dial Megan.

"Hello, Chelsea." She never calls me by my full name. She usually calls me Chels.

"Meg, I miss you. Are you still mad at me?" The answer is evident by the proper and stiff way she said, 'Hello, Chelsea,' but I ask anyway.

"Yes, Chelsea, I thought we were friends. It seems everyone in the office knew about you and Drew but me. ME Chelsea." Her voice cracks.

"I am so sorry. You would have had to keep my secret, and I thought it was too dangerous to tell you about Drew and me."

"Dangerous? Give me a God damn break! This is how you treat everyone."

"What do you mean by that?"

"Chelsea, you stiff-arm anyone who wants to get close to you. I can't believe it. You just sat at your desk two feet away from me, day after day, tight-lipped about you and Drew. How could you? We were friends."

"Meg, I was a complete ass. Please understand, I've never spoken up for myself. I've walked around like a scared deer, scanning the horizon, ready to jump away at any sign of danger. But I'm changing."

"Meg? Meg. Please talk to me." Foolish, shameful tears erupt from my eyes.

"I'm furious at you!" she breathes hard. "But I miss you too. I hate to admit it." Her voice softens.

"I thought it was the right thing not to tell you or anyone about Drew. I swear, Meg. It was all bottled up inside me. You should have known about Drew and me. I know that now. I'm truly sorry."

"Oh, Chelsea. A part of me wants to stay mad at you, but that doesn't do either of us any good. I love you, dammit." Megan sniffs. "Did you ever hear that story? Whenever my family argues, we end it with 'I love you, dammit.' It means I'm hurt, but I still love you. Agree to disagree, kinda thing."

"Thanks, Meg. I love you too, dammit."

We stay on the phone for almost two hours. I tell Meg everything. Everything about me and Drew. How she seduced me and how I loved the attention. Making sense of my feelings, knowing deep inside that Drew never respected me. Drew put me under her spell.

Megan is interested in Grandma and Josie and the journals. She agrees on the importance of positively changing my life and that Grandma sounds terrific. I tell her about the sexual abuse when I was young and that my suspicion is that my father abused me. That I'm in Walaletta and about Tito and how the lost journal may explain in all my family's secrets.

I tell her about my fear of traveling away from the West Coast with no one's help, but that it was also empowering. Meg understands why I'm anxious about using up my savings. Tears fill my eyes while explaining what happened in the bar with Jen. I'm too embarrassed to mention the men at the bar, so that story gets left out.

"Awe, Chels, you're doing the right thing. You got this. Don't let some old chick bartender push you around."

"Thanks, Meg. I'm so glad you picked up." We both say goodnight. I close my eyes, place my phone on my chest, and smile. "Love you, Meg," I say to the empty hotel room.

My phone buzzes in my hand. It's probably Meg. She probably forgot to tell me something.

CHAPTER 22

My phone shows Mom's number and her picture frozen on the home screen. It's the second time she's called tonight. She never calls this late. Something must be wrong. She might have twisted her ankle again.

On the other hand, if she's okay and just calling, I'll confront her about my father and the times I would block him out of my room with my dresser. Silence now as the call goes to voicemail. I'll call her back tomorrow when I'm ready. She won't be able to downplay or deny the truth like she always has. Now I have a real memory. Not just those flitting snips of memories, those little slices of images like a cut-up photo. Here's my chance, a real opportunity to learn the whole story. After all, that's what I'm doing in New Mexico – finding the truth.

Mom must know something, anything. She should tell me what she knows. I feel conflicted. It's late, and she's called twice. My concern wins, and I call her back.

She answers. "Chelsea, are you avoiding me?"

"No, my phone was hidden under some papers." This is my pat answer when I don't want to talk with her. "Mom, you okay?"

"Where are you?" Mom sounds buzzed, slurring a bit like she's been hitting the wine.

"You are calling so late, Mom. Is everything all right?"

"Oh yesss, I'm fine. I was out with those friends that we always celebrate our birthdays together. It was Sandra's birthday tonight. So, I'm home late. I've been thinking about you all evening. Did you get that promotion?"

"Ahh, promotion? Right. Um, I don't know. They haven't posted the position yet, at work. Not sure when." I can't tell her there will be no promotion, no advancement at Chausse Shoes, for me. Promotions are impossible when you're fired.

"Hm, okay. Well, how 'bout that photo of my dad? I didn't get it from you. Did you send it?"

"Mom, about that." She can't know that truth, either. That there was no such photo. I was only covering for what was in Grandma's journal. "I've wanted to ask you. Do you remember any stories about Grandma Eve and me? Like, pleasant stories?" I bite the cuticle on my thumb, waiting to see if Mom remembers anything good about Grandma and forgets about that photo she's been obsessing over.

"Chelsea, my memory is terrible. You know that." I hear her take a drink of something, probably wine. "About that photo of my father. Did you–"

"Mom, any memory at all?" I interrupt her while propping up the pillows on the bed. "Mom. It's important to me."

"What's with all these changes? You used to hate to talk about your shildhood." She lets out a heavy sigh. "Now, all you do is ask me about your shildhood. Tell me about my grandfather. Tell me about Eve. Jesus, this is tiring, all these questions."

"I know, Mom. It's stupid, but anything, any memory, will help me."

"Help with what? Chelsea, what are you up to?"

"Why do I have to be up to something, Mom?" The margarita that Jen had made for me tastes a bit diluted from the melting ice.

"Becauuuuse, you are always so secretive. It bothers me that you don't tell me the truth about what you're doing or what's happening.

Never. Not when you were young. Not when you were a teenager and definitely not now. Dammit, Chelsea! Why? You zip your lips. Why can't you tell me what's going on in your life?"

"Oh, you wanna talk about the truth? You want to do that, Mom? Okay then. You tell me what the hell happened to me when I was ten years old? What did my father do to me? Why did I pull my dresser in front of my door every night?" My cheeks start to burn. Angry tears fill my eyes. "Answer that one, Mother!" Choppy breaths spurt out of me.

I can only ask her these questions over the phone. I'm much braver than when I'm face to face. When I look into her eyes, I get scared and lose all ability to speak up for myself.

"Chelsea, I know nothing of that." She exhales a short, nervous laugh. "I'm sure you didn't pull your dress–"

"Stop it! Just stop it, Mother." I don't let her finish. "You never believed me! And you don't believe me, now." My heart pounds and my fists are so tight, my fingernails bite into my palms.

"I never once saw your dresser in front of your door," Mom says.

"Never once? Are you kidding me? How can you have a daughter and not know she pulled her dresser to keep her father out of her room, night after night? How, Mother? How? How!" I screech. "Mothers are supposed to protect their children! And you didn't. You didn't look out for ME! You didn't keep that monster away from me!"

"Oh, Chelsea. You need to calm down. Monster? Your father was no monster. He was depressed and quiet, but not a monster. It's ssooo late. I muss go to bed. I can't deal with all this."

"You couldn't deal with me back then, either." Infuriated, I yell at her. "You were always too busy. Always at work. Leaving me alone. Never there for me." The words spit out of me like they are rotten food.

"You never told me this before – this thing about pulling your dresser in front of your door. I'm baffled. Are you sure you're not making it up? Saw this in a movie, and now you think it happened to you?"

"Goddammit! I can't make this shit up! You know what? Screw you! I'll find my own answers!"

"My eyes are closing. I'm hanging up now, Chelsea." Her detached tone is as flat as the Mojave Desert.

"Mom? Mom! God Dammit!" Bitter, angry tears flood out of me as I lurch back and forth, holding my knees up to my chest. Balled up, alone on a strange bed in a strange town, I cry and sob. There's no controlling the profound, brutal agony of knowing your mom didn't protect you when you needed it the most. The one person in the world who is supposed to shelter and safeguard you from harm – didn't. Just didn't. How can that be? She couldn't deal with it? Couldn't deal with me. Her biting words tear into my heart.

There are tissues in the bathroom, and I see myself in the hotel mirror. My blotchy, chubby, red face stares back at me. My blue eyes stand out against the rest of the bloodshot color. Usually, I avoid mirrors, but this time I look at myself. My skin is pale, and my stringy hair is a mess from the long drive. The fat on my neck gives me a double chin. I poke at it and then take a deep breath out in repugnance. As I look deeply into my eyes, I think about my ten-year-old self and then about other ten-year-old girls. Ten-year-olds aren't dirty or guilty. They're just little girls. That's a vulnerable age, so trusting, so gullible. I was unguarded, unprotected. I had to pull my dresser in front of my door! Did I pull my dresser? Mom's not right that this action was in a movie? No! She's wrong. It happened. The memory scorches my mind.

On my right forearm is a scar. The raised, thin pale line is further proof I'm not crazy. I remember pushing so hard on my dresser one night that I slipped forward, and my arm jabbed against the sharp edge of a drawer. Rubbing my finger over the scar, I realize I have been ashamed of what it represented for years. Now, I'm glad it's here on my arm, the tangible validation.

Pushing in on the scar, I want to connect with my feelings and what it was like pushing on that old dresser. What did I do to entice my father? To make him want to. Oh God, the shame. I'm disgusting. I slap myself hard across my cheek. It stings. And then I hit the other cheek. And then, slap again and again until falling onto the bathroom floor, soar-cheeked and wailing. "Why?" A primal sound emerges from me. "Why? Why?" Why doesn't Mom believe me? She treats me like a child. My breath catches several times as my weeping slows.

I'm insanely furious at Mom. Dad was deeply disturbed when he kept trying to get into my room night after night. But Mom. I'm angrier with her for not speaking up for me, for not even opening her eyes and seeing what was happening. How could she not have noticed my dresser pulled in front of my door? The dresser would stay there all night. Did she never come in and check on me when she got home from work? Didn't she care if I was awake or asleep? Scared or confused?

Reaching up, I take a tissue, wipe my face, and blow my nose. The old tile floor holds me as I crawl out of the bathroom and hoist myself into bed. In a fetal position, I fall asleep alone.

The following day, it isn't easy to get going, and I pull the covers over my head. Facing another day when I'm broken seems impossible. I have always been this way. Megan said I don't let anyone in, push people away. Mom said I never tell her what's going on in my life. Maybe they're both right.

In my defense, some people are unsafe and should be pushed away, like a drunk father trying to get into your bedroom in the middle of the night. There are many people you cannot trust. They might take what I say and use it against me as Mom does. I've had to stay quiet for my safety, like my affair with Drew. But do I take it too far? Do I go to the point of total disconnection? Josie is the only person who might think differently of me. And maybe Grandma, if she was still alive.

Thinking about Josie, I text her and tell her about New Mexico and that Wallatetta is not too far from my hotel. There, that's reaching out. That's communicating. I'm not pushing her away.

Putting on my hiking boots has proven to be quite a challenge after such a long hiatus from hiking. My phone dings, and it's Josie texting. "Glad to hear, dear. How is New Mexico? Everything okay?" Her voice is soothing even over a text.

I explain my plan to go to the Pueblo after breakfast and ask her to send good thoughts to find Tito, that it might not be easy to find him. Josie texts.

> Your grandmother was powerful, Chelsea. Imagine that she's right there with you. You will be stronger. Keep me posted, dear.

My shoulders pull back, and my chest puffs up as I take a deep breath. Journals One and Two go smoothly into my backpack, and I march downstairs for breakfast.

I must find Grandma's last journal as it holds the truth. Either Mom decided not to tell me anything about my childhood, or she looked the other way when all this was happening to me. In either case, I know there will be genuine accuracy in Grandma's journal. I know it. It is here in this town with Tito. Leaving New Mexico without it is not an option. Tito Lujan had to have kept Grandma's journal safe. She asked him to do this one thing.

While eating my huevos rancheros, I check maps on my phone for the way out to the Pueblo. It's nine minutes away from the hotel, north of town. My stomach churns. Shifting in my seat, I try to get comfortable, but it's useless. Jen's words ring in my head. "Don't go digging into something you know nothing about."

Jen has a significant problem with Tito and the Pueblo. She has lots of baggage with her father. I can relate. It's like I'm pushing a grocery cart full of emotional baggage while carrying an oversized Santa Claus size sack over my back. Jen carries around the same unfortunate load. It weighs you down like a suit of armor. She's ready to take down her protection, but I may be getting close. No more pushing people away anymore. No more feeling isolated and alone, like a prisoner of war in solitary confinement.

Taking a bite of the soft, warm flour tortilla, I pull Journal Two out of my backpack. Grandma's words will help me. I don't feel so alone when reading her journals.

2/15/1989 Attended my first cooking class in Santa Fe! Have so much to learn. The instructor, Rudy, got mad at me because he told us not to touch our eyes when chopping chiles, and like an idiot, I did. Ugh, it stings – bad! I mean, super bad. My eyes watered and stung for a couple of hours.

Pushed through the stinging and Rudy's mean looks. Then, I nearly chopped off my index finger. It was bleeding all over the place until someone gave me a band-aid. He kept shaking his head, saying, gringa.

On the bright side, we focused on making rellenos. Learned the word relleno means stuffed. There are so many kinds of chiles to stuff with many different fillings and batters. Learned about traditional rellenos and rellenos associated with traditional celebrations. Took us all day, but we made four different types; New Mexican tempura rellenos, ancho chile rellenos, cream cheese stuffed jalapenos en escabeche, and chiles en nogada, which show off a walnut-based cream sauce. We arranged them on these bright blue plates. They were both beautiful and fabulous and quite spicy. My mouth needs to catch up with the New Mexico heat. Sour cream puts out the fire in your mouth.

I also had to ask why they spell chile with an e instead of chilli with two l's and an i at the end. Rudy said the spelling Chilli, England, and Europe mostly use. And Chile is by far the most commonly used in America's Southwest regions, particularly in New Mexico. Another participant, Andrea, brought up the third way to spell chile as chili, one l, and an i at the end. Rudy snickered and said, you mean that delicious food with meat, beans, and spices that you eat out of a bowl? Here in New Mexico, Rudy said, spell it chile.

Salsas and sauces day tomorrow. Hopefully, it'll go better. I'm pooped from all the chopping, note-taking, and blood loss. It's an excellent kind of pooped, though. I love learning new ways of cooking and all these fresh ingredients. Been reading these cookbooks like novels. I'm in love with cooking!

The flour tortilla sops up the remaining green chile and warms my mouth. Grandma's elation is palpable. It fills my body like helium in a balloon. She came out here not knowing anyone, not knowing how to cook, not understanding the culture. She just did it. Josie is right. Grandma was a badass. I will draw on her strength. I will find Tito, and I will find the lost journal.

With purpose, I stand straight up like a general in the Army, and my chair crashes behind me. My sudden movement and the weight of the backpack pulled over the chair, and everyone in the restaurant rubbernecks in my direction. I feel a flush that creeps across my cheeks, my sore cheeks. Cringing, I snatch up my backpack, place the chair upright, and hurry out of the restaurant and to my car.

My focus is on only three things – Pueblo, Tito, and Journal. I start my car and pull out of the gravel parking lot. My tires chew and grind the gravel. Get to the Pueblo. Tito. The lost journal. Pueblo Tito. Journal. Pressing on the gas, my car lurches forward as the road transitions from gravel to pavement. The back end of my car spins around as I attempt to make the turn onto the main street. Dust flying up behind my car makes the turn, only to find the back end of a pickup truck. I push on the brakes as hard as I can, but it's too late.

My car comes to an abrupt halt – metal against metal. I jerk back, then forward toward the dashboard. My lungs contract with such force that I'm afraid they will fold in on themselves.

By the time my eyes fly open, I realize what I've done. A man jogs toward my car.

I open my door and try to take off my seatbelt.

"Are you all right, miss?" He's a tall older man with deep wrinkles, olive skin, and a gray cowboy hat.

All I want to do is get out of the car. I'm disoriented, and the seatbelt button alludes me.

"Just sit there for a sec." The man pats my shoulder. His pressed jeans and shiny, black cowboy boots seem foreign to me. In Portland, everyone is either in business clothes or flannels and wrinkled khakis. "You were coming out of there goin pretty fast. Where were you goin in such a hurry?"

A small breath escapes out of me as words cannot be formed. The chilly outside air blows on the nervous beads of sweat building on my upper lip. My hands shake. I reach into my backpack for my wallet, but I'm trembling so badly that I can barely grip it.

Then another man and a woman come over to me.

"Do you feel okay?" the woman asks.

I nod my head, and finally, I'm able to release my seatbelt.

Wobbling out of the driver's seat to assess the front of my car, and see that it is wedged up under the back bumper of the truck. The dark blue truck looks virtually unharmed except for a few scratches on the silver bumper. My car, however, looks like a smashed soda can.

A police car drives up with the lights on, and a young, stout woman jumps out of the vehicle. She nods to the tall, older man with the cowboy hat. They shake hands, and he points in my direction.

As steadily as possible, I walk over to the two of them. The police officer holds out her hand, and I shake it. I'm aware of how sweaty my hand is as it touches her calm, dry hand.

"My name is Officer Lopez. Do you have your license and proof of insurance?" I offer my license and other paperwork to her. She takes it.

She studies my license. "Chelsea?" Looking into my eyes. "Are you hurt?"

"I think I'm okay." The man in the cowboy hat and boots opens the truck driver's side door. "I'm so sorry, sir. I was coming off of the gravel and wasn't watching my speed."

The cowboy nods his head but says nothing. He gives his license to Officer Lopez as well. I look at his name as he hands it to her. William is the only part I can make out.

The stocky police officer walks to her car and then back to us. She hands my license and paperwork to me. "Here you go, Chelsea. I'm gonna have to write you a ticket, you know." The officer turns to the older gentleman. "Do you want to pull your truck forward? Let's see if we can unstick these two vehicles."

His cowboy hat in the back window as he pulls his truck forward seems otherworldly, like this is a movie and I'm one of the actors. He parks the truck on the side of the street, leaving my dinky little car in the one lane of the two-lane main road. It's mind-blowing how the front bumper crumpled.

The officer crouches down and looks under the engine of my car. "No fluids are leaking out. Chelsea, do you want to see if your car will start?" the officer asks while motioning the local traffic around my car.

I get in and start it up. Officer Lopez waves me to pull it over out of the street. My hands shake so much it's hard to hold the steering wheel. I shut off my engine and walk back over to the officer and the cowboy.

Remembering the name on his driver's license, I apologize. "Again, William, I am so, so sorry."

"Well, you be careful, young lady. There are plenty of dirt and gravel roads around here." He tips his hat at me, turns, and walks toward his truck. He steps into the truck and pulls away slowly. Out the open driver's side window, he waves once to the officer.

"Stay outta trouble, Mr. T," Officer Lopez hollers as he eases down the road.

Then, the officer turns toward me. "Do you have anyone to call?" She looks at her notepad and taps it with her pen as she speaks. "Are you traveling with anyone? It looks like you live in Oregon."

"Yes, from Oregon, and no, I'm by myself."

"Vacationing?"

"No. I'm looking for someone. Someone my grandma used to know." I look at the officer and try to have a calm voice. "Do you know a man by the name of Tito Lujan? He lives on the Pueblo."

"Tito Lujan?" she snorts. "He just drove off. You hit his truck."

CHAPTER 23

The officer chuckles and points in the truck's direction. "Yep, there goes Tito Lujan."

"Wait, his license said his name was William." As I look down the narrow two-lane street lined with adobe commercial buildings with brightly colored signs, a quiver shoots through my stomach.

"Yeah, he's never gone by that name." Officer Lopez tears a piece of long white paper from a hand-held printer. "Here you go." She hands the ticket to me. Though the morning temperature outside is chilly, my cheeks burn.

"So that man in the cowboy hat was Tito Lujan?" I ask, shifting my gaze from the ticket to the street again. The dark blue truck gets smaller and smaller, and other cars pull behind Tito, camouflaging him even more.

"Can you tell me where he lives? It's important that I talk with him!"

"He won't sue you or anything for this incident. He's not that kinda guy. Most people here would rather jump out of a window than call an attorney."

"It's not about the accident, officer, though I am sorry, of course. I need to find him for personal reasons."

"Personal? Is that so?" Officer Lopez lifts her dark eyebrows and then lowers them, looking at my paperwork. "Sorry, it's against the rules to divulge any information about William." The officer over-enunciates his proper name. "Now, you drive carefully, Miss Chelsea from Portland. I don't want to have to write you another ticket." She turns with conviction and marches toward her police car.

I scamper to my wounded car and start it up. Another ticket would be no good, so I take it easy. As soon as the officer's car fades in my rearview mirror, I speed up. Pushing on the gas pedal, I hustle down the main street, eyeballing every parking lot with small strip malls and gas stations, looking for Tito's truck. He can't just disappear.

The road forks. Tito's truck is nowhere to be found. Trying to decide which way to go, I take the fork to the left. It's a residential street that seems to take me away from town. The pavement turns to dirt, and my car kicks up dust as I slow down to look all around for Tito. Each house is similar – flat-roofed brown adobes with blue doors and window casings. I thought it was just in the hotel, children's toy blue, but it's everywhere in this town.

"Goddammit!" How could he disappear? I jerk my car around and hurry back to the main street where I last saw Tito and head in the other direction at the forked road. I fix my eyes on every driveway. The road dead-ends into a fenced field with a paddock of chewed-down grass and mud. There were no structures in sight. The herd of cattle on the other side of the fence stop chewing and look at me. I buzz down my window and smell the sun-warmed earth mixed with cow manure.

"Do any of you cows know Tito Lujan?" The cattle swish their tails and get back to their monotonous chewing. "Guess not."

I look up Tito Lujan on my phone. There's nothing new. The same sites came up when I first learned of him. The Walaletta Pueblo site pops up first. It talks about Tito when he was a member of the Tribal Council several years ago. There are other Tito Lujan's out there in the world – an athlete, a singer, a scientist – but they are not my Tito Lujan. I just rear-ended my Tito Lujan. Just once, I'd like to do something right.

There's an article on the nineteen Pueblos in New Mexico. My reading confirms Pueblo refers to communities of Native Americans, both in the present and in ancient times. A Pueblo is a tribal nation, a body of land under a sovereign tribal governmental structure. The Pueblo community comprises related people with similar belief systems, spirituality, and lifestyle. It sounds like a nice place to live – everyone is getting along. Unlike the rest of the US, where belief systems vary, there are thousands of religions, and everyone lives separate and different from each other. I click out of the article and into maps.

My original plan was to visit the Pueblo and see if Tito was there. That was before the car accident, the police officer, and my ticket. Now, at least, I know what his truck looks like, and I'll remember that broad face and tall stature and the cowboy hat. Checking maps, I turn my car in the Pueblo's direction.

White Fir Road turns from town into the country before I can put up the window to stop the dust from hitching a ride. Barbed wire fences line the road on each side. Hardy weeds make an attempt at life coming up along the road and under the wire fences, but mostly there is bent yellow grass and small patches of snow under the pine trees. Every so often, breaks in the barbed wire fence expose a long dirt road leading to a house with a barn and free-ranging dogs. I pass a sign that says Walaletta Pueblo 8 Miles.

The Pueblo has a dirt parking lot marked visitors' parking, and there are a few cars and two trucks, but neither of them is Tito's. There is an orangey-brown sign that reads Welcome to Walaletta Pueblo World Heritage Site. Under the headline in blue reads, The Walaletta People welcome visitors as they have for over 1000 years. Towering above the sign is a steep, harsh, and craggy mountain. I spot the visitors' building and walk up to the ticket window. This place is way more organized than I ever expected. Then again, I'm not sure what I expected. Certainly, not a will-call type window to get a ticket to a Pueblo.

"Hello. How many in your party?" the young man says to me.

"Hi. Oh, it's just me." That assaulting question again. "I just want to walk around the Pueblo. I don't need a tour or anything. Are those tickets any cheaper? It's just that I'm traveling on a shoestring."

"It's the same price whether you take the tour with our tour guide or not." He looks at me with his dark brown eyes. "I'm pretty sure Lillian will be your guide. She's great! Very knowledgeable. She's a student at UNM. All of our guides are students."

"She sounds wonderful, but can't I just walk around myself?" My savings are low, and I'm worried about having enough money to finish my trip. "I have to buy a ticket?"

"Fraid so."

Fifteen dollars seems kind of steep, but it's a small price to find Tito. Once I find Tito's truck, then bingo! Tito will be there. Easy enough.

The man gives me a receipt and tells me to follow the signs to the Pueblo tour.

"Ma'am? There are specific rules for our Pueblo. Please do not talk to any of the residents if they do not make eye contact with you. If they don't look at you, they don't wish to talk to you. Stay with your guide, and ask before taking any photos. Also, please check out our native artists. You'll see signs for their businesses outside their homes. If the door is open, you may enter." He points behind me. "There's your group. If you hurry, you can join that tour and not have to wait for the next one."

I turn around and see a group of about six people following a young lady with long black hair pulled into a ponytail. She wears a burgundy-colored top and a black skirt with black flats.

The gravel jabs up through the sole of my sneakers as my pace quickens to catch the tour. I kick up a couple of dry stones, and they hit the back part of a women's shoe who takes part in the group. She spins her head around and looks at me just as I come to a slower pace. "Sorry bout' that," I whisper.

"No worries," she says softly with a gentle smile. She motions for me to come up with her and another woman she was walking beside.

As I maneuver up with them and keep step, both women smile at me. One woman is blonde, and the other is a brunette. Both are slim and are in their late fifties, maybe just a little younger than Mom. The blonde reminds me of what Grandma probably looked and acted like when she made this trek – pleasant, curious, and not Native American. Certainly, Grandma walked right here on this same gravel road, looking at these identical pueblo houses. My heart aches.

The crunch, crunch, crunch of the gravel under shoes goes silent as the tour guide stops walking. She turns, looks at the group, and nods at me. "The Walaletta People are proud and ask that you not take any photos unless you get permission. My name is Lillian, and please do not take any photos of me. You CAN take photos of the buildings, the land, and the surrounding mountains." She turns and starts walking again, and we all follow in step.

As we walk behind Lillian, I scan for Tito's truck, trying to remember the make and model. It could be a Ford or a Chevy, but for sure, it's dark blue, and it seemed to be relatively new and in good shape, except for where I dinged his shiny silver back bumper. My brain floods with all the scenes from this morning – the accident, Tito, and his truck. A line of trucks are parked in front of the Pueblo houses, but none are dark blue.

We stroll through the Pueblo. It's a cluster of homes, one connected to the other. There's no distinguishing line where one home ends and another starts. It's a beautiful blur of light brown adobe buildings with an azure blue sky, making the soft corners of the houses more explicit. I wonder if Grandma stayed here on the Pueblo with Tito while they were dating. Or was that against the rules? She'd stick out like a sore thumb as Grandma was a strawberry blonde – like me.

Lillian stops under a covered patio. She turns and starts her talk. "Welcome to the Walaletta Pueblo." She explains the living situation at the Pueblo and how people have lived there for at least one thousand years. She tells about the several wars waged on the people, uprisings, and the living conditions. There are around two hundred permanent residents who live inside the Pueblo walls. Their ancestors and families have gifted the residents their homes. She explains one must be eighty percent Walaletta to live within the Pueblo walls.

THE JOURNAL EFFECT

What Jen told me back at the bar was the truth. That Tito had upheld this law even though it meant she could never live there in their family's pueblo home. At first look, I'm not sure why she'd ever want to live here – dusty, sunbaked dirt roads, mud houses, no fast food in sight.

"Our sense of community is fundamental." Lillian's eyes sparkle as she lifts her chin. "The people who live inside the Pueblo wall show pride in their heritage by living here the way our ancestors did in the old days. Everyone lives without running water and electricity. No internet. No TVs. And they do most of their cooking in one of these." She points to an outside domed oven made from adobe. The black soot envelops the inside of the well-used oven. "Three to four homes will share one horno oven. The families cook most everything from breads and tortillas to meat in the horno."

The blonde woman standing next to me asks Lillian about the handmade wooden ladders that lean onto the adobe houses.

"Pueblo communities in New Mexico and Arizona center around the traditional homes, or pueblos, which are stone and wood structures covered in a mud mixture called adobe." Lillian walks closer to the home with the ladder. "The buildings were constructed into multilevel terraced apartments with access through the roof. There were no front doors. Most of these rooms were entered by a ladder through a hole in the ceiling. These ladders could easily be moved up and into the home to create a solid defense against invaders and unwanted animals. Now, most of the residents have installed wood doors, though some still use the ladder."

Lillian walks forward again. Her matter-of-fact, proud nature makes me feel a little jealous. She seems fearless and steady. I step up to walk beside her. She looks at me but says nothing.

"Hi. I'm Chelsea." I slow my pace to keep up with her. "So, do you know all the residents here on the Pueblo?"

"I think so. If not, I'll know some of their family. I live in town, not on the Pueblo, and commute to Albuquerque for school. I'm studying political science and international affairs." Lillian has beautiful olive-colored skin. Soft and smooth like her silky black hair.

"That's great! I was just wondering cause I'm looking for a friend of my grandmother's, Tito Lujan. Do you know him?"

"I met him once." Lillian turns away from me and stands next to a river that seems to cut the set of pueblo houses in two. She faces the group again. "This is our sacred river. It flows from the mountain range surrounding the Pueblo on the Northside." All of us look upstream toward the pine-dotted mountain that springs up thousands of feet above the Pueblo. A predatory bird cries out a shrill pitch, probably searching for food. "No one outside the Pueblo is allowed in the river, as this is the only form of water for the residents. They drink the water as it is pure and untouched from the mountain. It has been this way for a thousand years, for as long as the Walaletta people have been here." Wind feathers through the wild grass growing along the river as Lillian's footsteps crunch the dried leaves.

Just as she finishes her sentence, two young boys from the Pueblo run into the creek, giggling and splashing each other like two puppies. As a collective, the tour group turns their attention to Lillian, wondering if she will shoo the boys out of the sacred water, but she doesn't. She seems unfazed by their antics, as if normal and natural.

"For a thousand years, only Walaletta people have bathed in this water, fished, and drank from it. Therefore, we do not have any illnesses from foreign people contaminating the water."

Thistle weed heads stick to my jeans as I walk closer to the creek. I look down at the clear, flowing water and watch the boys playing and splashing. Grassy banks edge the shallow meandering flow over small stones.

"Does anyone have questions before the tour ends?"

A few other people ask their questions, and Lillian answers them in her assured but soft voice. It's melodic, like ocean waves. When there are no more queries, she tells us this is the end of the tour and to please honor the rules of the Pueblo.

After the other tourists give her tip money, I walk up to her. "Lillian, do you know which house Tito Lujan lives in?"

"Even if I knew, I wouldn't tell you. I'm sorry. I'm not trying to be mean or anything." She half-smiles. "It's just proper etiquette for people who live here. If Tito had invited you to his house, he would tell you which one is his." She nods at me. "Do you understand?"

"Yes. It's just I need to find Tito." I feel into my front pocket and pull out a five-dollar bill – the change from breakfast. "Come on. You can tell me. I won't tell anyone." I push the money into her hand. "Can you at least point toward Tito's house?" I say under my breath.

Lillian recoils and looks at me in astonishment. Remaining quiet for a moment, she squints and fiddles with her turquoise pinky ring, spinning it around and around as if contemplating what to do next. "This is not how to find what you're looking for." She shoves the money back at me. Twigs brush her legs as she turns away from the creek, and Lillian says goodbye to the tour group and marches away. I stand there, frozen, as she hoofs it over to the next awaiting tour. She looks over her shoulder at me, and seeing the disgust in her eyes cements the anchor of guilt for doing such a stupid thing. Lillian told us they were a proud people, and I shoved a five-dollar bill in her hand. This ridiculous behavior is just the thing Mom would do. I'm disgusted with myself. Lillian makes it to her next group. Apologizing would be best, but something catches my eye. Looking past the church where the group convenes is one of the roads that leads into the Pueblo. A dark blue truck enters the Pueblo with a small cloud of dust trailing behind.

"Tito," I whisper, racing over to the dirt road. The truck turns onto a road with a sign that says Pueblo Residents Only. There are too many bystanders to follow him into the restricted area, so I backtrack, watching his truck through some pine trees and other buildings. The truck flees to the other side of the creek.

Running toward the footbridge that goes over the creek, the two women I had met during the tour were standing under a shade tree. I slow to a fast walk and avoid making eye contact with them. Everyone here, both the tourists and the residents, all move slowly, deliberately. The people of the Pueblo move with a determined stride, each step filled with purpose. Seeing me run around the dusty terrain must be quite a sight.

The short stone footbridge that takes me over the creek looks ancient. The exposed rocks are shiny and slippery from overuse. As I'm about to step off the bridge, two snakes come out of the bushes and dart over my hiking boots. I jump straight up. A scream so deep within me forces its way out of my mouth. I land on the uneven rocks. One foot goes out from under me, my other ankle twists, and I go down into the mud and water's edge. My hands slap the cold water.

"No!" I snatch back my muddy, wet hands and jump away from the water. Maybe no one saw it? A group of tourists and the two young boys who were in the creek surrounded me.

"Are you okay?" the brunette tourist asks as she kneels beside me.

"I'm fine. I'm fine." I jump up, wiping my wet hands on my jeans. "There were massive snakes that slithered over my boots."

"Those are our little water snakes." The boys laugh and point at the creek. Those snakes are about a foot long, with skinny heads and maybe an inch around. They swim through the water, catching the current.

"I'm sure they were much bigger than those. Anyway, I'm fine. You all can go back to whatever you were doing." I hasten my steps, attempting to put as much distance as possible between myself and the sacred stream. Glancing over my shoulder, I witness her approaching rapidly, a storm of determination in her eyes.

"Excuse me! Ma'am!"

I pretend not to hear and continue with my trajectory away from the water.

"Wait! Chelsea, is it?"

Freezing, I turn around. "Yes." Using my most nonchalant look, I speak calmly. "Oh, hi, Lillian." My hands jam into my pockets.

"Did you touch the water? Everyone said they saw a splash when you tripped going over the bridge." Lillian holds her hand to her stomach as if it hurts.

"Two of your enormous snakes went over my boots, and they made me jump." Grandma flashes in my head. She must have gone over this bridge while she was here. My shoulders drop. What would Grandma say right now? Not Mom. Grandma.

"I'd like to say I didn't touch it." I step purposefully toward Lillian.

"Truth is, both my hands went into the water. It was not intentional, and I feel terrible. But just to let you know, I did wash my hands before the tour. I'm truly sorry," I say in a begging tone.

Doing the right thing usually costs rather than pays, but emerging from me rises someone Grandma would love. Someone Josie would like, as well. Though overshadowing, my better person inhabits the usual idiot, like bribing a nineteen-year-old with a whopping five dollars, rear-ending Tito, and making my chair hit the ground at breakfast in a thundering crash. If only I could rewind the entire day and start over. It's like there is a black, habitual cloud hanging over me.

Lillian looks around the Pueblo. Some residents come out to see what's happened. Two young men in jeans and dark t-shirts walk over to where we stand. "Chelsea, I'm afraid I will have to escort you off the Pueblo," Lillian speaks in an even tone.

"Need help, Lil?" one of the young men says while putting his hand on his hips. He's short, trim, and not exactly homely, but he's not handsome, either. Tattoos color both his toned arms. The other man is tall and skinny. His shirt hangs off his shoulders, exposing his clavicles.

"I'm okay." Lillian raises her eyebrows. "Right, Chelsea?" All three of them look at me. "You're gonna go back to your car right now. The tour's over." She nods yes as she speaks.

I rub my hands together, and they end in a prayer position. "Look, everyone, I'm here for one reason. Tito Lujan has something that belonged to my grandmother, and I need to get it from him. You all understand and respect family history. What I need from Tito explains some of my family history. History that my grandmother wrote and her words will put my life back together. Please understand." I scan the crowd. "Does anyone know Tito Lujan?"

The two men snap a look at each other, their eyes wide. And then they stare at Lillian.

"Chelsea, you have contaminated our water and must leave the Pueblo, now." She walks forward and motions for me to follow her.

"You can go right now, or Carlos here can put you in handcuffs. Is that what you want?"

I stumble forward behind Lillian. My eyes only see the dirt, gray gravel, and her dusty black flats. I can't bear to look at all the people who have come out to see the stupid klutz who polluted their water. I hope no one gets sick from my non-native fingerprints in the creek. My arms fold in front of me, pinning to my stomach.

"Wait a second, there," a man says.

Lillian and I stop and turn around in the voice's direction. A man emerges from around the bystanders. My mind races. The tall man with the round face and wrinkles of knowledge and hard decisions, the gray cowboy hat.

"Tito!" I launch toward him.

"Hold it." Lillian grabs my arm. "This woman put her hands in our sacred water. You all know what that means. She must leave now."

"Tito! I am Chelsea! Eve's granddaughter," I yell to him as he walks forward.

Lillian spins me around while the two young male enforcers flank me. Looking over her shoulder, she addresses Tito. "Sorry, sir, but you'll have to conduct your business with Chelsea outside the walls." Lillian pushes on the small of my back, urging me forward.

"Lillian, a moment, please," Tito says.

Tito walks to stand before me and studies the situation with a grimace expression. "Chelsea? Eve's Chelsea?"

"Yes, Tito. I am Eve's granddaughter. I've been looking for you. Grandma passed on last month."

"I got word of that. I'm sorry." Tito studies my face and body. "She was very special to me. You look just like her."

Lillian loosens her hold on my arm.

"Tito and Lillian, I apologize with all my heart for touching your water. It was an accident. The snakes. The slippery rocks. And, Tito, I'm sorry about the accident this morning." I take time to look both of them in the eyes.

Tito adjusts his cowboy hat. "Lillian is correct. We have rules. It would be best if you left our Pueblo now. We have to do a ceremony over the water to cleanse it."

"Wait! Tito, you have some of my grandma's things. I need the journal." I reach my arm out to Tito, but Lillian brings it back. Tito turns his back to me and walks away.

"Come on, Lillian, all I need is that journal, and then I'll be out of your hair. You'll never see me again."

"Rules," Lillian states as she and the two men pull me forward. I crane my neck to peek over my shoulder, but he disappears into the crowd. "Tito!" My scream echoes off the adobe houses.

CHAPTER 24

Lillian and the two men deliver me to my car like a five-year-old flanked by angry parents. So close to Tito... twice now!

I yank my keys out of my pocket and unlock the sorry silver beater with the munched-in front fender. I want to scream, but it's better to hold it together. "Again, I'm so sorry," I say to Lillian, placing my backpack on the passenger side. All three sets of eyes burn a hole in me, like in middle school when you jittery-walk to the front of the class to scribble the answer to a math problem. Gripping my car door for fear of falling over, I speak as calmly as possible. "What I've done is done, and I am truly sorry. My germs cannot stay in that water. The muddy handprints and any contamination my skin imparted into the river will disappear. The water moves. It flows over the rocks, naturally cleansing the water."

They stand there looking at me, stone-faced and unyielding. The rocky mountain jutting up behind them wears the same decisive expression. I hold out my hand to Lillian in a good-faith handshake. She refuses it and takes a step back, and the two men follow her lead.

A chilly February breeze assaults my face. The pure and cold air drills my ears like an ice sickle. I get into my car and close the door. The trapped warmth of the New Mexico sun acts as a heater, and it thaws the chill surrounding my heart and muddy hands. The trio turns and walks back to the Pueblo.

As their forms get smaller and smaller, my insides feel smaller and smaller. I have damaged and mistreated their sacred river, their wellspring of life, acting like a self-seeking fool, just like Mom. Why do I do that? She is the last person who should influence my behavior. I desire to be more like Grandma, like Josie. But inside me, lying dormant until the need arises, a switch flips, and I become the fool. An inherited behavior from Mom, as this is how she goes at life, like she needs to bully her way through every situation.

Terrible visions infect my mind. I'll break into Tito's house, going in through the roof and down the ladder, find Grandma's journal, and climb back up and out before anyone notices. Who am I fooling? I would only ruin that plan, like all the rest of my absurd strategies. Besides, that's something Mom would do.

I inspect my dreadful, mud-crusted hands. Pudgy, sausage-like fingers hold river remnants up to my fingernails, jammed with silt. Rubbing them together over the floorboard proves to be futile. The dirt pellets fall to the floor, and the dust flies up and around the car like little fairies.

Jamming my key into the ignition, I look up through the windshield. "Whoa!" Tito stands directly in front of my car, looking at me. I open the car door and leap out. "Tito?"

"Hello, Chelsea." Tito stands tall and stiff with his hands in his coat pockets. He's like a superstructure that a hurricane could not budge. "Did Eve tell you to come and see me?"

"Not exactly. Grandma's attorney did." I sway back and forth, hoping to warm up from the movement. "Actually, I hadn't seen Grandma Eve for a long time. She died before… Before I…" Crossing my arms is not enough to ward off the chill in my body. "It's freezing out here. There is a warm jacket in my car. Please don't disappear again, Tito."

"Chelsea, you must leave the Pueblo now. Meet me at the Cristo Café at noon tomorrow. It's just a little down the street from where you rear-ended me." He turns and walks toward the Pueblo.

"Wait, Tito." I don't take the time to get my jacket and jog the few steps up to him and grab his arm through his forest green rugged coat. "Do you have my grandma's journal?"

He looks at my hand on his arm. I rapidly jerk it away, hoping it is not another sacred rule – to not touch his arm.

"Yes." He looks up at the sky. "She asked me to keep it safe."

"Can you bring it with you to lunch?"

Tito says nothing. He turns and starts walking.

"Tito?"

Tito turns back toward me. "Eve gave it to me. She knew I would honor her request. From what I've seen and experienced with you, I'm unsure if you should read that journal."

"Tito, please! I've read all of her other journals. Grandma came out to Santa Fe to take cooking classes. That she came up to your Pueblo. I know she was miserable when the two of you couldn't make your lives come together. Tito, I need to read that journal. I must know what happened to me, my father, and my uncle, why my mom and Grandma Eve stopped talking to each other. There are so many unanswered questions."

"See you tomorrow at noon, Chelsea." Tito turns toward the surrounding corner of the brown adobe houses and steps out of sight

An overwhelming sense of relief cascades over me. It's as if a weight I've carried for far too long has finally lifted from my shoulders, allowing me to breathe freely once again, if only for a moment. The burden of uncertainty and anxiety is still present, but there is a tiny ray of hope bringing a smile to my lips.

The sky above the Pueblo walls is a super intense blue with one perfect white cumulus cloud hanging over the rocky mountain looks like a painting. The soft, chalky UFO shape contrasts the jagged outcroppings of the mountains below.

It's going to happen. Horror quickly replaces feelings of success and conquering the impossible. Oh God, it's going to happen. I'll be exploring the white-fiery center of my soul. Reading this journal will uncover my childhood details, and I will be digging around the places I've avoided, stirring up those emotions and feelings. I've spent my life staying out of that scary place that gives me nightmares.

I drive away from the Pueblo, past the orange and blue Wallaletta sign and the ticket window, past the unforgiving gravel road leading to the line of curious tourists, and past the contaminated river. As my car turns onto the main road, my foot presses on the accelerator – harder and harder until it's flattened. Juniper pine trees lining the two-lane road are blips on my peripheral radar. The divided orange line in the center of the road becomes a vicious blur. Eighty, eighty-five, ninety. My car shakes and moans in protest. I can barely hold the steering wheel, but it's the only real thing that feels real. I clutch it tighter, my knuckles turning white.

Something moves on the road up ahead, and I can't quite make it out. The car slows as my foot unpins the accelerator, and we glide to a respectable fifty miles per hour, a comfortable speed for my slight and listless car. On approach, three deer are crossing the road, and I come to a complete stop. It appears to be two adults and a youngster. The baby is small and has no horns. Her cute tail twitches as she runs.

The family crosses the road without incident. Both the parents look at me and shelter the young one from the potential predator like all parents should. The baby walks in between two bare and leafless deciduous trees and into a field of pine trees. Tag-team style. One adult keeps her eye on me, and the other follows the baby into the forest. I'll bet that little one feels safe, loved, and protected. That's how a family is supposed to act, not like mine.

Maybe Tito is right. Maybe I shouldn't read the lost journal. Maybe I'm unable to process what is in it. These thoughts flood through me as I pull into the hotel parking lot.

Exhausted, I fall asleep before eating any dinner. And then I hear that awful sound – Scratch, scratch, scratch. The sound jolts me awake. "Nooooo!" Not that nightmare, that terrible memory. My mind assaults the hope of sweet slumber. I put both hands over my ears, but the sound is inside me, inside my mind. Scratch, scratch, scratch. The grating and screeching of my wood dresser desecrating the wood floor as he pushes on my door.

In haste, I rub my face with my hands and will my eyes open, and the horrid sound stops. The hotel room ceiling has one large round exposed beam running the length of the room with a weaving of smaller peeled round logs regularly spaced away from the beam across the room's width. The pattern is perfect in its simplicity. I try to keep my mind on the ceiling instead of the scratching sound or the lost journal, but it's no use.

The hotel room clock reads 3:25 am. I feel dizzy and faint, and a sharp, stabbing sensation hits my chest. Slamming my head back down on my pillow, I pull the covers over my head and squeeze my eyes shut. I've blocked my memories all these years for good reason. It feels impossible to be this close to the truth of my childhood. If Tito gives me Grandma's journal, I'll have to read it. Then I'll know the truth and won't be able to go back. I'll be forever changed.

My lungs hunger for air. Flipping the covers off my face, I close my mouth and try to breathe through my nose. Calm down. This cannot blow into a full anxiety attack. Big, deep belly breaths. In through my nose and out through my mouth. Count. 10. 9. 8. Breathe. My choppy, quick breaths extend longer and longer. Beads of sweat form on my upper lip, and I wipe them away with the back of my hand. 7. 6. 5. Breath. 4.

What the hell am I doing here? This trip has been a complete disaster. And now Tito is about to give me the lost journal – maybe. Should I meet him at the café? Or not?

At 11:30 AM, I will myself to stand and feel the need to talk with someone who will tell me what to do right now. I know what Mom would say. Don't meet Tito. Don't go digging up old stuff. She'd say that Eve knows nothing about me or my family. That Eve was up to no good. Just pack up and go home, Chelsea. You're better off not reading that as all those other journals are chock full of lies.

I find the number of the restaurant and dial. A woman picks up. "Cristo Café." Nothing comes out of my mouth except for a determined breath.

CHAPTER 25

The hostess shows me to Tito's table, and I'm unsure if I should shake his hand or one-arm-hug him. It's awkward. I opt for neither and sit on the cracked, red booth seat across from Tito. Above our booth is a blue neon sign that says, Time for truth. It has a clock in the center of the words. It reads 12:20.

"Sorry, I'm late, Tito."

"I thought maybe you were standing me up," Tito states with little expression.

That thought crossed my mind, I want to say. "Tito. Gosh, where do I start? First of all, it's incredibly nice to meet you. I treasure anyone who knew my grandma, and thank you for keeping her journal safe."

The old pine table between us has visible years of use with notches and ancient coffee rings. There are two glasses of ice water and two sets of silverware wrapped in paper napkins, but no journal. "I'm so sorry for the way I've behaved today. I've acted like a fool, from hitting your truck to falling into your sacred river. Please, please forgive me."

Tito holds out his hands, palms up. "So, you're not like this all the time?" His light brown skin looks like wrinkled leather, and his eyes peep out from under two white caterpillar eyebrows.

"No. Well. Maybe sometimes. Only when I'm acting like my flaky mom." I take a sip of water. "My whole life fell apart recently, and I've had a chance to read my grandma's first two journals. When I learned of the missing one and that you had it here in New Mexico, I overcame lots of fear to meet you and find that journal. It's not like me. I'm usually measured and think things through, but reading Grandma's stories has changed me, hopefully for the best."

Tito shrugs his shoulders. "Like putting your hands in our sacred water. That's not showing your best self."

"Wait a second. That was an accident. Those snakes were–"

"Okay, okay. I suppose it could have been a fluke."

Our server walks up to our booth, and he asks what we would like for lunch. Tito gets the posole and recommends I get it. To drink, I order a coffee, and Tito gets an iced tea.

When the server leaves our table, Tito's expression is serious. "Chelsea, I have one question for you. Are you ready, I mean really ready, for what you will learn in your Grandma Eve's journal?"

My eyes avoid his intense stare, and I look down at the funky black and white tile floor that covers the café. The white part has yellowed from foot traffic and spilled drinks.

My breath catches in my throat. "That's just it, Tito. I don't know. I'm not sure of anything anymore." There, I've said it. It feels good, to be honest. "I could lie to you and say, yes, I'm ready, with enthusiasm. But we both know there is a ton of heavy stuff in that journal. Honestly, I don't know if I'll ever be fully ready." I search his eyes and wonder if he knows the truth – that my father abused me. That Mom covered for him all these years. That Mom made Grandma Eve go away.

The waiter sets down my coffee and Tito's iced tea. Tito squeezes the lemon into the tea and swirls it. He does not add sugar. I don't, either. Tito's thick, square face, surrounded by his white hair, gives him a mighty and valiant look. I can see why Grandma found him attractive. He's sturdy and steady. That part must have reminded her of Grandpa Doug. And he's not half bad looking for an older guy.

Tito takes a drink of tea, which forces his Adam's apple to move up and down as he swallows. "If you are wondering... I didn't bring the journal with me."

"What? Why?" The words burst out of me. "That's why we are meeting."

"Chelsea, based on your actions today, I thought it best. Eve asked me a long time ago to keep it safe, and that's what I'm doing. You do not seem like a safe person. Just the opposite. You seem unstable and impulsive."

"But. It belongs to me!"

Tito frowns. "No, it doesn't. That belonged to Eve."

"Her attorney said that I am the rightful owner. He said that you would have to give it to me."

"Her attorney, huh? Look, Chelsea, that's not how we handle things out here."

Sipping my bitter coffee, I look away and then back again. "Tito. I am not a child. Grandma Eve asked you to keep the journal safe. For me." I fold my hands and place them on the table. "And please forgive me, but you sit there all high and mighty, judging me. Have you never made mistakes? Never had such a strong desire that you would go anywhere and do anything to get it?" I point a finger at myself. "No, I am not perfect, but neither was Grandma Eve nor are you. Now, that journal has essential information, and it's for me to read."

The waiter places hot bowls of posole on the table and unloads hot sauce from his apron.

"Thanks, Joe," Tito says to the waiter.

The soup steams up between our faces, and the aroma of the earthy hominy balanced with the sting of green chili makes my stomach growl in hunger.

"Easy, Chelsea." Tito grimaces. "You're scaring everyone."

"Oh, that's a funny one. I'm the one who is usually scared, always fearful, and anxious. I'm the one who looks over my shoulder, always waiting for the other shoe to fall. Me! I'm the panicky little rabbit, staying quiet." Pulling my dresser in front of my door. My voice cracks as my eyes fill. Embarrassed, I look away, hoping Tito doesn't see.

"I understand these family stories are critical to you. Your Grandmother knew things about your father and your family that no one else knew." Tito slurps a spoonful of the soup. "She held a great burden all her life for the good of your family."

"For the good of my family? What do you mean by that?" I sniff.

Tito takes another heaping spoonful of the white hominy and reddish broth. "It's delicious, Chelsea." He gestures with his spoon. "Have a bite."

The soup with shredded chicken and green chiles smells delicious. Dipping my spoon in, I get a small bite with the fresh cilantro and sour cream. It's a distinctive combination of spicy and savory. I take another bite and follow with a drink of water. The warming chile flavor lingers in the back of my throat.

"I do not want to play this worthiness game with you, Tito. I'm too tired." My anger starts to dissipate. "I apologize for being angry with you. I'm angrier with myself for not reaching out to Eve before she died. I'm taking it out on you, and I'm sorry. This search, albeit not gracefully, has been difficult. Many things have gone wrong since I started this quest. Since Grandma died, I lost my job and my girlfriend. My best friend won't talk to me. I walked away from my apartment, have used up my savings, and can't confide in my crazy mom. But the worst of it? Do you want to know the awful part?" I bend my neck forward. "My Grandma died, and no matter what I do, she's never coming back. Her journals are the last semblance of her. It's the only way I'll know her. Her words. Her handwriting." Tears overflow, and I wipe them up under my glasses with my napkin. "When I was younger, my mom told many bad stories about Grandma, so I never reached out to her."

Now it's too late as Grandma is gone.

With arms crossed, Tito hangs his head as he listens.

My throat is dry, so I gulp the water. "I have these weird, foggy memories of my childhood and only a few of Grandma. There are some memories of fights she and Mom had, but that's it." My insides tremble as I grip my hands tight under the table. "Grandma writes in her Journal One that she would take care of me, play ball at the park, and make ice cream sundaes for us." Feelings of anger, guilt, and overflowing truth overtake me. "Tito, she's not around to ask all these questions. I'll never be able to talk to her about other regular or confusing things in my life. Never."

Wiping my eyes and straightening my shirt, I attempt to pull myself together. "I need to hold my own story in my hands. And I'm old enough to decide what to do with the details in that lost journal." I put my glasses back on and, with a shaky hand, spoon another bite of the posole into my mouth. My words hang in the air between me and Tito. He sops up the broth with a flour tortilla, so I do the same.

He takes a long drink of iced tea and gets up. Without saying a word, he strides out of the restaurant.

I look around in disbelief. Tito left me with the bill? No wonder Jen, my new bartender friend, hates this guy. Standing up and looking out the café windows, I don't see him. "Goddammit."

The server comes over with the coffeepot. "More coffee, Miss?"

"No. I'll take the check. I guess we are done here."

"Will Mr. Lujan take more tea?"

"Hell, if I know!" I bark. "Don't think so. It appears that he's left the restaurant."

"Um." The server looks around and points at Tito coming back toward me.

In Tito's hand is a brown backpack. He places it in the booth and then sits down.

"I thought you left."

"I wouldn't leave without saying goodbye." Tito motions for me to sit back down. "Would you like another coffee?"

"Okay." I feel unsure and exhausted. What is Tito up to? He gets up and leaves the table without saying a word, and now he's back with this backpack.

Tito motions to our waiter. "Hey, Joe? Two coffees, please." He looks intently like he is peering deep inside me. "Chelsea, I have been listening to you. Or rather, I've heard you, and boy oh boy, you remind me so much of your grandma. It's scary. Facial expressions. Your looks. Your hair. I feel like I'm sitting across from a young Eve. You know, we met in our sixties. We both lost our spouses to illness, and I immediately became infatuated with Eve. Beautiful inside and out, she helped me through a troublesome time." Tito cradles the backpack as if it were a newborn baby.

This time, I stay quiet and allow him to talk out whatever he needs to say.

"As the leader of the Wallaleta Pueblo, I had to make hard decisions. It's a tough balance between honoring the old ways and accepting the new. Some of the young people had good ideas, but I was too set in my ways to hear them. Flexibility is not one of my strengths."

Joe sets our coffees on the table. "Before Eve, I used to pour on the cream and two or three heaping spoons of sugar." He holds up his mug in a cheers posture. Our mugs clank, and we both say cheers. However, it's not the same kind of cheers as when it's your birthday. This dull cheer sounds more like when you're at a funeral. Tito seems to relax a bit. His softened expression puts me more at ease.

"Eve used to say, 'Why do we drink milk? We are not baby cows.' It always cracked me up. But then, I realized she spoke the truth. I never put cream in my coffee, ever again." Tito looks out the window. His far-off gaze tells me he's looking past the line of trucks and cars and into another time – a time when he and Eve were in love.

My shoulders slump. "I have very few memories of Grandma." My words drift off as my chest tightens again.

"I know, Chelsea." Tito touches my hand. His hand is warm and thick and grandfatherly. "That's why there is this backpack." He feels the side of the bag like a lover strokes the cheek of his sweetheart. "I went through my house this morning after, well, after Lillian escorted you off the pueblo." Tito clears his throat. "Anyway... I gathered all the things that belonged to Eve and put them in one neat place. I kept one memento. A friend gifted us with a wedding vase that we would drink from on our wedding day if we married. But that never..." Tito swallows hard and holds his coffee mug with both hands, gazing into the dark liquid.

"Tito, I'd love to hear more about that and any other stories you can tell me about Grandma." We share a look. "But maybe that's for another time?"

"Right. Okay." He lifts the backpack and hands it to me over the table.

The dark brown pack is heavy and sits down next to me. The top zipper opens after a couple of forceful tries. I look at Tito, and his mouth turns down as he scratches his upper lip with the back of his thumb.

The first thing I see is some fabric. It's a soft, silky blue and gray garment.

"Back in those days, women would wrap a scarf around their heads. Being Eve's favorite, she would wear it when we took long drives into the O'Keefe country. She loved it out there. Said it inspired her to be a better person."

There are a few books, and I pull them out individually. *I'm Okay. You're Okay. You Can Heal in Time, Reclaim Your Life. Recipes for a New Generation. NM Cooking 101.* "Cooking and healing," I say.

"Yep, that was her. She was always searching to master both. She spent hours reading by the river. Yes, that river. The one you know intimately. Luckily, I was the recipient of the cooking part." Tito pats his trim belly. "I had a bit more of a belly back then. Back when someone would cook for me." Tito's eyebrows press together as he looks down at the books.

I dig around the backpack. There is a metal spatula, a hot pad with the Santa Fe Cooking School logo, and a magnet with a 1940s woman on the back of a motorcycle. I look at Tito. "No journal?"

"I'll ask you again. Chelsea, are you ready for this?"

"I'm not exactly sure what is in that journal, but believe me, I need to know. Being afraid of everything, including the truth, has damaged me." My hands fold neatly on the stack of books on the table.

"Grandma needed to heal, and so do I."

Tito lifts his head in a quick motion and points at the backpack.

"Try that outside zipper." Hefting the backpack into my lap, I unzip a smaller outside section and see it. It's the same small, yellow journal as the others. It slides easily out. "I thought you said you didn't bring it to lunch."

"Wait." Tito puts his hand over mine, forcing the journal to close. "Read it in private. Eve wrote explicit instructions and passed them onto me." Pulling his bearlike hand back, he clears his voice again. He's holding back tears. "She told me you might show up one day, and when you did, you needed to read this journal out in some open space, a free and expansive place. You could choose anywhere you want, but she recommended Georgia O'Keefe country. It's not too far from here." Tito wipes both of his eyes. "I read her instructions every day after she left the Pueblo and returned to California. They're a little dogeared from being in my wallet for years. The instructions are now in that journal." Tito rests his elbows on the café table and hangs his head.

The backpack's weight presses into my lap like a two-hundred-pound person sitting on me. My chest feels like it could split open, revealing my unsafe and naked heart. I'm terrified.

"Chelsea, you're pale. You okay?" It's like Tito's concerned eyes see through me and into my ragged soul. He gets up and sits next to me, putting his arm around my shoulder. Feeling his warmth and caring, I bury my face in his abundant chest and start to sob.

"You're right. I'm not ready for this." I push the backpack toward him.

He pushes it back toward me. "You got this, Little One. That's what your grandma used to call you – Little One." Pulling out a handkerchief, he dabs my eyes and then presses the cotton square into my hand. "I believe in you, Little One."

Tito stands up, pulls out his wallet, and places a fifty-dollar bill on the table. With one hand, he squeezes my shoulder, then he kisses his index and middle finger, blows a kiss to me, turns, and walks out of the restaurant.

CHAPTER 26

Zipping and unzipping the smaller section of the backpack where the journal lives, I'm frozen in the café. Joe, the server, comes by and asked if I want anything else. I can't form words, so he takes Tito's fifty and brings back the change.

My phone vibrates in my back pocket. The feeling snaps me out of my funk. Pulling it out, I stare at the screen. It's a calendar notification that used to matter to me. Weekly review and meeting with Drew. My life in Portland seems far away. It's only been a couple of weeks, but it feels like years. My life and mind have expanded like balloons since I started reading Grandma's journals. That dim and cramped life before Grandma feels like trying on sneakers that are two sizes too small.

My instinct is to call Mom. I want to give her one last chance to tell the truth. If she knows I have Grandma's tell-all journal, she may finally cave and divulge what she knows. She'll probably say nothing new, but at least she's alive, and I can talk to her.

"Chelsea? Chels? Can you hear me?"

"Yeah, Mom, I can hear you." Zip. Unzip. Zip.

"Are you calling about our last conversation? Are you still upset with me?"

"Mom. I have Grandma's journals. All of them."

"All of them? I expected there was more than that one on her desk. You know, the journal that went missing? I figured Josie had taken it and lied to me about it. So, you took it?"

"Yes, I took it and two others when we were there. It's a long story, but I have the journal where Grandma tells our family secrets. I haven't read it yet."

"Chelsea, what are you talking about? What family secrets?"

"I wanted you to have the opportunity to tell me the truth before reading this journal."

"The truth about my dreadful mother, Eve. Okay, fine. She was delusional! She told me your father and uncle could not properly care for you. She threatened to take you away and not tell any of us where she was taking you. She was crazy! Cookoo! So, I got a restraining order against her. She couldn't come near you, or she would go to jail."

"Mom! Why would Grandma need to hide me? Was I in danger? I'm giving you one last time to tell me what you know." Unzip, zip.

"That's your grandmother's truth. That is not the actual truth. And why haven't you read this so-called truthful journal? What are you waiting for?"

She has a point. Why am I stalling? I should read the lost journal instead of talking with Mom – my stomach cramps. If I know the truth, that's it; I'll know the truth. I'll have the answers, and I'll stop drilling Mom-- something I've done for a long time. Without this hanging over our heads, I'm not sure what else we'd have to say to each other. But old habits are hard to kill, like murdering a friend.

"Grandma wasn't crazy, Mom. Everyone who knew her loved her. All her friends are good people. None of them are crazy."

"Well, whatever. I knew Eve. She was my mom, and she was bats. But you don't believe me."

"Mom? I have one question for you. Did Dad hurt me?"

"Oh, Chelsea, I don't think so. I saw nothing that would make me think he did. Your father was a good man, but he got weird after Uncle Jim died. He said he had to get away from us to get his head right. Your father would never harm you."

"You don't think so? Seriously, Mom! I need a straight answer, and once again, you dodge the truth. Why did Grandma feel like she needed to keep me safe?"

"Now, that one I will answer. Eve hated your father and said terrible, mean things about him. She never wanted me to marry him in the first place, and she kept up the foul talk about him after you were born. She couldn't let me be happy. You want the truth? There you go."

"Mom, you tell me the same story over and over. I have Grandma's lost journal. I've been searching for it. And she will say how Dad sexually abused me, how she told you, and how you turned your back on me. That she probably confronted Dad and made him get away from me. Goodbye, Mother."

"Chelsea!" Mom says as I end the call.

I stand straight up, sling the backpack over my shoulder, and march out of the restaurant. Stiff and resolved, I'm like a soldier called to the final bloody battle.

Back in my car, I unzip the backpack's front panel and pull out the instruction page. It's a single sheet of lined paper, yellowed and thin in the creases where Tito had folded it so that it would fit into his wallet. It's Grandma's handwriting.

Dearest Chelsea, my little one–

If you are reading this, I'm no longer on the planet, raptured up to heaven or wherever souls go when life completes. Never liked heights, so I hope my transition was gentle.

Gave my most crucial journal to Tito, but you know that as well. He's the only person I trust. He's a good man, a little rigid, but don't hold that against him. Please know I had to keep this information safe for the right reasons. The innocent must remain clear of incarceration. That's why I held firm and didn't tell anyone.

In the journal, I wrote the story of your childhood, your parents, and your uncle. It will be hard to read. Then again, you may already know what happened within your precious first eleven years of life. Great suffering plagues us, but I want you to know that you can learn from this and understand I love you. Your mom and dad love you, too.

I wrote this journal in the remarkable country between Abiquiu and Taos, where Georgia O'Keeffe hung out. The views are vast, and being in nature helped me get perspective on this horrific turn of events in our family. If you can, read it outdoors as nature heals. She is patient. That's her superpower. Nature waits and waits until just the right time to blossom and flower – just like us.

Okay, Little One, get outside somewhere, wherever you are in the world, and read. It's your story, but you don't have to wear it on you. Discover, grow, let go, and move on.

Feel my arms around you, always. And if I get the chance in spirit form, I'll send you a beautiful dream. Look for red-tailed hawks. Hopefully, it'll be me in my next life.

With the most love in my heart,
Grandma

"Grandma." My voice cracks. It sounds shaky and slight. I reread the letter and then press it against my chest. "Grandma. Why did you die?" Looking down at the backpack, the top of the journal peeks out. Okay, Grandma, I'll go out to this. I look at the page and search for the town she wrote in the letter. Abiquiu. How does one even know how to pronounce that word? I search maps, and sure enough, it's there. It's about an hour away.

I tuck the letter back into the journal. Touching the cover, I want to open it and read, sitting right here in my car outside the café and confirm all my suspicions. No, no, no. I shake my head back and forth and turn on my car. "I'm coming, Grandma."

CHAPTER 27

The vivid light illuminating each red-dirt mountain, each tree, and each bush seems supernatural, while the New Mexico sun glares off the hood of my car, stinging my eyes with its force and clarity.

The landscape is dotted with short, gnarly pine trees that gives way to a small town of flat-roofed brown adobe buildings. Rocky hills lift above the single-story town, accentuating the feeling that somebody used the same dirt from the hills to make the buildings.

I pull my car into the first, and what looks to be the only gas station in town. There are two pumps and a sign that says pay inside. A mural-bedecked coffee shop sits next to the gas station. Painted red and green chiles decorate the front. I grab a stocking cap from under the pile of clothes, extra shoes, and books on my back seat. Pulling on my Chausse Shoes logo cap, I take the backpack and rush toward the gas station and general store. I'm not going to let the journal out of my sight.

Under the antique Pepsi sign is the blue front door. Opening it sounds the bells hanging on the inside handle. The wood floor creaks under my sneakers, and a heavy-set, rather blank-faced teenager stocks the shelves with bags of birdseed. At the cash register stands a smiley middle-aged man. His tobacco-stained teeth stand out as his salt-and-pepper mustache curls over his upper lip.

"Need gas?" he asks in a cheery tone. A small lump pushes out on the right side of his lower lip.

"Yes, thanks. Pump number one." Pulling out my credit card, the thought of reaching my credit limit scares me.

"How 'bout a snack? Agustina just finished an enormous pot of calabacitas! I can get a bowl to go for you." The man holds up a to-go bowl.

"I'm not familiar with that. What is it?"

"Oh, it's delicious. Take yellow squash, zucchini, corn, and green chile, and cook 'em all together in a little chicken broth. Deliciosa!" He turns and spits chewing tobacco into an old Folger's coffee can.

"Um? I've never had that. I'm not sure if I have enough mon–"

"Trust me. We're known for it." He takes the lid off a pot behind him and ladles the steaming concoction into the plastic bowl. "I'm gonna throw in a couple of sopapillas and some honey. On the house."

"Oh, okay." The vegetable dish smells savory. It reminds me of when Josie gave me a bit of her lovage soup and how delicious it tasted. "Say, can you recommend a nice, quiet place in the country where I can read a book?"

"There's a lot of open country 'round here, but just make sure you're not on someone's land." He scratches and rubs his unshaven chin. "People get grumpy about that round here. Too many touristos lookin' to find themselves. Santa Fe attracts the woo-woo crowd."

"Shadow Ranch," the teenage girl stocking the shelves says in a monotone voice without lifting her head.

The man's face lights up. "Yes, Shadow Ranch! It's only a few minutes away. Here, I'll draw a map for you."

I pull my phone out and look it up. "An artist colony? You sure anyone can show up?"

"Yep, anyone can go and hike or, well, read like you wanna do." He pulls out a napkin and a pen.

"Dad, she doesn't need a map. She's got a phone," the blank-faced girl says, sounding annoyed.

THE JOURNAL EFFECT

"Thank you, sir. Yes, I see it here. Shadow Ranch." Showing him my phone, I insert my credit card into the machine. Hopefully, it goes through and doesn't decline. The machine beeps. Approved. As I walk past the teenager, I touch her shoulder and smile. She looks up at me for half a second and then looks away. "Thanks for the suggestion, and take care." As I walk out the door, a huge, warm smile comes over me, starting at my lips, and then it generates throughout my whole body.

Pumping gas, I realize I've never said to anyone to take care. Never. For the first time in a long time, or maybe forever, I feel and see with such clarity that it's like I'm in a movie viewing everything through the omniscient camera lens. The colors are more vivid. Sounds penetrate my ears with purity, and kindness fills me.

The roller coaster of extreme highs and lows over the past few weeks has chipped away at the old me, and surprisingly, these emotional fluctuations have had a profound effect. This recent turbulence of life is teaching me to confront my fears head-on, and in doing so, I have discovered newfound strength and resilience within myself. While the journey has been far from easy, I'm starting to embrace the idea that vulnerability and facing my fears are essential steps toward growth and self-discovery. In the past, I would have thought to say take care, and then would have stopped myself, worrying it sounded trite or dumb. My fears prevented me from living, being kind, and loving.

Down a long dirt road, I make it to Shadow Ranch, a compound of adobe buildings, each marked with little brown signs. The signs say either private or public. Some residents walk by smiling and chatting, ready for adventure in their expedition khakis and wide-brimmed hats.

Behind me lies an open field with picnic tables. I put on my heaviest jacket and take the lost journal out of the backpack. As the sun sets, its rays cascade across the landscape, illuminating everything in its path, while areas shielded by the encompassing mountains are in cool shadows. The impossible expanse sends a chill through me.

My mind spins. Once I read Grandma's journal, I will know what happened. Elation and panic fill me again as I sit at the picnic table. Chelsea, this is why you're here, to know the truth finally. Tito's words echo so loudly inside my head that it feels like they could bounce off the red canyon walls surrounding the artist's compound. "You got this, Little One."

October 7, 1997, Oh, where to start. I've been in Santa Fe and Taos for about six months, this time (much longer than planned). I've fallen in love with a place and a man. Initially, I came here for cooking lessons, and then fate takes you by the hand, and there's no looking back. I'm a much better cook. That's for sure. But I didn't expect to find someone like Tito. Let myself fall in love with someone incapable of loving me back. His lover is the Pueblo, and I can't change that. I've come to this resolve and will return home soon to La Jolla. Will miss the sunbaked, open-air, close-to-the-earth lifestyle that New Mexico extends, but I know it's best. Besides, La Jolla and the beach ain't half bad.

Today, there's something bigger weighing on me that I must get off my chest. Liz, Robert, Jim, and Chelsea.

Robert called the cooking school and left a message for me, but he left a number I didn't recognize. Worried and frantic, I called him straight away. Thought Liz or Chelsea might be sick or in the hospital. Robert told me that Jim was hurt in a hunting accident and died. Robert told me more. A lot more. Something horrible was happening, but I never saw this one coming.

It's really heavy. I'm not sure what to believe. I don't think I should write any of Robert's stories down. I'm afraid for him. If he tells the truth, he's damned. If he stays quiet, he's damned.

Talking to Tito will be helpful.

I slam the journal shut. "Fuck, fuck, fuck." My hands cramp into fists, and I put them to my mouth. "Do this, Chelsea. You can read on." I whisper into my fists, rub them briskly against each other, knuckle against knuckle as the friction creates heat.

October 8, 1999, The gurgling waters of the Chama River sing to me as I sit here, crying. This is the saddest thing I've ever written. After talking with Tito, he thought it was best to write it all down. Tito offered to keep the journal safe for my family and me. To not let the authorities get a hold of this journal and relinquish it either back to Chelsea or me one day.

Today, I write and dedicate this to Chelsea, my granddaughter. My sweet girl, I'm not sure when you'll read this, but I will tell you what seems to be the truth. Things happened to our family that are tragic and tough to understand.

Let me back up and tell the story the way I remember it.

Chelsea, when you came into this world, you were a bright-eyed, cheerful baby. A delight – no colic, only cried a little and loved picture books. And then, the terrible two's hit, but you couldn't help yourself. You were two. At four, curiosity came in. Constant questioning. "Grandma, what's this? What's that?" When you went to kindergarten, I found a little sweater that said CHATTERBOX on the front. You loved it! You were talkative, open, and funny. Six, Seven, and Eight came with the usual trips to the library, cartwheels in the yard, making Halloween outfits, and Christmas cookies. I spent as much time as possible with you while working full time at the hospital.

Liz and I were not getting along, even more than our usual clash. I couldn't understand then, but now it's relatively straightforward. We were two very different people.

Back to the story at hand.

A month after your ninth birthday, Liz and I had a terrible argument. Liz worked two jobs because Robert and Jim's construction business hadn't taken off as they'd hoped. The men had some free time, so they cared for you after school. I'm sure you remember that. I wasn't fond of either of them and didn't think they could give you the energy and love you needed. Neither Robert nor Jim could cook, so they would take you to unhealthy fast-food places to eat dinner.

In my opinion, dinner should be made at home, and everyone should sit down together. I offered to help, but Liz wouldn't let me. Angry and always at the end of her rope. She was consistently exhausted, and for good reason. She was a hard worker.

After work one afternoon, I went over to the house. Chelsea, you acted differently. It was weird. You acted shy and looked down and away every time I tried to talk with you – no more chatterbox. I brought a new soccer ball, but you wanted nothing to do with it. You loved to kick around a ball. Your pale face told me you hadn't been outside and had dark circles around your bloodshot eyes. I was concerned. Jim had his feet up, watching TV. At least, I think it was Jim. I always had to ask. Being identical twins, it was nearly impossible to tell Robert and Jim apart. I asked him about your curious behavior. He was flippant and thought you were acting like a normal kid. You were not acting normal.

Again, I told Liz, but this did not help our relationship. I'm sure I forced my opinions and wasn't empathetic of her stressed situation, but I saw my little Chelsea shriveling and sickly and expressed my concern.

A few weeks later, I decided to see if you wanted to go out for ice cream. I called the house, but no one answered. The front door was unlocked when I got there, so I let myself in. Called out for Robert, Chelsea, or Jim. Robert darted out of Chelsea's room, pulling on his t-shirt. Again, I thought it was Robert. He asked me what I was doing there, and I told him. He blocked me from entering your room, but you were whimpering and crying. He had made some excuses. Something about some mean girls at school and an F on a spelling test. I pushed past him and spotted you in bed, covers pulled up to your neck. When you saw me, you pulled the covers over your head. This was weird, so I sat down next to you and talked. Encouraging you to go with me to get ice cream, you declined. I started tickling your feet to get you out of your funk. You squirmed, and the sheet fell to one side, exposing your naked body.

I'm sorry to recount this, Chelsea. I don't know if you remember or not. I'm sorry if you're disturbed hearing my description of that evening. I want to be as honest as possible.

Not wanting to embarrass you, I walked over to your dresser and pulled out a blouse and a pair of jeans. You sheepishly dressed, but I couldn't get you out of your room. I had a sick feeling and went to the kitchen. Robert was having a beer when I confronted him. I asked him if he was doing anything inappropriate with you. He called me crazy and ordered me out of the house.

I told Liz that he might be sexually abusing you, Chelsea. That I had noticed you had been changing, and not for the good. She exploded, as usual. I told her she was too tired to see what was happening right under her nose. She defended Robert and put a restraining order against me. I couldn't get close to you, not at school or the house.

Wanted to whisk you away and out of that house, to keep you safe. I called Social Services and told my story to them. They sent a social worker to the house to check it out, but I never heard the visit results. Liz successfully kept me away with that restraining order.

So days turned to months. I sent you letters, books, and cute clothes, but I never heard a peep. Would call Liz, and she always hung up on me. Sent birthday cards and gifts for your tenth and eleventh, but nothing.

I could throw up right now, writing all this down. There are no excuses. I should have done more. I'm sorry, Chelsea.

When I talked with Robert yesterday, he told me the entire story. God, this is hard! This is what he told me:

Last week, Robert came home from repairing a toilet at a client's house and found your Uncle Jim on top of you on the couch. He ripped him off and punched him in the face. Jim, of course, denied doing anything. In a rage, Robert ordered Jim out of the house. Jim apologized and said he would never do that with Chelsea again, that he'd drunk some whisky and had gotten a little carried away.

Robert didn't tell Liz, didn't tell anyone. Your mom and dad had been having issues in their marriage, and he feared she would use that information against him. Probably not a smart move on your father's part, but we all do interesting things during desperate times.

That weekend, Robert and Jim had their annual hunting trip planned out in the desert. Robert wanted to cancel, but your Uncle Jim convinced your father to go on the hunting trip. Jim said he wanted to talk to him about you, Chelsea, so your father acquiesced.

"What the hell? It wasn't Dad? It was Uncle Jim?" My stomach stiffens and cramps, and I double over. The unusual red dirt under the table catches my attention. I sit back up, shaking my head back and forth. No way! This cannot be the truth. I pulled my dresser to stop Dad. He had said, "Come on, Chels. Let your Pop in your room." Or "Let your Pop rub your back." Or "Go to McDonald's with your Pop." He never called himself Uncle Jim.

Dearest Chelsea, I hesitate to write the next part down. Not here, not anywhere. I don't want anyone to find this journal as incriminating evidence. But this all needs to come out. YOU NEED TO KNOW! Tito will keep it safe until it is time for you to know. I trust him, and they have different laws on the Pueblo that are out of our jurisdiction.

Anyway...

While the men camped in the desert, Robert interrogated Jim. Jim confessed he'd been a little too close with you frequently. Robert had worried that Jim had an unhealthy attraction to young girls, but always looked the other way. As Jim admitted he had a problem, he fell apart and started sobbing. Your Uncle Jim picked up a rifle and stuck the end of the muzzle into his mouth. And your father stopped him before he pulled the trigger.

Later that night, your Uncle Jim started drinking whiskey, as he did on many occasions. He told Robert that he had been with you more than once. He went into detail about how he would go into your room for nearly two years now. Jim said you were not his first. That he'd walked some of the soccer girls home from the park, he'd tell them how beautiful they were. Jim would give them gifts and then ask for a favor in exchange. He said he wanted to help them understand how to have proper sex with a man and that he was helping them. I'm so sorry, Chelsea. This situation is all so disgusting!

I'm shaking as I write. I had to take a break and put my feet into the river. It's chilly but grounding. Back to the story.

On the phone, Robert told me he thought Jim would continue hurting little girls. That he'd groom these young girls, molest them, ruining their hopes of having a normal childhood. He regretted stopping Jim from committing suicide. That night, Jim passed out from the whiskey. Robert couldn't sleep.

On Sunday, the last day of their hunting trip, they still hadn't gotten a deer. So the two of them set out deeper into the desert. During the drive, Robert cooked up a plan.

Once they reached a good spot, both men had their routine. Get out of the truck, check the surroundings, and if it seemed like a suitable location, they'd retrieve their guns that hung on the gun rack in the back window of Robert's truck. Knowing their method, Robert held back and let Jim scout out the hunting spot.

Robert took both rifles out of the truck. He threw Jim's rifle under the truck so he couldn't get to it. Robert called for Jim, and as he walked back through the desert bushes, Robert told his brother he was sorry. Your father aimed at Jim's belly and squeezed the trigger. He missed his belly and hit Jim's upper thigh. Jim *went down. Robert wondered if he should shoot him again, but lost the nerve. He started having second thoughts, so he dragged Jim back to the truck to take him to the closest town. But the nearest town was 80 miles away down a bumpy dirt road.*

Your Uncle Jim didn't want to go to the hospital. He told Robert that he did the right thing to shoot him. Jim was bleeding badly. Robert put a blanket around Jim's leg, more to cover it and less of a tourniquet. Both men knew what was happening. Robert pulled out the bottle of whiskey, and each took a swig. Jim couldn't sit up any longer. Robert eased him across the truck's bench seat, cradling Jim's head in his lap. He kept telling Jim that he loved him and that he was sorry. Jim fell asleep.

With a final breath of air, Jim's heart stopped. Robert drove to town to the tiny desert clinic. He told them it was an accident, that Jim had been cleaning a rifle, and it went off. That they set up camp so far into the desert, he could not make it in time to save him.

The words on these pages are truly astonishing; it's difficult to believe what I'm reading. Uncle Jim abused me? Did my father kill him? I'm completely disoriented. This is not what I thought I'd be reading. Not at all. The sun has disappeared behind the encircling mountains, and the temperature has dropped significantly.

An older man stands next to my picnic table "Miss? Visiting hours are over. We close up the park at sunset."

I look into the man's eyes and start crying. A wrenching, gut-deep howl comes out of me. My body shakes as I pound my fists on my thighs. The journal tumbles to the ground. "This cannot be!" It's like I've lifted out of myself and am watching myself from above. "It's all wrong!"

The man jumps back. "Whoa!"

My arms convulse, and then, all at once, my body goes limp. I look at the man with a stony expression. "It was Jim, not my father."

The man keeps his distance from me and speaks irritatingly calm. "Miss? We can see you are not okay. What's going on?"

A group of older men and women have formed a semi-circle around me, and a white-haired woman approaches.

"Can I sit next to you?"

I nod yes, and sniff again, pulling my knees into my body and up to my chin. My lips flutter.

"There, there. It's okay."

"No! No, it's not okay!" My breathing catches. "I don't know what to believe."

The woman put her hand on my back, rubbing back and forth. "Wow, that sounds horrible. Is there anyone we can call for you?"

"No. I have no one."

Out of the crowd of people, a box of tissues appears. The woman next to me takes it and offers one to me. I blow my nose and take another tissue.

"I know what needs to happen," I say, standing up. The crowd takes a collective step backward. I turn and hug the woman sitting next to me with both arms, both arms. She hugs me back, a sweet, sincere hug.

"You sure you're okay, dear?"

"No, I'm not okay. I've not been okay for a long time." Tears overflow my eyes and I wipe them again with the tissue. The journal, lying for a few minutes on the ground, is covered in a fine layer of red dirt, and I snatch it up.

The older woman hands the tissue box to me. "What are you going to do?"

"I need to find my father if it's not too late."

CHAPTER 28

My beat-up car rattles down the dusty dirt road. They close the gates behind me for the night at Shadow Ranch. My whole life is turned upside-down, right on top of my head. Everything I thought was true was all wrong once again.

One day, my life was there, mine and mine alone. I knew where the fences were, the borders that kept me safe. And then, like a feral dog, I ran around looking for a rabbit. But instead of a rabbit, a bottomless rabbit hole formed, and there is no way around it.

Dad may have lied to Grandma and concocted a grand story so everyone would believe him. Then again, he only told Grandma about killing his brother. Why not Mom? Why not me when I became old enough to understand? He kept it to himself all these years. It makes no sense.

As my headlights illuminate the stop sign before the highway, I reach over, open the journal, and thumb through the pages. Instead of reading, I turn on my blinker and return to the hotel.

There is only one thing on my mind – finish reading. Wanting the truth gnaws at me like a hungry animal. Speaking of hunger, my stomach growls. Hours ago, the calavacitas and sopapillas tasted fabulous, just like the nice older man at the gas station said. It was tasty,

KELLY SIMMERMAN

but I'm hungry again. If I go into the hotel bar, Jen may distract me from reading, and she would ask about my meeting with her dad, Tito.

Passing the fancy hotel restaurant with the white tablecloths, I look down at myself. Dust and mud-covered sneakers, hair a mess from the stocking cap and wind, eyes puffy and red. They probably wouldn't let me sit down at those nice tables.

Against my better judgment, I walk into Jen's bar.

The cozy, shabby bar is quiet, short of a group of middle-aged women at a table with a bottle of white wine. Their low chatter and occasional laughter rouse a thought of Grandma. Maybe she shared a bottle of wine with her fellow cooking students here? She may have met Tito here for a happy hour if Tito would ever take part in a happy hour. It isn't likely. He doesn't seem like a happy hour kind of guy.

Jen flies out of the kitchen carrying a bowl of guacamole and chips. She winks at me while delivering the food to the women's table, and then she fast-walks over to me.

"Chelsea, you are quite the talk of the town!" she says under her breath as she flicks my arm.

"What do you mean?"

"Jesus, first you rear-end my dad, then you jump in the river, which leads to Lillian throwing you off the Pueblo! Everyone comes in with a story about the new chick in town."

"Oh, that. Yeah. Not proud of all that."

She sets a margarita down in front of me. "By the way you look, you could use this." Jen's eyes widen, and she shows her teeth in a shamefaced gesture. "Well, I guess you found my dad, huh?"

"Eventually. After I hit Tito, he drove off, and then finding him was a challenge." The margarita is a fantastic combination of salty and sour. "Then? Blah, blah, blah. You know the rest of the Pueblo story. You would not believe the day I've had."

"Sounds like a doozy." Jen offers me a menu while placing a plate of chips and salsa on the bar in front of me. "What'd you think of my dad?"

I avoid her question. "So, remember the story about my grandma's lost journal? I finally got it from Tito."

"Is that it?" Jen's face lights up as she points to Grandma's journal.

"Yeah, and I really need to read it."

"Say no more." She squeezes her lips together with her fingers and then opens them playfully. "Fish tacos taste great tonight." She presses her lips closed again.

"I'll take 'em." I smile at Jen and sip my margarita, licking the salt rim. She has no idea how deep Grandma's journal dives – the drowning of family secrets and pain pressing down on me. If Grandma writes the truth, then my family is more messed up than I ever thought. My uncle was a pedophile, my father was a murderer, and my grandma covered for both men. And Mom? Mom plays the clueless drunk, of course. And I'm the victim, hiding from everyone. Each of us plays our jackass roles to a tee.

"Not anymore," I mumble.

"What?" Jen uses a step stool to get a bottle of wine from one of the upper shelves.

"Oh, I was just thinking about my dysfunctional family. Some crazy shit here. Hard to believe some of it."

"Oh yeah? Like what?" Jen taps the counter. "Pretty sure MY family INVENTED crazy." Her deprecating chuckle turns dark.

"Tito told me to be careful with the information in the journal. That it could be damaging."

"Oh, talk about crazy. Try having Tito as your father. Somebody needs to pull the hardened metal rod out of Tito's spine. He's totally over the top with rules." Jen clears her voice as she opens the red wine and delivers it to the lady's table.

Chelsea, I need you to know that I didn't believe your father when he first recited his story. Had it in my mind that HE was the incestuous one. Never suspected your Uncle Jim, so I probed Robert for any and all evidence. He broke down and said all he had was his word.

He begged me to keep it a secret, fearing a murder prosecution. This has been hard for me. I'm honest to a fault. But his story sounds crazy but compelling, and after talking with him, I believe your father. He knew Jim's illness would plague his family and maybe other families, and Robert did not know how to stop him. Robert raged when he learned of Jim's actions. He said that killing him was the only option. I disagree, but I wasn't out there with a hunting rifle pointed at the man who had molested his daughter.

I wanted Robert to tell Liz. He told me he would hold off and let Jim's death blow over as there was an open investigation. Robert said he would tell Liz at the right time. I plan to honor his request for now.

As I write this, Chelsea, you are only eleven, and I'm not sure when you will read this journal. Hopefully, Robert will tell your mom, and you all can try to heal, especially you, sweet Chelsea. My deep desire is to see and talk to you, but Liz still has that restraining order against me.

Been searching my heart for whether or not to believe Robert. I go back and forth. But after closing my eyes for a few moments and listening to the beautiful Chama River, I feel Robert's story is true.

I remove my glasses and rub my gritty eyes. It can't be true. This is so confusing. I always thought it was my father coming into my room all those years ago. What did he say to convince Grandma? I try to conjure a memory of my father. It's bizarre, as I have avoided thinking about him for many years. Squeezing my eyes shut, I try. The only thing that comes to me is that annoying sound when he had walked across the wood floors in his work boots. His uneven gate clunk, clunking. He had been in a car accident when he was a kid and had broken his femur, giving him a slight limp.

"Everything Okay, Chelsea?" Jen tilts her head to the side. "I don't know you all that well, but you look pale. Did you finish the it?" Jen puts her arm around me in a sideways hug.

"Not yet." I rub my hands on my pant legs. "Not sure how much more I can take of it. It's pretty fucked up."

"Yeah, your eyes are bloodshot, too. It's been a tough day." Jen studies my face. "I have an idea. How bout you take a break from reading." She sits on the barstool next to me. "You've barely touched your dinner. I'll stay right here next to you while you eat." She looks around the bar. "Besides, it's dead tonight."

I hadn't noticed, but the table of women left. It was only me and Jen in the bar.

Jen picks up my fork and places it in my hand. "Here. Take a bite."

I take the fork, scoop up a tiny bit of the beans and rice, and slowly lift it to my mouth. The soft and tacky bite hits the spot and ignites my hunger. I pick up one of the tacos, take a big bite, and follow it with a swig of margarita.

"Atta girl!" Jen smiles, dipping a chip into the salsa.

"All these years, how could my grandma let me think my dad had abused me when it was my uncle?"

"Whoa. Is that what's in that journal?"

"Yes. Sorry. I can't stop my mind from churning." Spinning the barstool toward Jen, I reach out for both of her arms. "Jen, promise me." Squeezing her arms and searching her eyes, she feels safe. "Can you promise you won't tell anyone what I'm about to tell you?"

"Of course. Besides, who am I gonna tell? The only person we both know is Tito. And I sure as hell don't ever talk to him." She lets out that laugh-cough I recognize as her signature.

I tell Jen everything that is known to me at this point. When I was ten, using my dresser for protection, I thought my dad had been hurting me, but it turns out it was my uncle. I explain how my uncle died and then about Grandma and Tito's relationship, but she stops me there.

"Jesus, Chelsea. Now I need a drink." She goes around the bar and starts making margaritas. "No wonder you're a mess tonight." Setting two glasses on the counter, she fills both with the yellowy mixture. "So let me get this straight. Your grandmother and my father had a thing? A relationship?" Jen walks over to the neon green open sign hanging in the window and yanks on the power cord, unplugging it.

"Yes. That's why Tito had the journal. Eve, my grandma, had him keep it safe because of the tell-all details of a murder."

"Tito never told me about Eve." She clears her voice. "Then again, we are not exactly close. Never been. I always lived with my mom in Albuquerque and came here a few years ago. I had the crazy idea I'd get to know Tito, but he's not exactly the warm, fuzzy type."

I hold up my glass. "Well, here's to shitty dads." She nods, and we clink glasses.

"Back to what you had said about your grandma, dad, and uncle?"

"Yeah, I'm confused why my grandma let me believe my dad abused me when she knew it was my uncle. How could she do that?" I finish the last bite of my first taco. It's odd being mad at someone who you never really knew. I can't talk to her or work it out with her. The journal answers some questions, but it has brought up even more.

"Well? When was the last time you talked to your grandma?"

"Not since I was like ten."

"And you said you were ten when your uncle abused you?"

"Yes. And my uncle died when I was almost eleven." I'm doing the math, and Jen is, as well.

"Maybe your grandma knew the threat was dead and buried, so why bring it up?"

"Yeah, but–"

"That was her generation. There were no #metoo, no chat rooms, no blogs or social media. Besides, you never talked, so how could she know what you thought?"

"I guess… From Grandma's writing, it seems she loved me."

"Of course, your grandma loved you. But your mom kept you away from her, right? Isn't that what you told me? How was Grandma supposed to tell you the truth?" Jen pushes herself off the barstool and walks over to the glass door that leads outside. She turns the lock and strolls back to the bar. "I think that journal was her way of explaining everything. Maybe it was her way of loving you."

"Yeah, but why didn't she give the journal to me sooner?" I lick my chapped lips.

Jen opens a drawer behind the bar and places a lip balm on the counter. "Here, doll. Take this. As long as you are in New Mexico, you will need one of these close at all times."

"Thanks, Jen." The balm soothes my red, hot, burning lips.

"You know what you have to do?" Jen dusts bottles of tequila with a white bar towel. "You need to find your dad and talk to him."

"Oh, God. Just the thought of talking with Robert scares me to fucking death. I haven't seen him in, like, fifteen years."

"Aren't you curious? Now that you've learned the truth?" She angles a step stool to reach the top shelf bottles. "I would be," she murmurs.

"Will you make a deal with me? If I talk to my dad, will you talk with Tito?"

"I've tried talking with him, Chelsea. It does no good. Have you ever had a conversation with a cement wall?" Jen shakes the dust out of the bar towel.

"What if you just got to know him better? You know? Like what's his favorite–"

"Chelsea! Stop. I tried. I failed. End of story." She comes off the step stool, picks up our glasses, dumps the ice, and slams them into the dishwasher. "He's an unbending asshole. Only cares about himself and his precious pueblo. He doesn't give two fucks about me. Never has."

"I know how you feel, Jen, but at least you know where your father lives. When I met Tito this morning, I thought he was okay. Rather starchy and cold, but he wants to do the right things. Don't imagine he has murdered anyone."

"Tito sees two colors." Jen holds up her hand, showing two fingers. "Black and white." Jen's anger twists her mouth, emphasizing the wrinkles around her lips. "Life has many shades, Chelsea. That's the point I'm making with your grandma. Who knows why she did what she did? But if your father is still alive, you must find him."

"I will if you will."

"Oh, Chelsea." Jen shakes her head back and forth.

"I'll be right back." I push myself off the barstool and lumber toward the bathroom, holding onto the backs of the empty chairs along the way.

"Whoa!" I shriek. "How long have you been standing there?"

"Yes, there are more colors than black and white." Tito stands in the doorway between the bar and the lobby. "May I come in, Jen?" He takes his cowboy hat off and steps into the bar. "You two need to talk," I say, covering my yawning mouth. "I'm exhausted."

Jen walks toward Tito and me. "You okay, Chelsea?" She squeezes my arm and hands the brown backpack to me.

"Surprisingly, I am okay. Thanks to both of you." Looking at Tito and Jen, their family resemblance is strong – mostly in their eyes and the shapes of their foreheads. "I need to get a good night's rest before all of tomorrow's mishaps. I'm kinda known for those." I clear my voice.

"I'd go with adventures. And you have a father to find," Jen says with her hands on her hips.

"You found me," Tito says. "And that's not easy, 'cause I'm off the grid."

"Yes, I did." The backpack is heavy on my shoulders. "The grid. That's it. That's how to find Robert. Goodnight, you two." I turn and hurry out of the bar.

CHAPTER 29

*C*radling the journal in my hands, I read aloud, walking in a zig-zag around my cramped hotel room. My oversized, ratty Star Wars tee shirt, loose panties, and dirty socks – unconscious habits of living alone – are perfectly comfortable. Talking to myself is another habit that I do more and more. It's living alone, or maybe age. Or perhaps I'm just as messed up as the rest of my family.

Oct 9, 1999, Chelsea, you are twelve years old now. As you and Liz continue to live in Seattle, there is a great emptiness in my heart. Daily, I'm torn between telling Liz the truth about Robert and Jim and remaining quiet. This is a challenging situation. At the very least, Jim won't touch you or any other little girl again.

Leads me to the question – what is truth? Truth seems to be the perception of something that has happened. Robert's reality may differ from Jim's. Don't know what you think or feel, Chelsea. Wonder what your memories hold. What YOUR truth is. You were so young, and perhaps you have no memories. Doubtful, I know, but it's my secret hope that you have no recollection of what your uncle did to you. If you remember, you will carry the trauma until you take active steps to release the sickening, evil pain and forgive the critical players in your life who didn't provide you with proper footing and security. Your mom didn't know anything, at least, I don't think so. Your father reacted erratically but probably appropriately once he found out. Your predatory Uncle Jim met his maker and will have to answer for his horrible doings to you and potentially other little girls.

Oh, if only I could talk with you and your mom. Strip away all the ugly words between her and me and start fresh. End this state of limbo for all of us.

"Dam right, limbo!" I've been in limbo for almost twenty years. My family created a dangerous world. I see how I had no choice but to construct walls around me. My first wall was my dresser. It kept him out of my room. Sleepovers were scary in middle and high school, and I avoided them at all costs. There were not many offers except that one in seventh grade, though I think Lindsay Labuff felt sorry for me. Also, Lindsay's mom was the Girl Scout Troup Leader, and recruiting new meat, she took on like a career. Lindsay invited all the girls and me in our English class to her birthday sleepover. I said yes at first, acting normal and all. I never got her a present and didn't ask Mom if I could go. Waiting until the day of the party, I called Lindsay and told her something ridiculous, like my stomach hurt and couldn't make the sleepover. The fear of the men who lived in that house overcame me. There was the impending Girl Scout recruitment, as well.

Girl Scouts sounded like sheer hell – a bunch of get-togethers with a bevy of girls who would eventually judge me. I was sure I'd never sell enough Girl Scout cookies, eating up all the profits. And then there were the horrid uniforms. Nope, it wasn't for me.

It's weird reliving this now. I wasn't conscious of those fears then, only reacting to them. Those awkward behaviors and lying about the stomach ache were because I was anxious and embarrassed. And then, no other invitations came my way. Once your party pooper status gets out there, it's not forgotten, especially among teenage girls.

Then, the emotional walls went up. I became prickly. Always guilty and shy, with no close friends, still don't. I ate lunch in my homeroom reading sci-fi novels, usually Star Trek or Star Wars. The vulnerability wasn't safe and still isn't. You must be sensitive and exposed when you're with a friend. I've seen movies like Thelma and Louis and Bridesmaids. Captain Kirk and Spock were the best of friends when

Spock was dying in the Wrath of Khan. That kind of friendship means you must open up and expose your deepest fears. It's too hard.

My biggest fear was that someone would see into the holes my uncle had punctured into me. Peer into my darkness. My guilt. My gross, over-touched body. Memories rush into my head like they never have. I'm running to gym class, not because volleyball or tennis were my favorite activities. It's ninth grade, and we have to change from our regular clothes to shorts and a T-shirt. I ran, needing to get there and dress out before the other girls. Back then, I thought it was shyness and unpopular panties. The other girls would share hand lotion and boy stories, but I stayed quiet and laced up my sneakers, hoping they wouldn't notice me.

Unconsciously walking around the hotel room, I stub my big toe on the desk chair and jump up and down. "Shit! You stupid klutz!" I'm immediately hurled to the present, hobble to the bed, sit down, pull off my Wookie sock, and rub my toe. "Ouch." Pain reverberates up my leg and into my sad soul. My lonely, bitter persona. The little Chelsea who is showing herself to the adult Chelsea – whether she likes it or not.

Exhaling a large breath, I gingerly tuck my feet under the southwestern blanket, lie back on the bed, and open the journal.

Oct 10, 1999, Talked to Robert again, and he still hasn't told Liz. The investigation stays ongoing and open. Robert told me he hadn't been able to sleep. Nightmares keep him awake. I recommended he confide in Liz. He disagreed. They have constantly been fighting. He fears Liz would be the first to call the detective and tell the truth about how Jim died. Though I hate it, I need to stay quiet. Chelsea, I hope you understand. Your father is a decent man. He should not go to prison. Your predator will never touch you again.

"What the hell! Everyone stayed quiet!" I come by that honestly – being quiet because you're scared. Fear froze me, but they were adults. They should have known better. At some point, they should have let me in on the big family secret.

The hotel alarm clock reads 2:05 AM. My toe stops throbbing, but my body feels heavy in bed. My weary eyes burn, but I need to finish. There are only a few pages left.

Oct 17, 1999, Took a few days off from writing. Had to fly home to San Diego. Liz and Robert are flipping out. Your mother demands they move to Seattle, and your father won't. He wants to move to Denver. I haven't talked to Liz. I'm getting all this from Robert. We have stayed in touch, which is rare for us. Your dad and I haven't always gotten along. Over the years, he has shown me kindness and honesty.

Had coffee with Robert this morning, and he opened up to me. Your father is in terrible shape. He's having delusional thoughts. Thinks someone is following him. I told him to go to therapy, but he's too proud. Says he can work this out on his own. One can't kill another human and think they'll be okay, especially if that person is your brother and best friend.

Oct 29, 1999, Liz and Robert separated. This happened quickly, but I think they'd been having problems all along. Robert moved into a motel. They believe this is best for all of you. Robert says he needs to get his head straight and plans to stay with his cousin in Denver for a while. Says he can stay with him for a bit until he gets healthier. It could be for the best. He sounds weird on the phone, and I'm concerned about you and your mom. I mean, if he can kill his brother, who knows what he's capable of doing?

Oct 30, 1999, Called your house today. Left a message on the machine for you and Liz. It's about the twentieth time I've called. I called again just now and left another message. Was hoping you would pick up, Chelsea, as you should have been home from school.

Last night, I made cookies thinking they might be like an olive branch. That Liz would let me in and allow you to have one of Grandma's cookies. (Chocolate chip – your favorite.) I also wanted to see your Halloween costume.

Tomorrow, I'm going to drive over and check on you both. Don't care if Liz has me handcuffed. I need to see you. Make sure you're safe.

Oct 31, 1999, Knocked on your door. No one answered. Tried both the front and back doors. Locked up tight. Lights out. Frantically, I checked all the windows and waited in my car for you both to show up. Waited and waited. At midnight, I left the cookies on your front step and drove home.

Nov 1, 1999, It's 6 AM. I'm going over again right now.

Nov 3, 1999, Spending a night in jail gives you much time to think. Liz called the police when I drove up to the house. I'm still in disbelief that she'd call the police. It turns out I was wrong. Before the police showed up, I tried to see you. Liz wouldn't let me in. Staying calm was not possible. After all you've been through, I needed to see and hug you.

Liz said you'd be moving to Seattle soon, but she refused to give me the new address. I can't believe the way she's acting. It makes my blood boil.

I kept asking questions, but it was apparent Liz knew nothing about your abuse or that your father killed Jim. I didn't tell her, keeping Robert's secret.

Nov 10, 1999, There is a burning inside of me. I want to see you so badly, Chelsea. Life exploded, and I can't find a way to get to you without going to jail again. I'm sick about it. If I violate the restraining order again, it could be more jail time (not just one night) and thousands of dollars in fines. And then, if I violate again, it's five years in prison. I feel so God damned stuck! I'm so sorry, Chelsea.

"Goddammit, Mom!" Fury rises in me like a building on fire. I'm steaming hot and kick the covers off my legs. Dad didn't feel safe telling her about this most critical and pressing situation. I can understand the way he thinks about Mom. She was always checked out and unreliable, just like she is now.

They were married, but I knew Mom and Dad were not best friends, even as a little girl. Dad and Uncle Jim were best friends. I remember hearing them talk and laugh as they were loading the truck with tools in the garage. It's hard to believe Dad did that. He killed his best friend and twin brother. For me. To keep me safe.

How strange and awful what Dad went through, how he's felt all these years losing his brother, knowing full well what Jim did to me. To feel love for Jim and also great disgust. One day, you think you know someone, and next, you learn he's a sick person with a destructive mental illness. And then, to carry the burden and stress of this knowledge plus worrying, they may prosecute you for murder. Dad lost Jim and also me. And I lost both Dad and Grandma.

The only comfort is that now I know, or at least I think it was Uncle Jim. For twenty years, I've had suspicions, fleeting, jumpy memories. The two men looked identical. Everyone had a hard time telling them apart.

"Why keep this secret for so long?"

Dec 1, 1999, Dearest Chelsea, this is my last entry. I'm sobbing as I write. An emotional month this has been. You and Liz left this morning, and I don't know where she's taking you. Watched from across the park, making sure Liz didn't spot me. She loaded the car with suitcases and boxes. You brought your pillow, a backpack, and your tote with books. You always loved your books.

You are twelve now and will grow into a beautiful, intelligent young woman. I'm not sure when I'll see or talk with you again. I only hope soon. I'll get your new phone number from Robert. I'll keep chipping away at your mom. Maybe she'll soften one day.

Chelsea, the world is not always a safe place. Hopefully, you will have a chance to thrive with your uncle gone. I know you'll need to self-protect. You've been through hell. It's human nature. The downside to self-protection is that we shut down opportunities for connection. The severe and steady pain of distrust pushes people away.

I tell you this, little one, because I pushed loved one's away after your grandfather died. It felt like it was my fault. Even after a bunch of therapy, I still felt responsible for his death. No one would want to be around me once they saw my flaws and knew how messy my life and heart were, so isolating myself seemed like the correct answer.

Loneliness overtook me. My therapist encouraged me to be vulnerable. It feels terrifying and unstable. I had to let down my walls and stop showing the shiny, faux version of myself. Was so insecure, still am. But the more authentic I became, my friends responded in good ways. Was connecting better and noticed they weren't polished and perfect either, which was nice. We could connect. It's still challenging to be vulnerable, but practice may make perfect. Or at least, I hope so.

My therapist called me brave for opening my heart to my friends. I've thought about that quite a bit. Being brave does not mean you're not scared. I was not courageous that day on the mountain when Grandpa Doug died. Being a nurse, I performed the things I did every day. Being brave means you do something that scares you, and you do them anyway. *It's scarier to open and show my yucky flaws than doing open-heart surgery, at least for me.*

Hopefully, you will read this sooner rather than later. I will give Tito this journal to keep our family safe, primarily for your father. One day, you will meet Tito. I have asked him to search you out if you don't find him first.

My Little One – please know that I love you with all my heart. Though we cannot see each other, please feel my love. I will find you and your mother. Until then, every time I look at the moon, I'll know it's the same moon you see. And when the sun kisses my shoulders, I know it'll be kissing yours, too. We will be connected forever. Remember, you are never too old to wish upon a star.

With eternal love,

Grandma

PS: If you wonder why I never told you or Liz about how your uncle died, I knew I needed to keep the peace. Your family was torn to pieces all because of one person – Jim. Jim did the damage. Your uncle is no longer alive and, therefore, can't hurt you anymore. Robert moved to Denver, away from you and your mom. Safe up in Seattle, now. You need peace.

There are other reasons. First, I don't think Robert should go to prison for what he did. And second, he promised to let me know about you and your mom – your new address, the school you attend, and new friends. Liz is so mad at me. I know she'll keep up this restraining order business. When she fixates on something, she doesn't let it go. I don't know for how long. Until then, Robert is my only lifeline to you. He said he'd send pictures and updates about your life.

I'm covering for a murder, which makes me a part of the crime. There is no other way around my situation. I'm in a box with no other choice. I hope I'm making the right decision. One day, we will get to speak to you about the agreement between your father and me. Until then, I will moon gaze and dream of you.

I love you, Chelsea.

My tears hit the page. I want more. More of Grandma. More of her words. Flipping through the last empty pages of the journal, I moan in sadness. I've cried so much the last few days that it doesn't seem possible there are any tears left. And yet, they stream out of my tired eyes.

"I will not be the victim! Not anymore." I've been a victim for almost twenty years. No more. No more hiding behind a dresser. No more staying quiet. No more pushing people away. No more scared kid, the wallflower, the walking dead.

Climbing out of bed, I rush over to the old hotel window, throw back the drapes, and look up. A dark purple sky dotted with stars and a few puffy clouds are visible through the panes. No moon. I press my cheek against the cold glass, desiring to see the same moon as Grandma. The coolness soothes the fever of information overload.

After a few minutes, I shuffle back, pick up the lost journal and place it with care on the nightstand, and set my alarm for 8 AM. Tomorrow will be another big day of searching – this time, for my father.

CHAPTER 30

It will be impossible to make that first call. Understanding it was Uncle Jim doesn't erase the years of despising and avoiding my father.

Leaning hard against the back of the hotel chair, my head flops backward like my neck is not strong enough to hold it up. I'm thinking about contacting my father! My dad! It's been almost twenty years since I talked with him. I've been both disgusted and afraid – a little girl's fear. I'm not sure how long the abuse happened, as it was woven into the fabric of my day-to-day life. What was happening to me seemed normal, like you get used to the water you swim in.

A background-checking site is open on my phone. And there it is. *Robert Price,* I read. My heart tightens, but I can't quite discern the feeling. It's not dread. Not excitement, either.

I slide my credit card out of my wallet and tap it on the distressed hotel desk in my room. My savings is all gone and am almost at my credit card limit. The site says $29.99 is all it takes to access Robert's full address. I peer over at my suitcases. My packed bags lie next to the door, awaiting their next destination. Chills run through me, making my shoulders quake.

"Shit. I gotta do this." My card information goes into the background screening site, and I push purchase. A circle spins, and the site prompts me to wait for the information to compile. I bite on my thumb and squeeze my eyes shut. "Come on. Come on. Come on." My phone vibrates, and there he is.

Fifty-eight-year-old Robert Lane Price. A report generates online. The relatives listed are Elizabeth Price, James Price, and Chelsea Price. The information has no picture of him, probably because he's not on social media. I'm excited and also a little sick to my stomach. Reading on, the last known address for Robert is in Seattle. "Seattle! What the?" Two PO Boxes and one physical address, all in Seattle. It gives our old address in San Diego. But, no address in Denver. Mom had told me he moved to Denver when they separated. Grandma thought so, too. Mom said he sent divorce papers and checks from Denver. When did he move to Seattle? Or is that a ruse? He reported a Seattle address to throw authorities off his scent.

The last given address in Seattle is on the other side of town from Mom's house, the house we moved to when Mom and Dad separated. The place I grew up in with the dark blue wood siding, yellow front door, and the one-car garage that Mom's Honda Civic barely squeezed into amongst the old, rusty paint cans and dusty shelves. So, either the background screening site has it wrong or Mom lied to me about where Dad lived. Or Dad lied to Mom. A person could go mad thinking about this. It seems to be a routine thing in my family – lying and family secrets.

With all these secrets, my reality is false, even shattered. My truths are not the real truths. I've always felt suspicious of Mom, even resentment, but maybe she was the innocent along with me. It sounds like nobody told her about Dad and Uncle Jim and the so-called accident or the abuse. She's clueless, yes, but maybe that was her coping mechanism. Out of sight, out of mind, she would say. More of her favorites are – don't go poking around in what you don't know, and Chelsea, accept things the way they are. You can't change them, so why bother?

Head down, don't make eye contact, don't rock the boat, stay quiet. "Fuck that!" I can't do that anymore. I won't do that anymore! Feeling my body heat rising, I yank off my hoodie and hurl it on my suitcase. If Dad lived in Seattle, why didn't he ever call Mom? Or Me? They were divorced, but I thought she had kept track of where Dad lived. I know he sent checks to Mom twice per year. Mail has that date stamp that includes the city.

I need to ask Mom, but it drives me crazy when she acts clueless and tells me she doesn't know anything. I'm exhausted by that response. It's tiresome. She gives no answers, and then I end up furious. This routine is an old and tedious fight, but I must get the truth.

Staring at the background check on Dad, I see a phone number listed. My palms feel sweaty, and I wipe them on my jeans. I should call him, but what is there to say? Hi, this is your daughter that you abandoned years ago. Or hi, this is your daughter. I never looked you up before because, well, I thought you molested me. Or hi, this is Chelsea. So, you killed your brother, huh?

My phone rings, making me jump. It's Josie.

"Hi, Josie."

"Hello, Dear! How are your travels? I've been thinking about you, and there's something important that you need to know."

"It's been a roller coaster. One minute, everything is horrible, then the next bit of information feels like a special gift." That familiar lump builds in my throat.

"Are you alright, Chelsea?" Josie's tone is tender and caring. Her voice wraps around me like a warm blanket.

"I'm not sure. Sometimes my body wants to crumble into a million pieces, and then something happens, and I'm empowered again." I've only known Josie for a month, but I feel closer to her than anyone.

"It's so nice to hear your voice, Josie." I explain about Tito, the car accident and the Pueblo's River, and about Jenn, Tito's daughter. I tell her what was in Grandma's lost journal about Uncle Jim – left out the murder and the cover-up part. Now, I'm covering for my father, just like Grandma did. I told Josie that Uncle Jim had molested me. That part was hard to say, but once it was out, it felt good to release some of this family history to someone who cares.

"Oh, Chelsea, I am so sorry. Can you explain? Do you have a plan now that you've read the lost journal?"

"Well, I'm in the process of finding my father and will try to talk to him. I'm terrified. We haven't spoken in a long time, so I was figuring out how to start that conversation." Navigating the tiny room is easier in the daylight. The drapes are still open from last night's no-moon gaze. The bright sun lights up the gravel parking lot, and from the second story, I spot my car wearing its new booboo on the front bumper. "Pardon my language, Josie, but it's been a real shit show mixed with complicated stories and personal epiphanies."

"Wow. These are some difficult things to learn about your family."

I want to tell Josie everything, but Grandma kept it a secret from me and Mom, so respecting her wishes is essential. Grandma went to her grave with Dad's secret. I'm not entirely sure why. Blabbing about the murder and the cover-up is not my best option. Not until more information comes to light. I wonder, though, what Josie knows about the murder. Did Grandma confide in her?

"Josie? Did my grandma talk to you about my dad and uncle? Did she divulge? I mean, tell you anything about them?"

"Eve told me a little about your uncle, that he was a troubled man and died fairly young in an accident. She always said your dad was a good man but never forgave himself after his brother's fatality. I understand they were close." Josie sniffs. "Sorry, dear. I still miss Eve so much. Just thinking about her makes me cry."

"I know, Josie. You were best friends. Grandma touched many people. The lost journal had some stories about Robert and Jim. Do you remember Grandma telling you any more about my father?"

"She traveled to Mexico once, and I brought in the mail. There was a large envelope addressed to Eve. It was from your father. Robert, right?"

"Yes. Did you open the envelope?"

"Heavens no. I did ask about it. She said that he would occasionally send family photographs."

"How long ago was this?"

"Oh, eight or nine years passed. Eve framed a few, but your mom took them."

"Mom, huh?" I look over at the brown backpack. "There are some sweet souvenirs of Grandma's to share with you, Josie. Maybe I can visit someti–" What am I thinking? There is not enough money to put gas in my car. How am I supposed to get to San Diego?

"Of course, you can visit anytime." Josie's voice, that calming, soothing sound, washes over me, and my back muscles relax. If I were to dream up the perfect fictional grandmother voice, it would be Josie's. It's not false or fabricated like a made-up grandmother in a cheesy movie. Her slight French accent, with the brief rumble in her throat, resonates with her purpose. "Thanks, Josie, but I'm having a bit of an issue with my finances."

"What's the issue?"

"Um, money. Or actually, the lack of it. This grand adventure has taken much longer than originally thought. I've gone through all my savings." I bite the cuticle on my thumb again.

"Well, that was one reason I'm calling. You're going to be glad to hear. Eve had set up an account for you through a whole life insurance policy. I just got off the phone with her insurance broker. Sorry, I didn't know this earlier, but I have been slowly unraveling her finances. She set one up for your mother, as well."

Josie sends an email to me explaining the terms. "Oh, my God! Josie, is this for real?"

"Far as I can tell."

"One hundred thousand cash? The money is available any time?"

"That's what she told me. And they named you and your mom beneficiaries for each other. You know, just in case."

I crumple forward in disbelief and a crazy sense of joy, reading the email repeatedly. "I don't have to die to get the money from a life insurance policy?"

"Nope. The insurance broker told me that you could take whatever amount you wanted, and if you wanted to pay it back, you could. Or not. It's completely up to you. Just call that number, and they will send a check to you."

"A check?" I jump up out of the distressed pinewood chair. "Wait, I gave up my apartment in Portland and don't have an address anymore, Josie. Where can the check be sent?" Think, think, think. I tap my forehead. I could have it sent to the hotel in New Mexico, but that will take too long. I look down at my car, once again in its sorry shape. "Doubt if my car will make the haul up to Seattle from New Mexico after the accident, and besides, it's almost out of gas."

"How bout you have the check sent to me here in California?"

I think about that for a second. "That would be great, but then I would need to get it from you, and you are in the opposite direction of Seattle."

"Okay, here is an idea. Have the check sent to your mom, and I will get your plane ticket to Seattle." Josie is typing on her computer keyboard.

"Soooo, I am a bit confused. You grew up in Seattle, no? And your dad lives there? And now you need to go find him?" Josie's questioning voice sounds disbelieving.

"I know, Josie, it's completely effed up. I've been doing the same math, and one plus one does not equal two. Not in my family. That's why I'm a mess. Grandma's journals have opened a hornet's nest of questions, and my mind is buzzing."

"One issue at a time. Call that number in the email and have a check sent to Liz's house, and then you can go and pick it up."

"God, Josie, including Mom in all this will be a disaster. I've been avoiding telling her any of this until I had it all sorted out. She'll get mad at me for lying about everything. I know she'll discourage me from finding my dad. She'll be livid, knowing I've gone through all my savings. Every time we talk, it ends up in a fight."

"Sounds like someone I used to know."

"Yeah." I drag my hand through my hair. "Grandma said she and Mom used to argue all the time."

"Well then, how else can we get a check to you, dear?"

"I wonder if the insurance company can direct deposit the money into my bank account?" "In the meantime, I'll look for flights for you."

"Wait, Josie. I'm not sure if I can fly yet." The thirty-day hold may still be in effect from the altercation at the Portland Airport. Opening my calendar on my phone, I realize it had been thirty days on the nose. "Phew, it's okay."

My next call is to the life insurance company, which is a strikeout. The woman at the insurance company said they must send a physical check for security reasons. Thoughts flash through my mind. I could get a post office box in Seattle. No, that'll take too much time. And I'm sure you can't do that over the phone. Then a crazy thought hits me. Have the check sent to Dad's last known address. That's stupid. What if he doesn't live there anymore? What if he does live there, but he's a crook and steals my money? Who knows what he's become – what kind of hardened criminal? Growing up in Seattle, you'd think I would have a friend still living there. I search my mind for any answer. Finally, Mom's address is what I give the insurance company.

My flight confirmation to Seattle comes into my email. Josie booked it for me tonight out of Albuquerque. She also sent three hundred dollars to me through her bank. For an older woman, Josie's skills with technology impress me. I call her again.

"Thank you so much, Josie! You're like the grandmother I never... well. You know what I mean."

"And you, Chelsea dear, are like a granddaughter to me."

I tell Josie that they will send my check to Mom's address. "There was no other choice."

"Perhaps when you go to your mom's, you can work on not arguing. Try observing yourself as you speak to her. Listen to your word choice. And conversely, see your mom. Do your best to understand her."

"Sounds hard, Josie. Most times, I don't even make eye contact with my mom. It's difficult to see her if I can't even look at her?"

"You'll figure that out. Make clear requests and state your needs. And if Liz tries to deter you from finding your dad, don't blow up. Ask her why. Why is a fabulous word. And then, tell her your reasons for wanting to find your father. Chelsea, what is your why?"

"What is my why? I've been running so hard to find Tito and the lost journal. I've lost my why." I think for a second. "Truth. Truth is my why." In looking for the truth, many secrets have surfaced. Secrets Grandma held. Secrets Dad holds. Secrets I'm now keeping.

"How'd you get so smart, Josie?"

"Years and years of living on this tough but beautiful planet. Now, go catch your flight to Seattle!"

"Josie?" I swallow hard. "I love you."

"I love you, dear."

CHAPTER 31

It feels so strange sitting across the street from Dad's house in Seattle like I'm a private investigator, or worse, a prowler. A daughter should know where her dad lives, be familiar with his house, his neighborhood. A daughter should have some relationship with her dad. Is no relationship still a relationship if you are family? Shame engulfs me like a dark ocean wave. I should have been in contact with him sooner. That thought makes me queasy.

What is my plan? What is my why? I'm not ready to just walk up to Robert and say, what? Hi! Hello. Hey there. It's like I'm an awkward twelve-year-old, too shy to make eye contact with an adult. "Grow the fuck up, Chelsea." I hate myself right now, just sitting here in my rental car, talking to myself, afraid to move.

At eleven o'clock in the morning, he's probably at work. I wonder if he still works construction? The numbers on the house are easy enough to read – 3822 Blue Jay Drive. It's a small off-white wood-sided house with a charcoal gray front door. The modest house reminds me of Mom's. On the right of the house is a chain-link fence holding in two rather large German shepherds. They bark as the mailman walks by with his pushcart of mail.

A text from Mom comes in. She's thanking me for stopping by, that she wished I had given her more notice. I told her that work was the reason for my visit to Seattle and that an insurance letter would come to her address for me. She waved me off, saying her typical, whatever.

I need to find Dad first and ask him the whole slew of questions. The answers should come straight from the person who knows our history. From the horse's mouth, Mom would say.

The mailman is not important to me, but watching him gives me something to do as I'm avoiding the inevitable. How do I find out if this is genuinely Robert's house? Then a clear thought hits me. The mail. It will have his name on it. I sit up taller. But, it's against the law to look at someone's mail. I will not open the mail, I rationalize.

Now, all I have to do is stroll up to the door and casually open the rusty mailbox that's attached to the house, pull out one letter, and verify his name – all without waking up the dogs. And, hope to God Robert is not in the house and saunters out with his shotgun, just as I'm there with my hand in the cookie jar.

Slowly, I pull on the latch to open the car door. Harder and harder, until the handle fully pulls away from the door. Yanking on it again, I realize the door is locked. Of course, it's locked. I always lock doors. Here was another annoying habit that used to piss off Drew. Acting like a child, she would yank on door handles over and over. Just as I had done in the car, but she would overdo the yanking just to get my attention and make a point of how ridiculous it is to always lock doors.

I push the button, unlocking the door, and as quietly as I can, open the car door and swing my legs out. The empty glass iced tea bottle that was stored in the car door compartment flips out and hits the pavement with a clang, clang, and rolls under the car.

"Shit," I whisper, peering over at the mailman striding from house to house, going about his daily regimen. The rolling glass bomb went too far under the car to snatch it back.

Adjusting my shirt, I make sure to pull it down at the back to conceal my beltline. With an attempt to appear casual, I proceed towards the front of Robert's (or I'm hoping) Robert's house. It hadn't rained all morning, but just then, it started to sprinkle. There is a gray pebble path leading to his front door, and as I step on it, my heart jumps. It wasn't a flutter or a wave. This was like my heart had flipped over inside my chest like a heart attack. I take two tentative steps onto the eight-foot-long pebble path, and the dogs bark at me. They have that big dog sound like they could rip through that metal fence with their shark teeth and bite my body in half. I scamper up to the door, scan side to side for any onlookers, and lift the mailbox's small, rusty white lid.

While pulling out the mail, I can't help but stare inside the house through the side window. White sheers cloud my view of a small kitchen table and two chairs. Silver salt and pepper shakers sit next to vitamin and prescription bottles, like ten of them all lined up in a row.

The first letter I scan is addressed to Bob Price, the next to Robert Price, and the third to Resident. A sudden wave of dizziness hits me. My vision tunnels, blackening out around the edges. I throw the mail back into the old, thin mailbox, turn and dash back to my car. The dogs are still barking, but it sounds muffled, like I am underwater. After I'm in the driver's seat, I push the button to lock my doors and press my thumbs into my temples, massaging them, trying to calm myself down. I feel sick. The anxiety overtakes me.

"Big belly breaths. Big belly breaths." The breathing doesn't work. I unlock the car door, open it, and stick my head out low to the ground. After vomiting, my belly feels better, but the underwater sounds stay. Raising back up, a part of my hair sticks to my wet lips. Wiping my lips with the back of my hand, I push my hair back and away from my sweaty neck. Chills rattle my body, and I grip the steering wheel to steady myself.

A brown mini pickup truck drives past me and into Robert's driveway. I duck, flopping my head onto the passenger seat. Lifting slowly up, I watch an older man pull a cane and a bag of groceries out of the back of the truck. He sort of looks like the Robert I remember, except now he has silvery hair. He ambles up his front steps, pulls the mail out of the mailbox, opens the front door, and disappears inside.

Oh my God, I just saw my father. He looks so old, so frail. A fog of disbelief distracts me from my anxiety attack. For so long, I've not been able to even think about my dad, let alone see him or potentially talk to him. I thought this was possible, but now I'm unsure. The pain in my belly rages again as beads of sweat form on my forehead.

I can't go up to him, not right now. The enormous maple tree standing sentient in the front yard grabs my attention. Its large branches, like outstretched arms, swaying as if it didn't have a care in the world. Lucky tree. Looking up, I try to see the top, but can't make it out for the thousand shades of the green canopy. Three small birds dart in and out of the tree, probably playing tag, if birds do that.

One brown feather floats through the cloudy sky like a kamikaze whirlybird, landing on the pavement before me. "Feathers appear when Angels are near." Without thinking, I get out of the car, walk over, and pick up the delicate plume. A little feather blessing is exactly what's needed right now. I'm exhausted and stumble back to lean against the front of the car. Holding the feather up to the sun, I close one eye, and tiny shards of light stream through the shiny feather.

"Miss?"

I look in the voice's direction. It's Robert standing in the street a few feet from me.

"My God," he breathes. "Chelsea? Is that you?"

I gasp. There he is, standing right in front of me. Out of instinct, I want to run, but instead, my feet freeze as if glued to the street.

"Robert?" I squeak. We both stand there looking at each other like chess pieces, unsure of whose move it is. He, the king. Me, the pawn. Or were we both pawns?

"Yes." He takes a tentative step toward me with the aid of his cane.

I step back, raising my hand to ward off his approach, and brace myself against the rental car.

"Chelsea. It's you. It's really you." His raspy, clogged voice makes me think he has a cold. His clothes hang off his skinny frame, making him look much older than his years. Fifty-seven? Fifty-eight? I think to myself, trying to remember his birth year.

"What are you doing here?" He frowns and rubs the base of his neck. "I'm sorry. Where are my manners? Would... You like to come in?" He motions to the front door.

My mouth opens, but nothing comes out. "Um, fresh air is best." My cotton mouth gets the words out.

"Whatever you need, Chelsea." His mouth parts in what might be a smile. "But I'm afraid I won't be able to get outta the way quick enough if a car comes." He taps his cane on the blacktop.

We both say nothing. Don't move. And then Dad lightly speaks. "How 'bout the front step? Wanna sit down?" He raises his eyebrows with a questioning gaze.

This is my why. I have to get the answers, the truth. Pull yourself together, Chelsea. If Robert tries anything weird, I can push him down the stairs. He's so frail it would be easy. I put the little feather in my back pocket, shake out my hands, and take a small step toward the sidewalk.

"Look, I have a lot of questions. Are you ready to answer those?" My voice is sharp and pointed. I'm never this way. On the one hand, I'm proud of my new bad-ass self, and on the other, I'm terrified. My weak and shaky knees barely hold me up. Only a few more steps across the street, and we will be on the sidewalk in front of his house. As he walks in front of me, I notice his uneven gait. That didn't change.

"Yes, Chelsea. I'm sure you have a bunch of questions." He coughs and coughs a raspy, gross hack. I wasn't sure if he'd ever stop coughing, and then he did, leaving him hunched over. "I'm not long for this planet, and I want you to know everything. No matter what you think of me. You deserve to know."

CHAPTER 32

"Would you like a glass of water? Or gosh. I'm sorry. I'm not in the habit of entertaining. Oh, Chelsea, I don't know what to do with myself." He slowly lowers himself to sit on the front step and pats the cement next to him as he adjusts his blue and green Seattle Seahawks stocking cap. "The cement is kinda cold. You know, there might be a folding chair inside?"

"It's okay. I'll stand." Crossing my arms, I look down at the gray gravel and then back up at Robert. My heart pounds in my throat, and I swallow hard, pushing down the severe anxiety of standing this close to him. I expected I'd be off-balanced and confused, but my body feels like it may explode, like there's a time bomb inside my chest. Where to start? My mouth opens, but nothing comes out. You've come this far. Say something! "Um, Grandma Eve died. Did you know that?"

"I didn't know." He lowers his head and lifts it back up in a slow head shake. "When?"

"A few weeks ago. We cleaned Grandma's house out." My heart is pounding so much, but the blood isn't making it up to my brain. My mind is only capable of brief spurts of thoughts, making complete sentences impossible to form. "Um, actually, me, Mom, and Josie cleaned out her house after she passed."

"Were they speaking? Your mom and Eve?"

"No, they never talked. We didn't know Grandma had passed until after her celebration of life." I kick around at the gravel, nervously moving one dull, worn-down stone back and forth. My brain seems to be working a bit better.

"Shame they never made up."

The only way to keep my lips from trembling is to pinch them together. I'm in absolute disbelief that I'm standing here talking with my father. I feel light-headed and dizzy again. Lowering onto the grass next to the gravel walking path, I blink a few times as my vision is tunneled.

"Oh, let me go get that chair." Robert tries to stand but only gets halfway up and then sits back down.

"I'm fine. I'm fine. It's only a little dizziness. The grass is fine here." I'm anything but fine, and the prickly grass is cold and fucking wet. What the hell is happening here? I draw my knees up and wrap my arms around myself. Robert stares at me. "Look, this is not gonna work." I attempt to stand, but my head spins, forcing me back down onto the grass again. The black metal edging between the stone path and his grass bites the back of my thighs.

"This must have been hard, Chelsea. Thank you for being so brave." Robert scratches his forehead. "Not sure how you found me, but thank you for bringin' the news about Eve. It turns out she was a pretty special lady." His gentle husky voice sounds strangely familiar. "I'm gonna get that glass of water for you." Robert grabs the side railing to hoist himself to standing, takes hold of his cane, and walks unevenly into the house. The door closes behind him, but I can hear him talking to the dogs in a reassuring tone.

He's right. This takes bravery. I'm doing it.

It was terrible cleaning out Grandma's house. Mom made it a fiasco, and looking for Tito drained my savings. I lost my job, my girlfriend, and my best friend. It has been one hell of a month. And now, to top it all off, I'm talking to Robert.

Robert emerges, pushing the dogs back into the house. He barely navigates the stairs and hands me a glass of water. "I didn't know if you like ice, so there's only a few in there." As he passes the glass to me, he touches my shoulder. "I'm delighted you're here, Chelsea." I wince, and my body stiffens. The weight of his hand on my shoulder feels oppressive and dreadful, like an unbearable burden pressing down. He pulls back and clears his voice.

After taking a drink of water, clearer thoughts start to form. "This is weird being here with you. I need to talk with you, Robert, but I'm terrified and on the verge of a horrible anxiety attack." The wet grass soaks into my jeans, and it's getting colder. "I read Grandma's journals." I stare directly into his eyes, searching for truth. "All of them."

"So, you met Tito?"

"What!" Water sprays out of my mouth. "How do you know Tito?" Wiping my chin, I sit forward.

"Okay, so you've read THAT journal?" His voice shakes as he plops down on the stoop. "Eve eventually told me she wrote it. She said it was cathartic and wanted you to know the truth someday." He exhales a huge breath as he looks up at the tall tree in the front yard. We are both quiet for a moment.

Without looking at me, he speaks. "So that's why you're here." He coughs once and clears his voice. "I'm ready to go to prison, Chelsea. I should have turned myself in years ago, but Eve kept talking me out of it. She'd say that one day Chelsea would need her father. Even as screwed up as the whole situation was." Robert shakes his head back and forth again. "Well. When do the police show up?" He looks up and down the street and then finally at me.

"I'm not here to send you to prison. I'm here for the truth. I had thought one thing all my life, and then over the course of several weeks, I've learned that my horrible memories are all wrong." My weight shifts from side to side, and I pick at the grass. "I'm sitting here talking to you, and it's all surreal, like I'm living in a movie." A rush of heat rises in me. Speak up, Chelsea! Speak up! "I'm here for the goddamn truth, Robert! You know that thing nobody in our family tells? The truth!" A hunk of grass rips out of the ground, exposing the dark, wet soil, and I throw it across the yard with all my might. "Just tell me something real, something. Anything! Tell me the truth."

The need for truth is stronger than my fears. At any cost, I need to know. We both sit quietly for a moment. All the questions play out in my mind. Murder? Why the coverup? Why live in Seattle and never tell Mom or me? Why did Grandma go along with all this? But he needs to talk first. He needs to come clean and tell me everything.

"Chelsea, I've wanted to tell you for years." He grunts as he pulls himself to stand. "But I cannot sit on this hard, cold step any longer. I'll bet that ground is gettin' pretty cold as well. Do you think you could come inside?" He turns and stumbles into the house.

Robert talks to the dogs again, and then the door opens, and he stands in the doorway. "The dogs are outside, so they won't bother you. Please, Chelsea. Please, come in?"

Looking down at the gravel, I don't budge. It's not possible.

"I'll leave the front door open. See here?" He pushes the door wide open and positions a rock to keep it open. "Please understand, Chelsea. I'm... I'm sick and need to sit someplace warm and a bit more comfortable." He turns and walks at an irregular pace. "I'll put on a pot of tea." His words trail off, and all I hear is the clunk, clunk of his uneven steps – the sound of my childhood. Every night after work, he would clunk his work boots across our wood floors and into the kitchen.

I consider all my potential scenarios. Running to the car, speeding off, and never returning is one option. I could stay out here, but not much longer. The ground keeps getting harder and wetter under me. Hot tea sounds pretty good. God, if he has a candy bar, that would be amazing. Screw my diet! This is life and death kind of shit happening here. Going inside the house is the only way I'll get answers. Is he trustworthy? Was it Uncle Jim who molested me? Did Robert shoot him? My mind is a tangled mess of family spaghetti.

Sprinkles landing on my nose take me out of my thoughts. Squinting my eyes, I look straight up at the sky and let the light rain hit my face. It's refreshing on my red-hot cheeks. And then, Robert comes back outside with a blanket, a cup of hot tea, and two cookies.

"The rain is supposed to get worse through the afternoon, or so they say." He sets the tea and cookies before me and places the blanket around my shoulders. Once more, I tense up, bracing myself against the possibility of any physical contact. "Good thing you're here to eat up the cookies. The doc says sugar and cancer don't mix."

My gaze remains down at the gravel, though the blanket feels good. Tea and cookies? I don't remember him ever drinking hot tea. Then again, I don't have many memories of him. He used to drink coffee, as the smell used to be on his breath when he picked me up in the mornings. That's one memory. Another memory fleets through my mind of him, combing the tangles out of my hair. Looking back, that must have taken the patience of a saint. My hair was always tangled.

In the cold rainy weather, my nose runs. Reaching into both my pockets, searching for a tissue, I come up empty-handed. The inside of my sleeve works fine.

Robert opens his garage door and disappears inside. It's weird watching him after all these years. The passage of time has brought changes, both in him and in the dynamics of our relationship, making the experience entirely surreal. Then, he emerges from the garage with two lawn chairs. I look back down, hoping he missed me watching him. Out of the corner of my eye, he sets the chairs under the enormous tree in the front yard. He limps back into the house and comes out with his tea and another blanket. Robert plops down in one of the lawn chairs and wraps himself in the blanket.

"Hey, Chels. We'll stay dryer here under the tree. All of her leaves will keep the rain off us."

He wouldn't poison me. Would he? The raindrops get bigger and more frequent, so I pull the blanket over my head and take my chances with the tea. The steaming black tea tastes delicious and warm, and the cookie crumbles, leaving tiny brown bits on the saucer. I put the bite in my mouth. The flavor is familiar, but it's not one I've had in a long time. Not since my childhood. "Butter cookie." The words come out of me.

Robert clears his voice. "Yep, that's right. One of my all-time favorites. I used to buy 'em at the grocery but didn't like the frosting and would scrape it off. So I taught myself how to make 'em with no frosting." He talks behind me, but I don't turn around.

"You have cancer?" I ask, cradling the cup of tea in both my hands. The blanket tent is barely sheltering my head.

"I'm sorry, it's hard to hear you. Did you say cancer? Yes. I have throat cancer. It came back. The second time, now."

The rain comes down harder and harder, and I pop the second cookie in my mouth for fear it will become soaked as my whole body feels. Sitting here on Robert's front lawn getting drenched in the rain isn't working. Slowly, I look behind at Robert. He motions for me to come over and sit next to him in the lawn chair. Rising and taking baby steps toward the chair, feet shuffling, I reach the chair and pull it several feet away from Robert before plopping down. The chair almost tips over from the uneven ground, but I recover and move the chair off of the protruding root from the towering tree.

"Less rain over here under this big 'ole maple tree," he coughs out the words.

I nod in agreement and take the last sip of the now lukewarm tea. I'd be feeling weird if Robert had poisoned me. Wouldn't I?

"Still hungry, Chels?"

"No, I'm okay. Well. Actually, I'm not okay," I admit. "I'm confused about my childhood. That's why I'm here."

"It was a confusing time." He tilts his teacup back, takes the last sip, and sets the mug in the grass next to the leg of his chair. "First, Chelsea, I want to apologize. Things happened to you that were out of my control. Now, do you know about your Uncle Jim and what he did to you when you were younger?"

I nod. That's all I can do. My brain is drained of word-forming nutrients. Just thinking about Jim and what he did to me causes a complete body shutdown.

"Okay then. And you know what I did to Jim for that?"

"More details about that would be helpful."

Robert exhales. "I killed him, Chelsea. My own brother, my best friend. It was the only way he'd stop. Do you understand? I've never been a violent man, but I did what was right. And in the end, as Jim was dying right there in my truck after I had shot him with my hunting rifle, he said it was the right thing. He said he was wrong in the head and didn't want to go to the ER. He wanted to die. Of course, second thoughts plagued me. He begged Chels not to get him fixed up and to let him die in the wilderness. So, we drank whiskey until he fell asleep. And then, he never woke up. Never again." Robert clears his throat and sniffs. "Not a day goes by that I don't think about that last night with Jim." He wipes his eyes up under his glasses. "That was a long time ago, and I've told no one but Eve. Not a soul. And now, I'm telling you."

It should be more stunning to hear this story straight from Robert, but after reading about it repeatedly, I'm oriented to it. I look up into the tree. The birds that were flying in and out of the enormous oak tree that was our rain cover were now quiet. "Why didn't you ever tell Mom?" "Oh, boy. We were this close to a divorce at the time." He holds up his fingers, measuring one inch. "I loved your mom. It was me. The guilt and overwhelming sadness took me over like an unrelenting storm of despair. Each moment weighed down my heart and mind with remorseful thoughts, and every attempt to escape its grasp seemed futile. I became depressed and couldn't work. I didn't want to give Liz one more reason for hating me."

"Mom doesn't hate you." I look at his skinny face, sunken eyes, and the blanket pulled over his vulture-like head. "Mom hated Grandma. That's for sure. But she doesn't hate you."

The way Mom always protected Robert used to madden me to no end. I thought this guy molested his daughter, and Mom would never validate my feelings. She would always take his side, not mine. I pull the shifting blanket back over my head.

The splash of a car going down his street breaks the silence, and I think of what we must look like to the outside world. Two Jedi Knights with our robes pulled over our heads hunkered down, waiting out the rain for our next assignment.

Robert jams his hands into his coat pocket. "How is your mom?"

"She's fine. You know, she's Mom. Rather clueless and manic, and she drinks too much." I remove my glasses and wipe the raindrops with my shirttail, smearing the water around and making them even worse. Frustrated, I put them back on.

"Some things don't change." Robert shivers. "She was hittin' those rum drinks pretty hard." He pulls his knees and feet together and crams both hands under his legs. "I never remarried. Heck, never even dated after the divorce. It's wild, but my love for Liz is still strong."

Wait, he still loves Mom? After all these years?

"Yeah, well, Mom never remarried, either. She dated a few losers, but nothing ever came of it. Thank God. You still love Mom?" Making eye contact with him becomes a little easier.

"Sounds crazy, but I do. Back then, I was a mess and no good for her. No good for you, either. Your mother had such a big personality, and you were so cute. And me? Couldn't sleep, didn't eat, couldn't work. So, I decided to cut her loose so she could find a real man. Someone who could hold down a job." Robert's legs bob up and down.

"Are you cold?"

"A little bit," he says in a low voice.

He looks so sick. My heart starts softening. I'm not scared of this skeleton of a man. He's vulnerable, like a turtle on its back. Yes, he killed his brother, and he kept these secrets from me and Mom. And yes, Grandma covered for him. So far, everything lines up.

"Wanna go in?" I motion toward the house with my head.

Robert flashes a toothy grin. "Thought you'd never ask."

CHAPTER 33

Robert opens his front door and offers me to go inside, but I shake my head no. Not yet.

"You go ahead. I need another minute." Or an hour or a lifetime.

"Okay, Chels. Whatever feels right." He walks into the house, leaving the door wide open.

For comfort, I squeeze the car key in my pocket. My quick getaway is just right there. As I step toward Robert's front door, the car starts beeping. BEEP! BEEP! BEEP! BEEP! "Oh, no." Taking out the key, I swiftly begin pressing buttons to deactivate the car alarm. The alarm stops, but the trunk opens. "Unbelievable"

After securing the car, I scamper through the rain back to Robert's front porch and stare through the open door at the backside of him, limping into the kitchen. He pulls the stocking cap off his bald head. There is only one option, but I feel so stuck, like there's cement in my shoes. And then a passage in Grandma's final journal pops into my head. The one she wrote days before she died.

Feeling scared is normal. Bravery is rare.

I've always thought of bravery as laying down your life for another person or a cause, like when Han Solo and Luke Skywalker got the Medal of Bravery. Maybe courage is when you give up something you've always thought about for greater knowledge. Perhaps it's about walking through open doors when your body freezes from fear.

Robert clangs some dishes in the kitchen, then emerges and turns toward me. "Hey, Chels, I'm gonna let the dogs in. You'll love them. Bonnie and Bella. They're sisters. I got 'em from a rescue when they were just three months old." Robert looks at me. "Come in. You're soaking wet."

The weight of my wet clothes clinging to me and the dripping blanket is uncomfortable and suffocating, making each movement sluggish and cumbersome. Chills rattle me like an earthquake.

"Just leave that wet blanket on the porch. We'll take care of it later," he calls out from the kitchen.

I drop the rain-soaked blanket off my back and leave it in a lump on the porch. *Bravery is rare.* I take one step, brace myself against the doorjamb, and then take another step. And I'm inside. Keep calm. You've gotten this far. You can do this.

"There's a dry towel on the floor," Robert calls out from the kitchen.

The towel is dry and warm as I wipe my face and use it to dry and smooth my hair. I blot my pants and shirt, but it's no use. I'm completely soaked and dripping on Robert's front entry rug, looking less like a Star Wars character and more like an orphan seeking a place to call home, longing for the warmth and love of a family. And then, the two big shepherds come bounding in straight for me.

"Easy girls," Robert says in a deep, dog-calming voice. "This is Chelsea."

The dogs slow down and sniff at my wet sneakers. I simultaneously reach out and pet both and feel their wet, cold backs. One jumps up on me, placing her paws on my shoulders. Stretched out, she's the same height as me.

"Bonnie, get down!" Robert scolds.

"It's okay. I like it." However, I start to crumble under her weight. "Okay, girl. Maybe you better get down." The presence of the dogs normalizes this extreme and strange situation. I'm thankful for them.

I wipe their backs with the damp towel. Bonnie reaches around and gives me a gentle dog kiss.

"Wow, they're usually not this friendly. Then again, no one comes over." Robert pats the dogs. "Good girls. Now go on. We need to get this other one dry." Robert points to me and smiles. Now, I remember his closed-mouth smile. His extreme dimples run from his cheek down to the sides of his square chin.

There is a puddle of rainwater at my feet. "I'm sorry."

"It's all right. This house has seen plenty of rain. I live in Seattle, for goodness' sake. Would you like to take off your shoes? I'll get more towels."

If I take off my shoes, I won't be able to run out of the house. Then again, running barefoot is an acceptable option. It's just rain. Struggling with my saturated sneakers, I untie them and attempt to kick them off, but they cling stubbornly to my feet. Finding it difficult to remove them, I sit down on the floor and forcefully yank at them until they finally come off.

"Here you go." Robert offers me another dry towel to me. "Come on in, Chels." He turns and motions toward the kitchen. "I'll turn up the heat."

Patting my pocket for my rental car key, I take a small step forward. *You can do this. Let's go. You have questions to ask this man. You need answers.* And like someone was pushing my back, I'm forced toward the kitchen but leave the front door open a few inches, just in case.

"You can sit here." Robert pulls out a kitchen stool, one of two seats next to the tiny, uncluttered kitchen.

"I'm soaked. I'll stand."

"Well. Would you like some dry clothes? Um, I could put yours in the dryer. They'd be done in a jiffy."

"No! I don't want to. I mean, can't. No, just no. I'm fine." *I'm not getting undressed here! God no.* Placing the dry towel on the wooden chair, I sit on it, hoping that the cloth will absorb some of the wetness from my clothes.

Robert turns on the teapot once again. Without lifting his head to look at me, he speaks. "Outside you said you have some questions for me?"

"Yes. I have lots of questions. I've always had questions, but Mom wouldn't answer them. I'm learning she didn't know enough to have any of the answers."

"Nope, she knew very little. Eve and I decided not to tell her. She's always been too unstable. And, if she ever found out me and Eve were conspiring, she'd have hit the roof."

"That's the truth. Well, until recently, the truth about my childhood would have crushed me." I look down at the wood floor. "I've been terrified of you for years." My heart beats so hard that there is a swishing noise in my ears. "You let me believe it was you who had molested me!" My voice rises in rage. "How could you do that to, to your own daughter? How?"

His chin drops, and he crumples onto the kitchen floor. The weight of chronic grief pushes him down. And then Robert's shoulders bob up and down in a soundless cry. Both dogs rush to him, frantically licking his face. He props himself against the refrigerator door and wipes hard at his tears, swishing the wetness away. "I'm an idiot," he whispers. "A damn idiot, Chelsea!" His eyes are red with sadness and deep regret. "I should have told you when you were old enough to understand. I was a coward! A stupid, weak, gutless fool. I chose to give you up over going to prison." He pounds the floor with fisted hands. "Stupid!"

"Bella, Bonnie, come 'ere." I pat my legs to encourage the dogs from walking all over Robert, licking his face. Bonnie comes to me, but Bella stays attending to Robert, who looks entirely broken.

Robert sniffs. "She's my loyal one." He pats Bella's head. "That one," he says, pointing at Bonnie. "She'd follow anyone home."

I kneel on the floor with my arm around Bonnie. "It seems there was no good choice. At a certain point, you could have told me, Robert. Shit, I wish Grandma had told me."

"I was damned if I did and damned if I didn't." He raises his head to look at me. "And you know, you can call me Dad." He swallows hard and offers a desperate half-smile.

My therapist said I needed to dehumanize him by calling him Robert. So we took away Dad and replaced him with Robert. I needed coping skills, ways to deal with my screwed-up feelings, and strategies for managing severe anxiety. It didn't work, not really. Anxiety attacks still came over the years. And here I am, looking at this wisp of a man crumpled on the floor. This man that I loathed, demonized, and feared for twenty years.

The teapot on the stove whistles, and he struggles to get up. I jump up and step over his legs to turn off the burner. He surrenders back to the floor. Carefully, I pour the steaming water into the two mugs containing tea bags, giving both a quick dunk. Carrying the mugs down to the floor, I push one cup toward him, making a deliberate effort to ensure that our hands don't touch during the exchange.

"Thanks, Chels. This is the only stuff that helps my throat feel better. It's that CBD tea. Not the kind that'll make you loopy. Just soothes my cough."

He looks at me with the most tender eyes, but they're sad, like they've been touched too many times by storm clouds. There is pain and kindness and torment and decency. I hadn't wanted to find him before now because of fear and anger. "How... how far along is your cancer?"

"Well, the doc said it's stage four squamous cell carcinoma. They gave me a round of radiation and chemo, but the damn cancer persists." He coughs. "Asbestos, they figure. From all the construction materials I used to use every day."

Chips of ice melt away from my damaged heart as I feel sympathy for Robert. More than sympathy. More like overwhelming sadness. "What else can you do to heal?"

"Super Enjoyable stuff like grazing on vegetables and not eating sugar." He winks at me and then stares into his steaming mug. "Not sure what else. It's spread into my lymph. The doc wants me to continue treatment, but I have second thoughts. Not sure it's worth it. All these medical procedures are pretty spendy."

"Well, you should do all you can, including the treatments." You can't die. I just found you.

We stay on the floor for a few more minutes. Honestly, I'm profoundly conflicted and don't know what to do with myself. Do I hug him? No. Maybe I should reach over and touch Robert's arm? Oh God, no. To calm my hands, I pet the dogs who have settled on the floor next to us. And then, he tells me he wants to change into dry clothes. He turns over on his side, and with great effort, pushes himself to stand.

He lets out a groan. "I'll be back in a minute. I'm freezing, Chels. And once I get a chill, it doesn't stop." Using his cane, he walks back down a hall and out of sight. "Sure I can't get you some dry clothes?" he hollers.

Refusing his second offer, I sit in the chair beside the couch and wait, still sitting on the once-dry towel. My soaked clothes stick to me, but I'm not changing. What, wear his clothes? No way.

The family room is small, and the decorations are minimalist. He likes books. There are enormous stacks all over the room, with a built-in bookshelf on one whole wall. It overflows with books. I get up and squish-squash over to peek at the titles. Take Sharp Photos in Any Situation, The Photographer's Perspective, Sharpening Your Eye, Lightroom Basics. Well, he's into photography. No books on hunting or construction. I figured there would be some of those. There are lots of paperback novels and some titles relating to cancer from doctors and PhDs.

On the opposite wall are three small, older photographs of the ocean and surfers. The white edges of the photos have yellowed. My family used to surf when we lived in San Diego. I can't make out who the surfers are, but they are right in the middle of a fantastic curve of a wave. I can almost taste and hear the ocean. It's always been my happy place – the spray and mist from a breaking wave and the booming sound it makes.

There is a stack of mail on the TV stand, car keys, and a library paperback version of *The Diary of Anne Frank*. I flip it open to a dogeared page and read. "First, we make our choices. Then our choices make us." True words. On the wall next to his TV are more photos. My face drops from a gentle smile to stone. Studying them, I realize they are pictures of me in my sixth-grade uniform coming out of school. The other photo captures me getting my diploma at my high school graduation. Another image is hanging on the wall of me graduating from college at the University of Washington. Robert hobbles down the hall, but I continue to study the photos in bewilderment.

He rounds the corner and stands next to me. "Oh yeah. Um, well, that's why I moved to Seattle. I couldn't stand the thought of you growing up without me. At least I could watch from afar. Photography has always intrigued me. I would wait outside your school every day and take pictures of you and your mom." He coughs. "I'm sure it feels like an invasion. I'm sorry, Chelsea. You will be getting many apologies from me. It was worth it to stay connected to you, even if it was just through photographs and stolen far-away moments. Eve craved photos of you as well."

We both stand there looking at the framed photographs. Invasive? Maybe.

"I love you, Chels. I swear I never touched you inappropriately. You've thought that it was me through the years. It wasn't me."

I peer at him, his bald head with a few short, wispy gray hairs sticking out here and there. "Okay, Robert, prove it. Prove to me it wasn't you."

He drops his head again, limps over to the couch, and eases down. For as long as I can remember, he's had that limp – work boots clunk-clunking. Uncle Jim didn't have a limp. That's the only distinguishing thing between the twin brothers. Is that what he's going to say to me? Will that be his proof?

Did he limp? My memories are fuzzy, like looking through cotton. Remember Chelsea. God Dammit, remember! Did you see the man limping or not?

"Me and Jim were identical twins. We were the same height and ate the same food, so we were the same weight. We had the same blue eyes and brown hair. There were only two things physically different about us. That ATV accident when we were younger left me with a limp, not Jim. And Jim had a mole under his left eye, and I don't."

Robert points at his cheek under his eye. "He would nick it occasionally when he was shaving and wore a small band-aid 'til it stopped bleeding."

"The band-aid!" The memory of him lying on top of me floods my mind, and all I saw was the band-aid on his cheek. "The band-aid!" I stumble over toward the chair where I'd been sitting, but don't quite make it.

"You okay? Chelsea?"

The blood leaves my brain, and then the entire room goes black.

"Chelsea?" I feel Robert patting my cheeks.

Blinking my eyes open, I look up at him. He's holding me.

"There you are. Whew. Oh, honey, you fainted." Robert pulls me closer, rocking back and forth, fanning his hand at my face. "Was just about to dial 911!"

My body is limp. "Jim's cheek." My words come out on my breath. "Band-aid." My body releases all the pain I'd been holding for twenty years. My instincts of pulling away from Robert subside. He continues to rock me, and it feels good. I'm not afraid, not stiff, not anxious. My body wrenches with overwhelming sadness. Then Roberts starts, and we both howl-cry for the years we'd spent apart, for the wrong thoughts about what had happened. For love lost. For regrets. For far-away photos.

I wrap my arms around him, burying my face in his bony chest, and sob. He continues to rock me. The excruciating grief cuts both of us like a double-edged sword. My body surrenders to the primal need for love and touch from someone who loves me.

Love from my dad.

"Oh, Chels. I didn't think this day would ever come," he says, rocking and stroking my hair. "Do you know how many times I've picked up the phone to call you? A bazillion." He shakes his head back and forth. "I'm an idiot. I'm so sorry. I did it all wrong." His voice is deep and gritty. It sounds incredible with my ear to his chest. This connection is warm and safe.

After some time, I'm unsure for how long I sit up and wipe my eyes.

He smiles.

I've gotten his dry clothes wet where he was holding me. "Oh, no." I point at his damp shirt.

"Oh well. It was worth it to have you in my arms." He lets out a long, heavy breath. "God, Chelsea, it feels like I've been holding my breath for all these years."

We both close our eyes and release the profound, deep-seated agony and heartache. It pours out of both of us, out of our hearts and our bodies. Opening my eyes, I look at his weathered face and watch him inhaling and exhaling. I'm amazed at how comfortable and how stable I feel. He's right here, and I'm not afraid. He opens his eyes, but I don't look away this time.

It wasn't you. It was Jim. I fully believe it now. All my tense muscles melt, and the contrast between a few hours ago and now is palpable. I'm not clamping up or twitching, not dizzy or light-headed, or sick to my stomach. I'm just here looking at him, him looking at me. And it's okay.

"Dad?" I'm keenly aware that I've called him Dad. "I think I'm ready for those dry clothes now."

CHAPTER 34

"Do you cook, Chelsea?" Dad asks as I emerge from the bathroom in a pair of his sweatpants and a dry t-shirt.

"Me? Um, no. But Josie wants to teach me. You remember Josie, who lived with Grandma?"

"Yeah, never met her, but she and Eve were good friends."

"She's amazing. She said she'd teach me as soon as well. As soon as I got the answers to all my searching's, as she called it." I use my best French accent to sound like Josie. "Why do you ask? Are you hungry?"

"Little bit."

"I'm good at ordering takeout and delivery." My mood continues to lift. Robert's, I mean Dad's, sweet and unassuming demeanor feels comfortable, homey even. And it's nice to be out of those wet, heavy clothes.

"Alright, delivery it is, but it has to be healthy. No more red meat for me, anymore. Stick mostly to veggies. There's a nice little place close by called Homebound Restaurant. The roasted veggie avocado bowl is tasty."

"Sounds good. I've been trying to eat better, as well."

I'm amazed at this situation, casually browsing food options for delivery while he sits just three feet away from me. It feels like a mix of disbelief and nostalgia, as if time has folded in on itself, bringing us back to this unexpected proximity. The juxtaposition sparks a whirlwind of emotions, reminding me of the past and how life's unpredictable twists have led us to this moment. This would've never happened unless I had offered to clean out Grandma's house, found her journals, and then obsessed over them. A proud smile starts deep inside and washes over me.

"That's a pretty smile." Dad smiles back at me.

Just as I let that pleasant feeling sink in a little, I get sick to my stomach. What if this is all wrong? What if Grandma didn't know who was who – Robert or Jim? Nobody would know. What if he lied to her? What about the mole and the band-aid? Is he lying about that? Trust your gut, Grandma said. What does your gut have to say about all this? "Chelsea!" I yell at myself. Dad steps back. "Whoa!"

"My mind won't fucking shut up!" I rub my temples, demanding the intrusive thoughts stop. "I'm sorry, that yell just flew out of me. Please tell me your side of the story with all the details. Tell me exactly what happened!"

"Okay, okay, you're my strong girl. You can take this."

Dad thinks I'm strong? Nobody has said that to me, ever. I calm down again, and Dad is looking at me, tears streaming down his face. All these pent-up lies damaged both of us, causing profound and undeniable injuries to the heart and soul.

"Trust and easiness were happening, and then my stupid mind chatters a bunch of doubtful thoughts. How am I supposed to trust you?" My gaze rises from the multi-colored rug in the living room to Robert.

Robert's bony shoulders drop. "Oh, Chels, we gotta figure this out."

"All these years. You were the reason I had to pull my dresser in front of my bedroom door. You were the reason I've never had a good relationship with a man or a woman. You were the reason for my horrible anxiety and depression. You were the reason I tried to kill myself two days after my sixteenth birthday!"

"My God. I am so, so sorry. If only I could turn back time. This life should have been different. Please tell me how I can make this up to you?" He looks at me so intensely, like he can see into the holes in my body, bored by pain and guilt and my sick uncle. "If I could take back all that pain, I would. It seemed like the right thing to stay away from you and Liz. I should have just taken my medicine. Just gone to jail for killing my brother." He angrily swipes a tear from his cheek. "Wouldn't blame you, Chelsea, if you never forgive me. Hell, I can't forgive me."

"In my mind, it was you who abused me. Then I learned it was Uncle Jim." My head shakes back and forth, and confusion fills me.

"Let's just take this slowly. This is a lot to take in all at once." Robert sits down on the oversized worn-out couch. "We have all the time in the world."

"No, we don't. You're sick!" A chilly breeze fills the room from the open front door.

"Oh, I'm fine, Chels." He half-smiles. "I've beaten this cancer before. I'll kick its ass again."

He's not fine. He's pale and gaunt. Reptilian skin hangs off his arms, exposing his skeleton. I want to ask him if he ever looks in the mirror. Like me, I'm sure the answer is no.

"I'm worried about you." I slump over. "Jesus, how did this happen? Just a few days ago, I hated you. No. I despised you! It would have been too soon if I ever saw you in my lifetime. Now?" A sarcastic laugh belches out of me. "Now, I'm worried about you. Welcome to my effed-up mind."

"Chelsea, if you have a fucked-up mind, it's because of me and all my stupid lies and deceptions."

"Well, I won't argue with that one. And let's throw in your narcissistic, disgusting brother for the perfect trifecta." I flop back in the chair and look at the ceiling. "Oh, and we can't leave Mom out of this. She and her red wine."

"Wait a second. Your mom was innocent here. She knew nothing. She didn't know what Jim had done to you, to other little girls. Liz thought Jim died in a hunting accident."

"No, she wasn't exactly innocent." I shake my finger. "I told her you had abused me, and she did nothing. She didn't believe me, blaming it on a vivid imagination and that I would make things up."

Robert frowns. "Maybe she thought she could change your mind? Make you think it was just made up, not real? Maybe to save you from terrible memories?" He scratches the side of his face. "Both me and Jim were out of your life. She knew you were safe. Maybe she was trying to help?"

"Yeah, but I needed someone to believe and validate me. Mom constantly blew me off, and then that aloof response turned to anger. We used to fight like cats and dogs. Still do. She was the dog, of course – a mean bulldog. And then, one day, I stopped asking her questions about my childhood. It was useless. Outta sight, outta mind, you know? What did it matter?"

"It mattered, Chels. You matter, my sweetheart." He pulls the blue afghan off the back of the couch and puts it around his legs.

"Thanks, Dad." It's weird to call him that, yet the sound of it flows out of my mouth easily. Once the word, Dad, releases into the air, I feel my heart healing. I've never felt so calm, so at ease. It's like my shoulders were pinned up to my ears, and finally, finally, they can relax. I get up and walk over to the open front door, breathe in the humid, cool breeze, look at the rental car, and close the heavy door fully. Instinctive behavior urges me to reach up to lock the deadbolt, but I don't.

"Okay, let's order that food." I pull out my phone and order for both of us. He tries to give me a credit card number, but I refuse, knowing I've just deposited that fat check the insurance company sent to Mom's.

Dad's phone chimes while eating the takeout of roasted veggies and avocados. "That's my reminder alarm. I'm supposed to take like a hundred of those pills every night."

"Not a hundred," I razz back.

"Well, it feels like there are a hundred of them." He winks at me and opens a few of the pill bottles. He inspects the back of his hands. "God, when did I get so old?"

Not knowing what to say, I scrunch up my face.

He chuckles as he pops four pills in his mouth and follows them with water. "Yuck! Those red ones taste awful." He makes a face and then takes another gulp of water. "Hey, guess what? I'm never gonna miss another birthday of yours."

"That's right."

He fills his hand with more pills and gulps them down with water. I hope he's alive for more of my birthdays, but by the looks of him, it's not looking good.

My phone dings, and it's from Mom.

How is work? Are you coming here for dinner? If so, you'll need to pick something up.

"Oh man, it's Mom." The last bite of the brown rice is nutty and delicious. "I kind of told her a little lie," I admit to Dad. "Well, it's a biggie. She thinks I'm here on business. For my job. The problem is, my boss fired me around six weeks ago."

Dad raises his eyebrows as he gulps down another handful of pills.

I bite the cuticle on my thumb, expecting him to be disappointed in me for losing my job. He's quiet and allows me to talk. I like that.

"The way we fight, I thought it would be easiest to tell her it was for work. She doesn't know about Grandma's journals, about Tito, not even about you. I've gotten good at telling her what she wants to hear instead of the truth."

"Sounds like we've all become skilled at lying. I vow to you, Chelsea Price, that I will never lie to you, ever again." He holds out his hand. I hesitate for a second and then shake.

I want this with Dad. Yearning for a better connection, I wish for him to be a good man and for us to have a harmonious relationship filled with love and understanding. As I let these thoughts settle within me, the desire for a meaningful bond with him grows even stronger. I genuinely long for a positive and nurturing relationship, hoping we can bridge the gap and find genuine affection for one another.

"Now it's my turn." I look over at his pill bottles lined up on the small, rickety table. "I promise that I will never lie to you." His deep-set ocean-blue eyes are still as piercing as ever. My hand is out for him to shake, but he doesn't take it.

"Aaaannd?"

"And what?"

He raises one eyebrow and tilts his head. "What about your mom?"

"Really? I have to stop lying to Mom, as well?" I shake my head no. "That is not possible."

"Chels, come on. Look at what you've done! You and I are sitting here in my house. Talking. Eating. It's a miracle. We've cried. Hugged. You fainted."

Lowering my hand, I bite the side of my lip. "I'll... I'll try with Mom. No guarantees." There's no reasoning with her. Lying is the only way. If I don't, it'll be like World War Three. "Alright, I'll try. It's going to be hard, though."

"Do or do not. There is no try," Dad says in his best Yoda voice.

"Oh, my God! You love Star Wars?"

"Heck, yeah!" Dad holds up his hand for me to shake.

"Okay. Ugh, not even telling a little lie will be super hard with Mom."

"Patience you must have, my young Padawan." Again, in the Yoda voice.

"Alright, alright." We shake hands on our quest to be truth-tellers. Telling Mom the truth is ambitious and will require a ton of effort. "Sooo, how many more Star Wars quotes do you know?"

"Don't get me started!" Dad laughs, and it quickly turns into a congested cough. He excuses himself from the table by lifting his index finger. He can't get words out through the coughing fit. In the bathroom, I hear the cough getting worse and worse.

On my phone, Mom's message stares at me. I swipe it away and open my camera to snap pictures of all of Dad's prescription and supplement bottles, both front and back sides, and store the photos in a particular folder labeled Dad with a heart emoji.

He walks back to the table, holding a tissue to his nose and mouth. There are pinkish-red stains on the tissue. "Whew, sorry about that.

Sometimes those coughing fits turn ugly." His cheeks are red, making the bags under his eyes stand out even more.

"It's okay. Do any of these pills stop the coughing?"

"Not really. That tea does a good job, though."

"I'll make you a cup of your special tea, and then I should get going. I've got some things to talk about with Mom. She needs to know the truth. Just like I did."

"You mean about me?"

"Is that okay? And about Uncle Jim."

Dad runs his hand back and forth over his mostly bald head. "Yep, the truth is the truth. We may as well start with the big stuff. Do you think she can handle it? Just please go easy on her. She's a special person."

CHAPTER 35

Driving up to Mom's house brings back memories from my teenage years – some positive, some negative. The familiar streets and landmarks trigger a flood of memories, and it feels like revisiting a time capsule, creating a bittersweet sensation. Looking at Mom's house from the driveway, I'm reminded of the passage of time and the changes that have occurred since I left.

"Mom, let's sit down. There's something you need to know." She takes her glass of wine from the counter, pulls out a chair, and sits down with a humph at her sturdy, but scarred, kitchen table. I sit across from her.

"Would you like a glass?" Mom says.

"Not right now, but thanks." With a sense of urgency, before my courage wanes, I feel compelled to express everything on my mind. "I want to get all this out before I lose my nerve, and I'd love for you to stay quiet and please listen. Please understand and give me the space to speak without interruption."

Mom nods and takes a sip of her wine.

"I've not been fully truthful with you. I've told a few small… Um, okay, Grandma Eve wrote three journals besides that last little one left on her desk. I've read all of them and have them in my possession."

"I knew it! You took that one off her desk when we were cleaning her house. It wasn't Josie, huh?"

"Mom! Please!" I hold out my hand as if to say stop. "Just hear me out. Anyway, there was a ton of family information in those journals. The third one, in particular, was the most crucial, the most personal for me." She stays quiet, and her silence provides a comforting space, allowing me to pour out everything weighing on my heart.

I tell Mom everything about Dad, Denver, Seattle, and Uncle Jim, explaining Dad's fears and remorse. Sharing with Mom the intricacies of his emotions and the reasons behind his actions feels cathartic. All my words give her a deeper understanding of Dad's perspective and struggles. His health. The dogs. The pills. All the pills. The truth slides out of me as I paint the picture of our strange familial past.

Mom sits with her mouth wide open. She shakes her head back and forth. I can tell she's dumbfounded and confused. Her cheeks and neck are flush red, and she slips off the button-down sweater she always wears on rainy evenings.

"Mom, this is hard to believe, but I just came from Dad's house. It's like twenty minutes away, on the other side of town. He's sick. Really sick. He has throat cancer and takes all these pills. He knew all this about Uncle Jim and did what he did to protect me. Can you believe that? Whew, I know it's a lot to take in. I've been feeling baffled as well, but it's the truth. I feel he's telling the truth." Fixing my eyes on Mom, she looks angry, and it scares me.

I whisper to her. "Okay, you can talk now, Mom." She stays in a hushed daze, like she's forgotten how to speak. After a few seconds, she doesn't respond. "Mom? Um, there's more. Are you ready?" Mom nods. I tell her about Tito – Grandma's part and mine but skim the part where I drove to New Mexico alone but emphasized the sacred river part.

"Then there's my job, Um, Drew. Yeah, and Megan, oh, and Josie." I'm rambling because she's quiet, so weirdly lifeless. Her eyes are glassy, but I don't think the wine is the culprit. "Mom? Say something. You're freaking me out." I stand up and go into the kitchen. "Okay, I think I'm ready for that glass of wine. It's been one hell of a day."

Bringing the bottle to the table, I offer to refill her glass, but she puts her hand over the top of her glass, preventing me from pouring the wine. "Now, I'm really freaking out. Mom! Come on, talk to me. What are you feeling?" Still not a peep out of her. "Mom?"

After about two minutes, we are still sitting in silence – me drinking wine, and she is not. I can remain silent longer than she can. I'm used to staying quiet, staying safe. Keeping my mouth shut has been a lifelong strategy. Be the wallflower, blend in, and don't raise any eyebrows. Don't let anyone see you.

God, it's been like fifteen minutes. Maybe twenty. I tap my fingers on my thighs as I feel the wine tugging at my brain. Dad was right. No more lies. No more cover-ups.

"Hey, Mom," I say in my most gentle tone. She looks like she could shatter into a million pieces. "Look at me. Please?" I'm surprised at the words tumbling out of me. I guess I'm not the suppressed, stay-quiet mouse anymore.

She lifts her head and clears her voice. "Chelsea, you know I love you. Right? Only wanting the best for you. It might not have felt like it all the time. And Lord knows we have had our fair share of arguments, but I was all alone raising you. Your Dad vanished. He would send checks each month, but that was it. Raising you was on my shoulders."

"Yes, I know you love me, Mom." Moving over to the chair next to me, she takes my hands in hers. It feels so foreign. We never touch. Despite my hands feeling tense, I try to ease into this unfamiliar reaction, acknowledging the mixed emotions that have surfaced. She seems so exposed, so... might I say it? Sensitive.

"Oh, Chelsea. When you would ask me about the abuse, I could never imagine your father doing that. I'm so sorry."

We both sit there in silence, muted by our thoughts. When I try to talk to Mom about what Uncle Jim did to me, she shakes her hand in the air like she can bat down the notion. The memory prickles me, but I don't want this to become a fight.

"Robert lives here? In Seattle?" she squeaks out the words.

"Yes. Dad moved here shortly after we did, like when I was eleven-ish."

Her head drops again with her chin to her chest.

"Mom, it was messed up, but he wanted to keep tabs on us. Make sure we stayed safe. He feels awful about all that, but he feared you'd put him in jail for killing Jim."

"Why didn't he tell me any of this?" She pulls her hands away from mine. I'm relieved she pulled away first. I've never seen her so frail. So unsure. So vulnerable. I'm unsure how to respond. The one in charge, Mom, never once showed exposure or doubt. She fought through life and problems without flinching.

"Chelsea, why didn't he tell me? Talk to me? Confide in me?"

"Dad was afraid. Dad's actions were driven by his fears, which sometimes clouded his judgment and influenced his behavior in perplexing ways. Fear has a profound impact on our decisions and actions." My fears have been so strong and ingrained in my life that they had me doing some pretty strange things myself. "Mom, I told you somebody molested me." My cheeks burn. "And you didn't believe me, saying it was all made up, but it wasn't. Please tell me, why did you do that? A little validation would have been nice."

"I'm sorry, Chelsea. I couldn't believe it when you said your father had touched you wrong. He was such a good man. Upstanding. Hardworking, you know. We both worked so hard. He loved you so much. Goddam Jim! How could he do that? To his niece! I would've shot him, as well." Mom's face turns from soft and sorry to rage and deep hatred.

"I wish I could dig Jim out of the ground, yell and scream at him for hurting you, shoot him myself, and then drop him on the ground for the coyotes to tear apart. What a horrible thing!" She sobs. Her chest spasms in bursts. "Why didn't... God, why didn't I see it?"

My nerves make me want to chew on my cuticle, but Mom hates that. Instead, I sit on my hands. "Mom, I told you a long time ago."

"Couldn't believe it, Chels." She gasps for air and straightens her blouse. "Maybe I didn't want to believe it. Too hard, you know?" She looks at me. "Just too hard."

I bob my head up and down. I want to say I know how hard. It was me who endured the abuse. Me. I was scared, embarrassed, confused, guilty. Then all that turned me into a protected, weird, guarded, nerdy, unpopular slump of a person. The wine is going down too easy and fast. Mom still has half of a glass and hasn't taken a drink of it. My brain rambles with muffled thoughts and memories. We don't have the words to speak our feelings. We never have.

The dogs run, breaking the silence, and bark at the front door. "Lindsey! Stevie! Stop it!" Mom yells at the dogs. "It's so irritating. They keep doing that! I go to the door, and no one's there. It's maddening!" She crosses her arms. "Don't worry about them. They'll stop, eventually."

"They did this last time I was here, as well."

To stop them from barking, I get up, shove my hands in my pockets, and stroll to the door. "I'll take a look." It feels good to move. I've been more physically active in the last six weeks than ever before and am enjoying how my body feels. "Hey, you two. Hush. I'm sure there's no one here." Stevie and Lindsey quiet down as I open the front door.

I gasp and jump back. The dogs bark at the stranger and I do my best to grab a hold and quiet them. I step aside, holding the door open.

Dad winks at me as he limps across the threshold, clutching a small bouquet of daisies and carnations. "Hi, Lizzy."

CHAPTER 36

Chelsea's Journal
    April 11, 2019, Journal 1 of 3 (I'm committed to writing three journals, just like Grandma.)

Dear Journal – this is Chelsea. I decided to journal, like Grandma Eve. I'm not sure who will end up reading my journals. Most likely, I won't have any granddaughters. Then again, one never knows. The force is strong in me! (That's what Dad says.) And I've proven my strengths to myself over the last few months. Grandma's journals are the best. I'm a nerd, but I read them over and over as the past unfolds around me.

As one could expect, Mom freaked out when she saw Dad for the first time in twenty years. That was quite the day. We all had to endure its challenges and emotions. The weight of the situation felt overwhelming, and the uncertainty ahead made me question my strength and resilience. But Dad was humble and knew how to deal with Mom. It was like magic watching him calming her down with little effort.

While reading Grandma's journals, mind movies play out inside me, and I hear the voice that used to be me. As a baby, I was so small and curious about learning to walk. Then when I was five and going to kindergarten, and then at seven, learning of books and numbers and understanding cause and effect. And then, me at ten and eleven after the damage had been done. The memories jostle together like a washing machine. I see little girls now at the age of ten and think of their innocence. They don't ask for a predator to mangle their bodies and minds. They don't ask for that. I didn't ask for that. Though, now and then, I hear his voice – the voice of a damaged uncle. I try to clear it from my mind, to say to it, NO, you have no control over me, not anymore. Usually, it goes away. When it doesn't, Dr. Andrew is just a call away.

I've been in Seattle for two months taking care of Dad, hopping back and forth between Mom's and Dad's, spending a night here and there. I've been taking him to doctor's appointments and chemo treatments. After the treatments, we rush home and put on our Star Wars t-shirts and comfy sweats. After settling onto the couch, we binge-watch Star Wars movies and eat popcorn loaded with butter (I need to fatten him up somehow). Dad's favorites are the first three in the series, the classics. We say all the lines together out loud. Our current favorite is "Never tell me the odds." Dad loves Han Solo. I do, too.

Dad's living longer than they said he would. Whatever they think (insert eye roll). He's tougher than they realize – those doctors. Anyway, his stable health can be attributed to both my support and his rekindled, newfound love for Mom. My caring presence contributes to his well-being, while the renewed affection between him and Mom plays a significant role in bolstering his emotional and physical health. Yep, Mom and Dad hit it off again. Twenty years later. Better late than never (thank God they can't make any more kids.)

They are cute together. Last week, Dad moved in with Mom. Three's a crowd, so now I stay in Dad's spare bedroom at his house full time. Every time I go over to see Mom and Dad, it's like a circus of dogs – geez, four of them running around that little house. It feels homey and warm, though, and everyone gets along. It makes me happy to watch our little family.

I've been a little spacy lately, like I'm wafting through the gray space between childhood and adulthood. Even as an adult, I alternate from appearing like a seven-year-old craving Dad's attention to being a responsible grown-up woman who must eventually find a job. It's freaky, but new feelings have opened in me, like genuine happiness and contentment. I'm used to having the constant batter of negative thoughts that balloon into acute anxiety, so my newfound upbeat attitude is foreign but welcomed. I'm flowing with these new feelings and doing my best to keep good-vibe-killing suspicion at bay.

It reminds me of what Grandma said in Journal Two. She was sitting cross-legged on the sand, watching the ocean. She described the sunset as "unimaginably mighty and magnificent." Grandma wrote, "The ocean is patient yet powerful, commanding yet soft. And, if you don't flow with her rhythms,' she'll knock you down or drown you. You can't crush or stamp out the ocean. Feelings, either. You can only allow and trust their rhythms."

We've been unraveling all the secrets and deceits. Mom confirmed that Uncle Jim had a mole on his cheek and occasionally nicked it with his razor. That was enough for me. I remember the band-aid.

I still have the wretched memories of abuse, but knowing Dad didn't hurt me and stood up for me gives me peace. Maybe it's good that I will never see or speak to the man who fucked me up. I don't know. Emotional closure comes with telling Mom and Dad all the details, and they believe me – no more secrets. I feel less cramped around my wounds of humiliation, disappointment, and shame. God, I sound like an adult. Anyway...

I've been making Dad smoothies from Grandma's recipe in Journal Two. They settle his upset stomach. Mom drinks them as well. She says they help when she craves wine. She hasn't had a drink since the night I told her everything two months ago. Proud of her. She's more stable with Dad around and without wine. She's still ditsy and constantly picks at me to dress better and wear make-up, so some things may never change.

I talk to Josie daily and plan to move into Grandma's room. Well, at some point. I was going to say when Dad dies. But God, we all need to keep the faith that his cancer will go into remission. It's not out of the realm. Josie and I plan to cook together. She still wants to teach me, and I'm eager to learn! In the meantime, I've gotten good at smoothies and stir-fry tofu with veggies. The recipe that Dad likes. Mom even eats it.

I read Grandma's journals to Dad when he gets chemo treatments. The stories put him at ease. He fills in the parts of the story that he remembers, bringing them to life. I jot down his details and slip those pages into Grandma's journal. Again, for whoever rummages through my attic one day and finds these relics.

Dad helped me talk to Drew today. He encouraged me to act empowered. Dad has a saying – If you bite your tongue, all you get is blood. So, say what's on your mind.

Drew asked me to return to Portland just for a night or two. Hello? Bootie call! So, I finally and fully broke up with her. Me! I did it. Dad says my heart will be open for the right person – male or female.

It's been amazing spending time with Dad and even Mom (in little bits), but I'm lonely for someone my age. I am craving a little, you know, attention. It has to be the right person this time – no more treading water with disrespectful people like Drew.

Speaking of people my age, Jen, Tito's daughter, the most outstanding bartender in New Mexico, reached out to me last week. She invited me out to stay with her anytime. I'll take her up on the offer at some point.

Again, I can't schedule anything. It's all about Dad right now. The time we share is truly sublime, filled with moments of joy, connection, and a sense of contentment beyond words. It's a cherished experience that leaves a lasting impression, creating beautiful memories to treasure. I devour every second like its chocolate cake. He's so quirky and funny. We laugh when we can; when he's not in pain. That part is awful. Fuck you, cancer! Leave my dad alone!

April 15, 2019, we rushed Dad to the hospital this afternoon. It scared me. He couldn't stop coughing, causing him to vomit, and then he passed out on the bathroom floor. At the hospital, the nurse gave him something that made him sleep. I get sick looking at him in that sterile bed with a needle sticking into the back of his hand. I'm relieved he's not coughing anymore. Watching him, it looks like he has bad dreams. His eyeballs keep moving back and forth under his closed lids. Periodically, he jumps like he's having one of those falling dreams.

It's still being determined if they'll keep him overnight. The doctors haven't decided. Mom went home for a bit to get Dad an overnight bag and a change of clothes.

The events unfolded rapidly, leaving me little time to consider taking Grandma's journal from my nightstand before rushing to the hospital. The urgency and emotions surrounding the situation made it slip my mind, and now I regret not having it with me during this critical moment. Luckily, I have this new journal in my backpack. So here I sit beside him, writing just like Grandma did when Josie was in the hospital after that attacker hurt her.

It is a typical hospital room, sparse and functional, with stale air. An old TV hangs high in the corner, but I don't turn it on. The outside world seemed silly and absurd compared to what I was experiencing at that moment. Dad is hooked up to a sizeable mobile robot machine monitoring his heartbeat, breathing, and who knows what else. Next to the door are dispensers for rubber gloves and hand sanitizer, reinforcing my fear of germs and long-term illnesses. Looking at Dad, he's so frail. His pale skin is almost as white as the bed sheets.

Come on, Dad. Pull through this one. He will. We will share a smoothie and watch a movie soon.

Holding his hand – the one without the IV – I watch for any sign from him. His limp, colorless hand hangs in mine. For being so skinny, it's surprisingly heavy. Come on, Dad, wake up, smile, and tell me one of your dumb jokes. I peer up at him and order. Do it again, Dad. Kick its ass! I squeeze his hand harder and press it to my cheek. Do or do not. There is no try! Kick its ass!

He lies there, trapped in that bad dream. All we can do is wait.

CHAPTER 37

The wispy morning clouds painted in pinks and oranges light up as the sun starts to appear like a flower on the horizon. I blink toward the sun, feeling the August warmth on my cheeks. Tito's handwritten map takes me off the highway and onto a dirt road. Being my second trip, I've found that New Mexico has pretty much all dirt roads except for a few paved highways and maybe a couple of streets in town. The road skirts a small river, the Rio Chama, Tito told me last night at dinner as he drew the map. I pass by two men fly-fishing in dark green waders, and then I see the small pull-off Tito had mentioned. Eve's favorite place to park, he'd said.

Seeking reassurance, I checked with Tito that the Rio Chama River was not anyone's sacred river. He assured me that the river was free to be interacted with, as many people engaged in fishing and kayaking activities along its waters without any cultural or religious restrictions.

My chest has a profound feeling of heaviness, but admiring the rugged beauty helps me feel a little lighter. The name "Land of Enchantment" truly befits New Mexico, as I can now see why it's called that. The vast landscapes, with their expansive views and endless mesas, create a mesmerizing and enchanting experience that captivates the soul. It's like there's more sky in New Mexico than anywhere else.

Stepping out of the car, the combination of sweet and earthy smells of a morning river fills me with calm anticipation. I remove the backpack from the back seat and lock the car. "Come on, Dad." We head down the riverbank. The overgrown bushes impose themselves on the small footpath. Stepping over and ducking through them, I take care not to jostle my backpack.

And then I spot it, Eve's rock, as Tito put it. Tito said Grandma would return to his house after a day of writing with swollen, red eyes. She would look away and say it was nothing, but he knew better. He would hold her, and Grandma would cry into his shoulder. She didn't tell him what she was writing, that she couldn't tell anyone.

I untie the denim jacket around my waist and carefully lay it down on the reddish-brown rock, smoothing it out to serve as a makeshift tablecloth. The larger section of the backpack holds the urn of ashes, and I gently pull out the urn. It cradles in my hands as I hold it out in front of me. "Dad, you never visited New Mexico, but we talked about this those last few days." While in the hospital, I described the magical beauty of New Mexico. He wished he was well enough to travel, but we both knew he wasn't. The reality of his limitations saddened us, but we understood the importance of prioritizing his well-being above all else.

"Dad, I'm so glad we had three months together. What a gift. All those years when we were apart were a waste." My chin trembles. "Thank God I found you, Dad." I press the gold-colored urn to my chest. "None of us are perfect, but now I understand you did what you had to do, and I thank you. You are released from the lies and the secrets. Go in peace now, Dad." I open the top of the urn and kneel next to the river. "I love you. With all my heart." Shaking some ashes into the slow-flowing, languid river, I watch the dusty powder mix with the clear water. The intentional current carries Dad away and eddies around a large boulder that splits the stream. I watch until he's out of sight, and the endless supply of new water flows past me.

ABOUT THE AUTHOR

Meet Kelly Simmerman, a passionate bookworm turned prolific writer, whose literary journey began in a quaint independent bookstore in Santa Fe, NM. Kelly's love for reading evolved into a flourishing writing career, marked by over 100 articles in various magazines, covering a diverse range of topics from health to mindfulness, and equestrian sports to mental health.

Her digital presence shines on Medium (https://kellysimmermanauthor.medium.com) and through her blog about the enchanting Paso Robles, CA. Kelly's entrepreneurial endeavors, including founding an online child abuse training program, have not only impacted lives but also enriched her novel, THE JOURNAL EFFECT, adding depth to its narrative.

A member of both the Women's Fiction Writers Association and the Rocky Mountain Fiction Writers Association, Kelly is deeply committed to her craft, continually seeking inspiration through retreats and festivals. Balancing her writing life, she cherishes moments in Denver, CO, and Paso Robles, with her family and two dogs, finding joy in the mountains of Colorado and the vineyards of Paso Robles.

For a deeper dive into Kelly's world of words and wisdom, visit her at https://kellysimmerman.com and join her journey of captivating storytelling.

RATE THIS BOOK!

If you enjoyed this novel, please take the time to rate it on Goodreads and the retailer's site where you purchased it.
    Thank you,
    The Tumbleweed Books team

Made in the USA
Columbia, SC
12 February 2024